One Good Deed

Dave Rosi

Hard Shell Word Factory

Dedicated to my family

ISBN: 0-7599-0200-3
Published November 2001
Ebook ISBN: 0-7599-0197-X
Published August 2001

Hard Shell Word Factory
PO Box 161
Amherst Jct. WI 54407
books@hardshell.com
http://www.hardshell.com
Cover art derived from painting by Sonia Grineva

Part 1

I DIDN'T EXPECT to hear from my cousin Jake in August. So it shook me out of my summer spell on Crossroads Key, where the water was a milky blue and the hard road blazing hot and mostly silent. The annual ritual of family contact had always been in December. That's when I'd get his card, lately enclosed with one of those goofy family newsletters, inviting me to come up to Westchester for the usual rounds of Christmas house visits, present unwrapping and lots of booze. When had I been there last? It had to be seven or eight years ago by now.

But there it was, this little note folded up in a little envelope, almost lost in the pile of stuff I'd picked up from the post office box I kept in Miami. It said:

Joe,
I need your help.
Call me in New York as soon as you get this.
Jake, your cousin.

The "your cousin" part looked like it got scrawled in as a nervous afterthought, just so I'd remember who he was. Ah well, Jake was never known for any kind of epistolary elegance.

So I tried to imagine what the hell he needed my help for. It crossed my mind that he might be coming to the Keys and wanted a place to stay. But as best I could remember, he hated the sun, the salt water, and the summer heat. Besides, I thought, he and the Mrs. and the brood would definitely get drawn into the Disney World gravitational field before they'd ever find their way down here. Staying with me was out of the question in any case. I wasn't blowing my cover for anyone, anytime.

Then I remembered how he used to ask me about drug smuggling around South Florida, when he was doing some liaison work with DEA. But that had been a few years ago. He must have learned damn well then that whatever I knew, I wasn't going to share with him or his eager beaver brethren. Anyway, I'd been trying to keep my nose clean for quite a while and couldn't tell him much even if I tried.

I walked inside to the cooler behind the bar, grabbed a beer, and went back to sit on the porch steps. I kept turning the note over and over in my hands. Pretty soon, my gaze drifted out to the white causeway of

Highway 1, connecting the flat expanse of mangroves, and then beyond that to the swirl of blue water that ran slightly darker to the horizon. The sea was empty, except for a little sloop yawing in the channel. I looked down at Jake's note again, and then folded it up and stuck it into a crack in the steps. A piece of paper like that could, and maybe should, get lost pretty easily.

AS THE AFTERNOON slipped by, I hung out on the porch in the rocking chair, drank a few more beers, and felt the air getting more and more restless. A big bank of gray-black clouds had been building up in the northwest and, gradually, the day grew real dark. Suddenly, the sky was torn up by lightning and flooded with rain. The droplets drummed hard on the porch roof and a gust of wind swooped up Jake's note and blew it onto the gravel parking lot. I was half considering chasing what might as well've been trash, when Vera pulled up on her motor scooter. She waved like she had good news, but I knew it was just a little habit of hers.

"Thought you weren't coming back `til six," I yelled through the rain.

"Russ wanted to visit his father this afternoon," she said, "he's teaching him some kind of tennis thing. So we decided to forget about the dentist."

She turned off the scooter, pulled it back on its stand, and ran her hand through her short, soaked, yellow hair. As she dismounted, I noticed my piece of postal litter pressed against her front wheel spokes. In the next second, she noticed it, too, and bent down to pick it up.

"Vera, I'll take care of that." I stood up.

"Take it easy, Joe. I'm already half drowned."

She bent down and peeled Jake's note off the wheel. Then she squinted over it for a few seconds. I was glad I still had the envelope, with Jake's address, in my pocket.

"Hey, private correspondence," I said to her, as she stepped up on to the porch.

"Yeah, I'll bet. Cousin Jake, huh? And he needs some kind of special help in New York? Now c'mon Joe, don't you trust me yet to tell me you're some kind of spy?"

"Okay, Vera," I gave an exaggerated sigh. "I'll level with you. This job I've got here as general handyman, gofer and barkeep at your nonprofit establishment—it was all the idea of the boys in Langley."

"In Langley?"

"That's right," I said. "CIA."

"Uh-huh," she said, like she'd heard it all before, "so what is it you're really doing?"

"Keeping tabs. Real close tabs. On the unscrupulous practices of Pan American land speculators, Euro-tourist theme park refugees, and Canadian retiree fast food franchisees."

"Okay, Joe, you can play all you want. One day you're going to tell me what I've known all along, anyway."

"And what's that?"

"That you ain't no bartender type. You ain't no working man, neither."

"Is that so?"

"Yeah, that's so, like the way you talk sometimes. Just a little too fancy, if you ask me."

"Too fancy? So what do you want me to do, snort and grunt and use hand gestures?"

"You always think you can joke your way out of it, don't you, Joe? But I know better than you think. Something about you just don't fit, I said that from the first day you come to work for me. I said to myself, 'something about the man just don't fit'. It's not just the way you talk, Joe. It's...it's like you're supposed to be someplace else, altogether."

I turned my face away from that wide-eyed stare of hers, and found myself trying to picture how she could have looked twenty years ago. She must have been a fair-skinned, willowy lass I reckoned, who probably used to turn a few heads around on this little spit of sand and palm trees.

But the sun had baked that fair skin to leather and what must have been a real heart-breaking mane of light blonde hair, was now just a stringy, thinned-out, muddled cap. When she smiled, like she did now as I turned back to face her, she showed a crooked row of bad teeth and a road map of lines across her brow.

"Thinking up a good one, Joe?" she said, when our eyes met again.

"I don't know what I'm thinking, but, gee whiz Vera, don't you have something better to do right now than getting all nosy with me?"

"You're getting awful touchy." She laughed. "At least I'm not gossiping about you, the way ol' Larry's been down at the filling station."

"Larry? What the hell is he saying about me?"

"He thinks you're a fugitive," she lit a cigarette, "and that you killed somebody before you showed up here."

"Well old Larry's got himself a real outsized imagination now, doesn't he?"

"Oh, I don't know, Joe, but I suppose it don't make no never mind anyhow. I like you well enough, just how you are. That's why you get to work here."

"Now that's some kind of good luck. Isn't it?"

"Damn straight it is," she said, smiling. "Now why don't you tell me what that note's really about, huh?"

"You're not going to let go of this, are you?"

She didn't say anything.

"All right," I said, "the hell with it. I don't know exactly what the note's about. All I know is, it's from my cousin. He's a cop up in New York City, homicide detective last time I checked."

"You're a cop, too, aren't you Joe? Undercover, right?"

"Yeah, that's a good one. While you're at it, make sure I'm well paid, and getting laid by all the best women."

I CUT THINGS short with Vera and walked back into the bar. I paced around in there awhile, `til the rain passed and the full press of the day's heat returned. Then I decided I'd go ahead and give Jake a call. There was something about that note, and Vera as well, that was really beginning to gnaw at me.

I went over to the pay phone by the pinball machine, and dialed up police headquarters. It was a little before five and I figured Jake would still be there. The switchboard operator answered the phone, and connected me to a clerk who transferred me to a secretary who put me on hold for ten minutes. I was just about to hang up when Jake picked up the phone.

"Hello, Joe? Joey?" he said, "Is that you?" He sounded oddly happy.

"Yeah, Jake, it's me. How are you doin'?"

"Knee deep in shit. So what do you say? Your ass must be steaming down there, am I right? Gotta be 200 degrees in the shade?"

"More or less," I said. "So look, what's going on up there? Some kind of trouble or what?"

"Joey, you're always so nervous, you know that? No trouble, big boy. Just thought you might be interested in a little summer vacation, that's all. A few weeks of fun and games on the isle of Manhattan."

"For what?"

"I want you to help me in a little investigation we got going here, you'd be an expert consultant, see? I figure we can get you maybe three, four hundred bucks a day, you know? That's gotta be more than you can make down there, chief, legally that is."

"What's that supposed to mean?"

"Nothing, nothing. Hey look, Joey. I mean, I got an opportunity for you here, see? You really wanna give this a shot."

"So let's get to the point. What exactly is it you need me for?"

"It's complicated. I mean it's a...special situation. To tell you the truth I don't want to get into all the details right now, especially on the phone. No, you got to come up here, sport, and I'll lay it all out for you."

"Now that's a little vague, Jake. I mean, I'm going to take a trip up there just to get some details? About something I don't even know I'm interested in? You think I've got nothing better to do than jump through my ass for you?"

"Aw, now take it easy. You can't tell me you don't have some time to kill. Besides, I'll pick up the tab for the flight, all right? So what do you got to lose?"

"I'm not interested in playing games, Jake. Now just tell me what it is you want me for."

"You're an impatient prick, you know that? Look, we just want you to interview some suspects, that's all."

"What do you mean, 'suspects'?"

"Just what I said."

"What kind of suspects?"

"What kind, what kind," he said. "Murder suspects that's what kind, Joey."

"Why me?"

"Well...look...some of them are a little unbalanced and...."

"Unbalanced? What's that supposed to mean?"

"Joey, come on now, *unbalanced*, you know? Not playing with a full deck, see? And I thought, well, you know, with your background..."

"My background?"

"Yeah, with your background..."

"Forget it," I said.

"Now, Joey, slow down, all right? This could be an opportunity for you."

"What kind of opportunity?"

"To rejoin the human race, chief. Let's face it. You're dying down there, anybody can see that."

"I'm minding my own business and hurting no one," I said. "People can do a lot worse."

"Yeah, sure they can. But tell me something, what are you afraid of?"

"Who said anything about being afraid?"

"Aw c'mon, it's obvious. You're afraid something's going to come up and bite you in the ass. So you got to hide out and...."

"Hey, thanks for the analysis, doc," I said, "but I got to go now. Goodbye."

Then I hung up on him.

THE REST OF that afternoon and evening I was pretty rattled. I tried reading the paper, but I couldn't get halfway down a column. Some article with scientists arguing over whether we were heating up or cooling down, as a planet, that is. On the TV there was Bette Davis being an old hag in some lame English movie. It looked like she was suspected of killing the kids she was supposed to be a nanny for. There wasn't much to concentrate on there and my mind kept returning to Jake. I knew he meant well, and no doubt he'd gotten some prodding from the rest of the family. With both my folks gone, there were still a few people in the family who figured I needed some good looking-after.

But I couldn't see any way I was going to get involved in any murder investigation. And what about these suspects being "unbalanced"? What was he trying to be, delicate? Did I somehow need delicate handling?

I sacked out early that night, around ten or so, in my little room in the back of the bar. It was muggy as usual, and as a rule that didn't bother me. But that night I was shifting under the sheets every two minutes and my skin felt like it didn't fit right on me. Then I had this dream. In it, I woke up in my own bed, to what sounded like footsteps out on the front porch. I listened, holding my breath, and without a doubt there were footsteps, someone was just outside the house. I knew I had to get out of bed and find out what sort of danger there was, but my legs were like over-cooked spaghetti. Somehow, I was able to get up and barely get one foot in front of the other, to get out the front door and onto the porch. There, in the shadows, I saw Bette Davis like she was in the nanny movie, but with huge, glistening claws. She caught me out of the corner of her eye, smiled, and turned to move toward me. Her claws were growing longer and longer and I knew I was going to be impaled against the wall. I tried to turn and escape but my legs were still spaghetti-like. In a second she came up next to me and I felt the knife-claws running right through my gut. I managed to get my hands around her throat and bear down on her windpipe. For a second her malevolence dissolved into fear, our eyes met, and I wanted to let up. But then her lips curled up into this nasty, mocking grin and I squeezed her neck even harder. She gasped and hissed.

I woke up.

I saw the night darkness was just graying into early dawn, and the curtains swelled slightly in a puff of wind. It'd been a long time since I'd had that kind of dream. I'd always reckoned that if something stayed out of sight and out of mind long enough, you could come to believe it never happened. But now there it was again. I reached over and took a shot of Haitian rum from the night table and cursed my cousin Jake. Him and his damn extension of good will: "three to four hundred a day, that's gotta be more than you make down there, chief, legally, that is." As if I needed him to do my bookkeeping.

By the next morning I felt better. At least my skin seemed to fit pretty well again, except for some tightness at the back of my neck. Business was going to be even slower than usual at Vera's because Hurricane Amos was sliding off the north coast of Hispaniola and heading up our way. It was predicted to slam somewhere into the South Florida coast within the next forty-eight hours. I'd better get to boarding up the windows of Vera's place, but first I wanted to take a little morning row in an old dinghy I kept on the shore near the town marina. After I walked down to the beach and was about ready to push the boat off, I felt the sand and gravel voice of Horace Crassidy dirty up my ears.

"How 'bout it, Joe," He sounded vaguely threatening.

"Yeah, how are you doing, Horse," I said. I didn't look behind me, hoping to get into the boat and row off without further conversation. But fat chance of that.

"Got some real good blow in, Joe," he said.

I didn't want to know about it.

"Come in from Veracruz, two days ago."

I really didn't give a damn.

"Might could be just the thing for what's ailing you, Joe."

I turned around. I was in knee-deep water and he couldn't have been more than a few arms' lengths behind me.

"What do you figure is ailing me, Horse?" I wondered why I was taking his bait.

"Called small balls, Joe," he said, "could be a terminal condition, if you don't watch out."

"Why the hell are you so concerned?" Now he'd gotten my back up.

"You know damn well why. We could be making us some real easy money if you hadn't turned so goddamn chickenshit on me."

"Look, go play somewhere else, all right? I'm real busy today, I got to get Vera's place boarded up."

He started laughing, grunting really, like a pig, which seemed to suit him real well. "Now that's real important ain't it, Joe? She'd be liable to collect some real good insurance money if you didn't protect that shit-covered little rathole, huh?"

"There isn't any insurance on it, you moron, and it pays its way. Not that that's any of your damn business."

"Now don't push me Joe." His face darkened. Then he shook his head and tried to smile. "You know, it beats the hell out of me why you're working for that old dog anyway; shit, I can remember when she was one good looking piece of ass, many moons ago."

I climbed into the boat and put the oars in place.

"Yeah, I'm right happy you're taking care of her, Joe," he said, breaking into a high-pitched laugh. "I just hope you ain't too jealous about her still carrying the torch for me."

I pulled on the oars and tried to get some decent distance from him as fast as I could. I didn't want to believe I'd once worked, if you want to call it that, with that black stubble-faced, crooked-nosed, wild-eyed son of a bitch. But the fact is, I'd done a few deals with him, and it'd more than paid the rent for a while. But that's another story, at least for now.

I glided out in a jiffy over the blue glass and coral below, and in a couple of minutes I'd gone past the moorings and started to feel the slightest little chop at the bow. The stern of the dinghy was facing straight at Crassidy's anchored sloop—the Skink—and beyond it I thought I saw Vera walking down the ramp to the floating docks. Unfortunately, Crassidy was right about her feelings toward him. Who can explain why she, or for that matter anybody, would want that dung beetle. But there it was, she was his ever-ready would-be helpmate and servant. Every season I can remember, she'd scraped and painted that beast of a boat for him. As I rowed further out, I thought I could see her and Crassidy meet at the edge of the outer dock and stand together for a few minutes. I rowed harder and their figures faded into patches of color. Then she separated from him and moved up the ramp toward the parking lot. I let up on the oars and the boat slid quietly over a group of hovering barracuda. I wiped the sweat from my brow and took in the dazzling late morning sun.

When I look back now on that morning, I see it as one of the last few moments of a long anesthesia. All of what followed seems as abrupt and destined as the storm that was swirling up from the Caribbean and expected to crash into South Florida. I had lived with the illusion that if you kept your world small enough—mean enough, even—you could handle it all without too much worry, or regret. But I hadn't counted on events having a mind of their own, and recruiting whomever they wanted without warning or consent.

BY LATE AFTERNOON the next day, the weather report predicted the eye of Amos was going to land somewhere between Key West and Crossroads. The milky blue water had turned slate gray and was boiling and rocking and slapping out at the mangroves. The wind was moaning and must have been gusting up to thirty knots. You could hear the palm fronds scraping and whole groves were leaning hard, as if driven by some giant fan. The main highway carried a caravan of R.V.'s, mini-vans, passenger buses and various Florida and out-of-state cars up toward the presumably safe mainland.

I had driven down to the marina parking lot with a little trailer to pick up my boat, when I saw Crassidy stuffing all sorts of electronics and clothes from his boat into a battered blue Ford van. His shoulder length hair, usually heavy with an unwashed, greasy residue, was flying away from his ears in the wind.

"This gonna be one bad blow, Torento," he shouted to me.

"Reckon so," I said. "Where are you putting your boat?"

"Got a place on the north side, just east of the bridge. Then I'm haulin' ass to Lauderdale. Going to ride this one out with some sweet pussy and Jack Black, brother. What about you?"

"I imagine I'll stay right here. I'm not really sure where the storm is headed."

"Headed? It's headed right up your dusty ass, Torento. Hear me? That shack Vera's got you put up in is going to be floating in the Gulf of Mexico by tomorrow."

He seemed to get some special delight from this idea. "Now if you wanted to use half the sense you were born with, faggot, you'd be coming with me to Lauderdale and we'd be speaking with your Eye-talian friends in Miami on the way. Unless you really hate making money."

"What I really hate," I said, "is the way your face looks, Crassidy."

"You watch yourself now, Joe," he said. "Or I'll show how I can turn real ugly on you."

We just stared at each other. He looked just crazy enough at that moment, all mossy toothed and with his hair snapping around like some profane banner, that I figured it wasn't the time for further insults. I took a deep breath.

"Well, look, Horse, uh, you best get all packed for Lauderdale," I said, "and I need to get to my boat." Then I turned and started walking away.

"You know what, Torento?" he said to my back. "Old Vera's got some real dumb-ass idea that you could be some kind of secret agent, you know that?"

"Yeah, I know," I didn't pause. "She has some imagination."

"Some real charitable imagination, Torento, 'cause that's a whole lot better than being the chickenshit loser you are."

I kept walking.

"You hear me, Torento?" he shouted.

But I just kept walking.

"Chickenshit, fairy, loser."

The wind was howling and kicked up sand all around us. Best to keep a lid on it with Crassidy. I should have learned that a long time ago.

I TOWED MY boat back to Vera's place. I arrived there just as she and her kid were pulling up on her motor scooter. As I stepped out of the car, Russ was already running toward me, with his long red hair flying in the wind and his blue eyes and round freckled face all brightened up with excitement. He was a cute kid. About twelve years old.

"How ya doin', Russ? You're lookin' good in that poncho."

"My dad gave it to me, Joe...Hey, you scared of this hurricane, or what?"

"I respect it. That way I hope I don't have to get scared of it."

"Joe," Vera said, "you better stay with us in the big house. It ain't going to be safe in your room, that shack's liable not to be here tomorrow."

"Yeah, Joe," said Russ, "Mom said that house has been here over a hundred years, and been in storms bigger than this."

"Oh, I'm sure it has, Russ," I said. "That's a real good conch house. By the way, did you get that new chess set?"

"Yeah, Joe, brought it from my Dad's. Want to play? I'll set it up right now..."

"Give me an hour or so. I want to gather some stuff up from my room and around the bar."

"Better do it quick, Joe," Vera said, "or you're going to be pilotin' that bar right through the eye of this damn storm."

The wind wailed high and painful and whipped up a light rain that stung when it hit our faces. An early darkening was closing in on us. The air suddenly chilled my insides and jarred my bones.

Just then Crassidy pulled up in his dilapidated van, looking like some hybrid of war refugee and aging brain-pickled sixties burnout. He stopped several yards from us, rolled down his window and beckoned to Vera. As she walked over to him I heard Russ say, "He's a real asshole, ain't he, Joe?"

"That kind of talk is going to stunt your growth, Russ," I said.

"No way. I'm already the tallest kid in seventh grade. Besides, you know I'm right. Even my mother knows he's an asshole—sometimes she does, anyway."

"That's better than nothing."

"He uses her, Joe. Whatever he says, most likely she's going to do it. I think he's got her hypnotized half the time."

"I hope she works her way out of it," I said, "I reckon she ought to know better." Yeah, she ought to, I thought. But I didn't have much hope of her pulling herself away from that greasy-headed weasel.

The wind was shifting crazily and a big gust heaved us both back a few steps. Then Crassidy called out to Russ, "Hey you little sack o' shit. You best stay close on your momma's skirt so you don't get scared and wet your panties."

"I ain't scared, Crassidy," Russ said. "I ain't scared o' nothin'. You're the one who's headed out of here."

"I got better things to do, little man, than to be hanging around here watchin' people drown."

"Why don't you try joinin' them?"

Crassidy's old redneck face got real serious. "What'd you say boy?"

Vera got nervous. "Russ!" she shouted to him.

Crassidy opened the van door and started walking toward us. His eyes were bloodshot and weirdly dull and I knew he was high on some kind of shit, probably angel dust, which he once told me "builds up your brain real good." His face was twisted into a nasty scowl. All his boasting about time in the state penitentiary raced through my mind. He came up over Russ.

"Now that's a real good way to get yourself killed, talkin' like that, you goddamn little turd."

Vera tried to push herself between them and gave me a quick, pleading glance.

"Now Russ," she began, "you apologize to Mr. Crassidy right now."

Russ didn't say a word.

"Russ!" Vera cried.

The kid looked up at me, as if to ask, "Are you with me on this?"

I nudged him. "Apologize Russ," I said, "this isn't worth getting hurt over."

Crassidy grabbed the kid by the front of his shirt and lifted him up to his ugly pig eyes with one hand. "I'd say 'hurt's' a real kind word to be using," he said.

Russ turned suddenly white and I half-expected to see piss running off his dangling shoes. "I'm sorry, Mr. Crassidy," he squealed.

Then Crassidy dropped him at his feet. "Yeah, you're sorry," he growled, "you're one sorry-assed little fairy shit-for-brains frog-faced motherfucker. I ever hear a nasty word out of you again and I'm gonna slice you up for bait and go trollin' for sharks, you hear me?"

"Yeah," the kid muttered.

"'Yessir' you mean, you little pussy."

"Take it easy," I said.

He looked at me like he'd forgotten I was there. I figured it was definitely angel dust he was on.

"Mind your own damn business, Torento." He wiped some foam off his lower lip.

"Horse," I said. "I think you made your point, now the boy's scared half to death."

Crassidy looked around the parking lot and sucked some air through his teeth. He seemed to be considering what to say next. Then he turned to Vera.

"Damned kid," he said, "what're you raisin' anyway, some kind of damned animal?"

"Horace, I'm sorry," Vera said. "He gets real boisterous sometimes."

"Ain't gettin' whipped enough, as far as I can tell. Anyway, I expect I'll see you by day after tomorrow. Now get your butt over here and give me some sugar before I go."

Vera got over close to him, and got on tiptoes and kissed Crassidy lightly on his unshaven cheek. I thought I was going to throw up.

Then he got in his van and drove off, leaving a dirty little cloud just behind where he exited the parking lot.

"Well," I said, "Goodbye and good riddance to all that. Now I'd better get over to my room and grab some things."

"Y'all go ahead," said Vera, who suddenly looked sad and preoccupied. Then she turned and walked up the path toward the old conch house.

"Thought you were going to back me up there, Joe," said Russ, "thought me and you were going to whip his ugly ass good."

"You got the wrong guy, Russ. I don't get into fisticuffs with maniac collectors of guns and knives, especially when their brains are marinating in God knows what."

"Tellin' you, Joe. Me and you, we could have taken him out."

"Keep dreaming, kid. Anyway, since when did I become your bodyguard?"

We headed across the parking lot, up the porch steps of the shack, and across the barroom floor into my bedroom in the back.

This little nook, and free access to the liquor, made up my compensation in the summer. During the season, I could pick up a few hundred a week between tips and what Vera paid me under the table.

Russ picked up an old guitar I'd found in the dumpster and sat on the bed and strummed its strings. Normally it would have gotten on my nerves, but now it seemed like the proper accompaniment to the crying wind and creaking joints of this rickety room of liquor-fueled isolation.

"You know how to play this thing?" he asked me.

"No."

"So what do you have it for?"

"Figure I'll get around to learning it one of these days."

Russ moved his fingers up and down the neck and tried to improvise on some dissonant riff. I pulled an old suitcase out from under the bed, opened it up on the floor, and started to stuff whatever was mine into it. It was staggering, how little I had. Two shirts, a pair of khakis, a poncho, some boxer shorts and an old sport coat. From the desk drawer I took a spiral notebook that kept a rough inventory of bar supplies and a bank envelope stuffed with cash. I put everything in the case, snapped it shut and told Russ we were ready to shove off.

"You taking the guitar, Joe?" he asked.

"Yeah, stuff it in one of those plastic bags near the bar."

"You reckon you're really gonna learn to play it?"

"Yeah, one of these days."

"You're gettin' pretty old," he warned.

"Well, I never looked at it that way."

"How old are you, Joe, anyway?"

"Thirty-four."

"Wow, that's pretty old, Joe, seriously."

"Well," I said, "I'll try to get serious about it. Real soon."

We ran through the rain and mud up the path to the old house. Vera greeted us as we stepped up to the front door.

"Wipe your feet now, boys," she said. "Joe, we'll get you settled upstairs."

She wouldn't quite look at me when we got inside. I could see she was feeling sad and shameful about what happened with Crassidy. I'd been over the topic of her and Crassidy with her more times than I cared to remember and knew I didn't have anything new to say about it. Every time I told her to quit seeing him, she'd either tell me she was too scared he'd hurt her or she'd try to convince me that behind all that macho-Neanderthal posturing was a real "sweetheart" of a guy. Like I said, I had nothing new to say about it.

AS IT CLOSED in on midnight, the wind roared around the house and the windows rattled and chattered in an eerie chorus. Russ and I had a five game chess series going, with him ahead 2-1 and me down by a knight in the middle of game four. I didn't play half-bad, and it was my opinion that this kid had some real talent. Just as I was about to consider trading queens with him we were startled by the sound of a siren and a burst of flashing blue and red lights flooding through the front windows.

"What's going on?" cried Russ.

"Got me," I said.

I heard Vera shriek from the kitchen as I went to the door to see what the hell was going on. When I opened the door two cops in raingear were trudging up the front steps. I let them inside the foyer, and vaguely recollected seeing them around town. I think the town of Crossroads had three cops in all.

"Evening, officers," I said, "what's this all about?" They both just looked at me up and down.

"Ain't you Joe Torento?" one of them asked, round-faced, red-nosed, and just out of high school.

"That's me."

"You're a bartender." He squinted at me.

"Yeah," I said, "that's right."

"Who else is here?" asked the other one, older, dark-eyed, and pointy-faced.

"The owner of the house, Vera Parish and her son, Russ. But look here, officers, what's this all about?"

"Lookin' for Horace Crassidy," said the round-faced one. "He here?"

"No," I said. "No, he's not."

"You're a friend of his, ain't you?" said the pointy-faced one.

"I wouldn't exactly say that."

"Yeah, why not?"

"I hardly know him," I said, "just see him around, that's all."

"That right?" said round face, sounding dubious. "Y'all never did any work together, huh?"

"What!" I said. "With that nasty, unwashed son of a bitch!"

"Thought you said you didn't know him hardly," the pointy one deadpanned.

"I don't. I mean barely. What's all this interrogation about?"

"Why? You gettin' nervous?"

"I just don't know what y'all want," I said. "That's all."

"There's been rumors you and Crassidy were runnin' cocaine through here to Miami," said pointy face.

"I really don't know what you're talking about."

Russ had been standing in the doorway while we were talking and now the round-faced cop turned to him. "Your momma here, son?"

"Yeah," Russ said, "she's somewhere around."

"Brett, you go talk to her," said pointy face, "and take a look around. I'll be right here with Mr. To-ren-to."

After his partner left, he started up with me again. "Folks down at the marina said they seen you twice with Crassidy in the last two days, once by the beach and then once at the parking' lot."

"Yeah, could be," I said. "I got a little row boat I keep down there."

"So what were y'all talkin' about? This morning for instance."

"I don't know. Plywood, I guess, for boarding up the windows."

"He lives on a damn boat, Torento, so why's he talkin' about plywood?"

"I was," I said, "it was small talk, you know? Now look, officer, I'll be glad to cooperate with you in any way I can, but I'm telling you this man Crassidy is no friend and no partner of mine. And if you're looking for him here, you're wasting your time. He probably headed toward the mainland, like just about everybody else did today."

"That right?" he said, looking me up and down like he didn't believe a word I said. "And what about last night, you know where he was then?"

"Not the foggiest notion, officer," I said. "Nor do I care."

"Yeah?" He picked at something in his ear. "Well let me tell you a little story. 'Bout half-past four this morning we found a cabbie from Key West shot dead clean through his belly, layin' right there in his cab parked by Maury's Inn. You know where that is?"

"Just this side of the Three Mile Bridge, next door to the marina."

"Right. Now where would you start lookin' for a suspect?"

"I...I really don't know," I shrugged.

"How 'bout his last passenger?"

"Sounds reasonable."

"Damn right, his last passenger. 'Cause you see about three o'clock this morning this driver, some Yankee kid just out of college up there in Boston or somewhere near, makes a call from his car radio while he's parked in front of the 7-11 on Stock Island. He comes on the radio with the taxi dispatcher, jokin' with him, tellin' how he just picked up some stumble-down drunk shrimp fisherman out of Key West—who's now in the store gettin' a pack of cigarettes—and then he's headed up to Crossroads. The driver says this fella's got a gun and he's talkin' about blowin' somebody's damn head off. Now the dispatcher tells him to call the police, but the Yankee kid laughs and says there ain't nothin' to it and he'll use the fella in a story he's writing. Says he likes the fella's name—calls himself Horse. Now what do you think about that?"

"That's Crassidy's nickname," I said. "Most folks around here know that."

Just then, the round-faced cop returned. "Can't get nothin' out of her, Len," he told his partner. "She's just wailing and all hysterical back there."

"She seen Crassidy?"

"That's about all I got from her. Said she'd seen him today about four, just before he left for Lauderdale. She said he came by the house here."

Len turned to me. "Did you see him here, Torento?"

"Yeah, sort of."

"What do you mean, sort of?"

"I was taking care of some things," I said. "I more or less just waved to him."

"Why didn't you say that before?"

"Forgot, I guess. You didn't ask me when I'd seen him last."

"Don't play with me, Torento."

I shook my head. "No one's playing with you, sir."

"Don't play no games if you know where this boy is, Torento, you hear me?"

"Yes sir," I said.

"Or I'll run you in right now, as an accessory, you hear?"

"I hear you, and I swear I know nothin'."

He turned to Brett. "You get a look around?"

"Not yet."

With that, they left me in the foyer and went nosing around the house. Now, of course I wasn't going to cover for Crassidy. The fact was I really had no idea where he was. But why hadn't I told them I'd just seen him? I didn't know exactly, except that they'd rattled me, and I guess I just didn't like them, these two bumpkin Keystone cops. And I was still holding onto the shreds of some half-ass code about volunteering information to cops, even on a despicable thug like Crassidy. But wasn't this the time to let that go, especially if they were thinking I was his buddy?

They came back to the foyer after ten or fifteen minutes and Len looked at me hard.

"You watch out for this boy, Torento," he said, "and you get on the phone to us if you see him, hear?"

"You got it."

They opened the door to leave, and Brett turned around to face me.

"Looks like you did the right thing," he said, "ridin' things out right here."

"How do you mean?"

"Weather service is saying old Amos turned his back on us; he's fixin' to roll out to the Bahamas."

"Lucky for us," I said. "Good-night now."

I closed the door and leaned back against it. Crassidy's a murderer, I thought. Well that was no big surprise. God knows what led up to it. He must have been blind drunk and riddled with...who knows...? Angel dust, coke, acid—all of them and anything else he could find. There's probably a good chance he'd even blacked it all out.

I walked through the living room to the kitchen, looking for Vera and Russ. I heard Vera crying in the back bedroom. The door was half-closed and I poked my head in. She was lying with her face buried in a pillow while Russ sat at the edge of the bed.

"They left," I said.

Vera lifted her head up, all red-faced and teary-eyed. She sat up and wiped her eyes with her sleeve.

"Russ," she said, "go to the parlor now, I need to speak with Joe."

"I can stay," he said. "I know what all is goin' on."

"I need to speak with Joe privately," she said. "Now go into the parlor, I mean it."

Russ got up and walked with slow, heavy steps toward the door. When he got near me he said, "He's a no good son of a bitch, ain't he, Joe?"

"Reckon that's as good a description as any."

"By the way," said Russ, "you're gonna lose if you trade your queen."

"Thanks for the tip."

"You'll do better next series," he said.

"Appreciate the encouragement. I'll be out in a minute."

I closed the door and sat with Vera on the bed. She reached for a glass of whiskey on the night table and took a couple of big gulps. She looked drained and started to speak in a monotone.

"They won't get him," she said.

"Why do you say that?"

"Not before he kills me, anyway."

"What are you talking about?'

She smiled, weakly.

"I pushed the panic button, Joe, big time."

"What do you mean?"

"I mean I lost it, totally lost it."

"You're going to have to sharpen it up a bit, Vera. I don't know what the hell you're talking about."

She took another gulp, and tried to hold back her crying.

"Horace gave me a package to hold for him," she said, "'till he got back from Lauderdale. He wasn't gonna travel with it, and he couldn't keep it on the boat. It was a half a kilo of coke—what do you think that's worth?"

"I don't know. Maybe twenty-five, thirty grand."

"I figured that," she said. "Yeah, he's going to kill me."

"You flushed the whole damn thing. Is that what you're telling me?"

"Would have, but the toilet's too weak."

"So what'd you do?"

"Out the back door. Just tore it open and flung it to the wind and rain."

"Maybe you didn't get it all out."

She laughed. "You want to go check?"

I threw a raincoat over me and eased open the back screen door. A wild rain sodden gust pulled the doorknob out of my hand and swung the door wide open and smack against the house. I peered into the heaving, wind-riven grove of palms, feeling I'd for sure put myself on a fool's errand. Suddenly, I saw a scrap of plastic pinned down by the wind at the base of a palm tree. I ran over to grab it; it was no bigger than my hand. I licked it here and there on both sides and, sure enough, I got the expected bitter, numbing sensation on my tongue. I looked around there a little more, getting pretty disgusted and sad, and then plodded back into the house. Why the hell did she have to panic like that? Then again, who knows? Maybe if I'd seen the cops like that and had a stash in the house, I'd have done the same.

I threw the raincoat over a chair in the kitchen and went back to the bedroom. She was still sitting there on the bed, looking kind of numb and pathetic.

"It's gone all right," I said, "but look, did he say exactly when he was coming back for this shit?"

She looked up at me, vacantly, as if it was just dawning on her that I was there.

"Did you hear me? When is Crassidy supposed to pick it up?"

"Couple of days, uh, yeah a couple of days from now. Saturday, at noon. I'm supposed to meet him at Maury's in the restaurant."

"Perfect. I'll call the cops, and tell them I just remembered something. They'll nail him before he ever gets a chance to ask about the coke."

"You're going to snitch on him, Joe?"

"Snitch on him? I'm going to do everything I can to contribute to his lifetime incarceration, maybe even the chair if we get lucky. I mean...what do you mean snitch on him? He's a homicidal maniac and you're his next hit."

"Think he killed that cabbie?"

"Hell, yes. In cold fucking blood. Now what's going on, Vera? I mean, I know how you've felt about him, but look; he's one evil son of a bitch. He needs to be in a cage, if not put to sleep."

She started to speak, but didn't say anything. Then she took a sip of whiskey, and looked at me, real cold and angry.

"Well hurry up and call the damn station if you're going to do it," she said.

I went to the kitchen and phoned the station, and got the voice of Len at the other end.

"Hello, Len, I mean officer," I said. "Look, this is Joe Torento again. I'm calling you because I just remembered something real important."

"Yeah, what's that, Torento?" he said.

"I just remembered that Crassidy told me, this morning that is, while we were at the marina, that he was going to meet up with somebody at noon on Saturday at Maury's Inn, in the restaurant."

"Who?"

"Well, it's with a diesel mechanic. He was saying how he was having trouble with his inboard and I was talking about this boat I was going to buy. He said this fellow would look it over for me, if I wanted to meet them there, at Maury's that is, Saturday at noon."

"Uh-huh."

"So...you got to be there, got it? The restaurant, at Maury's, Saturday at noon."

"Right," he said. "Now tell me something, Torento, I got a question for you."

"Yeah, what's that?"

"Just want to know why you always sound so goddamn phony?"

"Phony?"

"Yeah, phony, like you're always talkin' bullshit."

"Well I don't know, officer," I said. "But this is no bullshit. Believe me."

He made a sucking sound through his teeth. "You know, Torento, you're one strange duck. Now I'm gonna take your tip, you hear? And I sure hope I ain't disappointed." Then he hung up.

"What's that all about, Joe?" I turned around, to see that Russ had come up behind me.

"Nothin', Russ."

"You gonna bust Crassidy, Joe? You got some plan with the police?"

"Not really. Anyway, let's get back to that game."

"I hope you get him busted. They ought to fry his ugly ass."

"Whatever," I said.

We returned to the living room and settled back into our chess game. Vera stayed in her room, watching TV. The wind's roar seemed to soften a little and I felt peaceful with the expectation that Crassidy would soon be behind bars.

Russ was playing very well and I saw I had maybe eight moves to checkmate. My mind drifted back to Jake and his so-called "opportunity." Three, four hundred bucks a day, he said, maybe for a couple of weeks. Well, I supposed I really could use the money. But what about this "unbalanced suspects" stuff, what was that all about? No, I thought to myself, I don't need to know.

Meanwhile, Russ was smelling blood. "Check," he said.

I looked over the board. Maybe my position wasn't as bad as I thought.

Then I saw headlights flash in the front window.

"What the hell?" I said. "The cops again?"

I got up and looked through the window, and made out a car with a light on top, but nothing was flashing. On the driver's side door I saw the words "All Dade Taxi" and a phone number. The car began to pull out just as the front door flew open. Then I saw Horace Crassidy, dripping wet and stinking of booze.

"What the hell are you doing here?" I heard myself say.

"Now that's some real hospitality, ain't it," said Crassidy, as he walked into the parlor.

Vera came out from the bedroom, looking like she'd drowned and washed up on the beach. She stood in the parlor doorway and opened her mouth to speak, but nothing came out. Crassidy wasn't so blitzed as to not sense something was wrong.

"What the hell's goin' on with you?" he hollered at her.

She stood there frozen, struck mute, looking like she'd been bled to whiteness.

"Answer me, goddamnit," he said. He trudged toward her, and I figured she'd be taking a bad beating before she could get a word out.

"Horse," I yelled. That got him to turn around.

"Now listen, Horse," I said, "she's real rattled and the fact of the matter is it's my fault, all right? Now I'm going to tell you up front that I already arranged to buy your stash for thirty-thousand, that's for the whole damn thing and consider it a done deal."

"Done deal?" he said. "What the hell you talking about? Where the hell's the money?"

"In your hands," I said, "by three o'clock tomorrow."

"Well that sounds real pretty. But...hey, wait a minute, where's my goddamn cocaine?"

"I got it locked up real safe," I said. "High and dry in a storage locker near Marathon."

"What the hell are you sayin,' Torento, you took my stash? What the fuck is going on here...?"

"Now, hold on. Hear me out."

"Goddamnit," he steamed. "Slimy, wop son of a bitch."

"Settle down and I'll tell you what's been going down. We got two visits from the police here this evening. Said they were checkin' to see if we were evacuating or not. Anyway, seeing as how I knew Vera had your stash here, I figured, just for safety, we better hide it off the premises. Just in case they come back and, uh, start gettin' nosy. You know they got a tendency to do that—with me especially."

Crassidy gawked at me, mouth agape and dead-eyed, bowlegged drunk. I wasn't sure what part, if any, of my scared-shitless bullshit story registered with him, and whether he would buy it. Then suddenly he seemed to wake up sharply, and fixed his gaze behind me.

"What you doin', boy?" he growled.

"Nothin'," said Russ.

"You put that goddamn phone down or I'll blow your damn head off!"

He ran across the room to Russ and flung him on the couch. Then he ripped the phone cord out of the wall.

"Now who you callin', boy?" he bellowed.

"Nobody."

"You a lying little shit," he yelled and backhanded Russ across the face.

"Damn it, Horse," I yelled. "Cut that shit out."

He pulled out a gun, and aimed the big, black barrel into my face. "You back off, Torento, or you goin' to be chewing on some lead real soon." Then he turned back to Russ. "You callin' the police, was you? You skinny little snake?"

Russ didn't say anything.

Crassidy turned to Vera. "You get your ass on the couch with your little lying snake right now!" he yelled. She crossed the room and huddled up close to Russ.

Then Crassidy beckoned to me with the gun and walked me over to the far end of the room.

"Now you listen to me, Torento," he began in a low, menacing whisper. "Just how goddamn stupid do you think I am?"

"Not very"

"This ain't no time for games, Torento," he said, with his voice suddenly shaking, like he was scared. "Now I don't give a damn what happened to that shit, long as I get my money, thirty-thousand, tomorrow."

"At three, like I said, I just got to go to Miami to get it."

"Why'd you change your mind?" he said. "About doing a deal?"

"Just got to thinking. I could sure use the money. Only thing is, I didn't expect you back so soon."

"Yeah, well it didn't work out with my little girl in Lauderdale. Then my van broke down. But that don't mean shit now does it?"

"Whatever," I said.

"Now I'm going to make something real clear to you, Torento. You fuck with me and them two are dead."

"I'm not going to fuck with you," I said. "Why would you even think it?"

"Understand me," he said, "you ain't back here by three, or if I see any goddamn cops trying to get in here, the little boy and his momma are dead, you hear me?"

"I heard you," I said. "Now why don't we all get some rest for a few hours. I'll leave when the sun comes up."

As best I could tell, Crassidy had bought my story. He went over and settled into a big easy chair, gun in lap, and kept watch over us that night. Russ napped with his head in his mother's lap, and I pretended to sleep in the old rocking chair in the corner. From time to time I'd blink a glance toward Crassidy and, to my disappointment, he never came close to dozing off.

I sat hidden behind my eyelids on that howling black night, and tried to assure myself I could really come up with thirty grand. I knew it would involve Danny—again—and hooking up with all that Cuban-Italian Mafia shit. I'd call him in the morning I figured, on my way up to Miami. I cursed myself for planning to get involved with all that garbage again. But what was I supposed to do? Crassidy was a fucking maniac and he had my back up against the wall. I only wished I carried a gun.

DAWN BROKE AND I caught sight of some fast moving clouds outside the window. The rain had stopped and there was a lone bird chirping in the palm grove. Crassidy sat upright in his chair, an evil mass of disheveled black hair, unwashed denim and mud-crusted cowboy boots. His cheeks rose up in some kind of malicious amusement when our eyes met.

"You best get that old box cranked up real soon, Torento," he said. "That's gonna be slow going to Miami and you got yourself a real tight schedule."

Russ and Vera rustled awake on the couch.

"You want some coffee, Joe?" Vera asked.

"I'm all right." I got up, grabbed the car keys, and headed toward the front door. Crassidy grabbed my arm as I passed him. His breath still stank of alcohol.

"Don't disappoint me, Torento," he smiled. "You ain't seen just how ugly I can get."

I went outside, cranked up Vera's old Saab, and started chugging up the overseas highway. I watched the sunlight starting to play on the blue-gray sea, and started running over various scenarios in my head. Calling the cops had a certain appeal, but I guessed that could deteriorate quickly into Crassidy shooting Vera and Russ, maybe even himself along with them. Or at the very least setting up some sort of stalemate hostage situation. Then I figured, why not just leave town? Keep heading north and call that scumbag's bluff. But no, he'd kill them. Just out of spite. And he'd get a real kick out of knowing how that would eat me up.

I pulled into Coral Gables around eight-thirty and rang up Danny from a phone booth. He was there and, true to his routine, had been up since six for his morning swim, meditation and all fish breakfast. He was surprised to hear from me and, at first, thought I was joking about the thirty grand.

"It's no joke," I said.

"You're serious."

"I'm serious."

He sniffed. "You're in some kind of shit, kid, serious shit, which by the way, I don't care to know about. Be here in an hour, we'll close a deal."

Danny Corona lived in a mansion on Biscayne Bay, south of Coconut Grove. I drove through a heavy iron gate, manned by two thugs in Ray-Bans, and went a quarter mile before parking in front of the massive pink and white Mediterranean-style villa. There were two Bentleys in the circle by the entrance and a goon in a three-piece white suit standing under the portico. He had a fat, beefy face and beady black eyes and I imagined he saw me and the battered, brown '77 Saab as a minor but unpleasant intrusion, as if a nest of palmetto bugs had been found underneath the terrazzo.

"I'm Joe Torento," I said. "Mr. Corona is expecting me."

He opened the door without a word and let me into the living room. Danny came out from the library and extended his hand.

"Always a pleasure," he said. His grasp was weak from a stroke he'd suffered about five years ago, and there was still a slight sag over the right side of his mouth and eyebrow. He must have been around seventy and you didn't have to look much beyond the tan and Ralph Lauren casuals to see a frail old man. It took a little effort to remind myself this guy ran the biggest crime family in South Florida. It took more effort to recollect that I was once welcome here as, if not exactly a member of the family, then certainly as somebody important. I'd been the boyfriend of his oldest daughter Enza. Only four years ago, but it might as well have been in another century.

"You look worried," he said as we sat down on the couch. "Somebody's after your ass, but I don't want to know who."

"Nothing like that," I said. "Just need to raise some investment capital for uh..."

"Joey," he interrupted me, "you're a nice guy, you know that? But you can't lie to save your ass. Now you're going to go over the loan details with Mario, I'm not going to get involved with that bullshit. But I'm telling you now, nice guy or not, this is all business, all right?"

"Got it."

"Don't fuck up, 'cause you ain't getting no special treatment."

"Got it."

He pulled back a little, and looked me over, shaking his head with disappointment.

"I thought you might have made something of yourself Joey, it seemed to me you had the stuff to be a...gentleman."

"I think I made a better impression on you than I did with Enza."

"Yeah," he smiled, "maybe. You know, she's got a son now, and she's living in Tampa."

"Good for her."

"She married a bank president. Real nice boy. To tell you the truth, she never mentions you. But what the hell, I'll tell her you said hello."

"Whatever," I said. I tried to smile, but inside I felt small and poor. I tried to gain some high ground by reminding myself that this palazzo was built on drugs, dead bodies and terror. But it didn't help too much.

"So what are you doing these days?" he asked.

"Running a little bar in the Keys," I said, "down in Crossroads, not too far from the Three Mile Bridge."

"Yeah, what's it called?"

"Vera's Place."

"Never heard of it."

"Well, it's off the main highway about half a mile. Then, uh, I'm getting into movie production, that's why I need some investment capital."

"What movie?"

"It's a love story. Set in Sicily as a matter of fact, Agrigento."

"Yeah? Terrible place."

We both knew I was full of shit, putting together some story to fabricate a little dignity. And he didn't see any use in calling me on it; it was too obvious what the scene was. I was a scared, hungry loser begging for money. And ready to risk my butt to get a loan that was going to bleed me dry in a matter of weeks.

"Well Joey," he said, "as always, a pleasure. Mario's going to take care of you in the office right now. Meanwhile, I got to get ready to fly up to Tampa, it's my grandson's second birthday. I'll give your regards to Enza."

"Yeah, sure, all the best."

I don't remember the exact details of the deal Mario offered me, only that I ended up borrowing forty grand to have something left over to start paying back the loan. Crassidy would have his damn money, and hopefully soon get picked up by the cops. I briefly thought of a scheme to get him to Maury's on Saturday, but I doubted he'd take the bait, and he wasn't so stupid as to not get suspicious about it. Anyway, I figured the only way to keep one step ahead of my new creditors was to give Jake a call and see if that offer in New York was still good. Say three or four hundred a day for, who knows, a month? Well, that'd at least keep my head above water.

I drove back real fast and, as I crested the bridge over Card Sound, a big flock of gulls took off from the girders overhead, like they'd chase away the last of the now distant hurricane's outer clouds. I turned up the radio to hear a blast of saxophone, some old, dancing Charlie Parker riff that tickled my brain and made me smile. Somewhere way back when, I remembered, my old man telling me that good things come when you least expect it. 'Course for all his damn optimism, he ended up with a big fucking bullet hole in his head.

But still, what the hell, he might have been right, at least some of the time. And anyway, how bad could it be in New York? Not worse than the time I'd let slip away in this dried up patch of fool's paradise.

I GOT BACK to Vera's house around two, and felt a sense of relief, accomplishment, even, that I'd pulled off this pay-off ahead of schedule. But when I walked in the door, I found Russ bound, gagged and lying on the parlor floor, and Vera sitting over him with a big bump and cut over her right eye. Before I could say anything, Crassidy came up behind me and pistol-whipped me to the floor. After I went down he started busting my ribs with his ugly, shit-kicking cowboy boots. When he stopped I managed to roll onto my back and look up at his sneering, beastly face.

"Lying, motherfuckin' snake" is what I heard him say. I tried to roll over onto my hands and knees but he kicked me good just behind my right ear and I must have gone out for a few minutes. When I came to, Vera was tying my feet together and Crassidy was counting up the cash he'd taken from my pocket.

"Vera," I managed to mutter, "what the hell is going on?"

"Joe, I'm sorry," she was crying, "I got to do what he says or he'll kill me and Russ."

"But I don't get it," I said.

She tried to stop her sniffling and tell me what had happened.

"'Bout an hour ago," she said, "the cops come by again, lookin' for you. Horace takes Russ and hides under the kitchen in the storage cellar. He says he'll kill Russ if the cops find out he's here. Anyway Horace heard the police talkin' about how you're supposed to meet him at Maury's tomorrow."

"Thought you were gonna nail ol' Horse for killin' that faggot cab driver, huh?" said Crassidy, while he counted up the forty grand.

"You got it all wrong, I began, "I was..."

"I ain't got nothin' wrong, pissant," he said, "'cept I was expectin' thirty thousand and now it looks like you done give me a damn bonus."

"Aw shit," is all I could mumble.

Vera sat me up and started tying my hands behind my back. "He's takin' us with him," she said, "said he needs hostages, just in case."

"Well, at least I need you for somethin' now, don't I," said Crassidy.

"So what'd you tell the cops?" I asked her.

"Nothin', Joe. Just said you'd taken the bus to Key West and you'd be back in the morning."

"Like I done told you to say, you double-crossin' bitch," Crassidy shouted.

"I ain't double-crossing you," she protested.

"Just shut your damn mouth and finish tying his ass up."

Crassidy got down behind me with Vera, stuffed two socks in my mouth, and gagged me real tight with a couple of torn old shirt sleeves. Then he bound my hands and feet together behind my back. After he checked all the fastenings he grabbed me by the collar and dragged me to the trap door in the kitchen that opened to the storage cellar. He opened it up and dropped me into the water that had flooded maybe two feet deep. I struggled to crunch up my belly and get my face just above the surface.

"You gonna die real quiet down there, Torento, like an old drowned dog. By the way, Torento, I killed that fairy cab driver, right after he done give me one real righteous blow job." With that he slammed the trap door shut and yelled, "Now let's haul ass!"

I held my face above the water, just trying to breathe. I heard a bunch of shuffling and then the back door creaked open and slammed shut. A minute later I heard a car start up, louder and more smooth sounding than the Saab, and it was coming from the back of the house instead of where I'd parked, out front.

Son of a bitch, I thought, Crassidy must have gotten one of his drug smuggling buddies to deliver a car to him. Ordered up via his trusty cell phone, no doubt. I heard the gearbox grind and listened to the engine rev and pause and vanish into the distance.

I took a deep breath and lay down below the water to rest my muscles. It looked like the only way I could get my face above the water was to put myself in a half sit-up position. That was about as high as I could manage with the way he'd tied me. I figured if I could fight off drowning, I had maybe twelve or fifteen hours to die from exposure. That water was dark and cold and there was a whole pitch-black room full of it.

In the first hour I was down there, I'd come up with a bobbing and dunking routine that let me inch my way back to the steep stairs that led to the outside hatch door. Once I got back there, I thought, I might be able to rest my back against the stairs and keep my nose out of the water. Of course then it would be a matter of dying from the water sucking all the heat out of me. But who knows, someone could come by, right? That's what I told myself. I mean, people did wander by the house, sometimes straying up from the bar. I remembered once, just last winter, some folks from Chicago knocked on Vera's door—thought she had a bed and breakfast going. But then again, that was during tourist season and now, well, let's face it, the bar's all boarded up and the island's nearly evacuated. Still, it could happen, I told myself. The state park is just down the road and people wander along the beach and footpaths, and occasionally come on Vera's property. I mean, I'm not going to fucking die here, right? I've been in tight spots, plenty of them, right? I'm not going to die in two feet of water in somebody's cellar, that's all there is to it.

I kept talking to myself like that, and little by little sliding toward those back stairs. Three hours must have passed until I got there and I rested against them just as I'd expected, feeling, I guess, like I'd just climbed my own private Everest. I tried to see if there was a way I could squirm up them, but it was impossible. I lay there a few more hours, in what I hesitated to describe as a deadly silence. There was nothing but my own breathing, and the lapping sounds of this cold bath against my chilly ears. Now it took every ounce of energy I had left just to stay leaned up against the stairs. I could feel myself shivering and weakening and part of me wanting just to pull under and give it up.

A few times I must have fallen asleep, because suddenly I'd find myself with water up my nose and I'd be coughing through the socks he'd stuffed in my mouth. As the hours passed by, weird images started to jump out at me through the darkness. I'd see some terrifying animal, like half snake and half vulture, flying at me with teeth sharp and bright as neon lights. Another time I thought Crassidy was strangling me. My body felt like a strange, squishy ball and I started to get confused about what was up or down, where I was or even who I was. I began to hum and moan through the socks just to give me something I could pay attention to. But that too was sapping my strength, and I had to stop and rest. And when I did rest the idea of death looked sweet and peaceful. "Sweet and peaceful," I said to myself, and kept repeating it, a lullaby that would carry me gently into death.

Then, suddenly, I began to hear voices; strange, otherworldly voices. Voices; laughing, teasing, high and low; voices that buzzed in some incomprehensible language. Then there was breathing, rapid, crazy, inhuman breathing. I heard myself moan and mumble curses and I banged my head hard against the cement steps, as if it could somehow make things clearer. It hurt like hell but somehow the pain sharpened me. That inhuman breathing, it...damn it, there was something above me, I thought, something, in fact, walking on the locked hatch door above me.

I listened, breathlessly, trying to figure out if I was hallucinating or not. Fuck no, I thought, some kind of animal is scratching and sniffing over the door. Then those voices again, I'd be damned if they weren't right outside, coming maybe from the back stoop, no more than ten or fifteen feet away. Some strange, buzzing mumbling, a man and a woman it seemed, sometimes laughing, both of them with a high cackle. But the language they were speaking, it wasn't English, that I knew.

My head started to clear in the excitement. There were people out there and, I guessed, a dog scratching at the cellar door. I started to make all the noise I could, splashing with my head, making high-pitched sounds maybe the dog could hear, moaning, humming, groaning, you name it. The dog began to cry and scratch and sniff harder over the door. Then I heard the voices coming closer, accompanied by footsteps in the brush. I splashed and groaned with everything left in me. The voices were right over me now, absolutely unintelligible through the door, but maybe with some sort of Slavic, yeah, Slavic sound. I heard knocking on the hatch door, knuckles rapping on the wood.

"Open the fucking door," I mumbled through the socks. "Open the damn thing."

There was silence above, momentarily, and then one of the doors slowly opened. I saw the dark outlines of what appeared to be a boy and a large dog. The dog began to bark dutifully and his voice echoed all around me.

I yelled out a muffled "Help, help me!"

Then I heard a low, manly voice say, "*Anya, posmatreet.*" (Look).

A woman's shadowy form appeared to the right of the dog. I smacked the water with my head and continued to yell for help. The dog let up on his barking and cocked his head slightly, as if he understood my situation. The woman opened the other hatch door, and the dog scrambled down the steps and splashed into the water beside me. He started to lick my face all over with his warm, rough tongue. I heard the man's voice again, clearly the voice of the figure I thought was a boy, calling the dog's name: "Senya, Senya, *shto*, ah—what who is there?"

Senya gave a mournful little howl and continued to lick me. The man, this very short man, began to step tentatively down the stairs. He kept calling the dog's name, as if to assure himself.

When he got to the last couple of steps, we could see each other's faces.

"Oh my God," I heard him say.

"Zhenya." I heard the woman's voice above. "What is it?"

"Oh my God," he repeated.

I nodded my head up and down frantically, trying to yell for him to help me. He slid his hands under my arms and started to yank me up the steps. In a minute, he'd landed me on the grass beside the cellar hatch. I felt delivered as a newborn babe, and was blown away by the little man's strength. They both got busy unfastening me and Senya, whom I could now see was a big black Lab, nuzzled and licked me and did his best to warm me up.

I heard myself gasping, "Thank you, thank you," the moment I was ungagged.

"You are welcome," the man said.

"Thought I was dead for sure," I said.

The woman said something to him in words I was starting to figure were Russian.

"*Nyet. Ne bezpokoyetce*" (No, don't worry), the man said.

"*Kak ti znaesh?*" (How do you know?) she said. It seemed to me she was worried that they were putting themselves in danger by rescuing me.

"Don't worry," I said. "You are in no danger. A crazy man tried to kill me but I'm sure he's far away from here by now."

"You speak Russian?" the woman asked.

"No, but I understand a little."

"How?" she asked.

"Took it for a semester in college," I tried a weak laugh. "Thought I was going to be a spy."

"Who are you?" she asked. Now she had the tone of a cop.

"Anya, let him rest a little," said Zhenya, "he is very weak." He had untied the last of the fastenings around my feet and I started to rise, to see if I could stand up. My knees buckled and my rescuers held me steady.

I smiled at them. "The name's Joe Torento. I'm a bartender, and, uh...very, very happy to meet you...all of you...and that includes Senya."

"He's very smart dog, yes?" said Zhenya.

"Oh yeah," I said, "very smart and very good."

They walked me around the backyard a bit and I got a little better on my feet. They asked me whose house this was and I told them how it was Vera's and how I'd been staying there during the hurricane. I didn't go into all the details about Crassidy, just told them there was a misunderstanding about money and I'd become the mistaken target of a vendetta. They didn't push me on it; it was as if they'd seen it all before.

Anya said they'd been driving up from Key West and had stopped at the beach just down the road to watch the stars and give Senya a chance to relieve himself. The night was so beautiful that they decided to walk along the beach, and then meandered up the footpath to Vera's yard. They'd just been standing there talking at the edge of the yard when they noticed Senya getting real excited about the cellar hatch door.

Zhenya said they'd have to get going very soon, because they were going to be staying in Miami at the house of a friend who was out of town. It was already getting close to two in the morning. It crossed my mind, just for a second, to have them stay at Vera's; but then I thought I must be crazy. First, I figured, there's some crazy outside chance Crassidy might come back, just to see that I was dead. And second, seeing as how I'm headed out of here anyway, and now close to broke, why not hitch a ride with them to Miami?

"Say," I said, "I'll tell you what, if you don't mind, I'd like to grab a couple of things in the house and ride up to Miami with you. I'm due up in New York for some business, and that'd get me on my way. Would that be all right?"

"And you'll not try to kill us, Mr. Torento?" said Anya. She seemed to be only half-joking.

"Hey, c'mon now, I never hurt a fly in my whole life. Besides, in the state I'm in you'd just have to get Senya to sneeze at me and I'd keel over."

"It's okay," said Zhenya. "Anya, he's okay."

They helped me into the house and I changed into my khakis and a white shirt and took about three hundred bucks I had in one of the pants pockets. Then I chugged about a gallon of hot tap water and stuffed some cold turkey in my mouth.

"You don't need a doctor?" Anya asked.

"No," I said, "I reckon you all cured me."

There, in the kitchen light, I got a real eyeful of her. She was tall, blonde, full-lipped and gorgeous.

Then Zhenya spoke up. "You know, Mr. Torento," he said. "You still look a little blue around the lips."

He couldn't have been over five feet and I could see he was bulging with muscles under his palm tree and toucan tropical shirt. "Built like a brick shithouse" came to mind.

"I'll warm up," I said, "all I ask is that you guys bring the car round front."

IN A FEW MINUTES we were tooling up Highway One in a banged up, half-rusted relic of a Toyota Corolla with Pennsylvania plates. Senya and I were crowded up in the back seat with a bunch of luggage, me with my knees near my chin and Senya with his tail wagging across my face and his head out the window, smiling and savoring all that brisk rushing air. On the A.M. radio Bobby Darin was singing *Beyond the Sea* and every once in a while I'd catch a whiff of Anya's beautiful, apple-scented hair. I couldn't figure out yet the relationship between these two, but they were one of the oddest couples I'd seen in a while. Were they romantic or something? Or was he just her midget uncle? She looked to be no more than twenty. He must have been forty at least. But what did it matter? Main thing was I was getting some miles between me and Crossroads and that had to be good. Though there was one thing I was obliged to do and, I thought, the sooner the better.

"Hey, Zhenya," I said.

"Call me Gene," he said, "that's my American name."

"Okay, Gene it is. Look, when you get a chance, pull over to a phone booth, I got one call I have to make."

"Now?" said Anya. "It's three o'clock in the morning."

"No, I know. But, uh, this is uh, that is, the people will be up, I'm sure."

"You're very strange man," she said.

"Not really. I mean...if you really get to know me...not really."

As we approached a gas station on the right, with all the lights out, Gene said, "I see a phone booth, there, in parking lot. Do you need money?"

"No thanks, I'm fine," I said, and ran out to the phone.

I still had the Crossroads Police number in my head and dialed it up real quick. The damn phone must have rung thirty times before someone answered it.

"Hello," a voice crackled at the other end.

"Yeah, hello. This Crossroads Police?" I said.

"Yep."

"Who's this?"

"Who's this?" He sounded like some cranky old man.

"This is Joe Torento."

"Who?"

"Joe Torento, you know me?"

"Don't believe I do. Now what do you want?"

I'd like to know who I'm speaking to, first of all," I said.

"Averell. Officer Averell."

"Okay. Officer Averell. Now look, Horace Crassidy, I reckon you know who that is?"

"Yes, I do," he drawled.

"Well he left town yesterday, and he's got Vera and Russ Parish as hostages, see? He left about three, yesterday afternoon. Probably headed north, what kind of car he's got, I don't know."

"How do you know so much about this Crassidy fellow?"

"I just know, all right. This guy tried to kill me. And now, he's got a gun and hostages you understand? Vera and Russ Parish."

"Where are you calling from now, son?"

"On the road. And I've got to get going. I told you all I know."

"Well sir, maybe you have, but I reckon you ought to come pay us a little visit, anyhow."

"I don't have time for that. So good-bye, and good luck in nailing Crassidy."

I hung up. I'd done what I needed to do and as far as I was concerned I'd washed my hands of Crossroads Key. I only hoped they'd nab Crassidy before any more harm came to Vera and Russ.

I climbed back in the car and we rolled on through the star shimmering night.

"Your friends were up?" Anya asked.

"Yes," I said, "as a matter of fact, they're real night-owls."

"Night-owls?"

"Yeah, you know, they like to stay up at night."

"I don't know this word," she said.

"It's a bird," I said, "the owl, he's got a round face and his eyes are set next to each other, in front of his face. He stays up at night and hunts."

"I see, my English is not very good."

"Sounds good to me. I guess you studied it pretty well in Russia."

"No, I speak it only since I came to this country."

"Yeah, and how long is that?"

"Two years."

"Well, I'd say you've got some real talent."

At this Gene began to laugh, and Anya did as well.

"She's very, very talented girl," said Gene.

Well, whatever that's about, I thought. But I did want to know more about her so I asked her where she was from and all that other small talk stuff. She said she came from a city called Yaroslavl, about three hours out of Moscow, and got to the States on a visa arranged by an American businessman, someone she'd become friends with while he was on assignment in Russia. She stayed with him awhile and now was living with some friends and family she had in Philadelphia.

"She's very clever girl, too, Joseph," Gene piped in.

She said something to him in Russian, which I didn't understand, but it didn't sound too pleasant.

He just shrugged his shoulders and got this sheepish look on his face. Obviously there was more to her story, but I didn't figure it was my place to ask.

We pulled into Miami around five in the morning and parked in the driveway of a little stucco box of a place on the southwest side. Just fifteen minutes from my new creditors, I thought, and this is as close as I ever want to get to them. After we got inside, it was clear that the three of us were way past being sleepy. So Gene broke out some vodka from the freezer and we sat around the living room all morning, toasting and telling long stories and lots of bad jokes—bad jokes that suffered all the more in the translation from Russian to English and vice versa. We all got real loose and warm and a little sloppy. Anya lay on the couch with her head on Gene's lap, and every once in a while would tousle his bush of thick black hair. They had a couple of tapes of Russian folk singers they kept playing over and over. At one point Gene said to me: "Joseph, this is Italian Mafia who try to kill you?"

"Gene," said Anya, "this is very stupid question, it is not your business."

"The guy who tried to kill me, he's his own private Mafia," I said. "I don't know anyone who would trust him enough to join up with him."

"But you should get somebody to kill him," said Gene. I know some guys in Philadelphia, you could do it very cheap."

"Well, I've got to worry about other things right now, like my business in New York. Anyway, the guy's wanted by the police."

"The police," said Anya with this look, like she'd just tasted something bad. "They are same as Mafia, only poor and stupid."

Gene got up from the couch and poured us another round. "Enough talk of Mafia and police," he said, "let's drink to our happy futures, and to our friend Joseph's good health and good business trip to New York."

We raised our glasses and kicked back another helping of *Stolichnaya*. And right away that was followed by another round.

"To friendship," said Gene, "and very bad luck to our enemies, especially enemies who try to kill us."

That was the last toast I remember, though there must have been a few after that. The next thing I recollect was waking up in the chair I'd passed out in, seeing that Gene and Anya had left the couch for the bedroom, and feeling like someone had taken a ball-peen hammer to my head. I got up real slow and trudged over to the bathroom. I looked like a fucking mess in the mirror; bloodshot eyes, hair matted over my ears and neck, beard and mustache flecked with pieces of lint from the chair I was sleeping in. I opened the medicine cabinet to see if I could find some aspirin. There wasn't any.

But, what I did see was a shaving kit and a pair of scissors. I looked in the mirror again, and then back at the razor and scissors. Yeah, I thought, it's time, way past time as a matter of fact, to shed this long hair, half hangdog look and get all the lost years and Crossroads Key behind me. I lathered up in a jiffy and shaved off my beard and mustache and then grabbed the scissors and gave myself a real short haircut.

That's it, partner, I told myself. Arrivederci to you and all the half-baked scams, sour deals, and sleazy bad times. Right down the toilet along with your black whiskers and your long curly hair.

Then I found some Visine to squirt in my eyes, tucked my rumpled shirt in my rumpled pants and walked back out to the living room. The dog woke up and looked me over real good from his spot by the front door. He cocked his head and let out a little growl.

"Quiet," I said. "Don't you recognize me?" He put his head back straight and went back to sleep. I went over to a little table and scrawled out a note to Gene and Anya, thanking them for everything and wishing them a good time in Florida, and safe trip back to Philadelphia.

Then I stepped over the dog and went out the front door and into the balmy air of early evening. I walked up the block and found a pay phone on Southwest Eighth Street, and gave Jake a ring at his home.

"Joey," he said, "all right, what's going on?"

"Not too much. But look, is that offer you made me still good?"

"Still good? Of course it is, Joey, of course. I was hoping you'd change your mind."

"Well, I'll tell you what, I could really use the dough."

"Beautiful, that's beautiful. And I'm telling you, Joey, this is a case where I can really use you. It's big, very high profile."

"No kidding?"

"Oh yeah. Now look, we'll start Monday, all right?"

"Yeah, Monday, okay," I said. "But, uh, let's see what's today...?"

"What's today? For Chrissakes, Joey, it's Friday. Now c'mon big guy, you gotta get your head on straight. This is a serious goddamn investigation here, okay? This ain't *Jose Cuervo* and reefer and walkin' around with your head up your ass."

"Take it easy, Jake. I just had a long night, that's all." My head was pounding.

"Yeah, long night my ass. I don't wanna be hearing about no more long nights. This here's serious business."

"All right, all right, don't worry about it."

"So get up here tomorrow. You book a flight into La Guardia and I'll pick you up."

"I'm not going to fly," I said.

"Why? What are you talking about?"

"I don't like planes, remember? I'll take the train into Penn Station. I should be there by, let's say Monday. I'll give you a call."

"You're nuts, you know that? You're going to waste a whole frigging day."

"You'll survive. I'll call you by Monday."

"Yeah, yeah, you fucking nut job," he said. "Good-bye."

"Good-bye."

I hopped a city bus to the Amtrak station and saw the Silver Meteor was leaving for New York at six tomorrow morning. The ticket ate pretty good into my assets and I hoped to hell Jake could advance me some dough when I arrived. I figured Monday was not a half-bad estimate for New York, because there was this little stop I had to make along the way, just a few miles north of Brunswick, Georgia. Call it a layover, if you want, with a few hours to kill taking a look at some old wounds. Who knows? Maybe I'd even open them up wide and take a look way inside them again. To tell you the truth, I hated like hell to do it. But I figured I had to. Yeah, I just had to, before I could return to who I was and who I'd been running away from. An old ghost of bad deeds past, he was somebody I'd thought I'd left way, way behind. A guy named Dr. Joseph Anthony Toricelli.

Part 2

WHEN I GOT to the train station I crashed out on one of the benches, and slept off the worst part of my hangover through the night. Next morning I woke up and got on the train about a minute before it left. Pretty soon we were rocking up the east coast of Florida. I sat back in my seat and watched all kinds of washed white houses and high rise hotels rush past the window; canals and four lanes criss-crossing each other in a big sprawling grid and spreading out all over were golf courses, shopping centers, twelve-plexes and lines of stop and go traffic.

A couple of hours out of Miami this nice old lady got on the train, sat across from me and started sewing up a storm. After awhile I asked to borrow some scissors she had, and went over to the bathroom to trim up some shaggy edges I could feel in my haircut.

When I finished and gave back the scissors to her, she smiled and said, "I see what you did, son, but I believe you were handsome enough already."

"Thank you, ma'am, but I could just feel it wasn't trimmed exactly right."

"You're probably off to meet your sweetheart, and just too busy to get yourself a haircut."

"Something like that."

"'Course if you don't have a girlfriend, I could introduce you to some real pretty girls in Palatka."

"That right? You got some friends up there?"

"Well, I should hope so. That's where I live. I'm just down here visiting my cousin in Jupiter."

"That's some real pretty country up by Palatka. Big green fields and dead quiet roads."

"Well it ain't what it used to be, son. Lot of that fine green country's getting turned up for housing developments. Too many Yankees, if you ask me. Just a pity what's happening."

"Reckon you're right. Soon they say Florida's going to have more people than New York."

"Lord have mercy, now that's a fact. All these damn Yankees, thinking they found themselves a paradise."

"It's sure one cheap paradise," I said, "compared with what they got to pay up there."

"Oh now that's a fact. I declare, that's what it's all about, isn't it? Money. Money, money, money. God's earth getting paved over for the love of gold."

"It's real sad, selling away what you can never get back."

"Oh yes indeed. You know you are just a marvelous young man, you are. And tell me, am I right? About you going to see your girl that is?"

"Oh, yes, ma'am, you sure are."

"I knew it," she said proudly, "and where's she from?"

"Well, ah, she lives in New York, actually."

"Lord have mercy. She a Yankee girl?"

"Well, no, ma'am. Actually, she's from Europe, Russia to be exact."

"Russian! Now isn't that exciting. Well how in the world did y'all meet?"

"It was at an international conference, in Washington last year. Her name's Anya, just felt something special for her the moment I met her."

"That's simply wonderful, wonderful. And what sort of work do you do? But, well I do declare, I don't even know your name. Mine is Mary Lou, by the way, and it's a pleasure to meet you."

"Same here, a pleasure. My name is Joseph, Joseph Toricelli. I'm a medical doctor."

"That's wonderful, Joseph. And is Anya as well?"

"Well, she's a scientist, working in cancer research."

"Marvelous. You know I've just got to tell you about my allergies. I was just in Boca Raton, seeing a specialist; you see I'm allergic to everything. Newspaper, cotton, plastic, ballpoint ink. Oh, it's simply a catastrophe. And nobody seems to understand it or do a blessed thing about it. I just itch. Well, you can't believe how I itch all over, it's the strangest thing!"

"Puzzling," I said. But this little game of mine was starting to give me a sick feeling and I could see we were heading into some real boggy places. Places where the just spit and shined shoes of Dr. Toricelli weren't quite ready to go. As a matter of fact, I started itching all over as she went on and on about her damn allergies.

"You know," I interrupted her, "this really isn't my area, I'm a radiologist, you see." I felt a strange sense of panic growing inside me. "I would suggest the Mayo Clinic in Jacksonville". I looked at my watch. "But please excuse me a moment, I've got to use the phone to check my messages, top of the hour you see."

"Oh yes, yes, of course, doctor," she said, looking kind of hurt.

I nearly bolted from my seat and started passing real quick through each car, imagining I'd burst into the locomotive before I was through.

I was struggling for breath and my skin was on fire. This doctor bullshit, it was a mistake I told myself, I should have known. There's no way I'm over it, I thought, and it's no accident that I've been holed up in Crossroads and vicinity for the last seven years. An animal's got to have his place right? Where you can be safe from predators, where you can nibble at a little food and sleep when you need to. No, I thought, this was a mistake going to New York, I'm getting off at the next stop. I thought I'd heard them say the next stop was Cocoa.

I kept running through the cars until I stumbled into the club car. There was only the bartender behind the bar, and it looked like I'd startled him. I must have had some kind of wild look in my eyes.

"Morning, sir," he looked me over carefully, like he wasn't quite sure what to expect.

"Well, yes," I said, "good morning. Next stop's Cocoa, is that right?"

He thought for a moment. "Yes, Cocoa," he said. "'Bout thirty minutes north, that's right, sir. That your stop?"

"Yes it is, sir. My hometown as a matter of fact."

"Fine place."

"Oh yes, real peaceful, tranquil, safe place it is."

"Yes," he said slowly, still looking me over, subtly, but nonetheless examining me. As if there were some strange energy coming out of me.

"So," I said, trying to loosen up a little, "what's there for breakfast behind the bar?"

"Well, a little bit of everything, sir."

"Hmm—I know, a screwdriver, vodka screwdriver, double as a matter of fact. Little hair of the dog, that's what I need."

"Will do, comin' right up."

He turned his back and started mixing. I looked around the club car, like I was being pursued. But absolutely no one was there.

"Here you are," he said, turning around. "Breakfast of champions."

"Cheers." I guzzled it in one swoop. "Oh yeah, now that'll really straighten things out." I licked my lips and felt the warmth of the booze rush up on me. "You know what? I think I'll have another."

"You're a thirsty man," he said, and went to mix another.

I felt my nerves quieting down a bit. It was panic, I thought, that's what it was. But, I'd be better when I got off at Cocoa. After all, who needed this bullshit? Yeah, Jake would be pissed I thought, but he'd get over it. Putting together another coke deal began to look viable. That'd get Danny paid off, maybe even ahead of schedule. Fuck it all, fuck the police bullshit in New York.

I grabbed my second screwdriver and settled into one of the swivel chairs near the window. The scenery whisked by and I sipped my drink and watched a few other people trickle into the car. After awhile a big fat good ol' boy in a three-piece suit plumped down in the swivel chair next to mine.

"Howdy," he said.

"Howdy."

"Mind if I take a look at your paper?"

"Huh?" I hadn't noticed the Miami paper on the table with my drink on top of it. "Oh, no, no. Be my guest."

He sat back with the paper, clearing his throat every once in a while. I continued to watch the scenery.

"Quite a case they got going down there in the Keys, huh?" he said.

I hardly heard him. I was thinking about how I could shape up this coke deal.

"Bunch of characters," he went on.

"Yeah? How so?" I asked, kind of absentmindedly.

"Drug arrests, assault and battery, hung jury on a rape case," he recited. "That's our justice system for you, set 'em free for more mayhem. Son of a bitch should have gotten the chair a long time ago."

"Probably so," I said. I was multiplying half-kilos times dollars and calculating a profit margin.

"'Course they're looking for a motive, police suspecting a drug ring," he said.

"Drug ring?" I said. "Really?"

"Yep," he said. "Look here." He put the paper in front of my face, and pointed at some photos. "Real couple of characters in those pictures, wouldn't you say?"

The second I glanced at it I inhaled a mouthful of vodka screwdriver and took a coughing fit. Bits of orange pulp got sprayed onto the good ol' boy's spiffy suit.

"What the hell." He stood up and backed off as best he could. He looked like he was going to cry. I caught my breath and between hacks spluttered out how sorry I was. I'd become the center of attention in the Silver Meteor Club Car.

"Terribly, terribly sorry," I said, trying to get my voice back. "Got a real bad spastic esophagus, she just binds right up on me. Going to see a specialist at Mayo about it today."

"Well you settle down there, son," he said. "You want me to fetch you some water or something from the bar?"

"Yes, please, water'd be just fine."

While he was at the bar I read over the sickening headline story. The first thing I saw was a photo of Crassidy, probably from his driver's license, and a police drawing of me, with beard, long hair, and thick eyebrows. They'd made my eyes way too far apart. Then I saw a photo of this dead cab driver, Francis L. O'Connor, a narrow-faced kid with short black hair, long sideburns and thick black frame glasses.

The article led off by describing the "slain cab driver" as a "recent graduate of Yale University" and the "youngest son of Michael O'Connor, flamboyant president and CEO of VitaCom International, the world's largest electronic media and publishing company, and the late Mary Beth Morrison, celebrated film actress who died tragically last year in an automobile accident." It went on to say that "Francis O'Connor was the nephew of Theodore Morrison, the senior U.S. Senator from New York; the grandson of Thomas Stearns Morrison, 34th President of the United States; and great-great grandson of Andrew Clay Morrison, famed 19th century oil and railroad baron."

The family was offering a $200,000 reward to anyone having information leading to the arrests of Crassidy and me. Holy shit, I said to myself, they got me tied in with the murder of a Morrison. This is going to be a tabloid-fucking circus. The story went on to say that the O'Connor kid had come down to Key West only a month ago. He'd taken a job as a taxi driver with the idea of supporting himself and "gathering material" to finish his first novel. The family had apparently expressed concern about their son driving the night shift, but he'd said it was all that was available.

The rest of the story was on the inside pages. The continuation began with the heading "Taxi Dispatcher and Writer's Diary Lead Police to Suspects". It looked like, in addition to the message O'Connor left with the taxi dispatcher, he'd also made an entry into the electronic notebook he carried, which the police were only able to unlock yesterday.

What he recorded was reported as follows: "5:15 A.M., Wednesday. I'm parked in front of Vera's Place, a total dive, gorgeous Horse Crassidy is getting his associate Joe Torento, I like the sound of that, to join us. Big Horse says 'there'll be all sorts of blow goin' on'.' I stopped right there and tried to figure out how the hell Crassidy could possibly be trying to hook up with me at that hour. Then the good ol' boy came by with the water.

"Here you are, son. My word, you lost all your color."

I tried to smile. "I'll be okay, just looking over this article."

"Go ahead, go ahead. I want to know what you think."

What I thought was that Crassidy must have started talking about cocaine and maybe sex with this kid. He'd probably already passed off some of his stash to Vera, and she probably went to hide it in her favorite place, that green metal box under the cement block under the bar. She'd always said she didn't want any stuff in the house, and must have only made an exception a couple of nights ago because of the hurricane. At any rate, Crassidy must have been pounding on the door of the bar that morning, thinking he could grab a taste for him and the O'Connor kid. He probably mentioned my name because he was going to wake me to unlock the door.

But I'd be damned if I remembered any noise in the night. And why hadn't he gone up to the big house to get Vera to unlock the door? Maybe he figured that was going to be too big a hassle. But as I read on, it only got worse. The police quoted Larry Albuquerque, the drunk who runs the filling station across from Vera's, swearing he saw Crassidy "peel out" of Vera's parking lot in his blue Chevrolet, around three on Thursday, with "somebody in the driver's seat that sure looked like Joe Torento." That drunk, near-sighted, bullshitting son of a bitch, I thought. He couldn't tell Vera from me, or from that mangy old German shepherd he kept that scared all his customers away.

The article ended by providing what details it could about Crassidy and me. Crassidy was described as "about six-feet-four, with a big belly, shoulder length black hair and a stubbly black beard." He was forty-seven years old and had a criminal record going back to age nineteen, when he was convicted of armed robbery after knocking off a convenience store. Besides a hung jury on a rape case and assorted assault and battery charges and drug arrests, he'd also dabbled in right-wing militia activity and had once been suspected of illegal possession of explosives.

Much less was said about Joseph Torento. Just a physical description: "about six-feet-two, medium build, shoulder length curly hair and a black beard and mustache." He was described by two individuals "who declined to be identified" as "a quiet man who seemed to keep secrets." No criminal record had been identified, though local police said Torento was "thought to be in a drug smuggling partnership with Crassidy." They also added that Torento had been "evasive and nervous" when questioned about Crassidy, and "kept changing his story" as to what he knew of his whereabouts. The "suspect's last contact with police was by telephone at 3:00 A.M. Saturday, when he alleged Crassidy had tried to kill him and had abducted hostages, as yet to be identified. This was thought to be another attempt by Torento to confuse the police in their investigation of the murder."

When I put down the paper, I felt like I'd been fast-forwarded into a nightmare. Except this was really out there, with a life and weird momentum of its own. I was just some fucking little pawn in the process.

"So what'd you think?" asked the good ol' boy.

But I was speechless.

"Them dumb asses. Bet you they had no damn idea who they were killin'. You wait and see, they're gonna get the chair."

"But, but..." I tried to say, "they're...presumed innocent, until proven..."

"Oh, c'mon, buddy. You want to go and get all technical with these boys? They are no count, no goddamn good white trash, you hear me? What they need is a real quick trial and a real speedy, no-frills execution. And this dead boy's daddy's gonna see to that, I can guaran-godamn-tee you."

Overhead the conductor announced we were coming into Cocoa. I was feeling hunted and ready to be trapped and suddenly, I found myself standing up from my seat.

"Well, nice talking to you," I said. "This is my stop."

"Thought you were goin' up to Mayo. That's in Jacksonville, ain't it?"

"Huh? Oh yeah, sure it is. But uh, got to make a stopover here in Cocoa. Anyway, good-bye."

I BOLTED OFF the train and started wandering up and down the streets around the station, trying to collect my thoughts. The bottom line, I tried to tell myself, was that Joseph Torento didn't exist anymore. No address, no driver's license, no credit cards, no tax returns, no phone or electric bills. No insurance policies, no car titles, no voter's registration. They could gather all the fingerprints they wanted, because I'd never been arrested and had no police record. My only official communication with the outside world had been through my post office box in the name of Joseph Toricelli, in Miami. That's a huge post office and I never had any specific dealings with anyone there. No one's ever going to connect Joe Torento with that box, and I'd close it out as soon as I got to New York.

But wait a minute, I thought, is that where I'm going, to New York? 'Cause just a little while ago, I was going to bag the whole thing, right? So where else am I going then? Not back to the Keys, not back to the Caribbean, and no....no, there's no way I can go back to that lost life of drug dealing again. That's a one-way ticket to Hell, without even having to die.

So what do I do? Is there any choice but to go to New York? I mean, at least there, maybe I really do have some kind of opportunity, to "rejoin the human race" as Jake put it. To try to do something useful, again. I can do it, I thought, I really think I can do it. No one will ever see Joseph Torento again.

As I walked down the street, I went by a little clothing store, and stopped to take a long look at my reflection in the display window. I passed my hand along my clean-shaven face, and ran my fingers through my freshly cut hair. I couldn't see how I bore any resemblance to that face, to that grubby, too wide face of Joe Torento in the police composite. I couldn't imagine anyone else seeing a resemblance there either.

Then I thought about how long I'd had that bearded, long- haired look. For all the years I'd called myself Joe Torento, as best as I could remember, but definitely after the last time I'd been anywhere in New York. Yeah, that was right, I thought. I'd always been pretty much clean-shaven in New York, except for a little stretch of time during med school, when I had a bit of a beard and longish hair. But that was years ago now, and I really doubted anyone there would have any clear recollection of how I looked then, and be able to connect me with that police composite. No, I'm okay, I told myself, I'm okay. There's nothing to worry about. I'd actually disappeared back into my real self.

By the time I finished thinking all this over, I was near the bus depot. I went in to ask about any northbound buses leaving any time soon.

"One leavin' for Savannah in fifteen minutes," the guy said.

"That by any chance stop in Doboy, Georgia?"

"Does if you want it to."

"Fine, give me a one way, please."

SOON AFTER I boarded the bus I fell asleep, and woke up several hours later, with the sulfurous stink of south Georgia paper mills in my nose. That meant we couldn't be too far from Doboy. That stench rocked my memory, and brought up images of the little cottage I'd had on the marsh, lazy afternoons with Janine and days spent at the hospital taking care of the vets.

The Doboy Federal Hospital was a big old rambling place that looked like an oversized plantation mansion. Lots of columns and cupolas and big green lawns stretching straight out to the wild marsh. It was an eight-hundred-bed neuropsychiatric facility that treated everything from chronic hebephrenia, depression and post-traumatic Vietnam vets to alcohol and drug problems, court-ordered medication supervision and garden variety malingering. The only thing that the patients seemed to have in common was that everybody smoked and by high noon in most of the day rooms you needed sonar and a compass to navigate from one end to the other.

I ended up there by accident. I'd finished med school in New York six months early, you could do that where I went, and this was the only place I could find that would take an intern in January. I'd never lived out of New York and I was real interested in neuropsychiatry, so I figured, what the hell, go for it.

I remembered the first day I met the crew there. The director of the place was a soft-spoken guy from Panama who did about a foot-long comb-over of his bald head that seemed to defy gravity. His assistant, who was my boss, a Dr. Lojoy, was an overweight, puffy-faced, burnt-out rummy who smiled a lot and was always calling me Harold, for reasons I never figured out. Besides me, there were three other guys in training: two from the Dominican Republic who, between them, spoke a hundred words of English, and a real nasty guy from Cleveland who had to go to one of those offshore medical schools and was always defensive about it.

As I was remembering all this, I noticed the "Welcome to Doboy" sign and jumped up to tell the driver to stop.

"Well you sure waited 'til the last minute, didn't you?" he growled.

"Sorry."

He let me off in the center of Doboy, in front of the Piggly-Wiggly, which had gotten a re-facing and a new drug store next to it since I'd last seen it. Otherwise the two blocks of downtown Doboy looked pretty much the same; little stucco and oyster shell houses down little side streets, that dead-ended on a thousand square miles of marshland.

I walked into the drug store to get a soda and immediately saw I knew the young guy at the cash register.

"Excuse me," I said, "but aren't you Sam Hemmings?"

"Yeah," he said, looking at me a little cautiously.

"You remember me? Joe Toricelli?"

His face lit up with a big grin. "Well hell yes, doc, of course I remember you. How the hell are you?"

We shook hands and hugged each other. Actually, it had been real easy to recognize him, because his back had been twisted up from a fall from a tree when he was a kid. He was badly listing to the right and his collarbone made about a forty-five degree angle with the ground.

"So, you the mayor of Doboy, yet?" I said.

"You remember when I used to talk about that, don't you, doc? Well, I reckon I'm busy enough here right now."

"How are your folks?"

"Daddy's drunk, as usual. Momma's remarried, lives up by Statesboro. She got herself a professor husband, doc. Real smart, just like you."

"Hey, and what about that science stuff I tutored you on, you remember any of it?" I'd done some volunteering in the school with the slower kids, one of whom had been Sam.

"Sure I do, doc. But to tell you the truth, I dropped out five years ago. But one day I reckon I'll go back for my G.E.D."

"That you ought to do. Definitely."

"And say, doc, what the hell are you doing down here, anyway? Ain't you some fancy specialist up in New York now?"

"Well, not exactly."

"What are you doing?"

"Just came back from South America. Doing some charity work down there. Wanted to pass through Doboy and take a look at the old place."

"That's great, doc. 'Course you know the old Federal Hospital ain't what it used to be."

"No? How's that?"

"No sir. They just got a few patients there now. Most of the place is closed up. Happened about three, four years ago now.

"I'll be damned."

"Yeah, things is even more quiet around here now. They even closed the theater and the motel."

"No more motel?"

"Yeah, but that's okay, doc, 'cause tonight you're stayin' with me. Remember where I live?"

"Sure, I remember." Down the end of Sapelo Road, edging the hospital grounds. I really appreciate the hospitality Sam."

"Least I can do for you. Why don't you go ahead down there now, make yourself comfortable? Door's open, I'll be there in about an hour."

"Thanks, Sam. Believe I'll do just that."

THAT NIGHT WE ate pork and grits and played checkers under the tin roof of Sam's little three-room shack. The TV had been mumbling in the background. When the eleven o'clock news came on, Crassidy's photo and the police drawing of me flashed on the screen.

"Couple of ugly looking freaks, wouldn't you say, doc?"

"Sure are. What's the story with them?"

"Hadn't you heard? Been on TV and the radio all day. They killed some rich Yankee boy around Key West and the family's offering a $200,000 reward for them."

"Lot of money."

"Well I'm going to keep an eye out for them, and if I see them I'm gonna call that 800 number they got set up. Imagine gettin' $200,000. I guarantee you they wouldn't see my ass at the cash register no more."

Next morning I got up early, washed and dressed real quick, and scribbled Sam a thank you note while I heard him snoring in the next room. Then I walked outside, along the long fence that surrounded the hospital property and up to the main gate. A guard waved for me to stop.

"Good mornin', sir," he said. He was a nice old black man in a blue uniform.

"Yes, good morning, I'm Dr. Toricelli. Just headed over to medical records, got to pick up some reports."

"Yes, sir," he said, and nodded me on without checking further.

I walked under a row of big oaks draped in Spanish moss and up the steps through the dark entrance. There was no receptionist at the desk and no hospital operator at the switchboard behind the big glass window. The long corridors on either side of the lobby were empty and lined with processions of barred windows. I walked down the north corridor, my footsteps echoing on the bare floorboards and plaster walls. I headed toward Ward 5.

The elevator was broken so I had to climb the five floors of stairs to the unit I used to work on. I got to the top landing, out of breath, and saw the familiar sign on the door: "Ward 5 North. Patients, Staff and Authorized Visitors Only". The door was locked and no one answered after I'd pressed the bell ten or fifteen times. I rapped on the door and the sound seemed to echo into empty space.

I found a few old nails on the floor and tried to pick the lock open. No luck. Next I tried throwing myself against the big metal door and it seemed to budge, just a little. I thought I heard something on the other side, like a door closing. I listened hard. Nothing.

Then I noticed a long strip of steel propping up the window by the landing. I grabbed it and wedged it into the space I'd made between the door and the jamb and yanked until the door broke open. When I stepped into that vacant hall, one arm of an L-shaped ward with rooms arranged on either side, it seemed to start speaking the memories of my year in Doboy. Part of me wanted to turn back, but I walked into the ward, and paced slowly toward the glass-enclosed nurse's station at the other end. As I passed each room I saw naked bed frames, grimy sinks and old towels and bed linen scattered on the floor. When I got just outside the nurse's station, I could see up and down each corridor of the ward, and over to the day room built out from the corner of the L. This was the spot where it had happened.

That whole fateful afternoon came back to me sharply. It was just Wilcox and me holed up in the isolation room. He was slipping in and out of his own brand of madness, going from Vietnam to the hospital ward. Sometimes he was in the jungle or looking for whores in the slums of Saigon, and sometimes he was talking about injections he was getting that were poisoning his brain. And for him, who was I? Charlie? His doctor? One of his dead buddies? That depended on his mental state. But never did he waver from the idea that I was his hostage.

"I'll kill you motherfucker," he'd been shouting, "motherfuckin' red bastard." He was right up in my face, clutching his AK-47, whirling around to check for an ambush, and then back on me with wild, strangely dead eyes. Then he'd start sobbing, then talking, talking to dead Vietnamese children. Crying, then angry, then confessing.

"I killed 'em doc—you understand me?" he'd yell. "Fuckin' V.C. teen-age girls, fuckin' shot and fucked dead, you hear me?"

"I understand you, Ab," I said. "It was fucked up. Bad, fucked-up situation. But you're tearing yourself up, you got to rest, man."

He'd look at me a minute, listening, wanting to trust, but then he'd explode in confusion and paranoia again.

"You red goddamn motherfucker, you tryin' to get out of here, huh? Is that what you're trying to do?"

"No, no way. Ab," I said. As a matter of fact he'd mined both exit doors. The cops were waiting on the grounds, trying to maintain a keep cool strategy.

He fell back again, into his fugue, back into his private nightmare home movies, while I cursed myself and the guy who was supposed to know better, Dr. Lojoy. We'd kept cutting back Wilcox's fluphenazine. We didn't think he needed so much. It seemed to be blocking the memories we thought he had to "work through." At first it seemed to make sense, Wilcox was way over-medicated on that shit and he could hardly talk and walked like some cheap toy soldier.

When we lowered it about fifteen milligrams he seemed to get human again, his emotions came back and you could have a conversation with him. But then we thought; let's keep lowering the dose. It wasn't even clear he should be on it, and we were worried about long-term side effects. We lowered him down to zip over six weeks and it seemed he got more and more alive. He would talk articulately, and was doing real well in occupational therapy. But then, real suddenly, he started losing his temper. He came back from a couple of day passes high from sniffing organic solvents and one time took a swing at an aide. I told Lojoy we had to do something, and he said get him back on a few milligrams, start with five. Wilcox refused to take the medication and I went back to discuss the next step with Lojoy. But Lojoy was out for the day and told me over the phone to hold off on things 'til the morning.

"Okay," I said, "you're the boss."

But the boss was nowhere to be seen when Wilcox broke into a million pieces that next morning, which was the first morning of the siege. And he was on indefinite leave of absence by the time the whole thing ended, on the afternoon of the next day.

But what about Wilcox? As I now stood there in the ward, I wondered if he was still alive.

Then suddenly, I saw a shadow flash and disappear from one of the doorways down the hall. I thought I was seeing things. I stepped toward the door and looked into the room. Nothing. Then I saw shadows move across the floor again, just as the oak branches out the window heaved in the morning breeze. I thought I was nuts. I had thought for a moment Wilcox could be in that room. Then I thought I heard something behind the open door of the room, somebody breathing.

I'm flipping my fucking wig, I told myself, but I had to look behind that door. As I stepped forward, a voice came from behind the door.

"Halt, intruder!" it shouted.

"Who's there?" I shouted back.

"Halt and show your identification. Have you made an authorized entry?"

"What?"

"Who are you?" the voice said insistently. It sounded vaguely familiar.

"A doctor. Dr. Joe Toricelli."

"Ah! I once knew a Dr. Toricelli. From Brooklyn as I recall. He was a student of mine. Bright young man, but without a deep sense of commitment to his medical responsibilities."

Now I recognized the voice. Fred Melleran. Delusional disorder, lifetime service-connected disability, former medic. Insisted for years he was the hospital director and a full professor at the medical school in Augusta.

"Melleran, is that you?" I said. "Fred Melleran?"

"Dr. Melleran to you, Toricelli, we enjoy no easy familiarity."

He strode out from behind the door, with his chin out and his nose high. He was naked under a stained and filthy long doctor's coat, which was only half-buttoned down the front. His long gray hair was a mass of grease and lint and stray black brush bristles. His beard was wispy and patchy and his fingernails were going on two inches. He walked barefooted toward me, holding an unlit pipe with a well-gnawed stem. He stunk of urine and body odor, but kept up the imperious air of a distinguished, pompous academic, considering me carefully and reveling in his presumed superiority over me.

"So Toricelli," he began, "came back to visit the old school, eh? Tell me son, have you made anything of yourself?"

"I'm a consultant these days." I'd learned a long time ago you had to speak with Fred on his own terms.

"Consultant huh? And with what institution are you affiliated?"

"NYU."

"NYU? Fine program, fine department. I suppose we can be proud of you."

"Thanks, Fred."

"You do insist on familiarity, don't you? Well..." he said, softening a little. "I suppose we are colleagues now, and you are a good alumnus, aren't you?"

An awkward silence followed. It was as if we were alone on a long elevator ride and had run out of things to say. Suddenly, he spoke again.

"Of course you recall the Wilcox case, don't you Joseph?"

I felt my belly go hollow, and didn't say anything.

"A bit of nasty business it was, Joseph, and certainly you can't take all the blame. Still, it must be difficult for you to live with the fact that you virtually killed a patient with your own bare hands."

Melleran's words carried me back again to that afternoon.

Wilcox had surrounded himself with the guns and ammunition he'd smuggled in from the last three-day passes. Thank God the cops knew the doors had been mined, but they figured they could mount an attack through the windows of the north corridor, gambling that they could take out Wilcox before he had time to react.

"Of course," Melleran went on, "you could be forgiven on the grounds of inexperience. And we all know Lojoy erred gravely."

But, as I said, Lojoy was nowhere to be found, though the hospital tried to beep him repeatedly. The hospital director was covering for him and called me at the nurse's station two or three times.

"You must try to keep Wilcox calm," he advised me, "and convince him to take his medication."

"Right," I said, "easier said than done."

But I remember trying to talk some sense into Wilcox, long shot that it was:

"Ab, you got to get some medicine into you, boy. Your mind's messed up and it's playing tricks on you."

He looked at me, furrowing his brows, as if he were trying to understand.

"Doc," he asked, "you got some medicine?"

"Sure do, Ab, right here in the cabinet. You could take a shot right now."

"I don't want no goddamn shot."

"Then you take some of these little pills, Ab. It'll quiet your nerves, you'll see."

"You ain't V.C. doc, are you?"

"I'm telling you the honest to God truth now, Ab, we're in the Doboy Federal Hospital, and you're going to see your way clear through this mess if you take your medicine."

"I could be dreamin', doc, couldn't I?"

"It ain't no dream, Ab, I promise you. Now why don't you take some of these pills?"

His eyes started to close a little and his face got kind of rubbery. Maybe he was burning out, I thought.

"Hell yeah, doc," he sighed, "go and get the damn pills."

I scrambled over to the medicine cabinet and pulled out a bunch of five-milligram fluphenazine pills. I handed him a couple with a cup of water, hoping this two-day nightmare would soon be over. He took the pills and cup of water into his hands slowly.

"Doc, you ain't V.C., right?"

"I'm Dr. Toricelli. Remember? From Brooklyn."

"Yeah doc. But you didn't know Johnny Russo did you? He was from Brooklyn."

"No."

"Poor bastard. He killed himself, two days after we burned up the village. He knew after what he done he had to die." Then he began to sob again, right there with the pills and the cup of water in his hands.

Again he asked, "You ain't V.C., are you doc?"

"No, Ab. Just Doc Toricelli here with a little bit of medicine."

"What kind of medicine?"

"Little bit of Prolixin, Ab. It's going to quiet your nerves."

"Prolixin? Ain't that the shit Lojoy was givin' me?"

"Yeah, it is."

"That's the shit that messed me up, I ain't takin' that shit."

"Ab, that's not exactly right. You were on too much of it once and that slowed you down. But when you don't have enough of it you get sick, uh confused, nervous. Like now."

He squinted at me. "You tellin' me the truth, doc?"

"I swear, it's the truth."

He stood there holding the water and the pills, looking to one hand and then the other and then to me and back at his hands again. He licked his lips and then looked up at me. I kept a friendly smile on my face, but inside I was screaming, "Swallow the fucking pills you crazy son of a bitch."

"Doc?" he asked, softly.

"Yeah, Ab."

"Doc, I think you're scumbag V.C. you know that! You're a lying red motherfucker, you hear me?"

I stepped back. "Take it easy, Ab."

"You're a lying son of a bitch. Goddamn Mussolini cocksuckin' red motherfucker."

He came towards me; crazy, screaming, spitting; lifting the butt end of his AK-47 up to his shoulder. I kept stepping back toward the wall.

"C'mon Mussolini cuntface wop faggot. C'mon," he bellowed, so his voice filled up the whole empty ward. Then he lunged out at me and slammed me across the head with the butt of the rifle. I went out cold before I hit the ground. I woke up maybe an hour later, crumpled on the nurse's station floor where he'd dragged me.

Wilcox had his back to me, guarding the door to the nurse's station like some deranged sentry. He was singing a Credence Clearwater Revival song and taking aim at all sorts of imagined intruders. Every once in a while he'd take aim and then scan the gun up and down the rows of windows on each corridor. He seemed to have forgotten about me. I lay there for maybe an hour, watching him march and aim and survey the ward from his strategic corner, as if he were making battle preparations.

Suddenly I heard a crash down the north corridor. Wilcox whirled and opened fire. At who? The cops, it had to be the cops. Fire was returned and splinters flew and glass shattered around the nurse's station. Wilcox dove down and landed two feet from me. He hadn't been hit. The groans down the hall told me some others hadn't been as lucky. Then I saw five, maybe seven, uniformed men bound through the windows into the hall. Wilcox sprang up and mowed them down before they knew which way to turn. He peered down the other hall to check for another attack, and I saw my chance.

I sprang up with only one purpose in mind: to take out Wilcox, by whatever means necessary. This bullshit had to end.

I jumped on his back, locked both arms around his neck, and squeezed just short of breaking his neck. He bucked like a wild bull, dropped the rifle, and reached back and started scratching and pulling my hair. I bore down on his neck, waiting to hear something snap. He fell to his knees and then forward on his belly to the floor. But he was howling terribly and continued to buck, almost throwing me off him. I got my chest over his head and started smashing his face to the floor, over and over and over again until all his heaving and squirming stopped. I rested for a minute, exhausted and ready to pass out. Then, without any warning, he threw me off of him and rose up unsteadily to his feet, a blood-spattered beast, front-toothless and spluttering out foul-mouthed promises to kill me. I snapped to my feet, feinted right, swung low to the left, picked up the barrel of the AK-47, and crashed the butt end into the left side of his skull. He fell, for the last time, and it was only at that moment that I feared I might have killed him.

All this raced through my mind as I stood there before Melleran.

"Yes, Lojoy erred gravely," he repeated, "but we must reflect on the seriousness of your mistakes. The case had been mishandled for several weeks and you knew it."

"I wouldn't go that far," I said. "Plus, Lojoy was supposed to know what he was doing."

"Oh, is that so? So you were just taking orders, right, Toricelli? The words that have served as the last refuge of many a scoundrel. And, perhaps, as a young intern, we could say your naiveté exonerated you, technically. But you knew Lojoy was a drunk and an incompetent. And ultimately Wilcox was your patient. You had the legitimate option, in fact the obligation, of seeking consultation with another senior clinician. Did you ever do that?"

"No."

"No, you did not. But that is only where the mishandling began, Joseph. You also failed to check on whether Wilcox's person and belongings had been properly searched on return from each of his last three day passes. Isn't that true?"

"Yes."

"And on the morning the siege began, when everyone could see the terribly agitated state the poor man was in, what did you do? Instead of calling in security, you, in your grandiosity and imagined heroism, decided to meet one on one with him in his room. Thereby allowing him to hold you hostage at rifle point while he ordered the entire evacuation of the ward."

"I thought I could talk him down," I murmured.

"Talk him down?" Melleran roared with all the righteousness and anger of a prosecutor. "The man was in a manic, psychotic rage and was probably under the influence of hallucinogenic drugs!"

"It was easier to see that after the fact."

"No, Joseph," he intoned. "No. Granted you were young and inexperienced, though you were several months into your internship. But you grossly underestimated the danger of the situation, and did not act responsibly to help the patient. Primum non nocere, Joseph, first do no harm."

Melleran took a few puffs from his ragged, unlit pipe and pulled his tattered white coat a little closer around his unwashed torso. He seemed lost in reflection. After a pause of silence, he continued.

"Eight policemen died that day, Joseph. And your patient is beyond any further harm...or help."

"What exactly do you mean, Fred? What happened to Wilcox?"

"But, haven't you done any follow-up, Joseph?"

"I didn't have the stomach for it. I know he got transferred up to Augusta. But then I left town, not too long after that."

"So you did. Well soon after Augusta he was transferred up to Washington, D.C., at Pershing Memorial, where he remains to this very day, hooked up to a machine."

"Yeah?"

"A ventilator to be exact. He's brain dead but breathing. The family insisted upon it, as part of the final settlement."

"I see. And how do you know all this?"

"How do I know?" he yelled. "I'll have you know that as medical director I make it my business to know about every patient and their family!"

I looked at him, sadly. "Right, Fred," I said.

His face darkened, he shuddered and shrank under his white coat, and mumbled something to himself. Then he swelled up his chest, jutted out his chin and held up his nose.

"Well, I'm off to rounds in a moment, Joseph," he said, reaching out his hand, "good luck to you."

"The same to you, Fred," I said. I shook his hand. He turned back into the room and I went out the exit door and down the stairs.

I FOUND MY way back to downtown Doboy but I have no recollection of the walk. I was dazed and discombobulated and wasn't sure if I was dreaming or awake. I went into the drug store to say good-bye to Sam and waited to hop the northbound afternoon bus. When I got to Savannah I hung out there for a few hours before catching the evening train to New York. Somewhere in there I figured I needed an epilogue to the Doboy story, and I decided I would pay a visit to Wilcox, for better or for worse, when I pulled into Washington.

As the train rolled up the low coastal plain I tried to make some sense of all the memories, regrets and sorrows swimming through my head. I'd shitcanned it all after Doboy, and following that, everything just went straight to hell. I left town a couple months shy of finishing the intern year, and drifted down south to the Caribbean. There, I got hooked up with a girl who introduced me to a couple of guys shipping coke up from Aruba on cruising yachts. I'd already come up with the tag of Joe Torento, and that's how I became known in that nasty little world of drug trading. I was convinced that there was no worse piece of shit than I, and that I might as well just take whatever I could from the world.

Back then I tried not to dwell on the fact that this white powder was killing a lot of people and fucking up a lot of babies. I didn't even feel too bad when some counterfeit bills we passed off to some of the big boys in Bogotá caused the execution of a couple of guys I'd known. You want to play the game, then you got to accept getting hurt I figured. Pretty soon I got to know some of Danny Corona's people in Miami and, for a while there, I was living pretty high on the hog while taking care of distribution details in and around South Florida. That's when I got involved for a time with his daughter. We'd fly to Europe in her private plane and put on wild all night parties at her place in Coconut Grove. After we broke up, I lost my privileged position in the family and drifted on down to the Keys. I'd still use the Corona connection sometimes, and that's how I got involved with Crassidy. I was the middleman between the shit he was bringing in from Mexico and the wholesaling of it in Miami. But, as another couple of years passed, I got more and more disgusted with myself and the whole damned scene. One day, I figured I'd put it all behind me, so I settled in at Crossroads and became a bartender at Vera's Place.

And I was doing pretty well at steering clear of evil dealings. Until this last episode, with Crassidy's lost stash.

But now, I thought, that I'd come back to Doboy and come back to face the old ghosts, well maybe, just maybe I could salvage something, and try to get some things right again. Joe Torento was dead, damn it, and all history of him was hereby erased. No one from now on would ever know who I was.

We must have been a couple of hours out of Savannah while I was thinking all this stuff, and I was ready to go up to the club car for a drink. When I got there, who did I see but the bartender I'd seen last in Cocoa. I got real nervous. I guess I thought he'd figure out who I was. So I sat down quick in one of the swivel chairs, away from the bar, and picked up a newspaper. He seemed to look up at me just as I looked down at the paper. And when I'd look up at him, he seemed to look away. I looked down again and decided I wasn't going to look at him again. Did that son of a bitch somehow recognize me from the police drawing? No, I'm getting paranoid, I thought. Fuck it, I'm going to go right up to him and order a drink.

I got up, and as I approached the bar, said: "Hi, how're you doing tonight?"

"Fine," he said. "Say, you look familiar."

"Yeah?"

"Yeah, where'd I see you...yeah Cocoa, yesterday morning wasn't it?"

"Oh, yes, that's right."

"That's your hometown isn't it?"

"Yeah, right," I said, "good memory."

"And you had a little problem, chokin' up there, didn't you?"

"Oh, yeah. Well, that's fine now. Got some medicine for it. And, uh, ready for a little gin and tonic this evening."

"Sure thing. So where you headed to now?"

"Oh, uh, got some business up in Washington."

He turned to fix things up and I caught sight of my picture in the newspaper lying on the bar counter. The headline read, "Police Widen Search for Suspects in O'Connor Slaying; Morrison Family Grieves Over Latest Tragedy." The bartender turned around again, and saw me looking at the paper.

"That's a real shame isn't it?" he said. "Boy seemed to have everything."

"Yeah, it's awful."

"But they'll find those fools, you wait and see."

"'Course it's not clear they're both involved."

"Well, that's not what the papers say. Looks real clear from the evidence in the boy's diary that after they picked up this other character Torento, that's when the boy got killed."

"Don't believe everything you see in the paper, it's no accident that they call journalism the second oldest profession."

"What's that supposed to mean?" he asked.

"Figure it out."

I went back to the swivel chair and sat down with my drink. I was pissed at the papers and pissed at myself for feeling so rattled. That guy couldn't have any idea who I was. Joey Torento was fucking dead. Let him rest in fucking peace.

THE TRAIN GOT into Washington about six the next morning and I hopped a cab to Pershing Memorial, just across from Rock Creek Park.

When I entered the huge Art-Deco lobby there were people rushing all over the place. I heard a guard saying, "I.D.'s, passes, I.D.'s, passes" and saw a stream of people rushing through a narrow gateway. I went over to the information desk to get Wilcox's room number. "Who are you?" the lady at the desk asked.

"Dr. Joe Toricelli," I said, "just paying a...courtesy visit."

"1225," she said.

I slipped into the Doctor's Lounge on the first floor, pulled an old tie out of my sport coat, and fumbled through a Windsor knot. I looked at myself in the mirror. "Do you really need to do this?" I asked. "And what are you going to do if he somehow recognizes you?" I fastened up the knot and tried to smooth out the wrinkles in my shirt with my hands. I took a last look in the mirror.

"Presentable," I said to myself. "Now go see what you did."

When I got up to the twelfth floor, I suddenly got weak in the knees and couldn't make it down the hall toward 1225. I leaned against the nurse's station counter and tried to breathe deeply. I must have been white as a sheet but no one noticed because the shifts were changing and everybody was running around "checking out" to each other. I saw the chart rack against the wall, and went over and pulled out Wilcox's file.

I opened it up and scanned the details on the order page. Good, I thought, this guy wasn't on any ventilator. Melleran was full of shit. I flipped a few more pages. Fuck it all; "near-complete damage to forebrain functions, chronic vegetative state." Just then a nurse approached me.

"Can I help you?" she said, real businesslike.

I closed up the chart and put it back in the rack. "Uh, no thanks. Doing a psych consult but it looks like I've got the wrong Wilcox here. Must be on another floor." I wasn't ready to get into any conversation with her.

She turned back to her work and I scooted down the hall looking for Room 1225. I found it around the corner with Wilcox and another patient's name on the door.

I stood at the doorway, ready to go in, but my feet wouldn't move. I was scared shit. But of what? The poor bastard wasn't going to recognize me and get upset. What was I so afraid of? To face what I did? You've got to, I said to myself, you've got to fucking face it. Just then, a group of med students and residents and a tired looking attending doc came down the hall and approached Wilcox's room.

"Nothing acute in there," one of the residents said.

"Never is," another one joked.

They all shuffled by, ignoring me, as I stood there frozen. Then I took a deep breath, and went in.

In the first bed was a young woman sleeping. In the far bed by the window, lay Wilcox. His eyes were open, and he was looking up at the ceiling. His dark brown hair was neatly trimmed and he still wore an earring in his left ear. The TV was on over the foot of the bed, but there was no sign he was paying any attention to it. I stepped forward slowly, past the sleeping young woman, to Wilcox's bedside. He didn't seem to notice I was there. I reached up and drew the curtain around the bed, so I wouldn't be seen by anyone passing by the room. Then I whispered: "Wilcox, Wilcox, can you hear me?"

He blinked a couple of times. Was it just coincidence?

"Wilcox," I said again, this time louder, and I squeezed his hand in mine. This time not even a blink. I leaned over and gazed straight into his eyes. "Wilcox, you hear me?" He looked right ahead, at nothing in particular.

I studied his face and it seemed to me that traces of that fierce, paranoid look remained, in spite of all that brain damage. I touched his forehead and ran my hand down his cheek. I don't know why. Maybe to see if there would be any response, maybe to comfort him, as if he were a child.

"Wilcox," I heard myself say. "Look, saying I'm sorry doesn't mean squat at this point, but it's all I can say. I'm sorry, brother, I'm sorry for what I did to you."

Then he blinked again. Damn, I thought, could he have heard me? Could he have understood me? I believed, somehow, that he could. I wanted him to know, if he really could understand, that I was going to make good for him. That I was going to make good out of what happened to him.

"Ab, I'm making a promise to you...right now. All the bad that's happened to you...I'm going to use it to teach me. I'm going to use it to teach me to make good, to make good wherever I can, and to do the right thing by folks, whenever I've got the chance to. This I promise you, Ab. One hundred percent." I looked at him, and his face was real still. And I believed that, somewhere, he was listening real intently, to understand what I had to say.

"Ab...Ab," I said, "I'm with you, Ab, every day. And...and I'll do everything in my power to help you, and to keep on top of whatever treatment possibilities come up. I'm with you, Ab. So you rest here, and you keep hope alive in your heart. I'm with you...heart and soul."

He blinked again. I clasped his hand. I wanted to believe so bad he could hear me. I clasped his hand tight and then I let him go.

"I'm going to go now, Ab, but I'll be back, that I promise you. So you take care now."

I turned around and drew the curtains back, and started to walk out. But a tall, long nosed guy with thinning white hair grabbed my arm as I passed the young woman's bed. The thought of him being a cop raced through me and for a second I thought of bolting. But how? And to where?

Deny everything, I told myself, deny everything.

"Doctor," he said, and looked at me with this steely gaze. "I need to talk to you, right now."

"I'm very busy at the moment," I said. Look like a doctor, and act like a doctor, I thought.

"I understand, doctor, of course," he said, now strangely breathless and clamping down hard on my arm, "but it will only take a minute. I know you're a very busy man."

"Okay," I said, "Okay."

"You..." he began. I saw now that his jaw was trembling and his leathery face—I guessed him to be around sixty—was covered with hundreds of tiny droplets of sweat. He kept shifting his weight from one foot to the other as he spoke.

"You..." he said again, "You...your voice, something about your words, doctor, to your patient, I mean. You made me think...I...I don't have to, do I?"

"Have to what?"

"I...I don't want to speak here, I mean out here. Please." He nodded and looked over my shoulder. "Let's go back, in there, please, into the bathroom."

We shuffled back past Wilcox and went into the bathroom opposite the foot of his bed. My new friend or, patient, or whatever, closed the door behind him.

"Doctor," he said, trying to pull himself together, "and you are Dr.—?"

"Toricelli."

"Yes, I'm terribly sorry, Dr. Toricelli. Well..." his eyes darted around the small room, as if he were a newly caged animal. "Well...before I go on, before I go on, Dr. Toricelli...yes, before I go on...damnit, I need a cigarette. I must have a cigarette. Please, if you would, Dr. Toricelli, I understand it is absolutely against hospital policy, but I need...I need to smoke a cigarette right now. Would you help me with this window? Please?"

"Sure," I said, "no problem."

We both pushed and heaved for a few seconds at this little window, which was probably stuck from new paint. Just as we jerked it open, I heard a heavy, metallic sound come up from the floor. We both looked down, and there was a .357 Magnum lying across the tile. We looked up at each other and he started to laugh, in these short little squeaky gasps.

Then he said: "That, of course, is mine, doctor." He bent down and picked it up, and then looked it over, as if he was considering what to do with it. Then he lay it down on the windowsill.

"It was my friend, doctor," he said, "my very trusted friend. Until a few moments ago, when I heard your voice by the bedside."

"How do you mean?"

"How do I mean?" He paused to light his cigarette. "I mean that I came here to say good-bye to my daughter, the young lady in the other bed there. Beautiful girl, she'll be twenty-four next month. Had a bad time of it with heroin, overdosed last month. Papers had a field day with it. The doctors saved her, but there isn't a goddamn thing they can do for her now. Moved her up here two weeks ago, from the ninth floor. She doesn't say a word, doctor. Just sleeps and eats and...stares."

"Terrible situation," I said.

"Yes it is," he said, "and frankly, given the state of her brain, she's better off dead. God forgive me."

He took a deep drag off his smoke, and blew a big cloud out the window.

"But it's funny," he went on, "just this morning I convinced myself her 'situation', as you called it, was all for the best. I could say good-bye to her, and she wouldn't have to face her old man blowing his brains out. Just a few steps from her bed. Yes, I was going to do it right here where we stand. Less mess that way, I thought, right here in the hospital. And housekeeping could clean up all the loose ends. As a matter of fact, doctor," he said, looking at his watch, "according to plan I should have been dead five minutes ago."

"But why? What's so horrible that you'd want to do such a thing?"

He smiled. "Do you know who I am?"

"No, I don't believe you introduced yourself."

"And I don't in any way look familiar to you?"

I looked him over. "Not exactly."

"Remarkable," he said, extending his hand. "I'm Timothy Landsdowne, doctor. Very glad to meet you."

"Yes, you're welcome."

An awkward silence followed. Then he said, "The name doesn't mean anything to you, doctor?"

"No."

"Remarkable."

Another awkward silence followed, before I said: "You seem a good bit calmer now."

"I am, I am." But, doctor, I don't want to sound immodest, but I'm not altogether used to ah, introducing myself. You see I'm Senator, former senator that is, Timothy Landsdowne. I'm currently the President's Chief of Staff."

"I see." I did recollect the name, though up until a few days ago I hadn't gone in much for following the news. I felt like pretty much of a meathead not knowing who he was, but then again, my embarrassment wasn't exactly the main thing at that moment.

"I'll try to get to the point, Dr. Toricelli, about my predicament. I am being blackmailed and I simply cannot live with the available choices. I can either be owned by a ring of pigs who will sell my secrets to the highest bidder, or if they expose me, I can end my career in disgrace, with charges of espionage and likely imprisonment to follow. I think you can see the appeal of suicide."

"Maybe, but I'd need to know more details."

He laughed. "Yes, yes, I'm sure, doctor. But I'm not altogether inclined to go into them...right now anyway." He took a long drag from his cigarette and blew the smoke out to the warming morning air. The Capitol dome and Washington Monument were visible on the horizon and the gun's metal glistened in the sunlight on the windowsill.

"All sorts of details, doctor," he continued, "more sordid and varied than you can imagine. But they're of secondary importance at this point. I need to know what to do, now, right now."

"Give me the gun, that's number one. Then you've got to promise me you won't make any decision to die until you've hashed this out with a shrink."

"Hah, that's concise now, isn't it?"

"Look, uh, Mr. Landsdowne, as far as I can tell, there's no

emergency about killing yourself. On the other hand, if you do; well, obviously it's an irrevocable decision. So why not take the time to talk all this stuff over with somebody? You've got nothing to lose by doing that, am I right?"

"You are. I suppose."

"So," I said, and took the gun and put it in my coat pocket, "promise me you'll call a shrink this morning and get moving on this, okay?"

He smiled. "I like you, Dr. Toricelli. But why should I call anyone? I've got you as a doctor, don't I?"

"Well, that's not going to work. You see I'm just here on a courtesy visit. I'm based in New York."

"But, but I could call you. Why I could come up there, quite easily as a matter of fact."

"Yes, well...but you see I'm really not taking on any new patients right now. And my calendar is very full, for several weeks. I'm a consultant, and I'm very, very busy."

He suddenly became downcast and I got nervous that he'd slip back into that hole he'd just come from.

"But look, Mr. Landsdowne," I said, "you call up the psychiatry department right here at Pershing. That's a start. And uh, here's my number in Yonkers," I scribbled down Jake's number. "I'll be there tonight and you call me if you have any difficulty hooking up with somebody. Agreed?"

"Agreed."

I was relieved to see him brighten up again. We came out of the bathroom and shook hands at the foot of his daughter's bed.
He wanted to stay there a while longer, which seemed okay to me. And so I zipped out to catch the next train to New York.

I JUST MANAGED to hop on an express, due to arrive into Penn Station at one o'clock that afternoon. I gave Jake a call as the train pulled out of the station and asked him to meet me when I arrived, if he could. He was a little pissed off at the short notice, but said he'd come pick me up.

As I settled into a seat, my brain was whirling with images and memories of where I'd been and where I might be going. I told myself, tried to reassure myself, that Landsdowne would be okay. Especially without his gun. I'd emptied the bullets out of it into the men's room at Pershing, and tossed the thing into a reservoir off Georgia Avenue, on the way back to the train station.

Landsdowne's not going to kill himself, I thought. It was one of those moments of panic, that's all. He'll get somebody to talk to and, well, I felt good that I'd given him Jake's number, just in case.

Seeing Wilcox, that was another story. I felt all ripped up inside over that, just like the day it happened, or pretty close to it. He was destroyed all right, vegged out courtesy of my nasty, skull-crushing hands. But still, there was something that had gone on back there, even though I knew it didn't make any medical sense. It was like he sensed somehow what was going on, that it was I who was by his bedside.

I knew the chart said chronic vegetative state. That meant basically brain dead, except for the centers taking care of his heart and lungs. The fact was, I'd killed the poor bastard and no amount of speculating about what he could or couldn't be aware of was going to hide that one simple fact. "That you just got to live with," I muttered, "you just got to live with it. And make good, make good."

Then, out of the corner of my eye, I caught the guy sitting across the aisle from me staring at me. Looking me over real good, like I was some kind of specimen. I looked straight back at him, and he stuck his nose back into his tabloid, where I saw the name "Torento" in big letters marching across the front page. What the hell was he looking at? Nothing. Nothing. Just at some guy talking to himself, that's all. To hell with Joe Torento. He was a useless, cowardly fuck who up and disappeared into the early morning vapors over Miami.

My thoughts shifted over to Jake and what was awaiting me in a couple of hours. Last time I'd seen him was the Christmas before I'd busted Wilcox's head, which would now make it about seven and a half years. His first son, Frank was his name, was just born then. Now he and Nina had two little girls as well. At least that's what I remembered from the last Christmas card.

I'd never exactly explained to him what had happened at Doboy. Or why I never got around to seeing him or any other family in the last seven years. But I guess he'd kind of read between the lines and got the idea that something bad had happened while I was in Georgia. Then he just accepted that I'd sort of...lit out for the territory, as Huck Finn once said. He knew me well enough not to ask about the specifics of what I was doing around Miami, but I don't think what he suspected was very far from the truth.

I suppose it's pretty much impossible to hide stuff from a guy who's known you all his life and was the closest thing I ever had to a big brother, or any kind of brother, for that matter.

We'd grown up next door to each other in Brooklyn. My mother and his were sisters and they'd always been very close. They both married cops and bought houses next to each other on Carroll Street. Jake's old man retired a while back and he and my aunt moved down to Arizona. My old man died when I was five, a real hero's death they said, busting some punks in a heroin deal in the Bronx. Some hero, I often thought, getting his head blown off in an ambush in some fallen down tenement. My mother miscarried the next week, after being pregnant about four months with who would have been my sister. She never remarried and we stayed in the house on Carroll Street and sort of became part of Jake's, and Aunt Norma's and Uncle John's family. My mother died about eight years ago. She had uterine cancer and went very fast. Her funeral was around Thanksgiving, the last time I'd seen all the relatives together.

Jake and I had kept in touch off and on in the last seven years. I'd call him two or three times a year, usually after I'd get some note or card from him at the Miami post office box. He was always asking me to get back to New York and would tell me about all the money I could make if I finished my training. He was always looking after me; always worried I'd lost my way for good and was going to miss all the good opportunities. I never paid much attention to what he said or wrote, but just took it as his way of telling me he loved me. As the train rolled on I got drowsy, and soon I dozed off, as all those thoughts and memories played gently on my mind. I must have napped through most of the rest of the trip, because the next thing I remember was seeing the profile of Manhattan over the ridge that runs up from Hoboken.

Part 3

I TIGHTENED up the knot in my tie and stood up for a minute to tuck in my shirt. In a few minutes the train slipped under the Hudson, rushed on through the darkness, and then gradually slowed and squeaked to a stop.

"Pennsylvania Station, New York," blared over the p.a. system, and I got up and walked off the train.

I took the escalator up to the big waiting room and wandered around looking for Jake.

I walked over to a guy with his back to me wearing a blue baseball cap.

"Jake?" I said.

The guy turned around. "What?"

"Sorry," I said. He was about Jake's height, a couple of inches shorter than I, but...well I guess I was a little nervous that day.

I drifted over to a newsstand, hoping I'd see some good news about Crassidy. But no way. The headline in the *Herald* got me sick. "Butch Crassidy and the Crossroads Kid," it screamed out, over pictures of me and Crassidy. I was shaking my head when I felt a hand grip my shoulder.

"Joey," I heard Jake say.

I turned around and he gave me a big hug.

"Joey," he said again. "Looking good, still the same Joey."

"All right Jake," I said, "good to see you, man, you're looking good, too."

But that was bullshit. His round, cheeky face looked awful, tired and puffy, so that he looked like he was about ten years older than his age, which was coming up close to forty. His once thick black hair was getting thin and a little gray, and he'd grown out more than a few sizes around his waist.

"Yeah, well I don't know how good I look, Joey, but uh...Hey, Frank," he said, looking down at this little pug-nosed kid wearing a Yankees cap, "say hello to your Uncle Joey."

"Hi, Uncle Joe." The kid seemed a little shy.

"How are you, Frank?" I shook his hand. "You're bigger than I expected. How old are you now?"

"Seven," he said, "but I'll be eight pretty soon."

"Well, you're getting up there, that's for sure," I said.

"You like Derek Jeter?" the kid asked me.

"Uh, Derek Jeter? Well, I'm not exactly sure who that is."

"Hey, Uncle Joey's a funny guy," Jake piped in, "he's making like he doesn't know the best shortstop in baseball, not to mention the best all around guy in the Yankee line-up." Jake looked at me and opened his eyes wide, as if to say, "What the hell's the matter with you?"

"Right, right," I said, trying to go along with the cover-up.

I learned more about the Yankees from Frank on the parkway up to Yonkers. By the time we pulled into Jake's driveway I could have given you the batting line-up, most of the important batting averages and who had the most home runs or RBIs or the lowest ERA.

We got out of the car and walked across the toy-strewn front lawn. Nina and two little blond-haired girls came out the front door to greet us.

"Say hi to your Uncle Joey," their mother instructed them.

"Hi Uncle Joey," they sang together.

"How are you, Uncle Joey?" Nina smiled and hugged me. She'd put on a little weight, but otherwise hadn't changed too much; still the same smiling brown eyes, turned up nose, high cheeks and short, jet-black hair.

She put my face between her hands, and pulled back and examined me.

"You look good," she said, "very healthy. You'd never know it with all the stories Jake is telling me."

"Yeah, like what?" I laughed.

"Never mind that now, Nina," said Jake. He sounded real sharp with her.

"What's your problem?" she snapped back at him.

"Mommy," the taller girl said, "I want to show Uncle Joey his room."

The little girl took my hand and, with her sister, led me and Jake and Nina and Frank up to the guest room. I had a strange feeling of unreality, as if I'd suddenly and mistakenly landed in a play and got handed an empty script. I wondered if I could really live here, even temporarily.

"Very nice," I said. "Very nice room you've got for me here."

"Okay, okay," said Jake. "Enough for now with Uncle Joey. You're going to see him in a little while for dinner. Me and Uncle Joey are going to talk now."

Jake took me down to the basement family room and closed the door behind us. Then he went over behind the bar.

"Beer, Joey?"

"Sure, thanks."

He handed me a can of Bud and I ripped it open as I sat on a barstool.

"It's great to see you." He opened a beer and leaned on the bar. "It's really great to see you. I missed you, you know what I mean?"

"Yeah, I know what you mean," I said. "I missed you too."

"Hiding all these years, huh Joey? Somewhere down in Margaritaville, right?"

"Something like that."

"Well look, I ain't going to get nosy, not yet anyway. I'm just glad you're back, big guy."

"I know. I am too."

"And, uh...look, we got a lot of catching up to do. But first I got to bring you up to speed on this case. What do you say?"

"Yeah, sure," I said. "Lay it on me."

Jake went over to sit in the big La-Z-Boy, rubbed his eyes, and then sat back and clasped his hands behind his head.

"It's like this, Joey. A week ago last Friday, a doctor was murdered in his office on Park Avenue. The guy was a very big shrink, and as soon as it hit the news, all kinds of important people started screaming out for us to find out who did it. A rumor started going around that there's some maniac killer in the neighborhood. Two weeks before the doctor got hit, an old lady was stabbed to death, while she was opening up her flower shop in the morning. This was just around the corner from our dead shrink. A month and a half ago, a fourteen-year-old girl got raped and beaten, on the way to school, over by the reservoir gate at 90th Street. So by now, the whole neighborhood, for that matter the whole friggin' city, is going bullshit. The *Herald* is playing up the serial killer theory, and the *Register* is breaking the mayor's balls that crime's going out of control; right in what's supposed to be such a nice, safe neighborhood."

"So is there any evidence that the crimes are related?"

"No, but who knows? Could it be one of the patients of this doctor? We got to check out all the possibilities."

"What's the psychiatrist's name?" I asked.

"Epstein, Dr. Horatio Epstein."

"That name sounds familiar, vaguely."

"Vaguely? Now c'mon Joey, I thought you were studying this stuff once. I mean the guy's written about twelve books, you know? He's a world famous, uh, psychon...uh, whaddaya call it...?"

"Psychoanalyst."

"Yeah, exactly. The guy was a famous psychoanalyst, see? Treated a lot of big shots, socialites, movie stars, you know what I mean?"

"I'm getting the picture Jake. You got another beer?"

"Sure, sure. Reach over under the bar and grab yourself one. So you see Joey, this is very high profile. And believe me, the mayor's making it high priority. He's still real sensitive about people saying he made a mistake when he shitcanned the Commissioner a couple of years back.

"Yeah, why did he do that?"

"Hey, Joey, don't you know nothin' no more? I mean, don't you read the papers?"

"No."

"Well, even in Miami they must have heard of Commissioner William O'Neal. The mayor fired him 'cause he was taking too much credit for crime going down, get it?"

"Yeah, sounds like a good reason to fire him."

"Well, that's politics, Joey, not your specialty, I know. But your cousin here's got a little talent for it, which is why you got this job, okay?"

"Yeah, yeah, okay—but about this job," I thought about Joe Torento's recently established Most Wanted status, "I sure hope there isn't any red tape for me to go through here, 'cause if there is, I'm sure as shit not going to take the job."

"What red tape, Joey? What are you talking about?"

"I'm talking about interviews, that's what. Employee screenings and all that shit. There's no way in hell I'm doing it. I'm not explaining anything about myself to any police personnel department dipshit. Is that clear?"

"Hey, don't worry about it, sport," he said. "You're already in, okay? Just on my say so, that's all. You're working as a medical consultant to the police department and you're dealing directly with me. You see? Now what could be more simple than that?"

"And that's it? Nobody else is asking any questions, is that right?"

"Nobody, chief," said Jake, laughing, "and I'm the one who cuts you your check at the end of the week. So look at that. You just went from Chumpville to landing yourself a place on Easy Street. All 'cause your cousin here is carrying the big stick. See?"

"The big stick," I said, shaking my head, "what a bunch of bullshit."

"Hey, it's a fact Jack," said Jake. "That's all there is to it. But anyway, you know what my hunch is about this case?"

"No, what's your hunch?"

"I don't think the murders are related, but I do think Epstein got knocked off by one of his patients. I mean, this happens, right? I been doing a little reading on it. You get some real whacko paranoid type, right? He gets the idea the shrink's trying to control him, right? That the doc's the one who's causing all their bullshit. So things get real heated up and—Bingo—the doc gets his head blown off."

"Yeah?" I said. "By the way, is that how Epstein died, with his head blown off?"

"Nah, he got strangled. Probably with a tie. But not his own, as far as we know."

"I see. Look, Jake, what you're talking about here, getting killed by a patient, especially with the setting this guy practiced in, it would be very, very unlikely. So, I mean, I hope you're checking out other possible suspects; friends, family, whatever."

"We're checking out everybody, professor, believe me. And so far the family and the few friends he had are coming up real clean."

"Okay, but I still say a patient killing him is a real long shot."

"All right, Joey, a long shot, but it's possible, right? Look, the guy's strangled right there in his office on a Friday afternoon. There's no theft, no sign of break-in, no struggle. The building lobby and private entrance are secure and video-monitored. No one's coming in or out of his office suite except patients."

"Well, if you're so hyped up about this hunch, do you have a suspect?"

"We've got some patients we're taking a second look at. The guy's got a lot of patients, and that Friday he probably saw half a dozen."

"Who's interviewing the patients?"

"Me. And we got some forensic specialist from Charity Hospital. But that's where you come in Joey, you're going to be my special forensic assistant, see?"

"Sure, so long as it doesn't mean I'm taking orders from you."

"Oh you'll be doing plenty of that, buddy boy," he said, laughing. "And you're going to like it. This is going to be your big break, Joey, this is going to..."

"Jake, Joey, dinner!" I heard Nina yell.

"The boss is calling," said Jake. "We'll pick this up again later. Let's chow down."

We went upstairs and sat down to a big five-course dinner, with lots of pasta and fish and meat; and afterwards tarts and liqueur and all kinds of sweets. After Jake and Nina put the kids to bed, we all went to sit out on the patio, with cups of espresso and a bottle of Amaretto. Jake was a lot more looped than I'd remembered him getting, and Nina seemed uptight and ready to tangle with Jake over any little thing. Jake seemed mainly to try to ignore her, and sip a little more Amaretto and talk about the Yankees.

We went to bed pretty late that night, and I remember lying in bed for a while before I fell asleep, thinking about what could lay ahead for me with these two murder cases; both the one I was cast as a suspect in, and the one I was called to help solve. I kept thinking to myself that Joe Torento's dead, and that's all there is to it. He's gone, without a trace, and you've got nothing to worry about now. And yeah, I could get myself to actually accept that; but then the idea of spending my time around police headquarters, while I was being hunted down myself, spooked me more than just a little bit. But c'mon, I thought, there's absolutely no way in hell anyone could be looking for me there, and it's got to be impossible that anyone could recognize me from that police drawing anyway. No I thought, there's basically no risk. And besides, soon they'll nab Crassidy and rescue Russ and Vera, and any suspicion of my involvement in the O'Connor kid's death ought to get totally blown away.

So I was safe. Safe enough, anyway. But then, I saw there was something else that looked a lot more important to me that night, than just being safe. No, the important thing, the really important thing, was that I was getting a second chance. A chance to do things right, and to actually do something good. To make good on the promise I'd made...to Wilcox, to myself, to whomever. To do good and to do the right thing, whenever and wherever I could.

NEXT MORNING Jake and I got up early and drove into the city. His mood was sullen and he had the weather-beaten look of a real bad hangover. He didn't want to talk much.

We drove down by the scene of the crime, Park and 87th, and Jake pointed out the door to Epstein's office. It was a private entrance just to the side of the lobby entrance of a big, elegant apartment building.

"Anybody in there now?" I asked.

"He shares the suite with another shrink. I think he's out of town till tomorrow."

"Yeah, what's his name?"

"Roland. Dr. Bertrand Roland."

"Now that name definitely rings a bell," I said.

"Oh yeah," said Jake. "He wrote all those books on women and, what the hell does he call it, uh, oh yeah, self-esteem."

"Right, right."

"Yeah, Nina knows him. He's on all those fuckin' talk shows."

"Weird combination," I said. "Roland and Epstein in the same office."

"Yeah? I don't know. But Roland's the one who found Epstein. Came in the next morning, on Saturday, and found him dead on his ass on the floor."

We headed downtown to Police Headquarters, and Jake took me

over to personnel, just to sign a couple of tax forms, so I could get paid as a police department "expert consultant." Then we went upstairs to the tenth floor, first to a reception area where he introduced me to a couple of secretaries, then on to an adjacent office, to meet the forensic psychiatrist who would be "directly supervising me."

She got up from her desk and walked over to greet us as we came in. She looked to be my age and was a real knockout, with dark eyes and thick wavy black hair falling over her shoulders. She had full lips, long legs, and a lean, athletic shape. I forgot about all the stacks of files, dingy walls and gray furniture around us, and started dreaming of the two of us walking on some moonlit tropical beach.

Then I heard Jake say, "Uh Madeline, that is, Dr. Moore, meet Dr. Joe Toricelli, our new forensic consultant in the Epstein case."

She thrust out her hand to me, and shook my hand, in fact, my whole arm, like it was one end of a jump rope. "Welcome aboard," she said, "we'll need to get you to work as soon as possible."

"Good," I said. Something about that handshake shattered any dreams of moonlit beaches.

"Now I'm very squeezed for time," she said, "but I'm going to update you on what I've done on this case in the last week. First of all, I have assembled a roster of Dr. Epstein's active patients and have prioritized them by levels of likelihood to act out violently. At the top of this list is a young man who is schizo-obsessive with manic and narcissistic features. He has a history of violence toward his parents and was very agitated around the time of Dr. Epstein's death. I have already seen him once and you and I will be seeing him together for a second interview. I presume you've had extensive experience in forensic interviewing, is that right?"

"Well..." I said, obviously hesitating. "I wouldn't say that, exactly."

"Mm-hmm," she said, with her lips pressed together tight, "well, in that case, I will conduct the interview and you will take notes. You should be able to handle that, shouldn't you?"

"Yeah," I said, feeling kind of peeved, "I think I can handle that."

"Now, the second thing I have done," she said, with this little smirk on her face, "is to have made a diagnostic analysis and summary of the twenty-four patients Dr. Epstein was seeing actively. I have interviewed each one of them personally, both counseling them in regard to the loss of their doctor, as well as making a general psychological assessment of them. They understand they are not murder suspects per se but, through their observations and general familiarity with the office environment, may help us to understand how and by whom Dr. Epstein could have been murdered. Your contacting them for a follow-up interview, the procedure for which I have completely manualized and will go over with you, will not come as a surprise to them. Now, are there any questions, or are you clear about things so far?"

"No questions," I said, "all clear so far." But the only thing I was clear about was that I felt like taking the next train to Miami. And I did have one big question, not for her but for myself, which was just how miserable was I going to be working with, or under, this Dr. Moore? Her condescension, all business attitude, and her stuff about "manualizing" procedures was all really rubbing me the wrong way. I looked over at Jake, who was standing by the window and looking out, and didn't seem to be paying any attention to us.

"Take this manual, Dr. Toricelli," she said, reaching over to her desk and handing me a fat, loose-leaf book entitled "Forensic Procedures in Psychiatry, by Madeline Moore, M.D."

"Take it, and study it thoroughly, cover to cover."

"Sure," I said. "Thanks. And, uh, you wrote all this, huh?"

"My name on the cover would indicate that," she said, "wouldn't it?"

"Right, I guess it would," I said, feeling like an idiot.

"Now I need to know, Dr. Toricelli, what exactly has been your experience in forensic psychiatry?"

"Well...nothing, actually."

"Nothing? What about in your residency, didn't you have a course in legal issues? Perhaps visits to prisons or state hospitals?"

"No," I said, and looked over to Jake again, who seemed to be fixed on looking out that window.

"What about post-residency training," she said, "fellowships, psychoanalysis, consultation involving court cases?"

"Nothing like that, Dr. Moore. But you know, frankly, I think the main issue here, in terms of qualifications, that is, is some general medical and psychiatric knowledge. I don't think it will be too difficult to spot the murderer, if he or she is, in fact, one of the patients. I mean, if it's a patient, they'll find it very hard to keep a secret."

She looked at me and shook her head slightly. "Just what is the basis of your assertion?" she asked.

"Common sense. If a patient killed Dr. Epstein, it would be a crime of passion and, in all likelihood, terrible guilt will follow the act and the murderer won't be able to keep it to him or herself."

She laughed at this, without bothering to hide her contempt. "Your common sense sounds very...poetic, Dr. Toricelli," she said, "but in this investigation we will do better to rely on carefully constructed, scientifically informed evidence."

"Well, that's just my opinion," I said with a shrug, "but, uh, you're the boss."

When I said this, her tone seemed to soften ever so slightly.

"Tell me, Dr. Toricelli," she said, "where did you train?"

"Doboy," I said. "Doboy, Georgia Federal Hospital."

"Doboy?" she said. "In psychiatry? I don't believe I've ever heard of it."

"Well it's a real well-kept secret," I said, "but it was really quite a place for learning about, well...among other things, violent behavior."

"Yes," she said, and seemed already to be thinking about something else. "And that reminds me, I'll need your C.V."

"C.V.?" I said. "I don't have a C.V."

"Well get something typed up," she said. "I'll need it in the morning, for my files."

Then she looked at her watch. "I have rounds at Charity in twenty minutes," she said. "I will meet you again at nine sharp tomorrow right here. You will read the manual today, and I will review it with you tomorrow. That should get you on the way to developing some level of...competence."

"Competence?" I said. I felt like she'd hit a raw nerve.

She looked at me with just a hint of a smirk again. "Yes, competence, Dr. Toricelli," she said. "We all have to show competencies in specific areas of practice and expertise, don't we?"

"I couldn't argue with that," I said, smiling just a little too wide, "and anyway, you're the boss."

"Yes...well you're repeating yourself now," she said. "I will see you tomorrow morning at nine sharp." With that she whirled around and walked out the door.

I looked over at Jake, who was still real interested in the window view.

"Hey, thanks a lot, asshole," I said to him. "Some plum job you got for me here, huh?"

"What do you mean?" he said, turning around to face me.

"I mean, I don't exactly call this 'Easy Street,' playing some dumb shit errand boy for this control freak bitch."

"Hey, take it easy, Joey, you don't know how many strings I had to pull to get your ass in here. Face it, your experience is a goddamm joke. Not that I don't respect you, don't get me wrong."

"Don't get me wrong?" I said. "And just how the fuck am I supposed to take that kind of statement?"

"Look, sometimes you just gotta swallow your pride, know what I mean? You're here because of my connections, not because of your goddamm resume, or whatever the hell she called it. And she knows all that, see?"

"Yeah, so?"

"Well, let me put it to you this way," he said, "just look at this as your ticket out of Palookaville. And quit all this egotistical bullshit, all right?"

"Ah, fuck it all."

"All right, Joey?" he said. "You hear me?"

"All right, all right. Like I said, fuck it all."

"Atta boy," he said, laughing. "Anyway, look, I got a 10:30 meeting with the commissioner and then I got some internal investigation bullshit this afternoon. So why don't you take some time here to read her book?"

I looked down at the ugly blue-covered mass of paper, which I'd laid down on her gray steel desk.

"Yeah, I'll speed read that tonight, Jake," I said. "But meantime, I think I'll nose around up there at 87th and Park."

"At Epstein's office? To do what?"

"Look around a little, you know? Let my imagination play."

"Joey, look, your job here is to interview a few patients, and enjoy getting overpaid for it, that's all. So who are you supposed to be, Columbo now?"

"C'mon, Jake, I just want to look around the place a little. It'll help me when I'm talking with the patients later, you know what I mean?"

He gave me a tired, blood-shot post-Amaretto look, and then muttered, "All right, what the fuck," and reached in his pocket and tossed me a set of keys.

"I been carrying these around since yesterday," he said. "The blue top and the red top ones open the street entrance to the suite, the silver one opens the inside entrance, which is immediately after that, and the gold colored one opens the waiting area to his office. His actual office is off limits right now, so all you're going to see is the corridor, his waiting room and the bathroom next to it."

"That's a start. I'm going to go up there right now."

"Just be careful. And meet me back here at 4:30."

"You got it," I said. "Later."

I TOOK THE Lex line up to 86th Street and got out drenched in sweat, after riding in one of the so-called air-conditioned cars. I probably looked a little wasted to the two doormen in front of Epstein's building, because they looked at me warily as I approached them. But they brightened right up when I told them I was from NYPD. We started chatting it up about the good dead doctor and one of them started joking about how they'd all miss that big Christmas tip from him.

"Gee, you guys are real sentimental, aren't you?" I said.

"Oh, he was a good egg, he was," said one of them, with a slight

Irish brogue.

"But a real weirdo," said the other, a bald, stocky guy who talked out of the side of his mouth.

"How do you mean?" I asked.

"The guy was in his own world," said baldy. "He'd walk right by you and you'd say to him 'Hi Doc'; and he wouldn't say nothing, wouldn't even look at you. Sometimes he'd be talkin' to himself, you know? Like some of the patients he was seeing. Hey, it takes one to know one, huh? Am I right or am I right?"

I turned to the Irish guy. White haired, older, he looked like he could be cast as some kind of senior statesman type.

"Did you know very much about Dr. Epstein?" I asked him.

"No, no, not I, officer," he said. "As I said, he was a kindly sort. Which I'll tell you, confidentially, is more than I can say for his partner."

"Partner?" I said.

"Oh yes, yes. I believe he is still out of town now, you know, Dr. Roland is his name. Oh, they clearly didn't like each other, they bickered over everything. Even how their mail should be sorted. A bad marriage those two, oh yes. They owned the place together you see."

"Yeah?" I said. "So any ideas on who killed the kindly and strange Dr. Epstein?"

"Well, I was here that day," said the Irish guy. "Ernie here was on a long weekend."

"Big Bronx holiday," said Ernie, "can't beat it."

"That day," the Irish guy went on, "seemed quite normal. I saw perhaps six or seven people come in and out that door."

"And did anyone look strange that day?" I asked. "You know, nervous, crazy, whatever?"

"Well, of course many of them are liable to look nervous, officer. But no, no, nothing unusual."

"But wait a second, Frank," the Bronx guy butted in. "What'd you tell me this morning, remember?"

"Ah, yes, well it's probably nothing, but, yes, it was a bit unusual that I saw Dr. Roland step out of a limo that Friday afternoon, around three. He's such a frugal man you see, and it just struck me as strange that he would use a limo."

"Frugal?" I said.

"Cheap bastard is more like it," the Bronx guy barked. "Ten dollar Christmas bonus for the last ten years. You believe that?"

"Ernie, now..." the Irish guy whispered.

"Aw, c'mon, Frank, this ain't exactly confidential. Cheap bastard that's all, that's why the limo stuff sounds whacky."

"Do you remember anything else about Dr. Roland, or the limo that afternoon?" I asked. "Like the name of the limo company, or if Dr. Roland said anything that you can remember?"

"No...no, nothing, officer," said Frank, "really nothing more than what I've said. Simply, that he stepped out of a limo, a black limousine, that's all."

"Okay," I said, "well, if you do remember anything then you'll call us all right?"

"Yes, of course officer uh...what did you say your name was?"

"Toricelli," I said. "Dr. Toricelli, police medical consultant."

"Ah, yes, Dr. Toricelli," he said. "I certainly will call you if I remember anything else. We've already been given the number to Homicide. Now, if you'll excuse me, the mail's here and I must bring it to the back."

"Sure, sure," I said, "go ahead. And good talking to you. I'm just going to take a peek inside the office suite now. See you later."

I went over and unlocked the outside door of the suite, which gave way to a small entrance foyer, which had doorbells for both Roland and Epstein. Then I unlocked the inside door and walked into a grim, drab, L-shaped corridor. Just to the left at one end of the "L" was a locked door that said, "Waiting room, Dr. Roland."

Straight ahead, at the other end of the "L" was a door marked, "Waiting room, Dr. Epstein."

The place had a quiet, closed-in feel to it, and seemed an unlikely scenario for a murder. I went down to Epstein's waiting room door and unlocked it. I entered into a tight little room with an old couch, a couple of chairs and a door marked "Bathroom." Just to the side of the couch was the door to Epstein's office. I turned its knob and pushed, but it was dead-bolted with one of those old-fashioned locks. I peeked through the keyhole and saw light spilling onto a deep red Oriental rug. The desire to get in there suddenly grabbed me. I began scavenging around the place for a pin or a nail or something to pick the lock with. I found a big paper clip under one of the chairs, unbent it here and there, and in a few minutes I'd picked the lock open.

As I walked in, I saw the office was rich with old leather chairs, modern art, huge bookcases and a table for tea and coffee. Journals were neatly lined up in a glass case and an old raincoat hung on an ornate wooden coat tree. He had a CD collection with lots of Mozart and Bach and opera, and the wall over his desk was covered with diplomas and certificates. He had studied and trained at all the best schools and he'd been president of the Manhattan Psychoanalytic Institute.

His own books held a special place in a case near the fireplace. I looked over the titles: *Specific Techniques in Narcissistic Pathology*, *The Hollow Self: Explorations in Borderline States*, *Fame and its*

Vicissitudes—Studies on the Psychological Burden of Celebrity. On the back of the last title I saw a profile picture of Epstein—glasses, graying hair and a beard, and a long, delicate nose. I looked over to his leather chair behind the desk, allegedly the exact scene of the strangulation. Jake had told me he was a flabby, small guy, and I supposed it wouldn't take much to overpower him. I wanted to get into his desk, but I figured I'd already done enough trespassing for now. So I closed the office door, re-locked the bolt, and left the suite.

Out on the street I waved goodbye to my doormen buddies and headed over to Fifth Avenue and down near the museum. I killed a couple of hours staring at old statues and trying to get used to the idea of being back home, back again as Joe Toricelli. All that stuff down in Florida and the Islands was behind me now I figured, secrets stuffed deep down where no one was going to find them. "I'm all right, aren't I?" I found myself asking one of those old Cretan statues. The weird little smile on his face seemed to tell me he thought I was.

THAT NIGHT, BACK at Jake and Nina's, was a poor repeat performance of the evening before. The food was reheated and the booze was flowing twice as fast, at least on Jake's part. After the kids went to bed, and we went out to the patio, any conversation that got past three sentences seemed to be another opportunity for Nina to pounce on Jake. She unloaded a catalogue of complaints on him, from too little money and too many chores, to the house falling apart and Jake ignoring the kids. Jake just sat there like some soggy, half-witted old dog, way past trying to protest the kicks and curses, he looked like he'd come to believe he deserved.

"Joey," Nina said to me at one point, "you're lucky. Stay free, and remember...little by little, at first so you don't notice it, a person can ruin your life. The very person you're supposed to trust, more than anybody else in the world."

I just listened, and figured if this was the way it was going to be, and every indication seemed to confirm that, then my ass was out of here real quick, and into whatever dive I could find in the city.

Nina quieted down a little by the time she was serving coffee, and it probably helped that Jake was half-passed out in his chair. I eventually crept up to the kid's computer room and spent the last part of the evening cooking up a one-page resume for Dr. Moore. I didn't want to guess at what her reaction would be. I just hoped that with old Jake nearby tomorrow, his presence would contain whatever outrage was bound to erupt.

NEXT MORNING, Jake and I got up early again and we headed down the parkway by 7:30. Again, he was pretty quiet in the car. After a few miles, I decided we ought to have a little chat.

"Pretty rough night last night, wasn't it?" I said.

"Oh yeah," he said, with this real husky voice. "But you know, we oughta get some breakfast or something. Or at least some coffee."

"Yeah, well, let's get into the city first. By the way, you all right driving?"

"Yeah, why not? Something the matter?"

"You look real rough, that's all. With all the booze you swilled last night, you probably still got some on board."

"Yeah," he rasped. "I fucking wish."

We cruised past Van Cortlandt Park and down into Riverdale, and he didn't say anything else. I figured I might as well be blunt.

"What the hell is going on between you and Nina?"

He snorted, and then cleared his throat a couple of times.

"Bullshit," he said, "that's all. A whole lotta screwy bullshit."

"What exactly does that mean?"

"I'll give you three guesses, Joey."

"You got a girlfriend."

"Bingo."

"Not that it was too difficult to figure out."

"Yeah? Well then let me tell you, you're not exactly right. You see, I had a girlfriend. Now it's fucking history."

"And Nina's raking you over the coals for it, huh?"

"Oh, that she is," he said, "big time."

"Well what the fuck do you expect?" Your wife finds out you're cheating on her, she's got a right to make your life miserable, doesn't she?"

"That ain't even it, Joey, believe me. No, it's really...it's really all about the pain of knowing what you could have had."

"So what is it you could have had?"

"Well, I'll tell you, Joey. I'll tell you what I could have had. I'll try to make a long story short. This girl, this girlfriend of mine, fucking beautiful girl Joey. Ida Louise. I mean gorgeous. I met her at a bar about six months ago, down in the Village."

"What were you doing hanging out at bars in the Village?"

"Nothing. Believe me, I wasn't looking for trouble. I was working late one night in the neighborhood, and stopped in this place to grab a drink. So anyway, I'm standing at the bar and I see this unbelievable broad down at the other end. She's with a guy but, you know, she's more interested in looking at me."

"Really? Bad sign already."

"Why?"

"It's obvious. Sooner or later she's going to do the same thing, when you're out with her."

"That's a lot of bullshit," he said. "But anyway, the guy she's with goes out to make a phone call, and I come over to talk to her, and uh, well it's immediately obvious we're meant for each other."

"Uh-huh. And does her boyfriend agree, or doesn't he even come back?"

"Eventually he does come back. But by that time I already got her phone number, and by the next Friday night, she's dumped the guy and we're out on our first date."

"Things moved pretty fast, huh?"

"Hey, I'm telling you, Joey, this was the real thing. We just hit it off and started seeing each other three, four times a week. It was just something between us, you know? Chemistry. I mean we loved all the same things; Chinese food, Howard Stern, the Staten Island ferry, John Grisham, carriage rides through the park, you name it. Bottom line, Joey, is we were in love."

"Gee, that's beautiful. And no problem working this around your family, right?"

"Well there we ran into a little problem. You see, we wanted to get married. I told her she'd be able to quit her waitressing job and work on acting full-time."

"So you were going to divorce Nina and marry this...actress? You were serious about this?"

"Sure I was, and I'm telling you she could go places, Joey. She's got a lot of potential and her whole life in front of her."

"Yeah. How old is she?"

"Nineteen."

"Nineteen?"

"But very mature."

I didn't say anything.

"So anyway, Joey, we wanted to get married. But I couldn't just ditch everything overnight, right? Shitty as things are between me and Nina. So I tried to stall a little, know what I mean?"

"Yeah, so?"

"Well, Nina's getting the feeling something's up, right? I mean, I'm out of the house almost all the time. And Ida's bitching at me 'cause she says she's not getting enough attention. So then she does something real stupid, she calls up the house. I told her to never fucking do that. Anyway, Nina answers the phone and Ida hangs up. But the problem is Nina's got the number on caller I.D. Now Nina's real sneaky, and she doesn't call back right away. She waits till the next day, and gets Ida's roommate on the other end. Nina asks if Jake's there and the roommate says no, Ida and Jake went down by the river, and they'll be back in an hour. Well, need I say more? I come home that evening and I'm cooked."

"So then what happened?"

"Well, a couple of days later, I talk over the situation with Ida. She gets all upset; guilty, crying, crazy, and then she just shut down. She don't want to see me or hear from me anymore. It's over, she says, because I ain't going to leave my wife and she, all of a sudden, feels like she's sleeping with her ol' man."

"It figures. So when did the two of you break up?"

"Two weeks ago. And she won't return any of my fucking phone messages. Then, a couple of days ago I seen her on Bleecker Street, with some punk with a ring in his nose. She don't even look at me."

I didn't want to, but I started to laugh.

"Hey, this ain't funny, Joey. I'm telling you, I ain't been worth shit for the last two weeks. I'm in fucking hell. I ain't worth shit at work. And at home, well you see what it's like at home. So I need you here, Joey. I need you here, right now."

"That's why this job was such an 'opportunity' for me, right?" I said.

"Don't bust my balls, okay, *keemosabie?* And did you have something better going on down there in the Everglades, or wherever the fuck it was you hung out?"

"Not exactly. But look, all this shit is going to work itself out. You're not the first guy looking at forty and family responsibilities who wanted to run away into some friggin' romantic fantasy. But you're no Paul Gauguin see? Or some fucking movie star. You're just a regular guy with a regular family from a regular neighborhood in Yonkers, who got in over his head with a girl who isn't grown up yet. It'll all settle down, you'll see."

"Yeah?" he said, sort of surprised and half-absent mindedly. "You think so?"

"Yeah," I said. "Guaranteed."

He got very quiet, like he was thinking it all over while we rode under the GW Bridge and along the west side. I felt bad for the poor bastard, I really did.

After a while he said, "So Joey, who the hell is Paul Grogann?"

But before I could answer, he'd drifted into the left lane and almost sideswiped somebody.

"Never fucking mind, all right?" I said. "Just keep your eyes on the road."

We finally got downtown and parked the car at Police Headquarters. Then Jake ended up wasting a lot of time getting a bagel and coffee, and going to fill a Valium prescription. He popped three of them in the elevator on the way up to meet Moore.

"Can I see the bottle?" I asked.

"Here," he said.

"It says take one pill every six hours as needed."

"No kidding?" he said. But his mind was already off somewhere else.

We walked into Moore's office at quarter after nine, and she looked real pissed off.

"You're fifteen minutes late," she snapped at us. She was dressed in a white doctor's coat and was sitting behind her desk.

"I'm sorry," I said. "We hit some bad traffic on the west side."

"Nothing unusual about that," she said, "just plan for it next time."

I was about to tell her to lighten up a little when my eye caught something about the O'Connor case in the *Register* on her desk.

"Do you have your C.V., Dr. Toricelli?" she asked.

"Oh yeah, sure." I pulled an envelope with her name on it out of my coat pocket and handed it to her. Then I sat down by her desk and prepared for the worst. I didn't have to wait long.

"Is this a fucking joke?" she asked, after she looked at it a few seconds. "Is this your complete C.V.?"

"Yes, it is," I said.

"You never completed a residency in psychiatry?"

"That's right."

"No certifications, no other training?"

"No."

"You're not even licensed to practice medicine in New York?"

"Had no reason to be."

"Dr. Toricelli," she said, "if that's even a title that is relevant, you have not been involved in any medical activities for almost seven years. You were never fully licensed to practice medicine anywhere, but had provisional status in Georgia as an intern at a Federal hospital. You are essentially without formal training or any mature clinical experience." Her face was getting very red. "You have no level of...of sophistication," she went on, with her voice rising in pitch, "for a job which involves interviewing patients under the most complicated of circumstances. Wouldn't it be prudent of you to consider that you're stepping into shoes just a few sizes too big for you? That perhaps remedial work in medical school would be an appropriate level of activity for you?"

I opened my mouth to speak but nothing came out.

"I can tell you right now," she said, "that your application for this position is denied. We will hire an assistant from the Forensic Institute, as had originally been my plan. So I will now bid you goodbye, Dr.

Toricelli."

Then she looked behind me, to Jake, who'd been standing by the window. "And Lieutenant Roma," she said, "I would like to have a few words with you, as soon as Dr. Toricelli leaves, in private."

I got up and turned to walk out the door. I shouldn't have been surprised by any of this, I thought. And I asked myself; who needs this horseshit, anyway? I wasn't sure what I'd do next, and I was awful curious about what that latest *Register* story said. But where was I going? Not back to Florida, or anywhere near there, right? Even if the FBI didn't find me there, Danny and his boys sure as hell would. No, I told myself, I've really got nowhere to go. And besides, what about that second chance I'd told myself I was getting here? To do something right, to do something good. No, I thought, I've got to stay. So then, I turned back around, and faced Dr. Moore.

"Dr. Moore," I said. "Your reaction to my qualifications, or lack thereof, is understandable and...justified. However, I'd like you to reconsider...based on...my commitment to this case...and, I believe, some new information, that I just picked up yesterday."

"What are you talking about?" she said. Even Jake stepped back from the window, and seemed to perk up from his Valium haze.

"Well," I said, "in speaking to the doormen yesterday, at Dr. Epstein's building, I learned that his partner, Dr. Roland, did something very unusual on the day of the murder. He apparently ordered a limo and..."

"You have no business being involved in this case at any level without my authorization!" she shouted. "And your presumptuousness is only outweighed by your lack of competence. Now I believe I've indicated to you that we have nothing further to discuss." She got up, strode over to the door and opened it for me to go.

"Joey," mumbled Jake, "go ahead. But wait for me outside there."

I walked out the door and stood over by the secretaries' desks, just a few feet down the hall. From there, I could hear Moore giving it to Jake left and right. She was yelling at him and threatening to call the commissioner, the mayor, and even the FBI. She called him a cretin, said he was corrupt, nepotistic, craven, brain-dead and sociopathic.

The two secretaries looked up at me while this was going on. I just shrugged and said, "Hell if I know what's happening."

"She's a bitch on wheels," said one of them.

"She's been like that since she got here last week," said the other, "and if you ask me, she needs some kind of therapy."

They both laughed at that idea.

Then Moore's office door swung open and Jake lumbered out, looking haggard and pummeled.

He said, "Let's go."

"Where?"

"Down to feed the pigeons. C'mon."

We took the elevator down to the street and bought a loaf of whole wheat at the corner deli. Then we sat on a bench in city hall park. Jake flung bread to the birds and talked to me.

"Joey, I didn't know you don't even have a freakin' license. I mean, get one for Chrissakes, make my life easier."

"Jake, that's going to take weeks, if it'll even happen at all. What's the difference anyway? This job you got me, it isn't practicing medicine."

"Aw shit, it ain't just that. She's just so fucking bent out of shape about you, it's unbelievable. What I'm going to have to do is put in a call to my man in the mayor's office. Most likely we'll get everything straightened out. And if push comes to shove, we'll shitcan her and get you a new boss."

"Maybe that's going a little too far," I said. "It's probably not the best idea."

"Fuck the best idea. I just don't need any more bullshit right now. Any more bullshit and I'm going to fucking bag everything."

He lit up a smoke and crumpled the pack on the grass. The bread was all gone and the pigeons started to thin out. A warm gust blew down Broadway and the trees gave a low sigh over the din of traffic.

"What's that supposed to mean?" I said. "Bag everything?"

"Nothing. Don't worry, doc, I ain't going to take the gaspipe. Ah, who the fuck knows what I mean?"

As he sat there on the bench, it was obvious he hadn't shaved that morning. The dark stubble exaggerated the bags under his eyes. I remembered how full of bravado and bullshit he used to be, boasting about all sorts of connections and brewing opportunities, trying to impress everybody with souped-up tales of power, intrigue and big decisions. Now he was little more than a burnt-out civil servant, drifting into the doldrums of mid-life disappointment and disillusion. And not wrapped real tight.

The air stilled and the sun moved out from behind the trees and began to bake us.

"Look, Joey," he said. "I'm going to go talk with Al, right upstairs there." He pointed back at City Hall. "We'll get everything straight. You hang loose today and I'll meet you back at the car this afternoon, say about four."

"You all right about this?" I said. "I mean, about me being on the case?"

"Fuck yes. Don't worry, all right? I'll see you at four."

"Whatever you say," I said. "Good luck."

AFTER WE PARTED, I took a stroll down Nassau Street and hoped everything would work out with me staying on the job. As I passed a corner newsstand, I picked up a copy of the *Register* and went to sit in a little coffee shop and read it.

The headline said: "Car of Suspects in O'Connor Murder Found in Miami." The article said a blue Chevrolet sedan, matching the description of witnesses in Crossroads, had been found on Biscayne Boulevard in Miami. Crassidy's fingerprints were found on the steering wheel and dashboard and the Florida driver's license of "Vera Parish, reportedly Joseph Torento's employer," was found under the front passenger's seat. A match between "probable Torento fingerprints" on different items in my room back at Vera's and other prints found in the car "was not definitive at this time." The car's serial number indicated it'd been stolen out of Brownsville, Texas, about a year ago and currently had a phony registration and a license plate from Fulton County, Georgia. I remembered being in that car about two weeks ago, getting a ride back from the marina with somebody Crassidy said was a buddy of his. Some Mexican guy, if I recollected right.

The article went on to repeat what had now become an established assumption: That Crassidy and me had kidnapped Vera and Russ as part of our getaway plan.

The rest of the story was on the inside pages, next to an article reporting details about the O'Connor kid's memorial service and what people had thought of him. His uncle, the senator from New York, "praised his nephew as 'a sensitive and caring young man.'" His older brother, Robert, "a respected independent film producer" said the loss "was as sad a thing as I could imagine...Francis had gone to Key West to work on the novel he'd started as a senior at Yale, he was totally dedicated to it and the parts he'd read to me were pure gold."

I had to say I felt really bad for the kid. But my sympathy got short-circuited when I turned the page and saw another police rendering of myself staring me right in the face. Son of a bitch, I thought, this one was a little different than the last one, a tiny bit closer to what I look like, especially around the eyes. But still, I told myself, it's nowhere near what I really look like, even if I still had the beard and long hair. No, I thought, nobody can recognize me from that. It's impossible.

Nonetheless, I looked up from the paper, and could have sworn two people at the counter had been staring at me. Then I tried to calm myself down. You didn't do anything, I told myself, and besides Joe Torento doesn't exist anymore. They're going to nab Crassidy and rescue Vera and Russ, and everything's going to settle down, you'll see, you'll see.

And that's pretty much what I kept telling myself, while I wandered around downtown and took a snooze in Battery Park. They couldn't find a guy who didn't exist; they just couldn't.

When 4:00 rolled around, I went back to meet Jake at the car. The minute I saw him, I could see he'd brightened up.

"You're in, Joey," he said to me. "That bitch is going to go ballistic tomorrow, but I don't give a shit. She's either going to work with you, or she's gone."

"How'd you do it?"

"Joey, Joey, c'mon. How many times I gotta tell you, it's all about knowing the right people. 'Bout time you learned that, isn't it, chief?"

"I guess so," I said, feeling happy to be seeing flashes of the old Jake. Beaten down, maybe even half-broken, but still able to make the same old noises.

However, when we got back home that night, I wasn't surprised to see him losing another round of the badly matched fight between him and his wife. When Nina started asking me outright what I thought of the whole mess, I decided I was definitely moving out, to some little sub-let in the city.

NEXT MORNING, driving down the parkway, I told Jake what I was going to do, and that he couldn't expect me to be running interference with his wife for him. He looked kind of hurt but said he understood. When we got into Moore's office, at about ten, she was sitting at her desk with her lips pressed together and her hair pulled back tight. She'd gotten the news about my staying on the job via a voice mail message from Jake the night before. I hoped there weren't going to be any further scenes.

"Good morning, Dr. Moore," said Jake as we walked in. "I'm just here to drop off Dr. Toricelli with you." Then he turned to me and said, "Any problem, you give me a call. I'll see you later."

"Yeah, fine, Jake," I said, "take it easy." Then I turned to face Moore.

"Well," she began, "it's obvious how the wheels of power are greased, and it appears you have neither the shame nor the self-respect to remove yourself from this case. So let's get moving."

"Dr. Moore...Madeline," I said.

"Don't ever call me by my first name," she said. "We do not now, nor shall we ever, enjoy any level of familiarity or collegiality. You are a disgrace to the medical and psychiatric professions. The only reason I haven't resigned is because I have a deep commitment to solving this case."

"But maybe..."

"Dr. Epstein," she interrupted me, "was my teacher and mentor and, out of my respect toward and admiration of him, I want to solve this case."

"And I want to help you. Dr. Moore."

"Is that so? Well, your role will be limited, mainly mechanical, and highly supervised."

"Whatever you say is appropriate. I'm at your disposal."

She looked me over for a few seconds, as if she was trying to decide if I was on the level, and if I really had anything to offer her. Then she shook her head and I stood there in silence over her desk. She shuffled some papers around while I stood there like a dumb ass for several minutes. Then, suddenly, she said, "I have a list of patients Dr. Epstein saw on the Friday he was murdered. He had six appointments in all. As I hope you are clear on by now, the Medical Examiner's report estimated Dr. Epstein was killed in the late afternoon, not long after his last appointment ended. Two of the patients he saw that day, one of whom was his last appointment, are scheduled to be interviewed today. I will interview them while you take notes relevant to the manualized assessment. You did read the manual, I presume."

"Yes. I did," I said, lying through my teeth.

"Well, frankly I find that hard to believe. In fact, you may do poorly enough in your assessments to bring in fresh evidence to get you fired."

"Maybe. Or I might just convince you that things aren't always what they appear to be on paper."

"Really? What I've seen so far is perfectly consistent with what's on paper."

"Anyway," I said, "when is our first appointment?"

"In three and a half hours, at two o'clock. I will be leaving momentarily to make rounds at the clinic. I should be back by one-thirty."

"I'll just take that time to review some key points from the manual," I said.

"You do that, Dr. Toricelli." She sounded doubtful.

After she left, I sat down at her desk and decided, what the hell, why not look over the manual. It was not only all written by Moore but about half the bibliography was made up of papers she had authored. She'd sure done one hell of a lot of thinking and research in forensic psychiatry. Trouble was, though, most of the stuff in the manual looked dry and dead and totally useless to me. The chapter on patient assessment was a weird stew of psychological and psychoanalytic jargon that tried to quantify the interview with the suspect/patients along different kinds of scales; violence, sociopathy, primitive transference fantasies, et cetera.

There were a whole bunch of questions, which should be addressed "explicitly" or "implicitly" to the patient. The chapter went on for thirty pages and was followed by another twenty or thirty pages of appendices. From what I could tell, the whole approach struck me as some kind of pseudo-scientific bullshit that could end up doing more harm than good in trying to size people up. But, bad as I felt about the whole thing, I spent a couple of hours studying the assessment scales, just to show Moore I could play on her team.

Around one o'clock or so the phone began ringing on Moore's desk and wasn't getting picked up when it rang through to the secretaries. I looked outside the door and saw both of them were out for lunch. So I picked up the phone and it was Moore on the other end.

"I have an emergency at the clinic," she said. "Tell Marisol to cancel the two o'clock appointment and re-schedule for tomorrow morning."

"Good enough," I said. But the problem was, Marisol, and the other one, Gina, stayed out way past their lunch hour. By the time I found the patient's number and left a message, she'd already left for the appointment.

The only information I had on her was what was on the interview sheet. Her name: Wilhelmina Frontenac. Her age: 25. And her occupation: Actress, Dancer.

A little before two I went out to the waiting area to tell Ms. Frontenac the appointment had been canceled. There were about a dozen people out there so I just said, "Ms. Frontenac" to the group. This tall, auburn-haired, designer- dressed woman rose up from her seat. She looked like somebody off the cover of *Cosmopolitan.* She strode right up to me and reached out her hand.

"Pleasure to meet you," she said in this very light foreign accent, "and you are?"

"Toricelli," I said. "Dr. Joe Toricelli."

"So," she smiled, "shall we begin?"

I led her back to Moore's office and gestured for her to have a seat by the desk. Then I settled into Moore's chair behind the desk.

"Ms. Frontenac," I said, "I'm very sorry for the inconvenience, but we had to cancel your appointment at the last minute."

"But why?"

"Well, you see our director, Dr. Moore, she's supposed to do the interview. But right now she's taking care of an emergency. I left a message on your machine, but I guess it was too late."

"But you are here, Dr...Toricelli, and I am as well. Surely we can get this over with. I don't know when I can come back."

"Right," I said. "But you see the problem is I'm not really authorized to interview you. I'm an assistant or...an associate and uh...well the director really needs to be here for this."

She seemed to settle more into her chair as I said this. "I really don't understand, doctor. I am here and I am sure there is nothing very complicated about this."

"Well, you may be right, but the director needs to be here. That's the policy."

"But you know, you act like such a boy, Dr. Toricelli. You are afraid to do things on your own?" She pulled out a cigarette and lit up. "Do you have an ashtray?"

"This is a no smoking...ah, the hell with it." I handed her an empty coffee cup. "Okay, I don't guess there's any harm in doing some preliminary questioning."

She threw back her hair and crossed her legs and smiled. "So, what do you want to know?"

"Well, first of all, you understand that the purpose of this meeting is to get any information we can about the circumstances of Dr. Epstein's death. The records show you had an appointment with him the day he was murdered."

"I understand, Dr. Toricelli. Everything was already explained to me last week, when the police first talked with me."

"Right, of course."

"And I suppose I could even be a suspect, yes?" she smiled.

"That's jumping ahead a little..."

"Why not?" she said. "I could have become crazy with jealousy when I learned he'd be leaving for vacation in two weeks, and may try to reconcile with the bitch wife who is divorcing him, and so I decided to kill him."

I wasn't quite sure what to do with this.

"So, shall I go on doctor? Do you want to know what I know about his wife or shall we go directly to how he propositioned me?"

"What?"

"Oh, come on, Dr. Toricelli, don't try to look so startled." She looked straight into my eyes and exhaled a long stream of smoke.

"That's a very serious accusation, Ms. Frontenac. Can you be more specific?"

She laughed at me like she was getting a real kick out of my trying to sound official.

"Why should I?" she said. "You won't believe me anyway. I'm sure your reverence for the esteemed Dr. Epstein wouldn't allow you to take me seriously. But your Dr. Epstein was a quiet little pig and he liked to spend a lot of the session time looking up my legs."

"So then why did you continue to see him...for how long?"

"Over one year, one or two times a week."

"So why, then? Why'd you stay with him?"

"Because he knew me, that's why. Because he knew the whole story of my life and he listened and he understood and...he liked me. And he never told me any bullshit. He wasn't shy about me being beautiful. At the beginning he even said he could hardly concentrate on what I was saying. He was a very sweet man, a sweet...old fart, with a terrible bitch of a wife."

"How do you know about his wife?" I said.

"Because I could hear her from the waiting room, shouting at him in the office. 'Horatio, that jacket is filthy; Horatio, lose that lard ass, you look like a fat old woman; Horatio, you've wasted your life studying bullshit and hocus-pocus.' God, she was horrible." Then Ms. Frontenac suddenly bit her lip and started to get teary-eyed. I handed her a tissue.

"But he's gone now," she said, wiping her eyes, "and he was somebody I could really trust."

Then, that stunning face, that just a minute ago was all high cheekbones, piercing eyes and hot, sexy lips, suddenly shrunk down low into a soft, sad little girl's pout. She looked like her favorite stuffed animal had just been taken away from her.

"I'm very sorry for what happened," I said.

But she was crying and caught up in her own world, and didn't seem to hear me. After a while she looked up. "What else do you want?" she said. "What else?"

I wasn't sure. I couldn't imagine this woman strangling Epstein. I mean, I really felt that she really cared for the guy. And the stuff about her being jealous about his vacation, where he might reconcile with his wife? That had to be all provocative posturing. But what about this proposition thing? Was that on the level? Did it mean anything?

I figured I better follow up on it. "Ms. Frontenac, obviously Dr. Epstein meant a lot to you and I know losing him hurts you real bad. Now, with all due respect, I feel I've got to follow up on something you said a few minutes ago. I mean about him propositioning you."

She quit wiping her eyes and made a fist around the tissue I'd given her.

"Dr. Toricelli," she said, in this real hard tone, "you have a filthy imagination. What makes you think you can talk to me like that?"

"Ms. Frontenac, unless I misunderstood you, you told me Dr. Epstein had propositioned you."

"Dr. Toricelli, if you go on like that I will report you to whomever you say is in charge here. Ah, your director! These are absolutely filthy insinuations and I will not tolerate being subjected to them."

What the fuck was going on here? I thought. One of us is nuts, and I don't think it's me. But best to try to calm her down, I figured.

"Look, I'm very sorry," I said, "sincerely sorry, Ms. Frontenac. There must be some sort of misunderstanding on my part. Please accept my apology."

She studied me real carefully, like she was trying to weigh my stated sincerity against the look of surprise, which must have been on my face. Then, in kind of an eerie and seductive way, she said, "Is there anything else you want from me doctor?"

Anything else I want? Well yeah, how about an explanation for your weird behavior. But no, I thought, I'm not going to touch that one, not today anyway. No, let's change the subject to something I hope is a little more safe.

"Well, uh...before we wrap up," I said, "can you tell me a little bit about the work you do?"

"Just a little bit, doctor?" She laughed. "And why is that important?"

"Don't know that it's so important," I said, "just trying to round out a picture of you for myself, that's all."

"And am I a suspect, Dr. Toricelli?"

"Not that I can tell, but you're a witness to some part of Dr. Epstein's last few hours."

"Well, Dr. Toricelli," she said in this deep, sexy voice, "if you really must know what I do...I'm a dancer."

"Yeah?" I said. "What kind of dancer?"

"That I would leave for you to judge," she smiled. "You should really come by and see a performance sometime." She pulled out a card from her purse and handed it to me. "Club Daylight. For the Discriminating Gentleman. 4747 East 18th Street."

""I think I get the picture."

"Oh you do, do you, doctor?" she laughed. "And what is it that you see?"

"The kind of place you work at."

"Oh, I don't think so doctor. I wouldn't trust such a nice, boring imagination as yours. You must really come by and get a full taste of this club. Unless, of course, you feel it may be too...how shall I say...? Stimulating for you."

"Maybe I could use some stimulation," I said. "I'll keep it in mind. Okay? Seriously."

"Oh, I can see you're very serious, Dr. Toricelli, such a serious young man."

The way she was teasing me was really starting to turn up the voltage in me and she didn't have any trouble seeing it.

"Will there be anything else you will want from me today?" She got this real sexy pout on her face.

"Uh, no, no," I said, trying to hold onto my mind. "That's going to wrap it up for today."

"Are you sure, doctor?"

"I'm sure," I said, "and I'm sure we'll be in touch."

I stood up to see her to the door. "So thanks, thanks, Ms. Frontenac."

"See you doctor," she smiled, as she walked out.

"Yes, see you," I said.

She left me under some kind of spell after she was gone.

The sound of her voice, the smell of her perfume, the image of her piercing gaze and the long legs, all of this was burning inside my brain. What about that weird angry denial of hers? She had said, "proposition," hadn't she? Or had she? But my mind was too steamed up and my feet too unsteady for me to focus on it anymore. I sat back down in Moore's chair and looked at the card again: "Club Daylight. For the Discriminating Gentleman." On the back she had written her home phone number. I wanted to see her again but I wasn't sure why. I hoped to hell she wasn't involved in knocking off Epstein.

But be careful, I thought to myself, because one way or another she sure seemed to spell trouble, and more of that I didn't really need.

WHILE I SAT BACK turning over the card, Moore walked into the office. She felt like a bulldozer crashing through my private grove of thoughts and ruminations.

"If you'll excuse me, Dr. Toricelli," she said, "I will need my desk now."

"Huh? Oh yeah, sure, sorry, I..."

"We have a three o'clock appointment with another one of Dr. Epstein's patients. So please let's move it because I've got a call to return before we start."

I got up, took a chair near her desk, and flipped through her manual while she talked on the phone. I was hoping she wouldn't be too pissed off that I'd gone ahead and met with Ms. Frontenac. At any rate, I didn't have time to tell her because when she hung up the phone the secretaries buzzed her, and told her that the patient, a Nathan Volknick, was waiting to be seen.

She stood up and tossed me the information folder on him. "I will bring the patient back here for the interview. Please pull up that other chair to the desk for him. Your job will consist of sitting where you are now and taking notes on the interview."

While she went out I organized the chairs and perused the folder on this patient. The information sheet said: Volknick, Nathan. Age: 28. Occupation: Unemployed.

Moore walked back in with a tall, gangly young guy dressed in black jeans, a white shirt, and a skimpy blue sport coat. He had short, curly black hair, thick, wire-rimmed glasses and a scruffy looking goatee. His complexion was stone pale; like he'd spent the last ten years hunkered down in somebody's basement.

"Mr. Volknick," said Moore, "this is my assistant, Dr. Toricelli. He will be taking notes during our interview."

I gave him a friendly nod and smile.

"Now if you'll sit here, we can get started," she said.

Volknick plopped down in his chair, and Moore went back behind her desk.

"Now first of all, Mr. Volknick," she said, "I need to be sure you understand the nature and purpose of our meeting today. Can you tell me what your understanding of it is?"

"You want to ask me," he started up in a monotone, "about anything I could know that could help you find out who killed Dr. Epstein."

"Exactly," she said. "Very good."

"I don't know anything about it."

"No, of course not. We don't expect you to know anything about it. But you may know something about Dr. Epstein's office routine, or other people you have seen in the office suite."

"Just start snitching on people, right?" he said. Then suddenly, he stood up, looked at the ceiling, mumbled something to himself and then sat back down again.

Moore flinched and took a deep breath. She probably thought he was going to take a whack at her. "Mr. Volknick," she said, "I will ask you to stay seated please, for this interview."

"Why, are we in school?" he said. Then he tapped her desk twice with his fingers and crossed his arms over his chest. He seemed to be literally trying to hold himself together.

"Let's try to go back to that afternoon, Mr. Volknick, now two Fridays ago."

"I told you," he said. "I don't know nothing. Noth-thing, you hear me?"

Moore started to squirm in her seat.

"Mr. Volknick, I understand that you came here to cooperate today. Of your own free will, is that true?"

"And now you're calling me uncooperative, is that it?" He stood up again suddenly, and seemed to try to suppress shouting something at the top of his lungs. Then he dropped back down again in his chair.

"Mr. Volknick," Moore was now slightly red in the face, "I asked you to remain seated."

He mumbled again. Then he repeated, "I've got nothing else to say, noth-thing."

I was feeling pretty bad for Dr. Moore. She was looking too rattled to have a conversation with this guy and he was too scared to talk about anything with her. I figured I'd go ahead and jump in. What'd we have to lose at this point?

"Mr. Volknick," I said. "Excuse me for interrupting but, I just wanted to say, uh, we really appreciate your making it down here today. I know it's got to be real rough for you losing your doctor like you did."

"Thank you Dr..."

"Toricelli," I said, "Joe Toricelli."

"Yes, Dr. Toricelli. I think I'm in a state of shock." His eyes darted up to the ceiling and then down to the floor.

"I can imagine," I said. "And even more shocking to think, as I guess you know, that you last saw him just a little while before his death."

"Yes, exactly." He tapped his chin three times with his right index finger, and then crossed and uncrossed his legs. "I saw him at four-fifteen that day, just like I have been for seven years, every single Friday."

"Was there anything remarkable about the meeting on that day?" I asked. "Anything you remember about Dr. Epstein or anyone else you saw there?"

He got this lost look in his eyes and wrinkled his forehead.

"I'm sorry doctor," he said, "can you repeat..."

"Yeah, sure. Maybe I was a little wordy there. Now, anything you remember about Dr. Epstein that day?"

He paused for a few seconds. "Well, he was nice. He was always nice."

"Uh-huh."

It didn't look like he was going to elaborate.

"Do you remember anything you talked about?" I asked.

"Uh...well, the Mets. Yeah, but Dr. E. was a Cubs man. He's from Chicago, you know?"

"I see. Anything else?"

"He gave me more Prozac. He'd raised my dose again. To a hundred twenty milligrams, yeah."

"What's the Prozac for?"

But Volknick didn't seem to hear me. He was mumbling something to himself. He tapped the desk once and cleared his throat with a grunt. Then he looked at me blankly. "Can you repeat the question doctor?"

"Well, let me ask you this: Are you on any other medication... besides Prozac?"

"Yeah, Risperdal ten milligrams. Every evening before going nighty-night."

"What's that for?"

"Voices." He looked up at the ceiling.

"Voices?"

"Oh yeah. Bad voices. But they're quiet now."

"Do you remember what they said?" But, before he could answer, Moore's beeper went off. She scribbled down the incoming number. "I'll take this outside," she said. "Excuse me."

Volknick scrutinized Moore as she walked out, then looked back at me.

"Why do you want to know about the voices?" he said.

"It might help me to understand you a little better," I said.

"I don't want to talk about the voices, doctor."

"That's all right, that's private anyway. It's probably the kind of thing you'd only feel comfortable discussing with Dr. Epstein."

"Dr. Epstein didn't feel comfortable about my voices. But Dr. Epstein felt very comfortable with my family's money."

"Yeah?"

"Oh yeah. He really liked the check for two hundred fifty dollars I brought every time I came to an appointment."

"Two fifty an hour, huh?" I laughed. "I guess the best doesn't come cheap."

"That was for twenty-five minutes, doctor."

"Twenty-five minutes!" I more or less shouted. "Holy..."

"Dr. E. really likes my family's money," he said, sort of mechanically, like it was a well-known slogan. I imagined him saying it over and over on his way to and back from Epstein's office.

"I guess he likes, or liked, getting paid. But he must have also felt a strong commitment to you. No?"

At this he stood up again, then sat down and cleared his throat.

"Dr. Epstein didn't give a shit about me," he said. "He didn't give a shit about Nathan. Nathan, he didn't give a shit about you. He only liked the money. Do you understand, Nathan? He only wanted the cock-sucking money."

He kept going on with this stuff at high volume over and over again, like he was repeating or echoing someone's voice. Whose voice, and whether it came from inside his head or from someone else, I couldn't tell. But he was getting more riled up; standing and sitting several times, gritting his teeth, sometimes sort of growling to punctuate his announcements about "Nathan" and "the cock-sucking money" and how "Epstein didn't give a rat's ass." I thought to myself, "This guy's going to blow his top right here in police headquarters."

"Mr. Volknick, Nathan," I said. "You, uh, you need to quiet down a little. They can probably hear you all over the tenth floor here, the way you're going on."

He suddenly stopped and gave me this weird, twisted smile. "Yes, doctor," he said, "whatever you say."

"You really got upset there, didn't you?"

"Not really, doctor," he grinned. "I'm okay, really I am, doctor."

We sat for a few minutes, without saying anything.

"Do you get upset like that a lot?" I asked.

"Doctors upset me, doctor. Doctors just seem to upset me, it's nothing personal."

"Yeah? Did Dr. Epstein upset you?"

"Dr. Epstein? Me? Did I get upset?"

"Yes, did you used to get upset with Dr. Epstein?"

He paused, and seemed to be thinking. Then he whispered, "I didn't like Dr. Epstein."

"Really? Why not?"

He started to laugh—to sort of cackle. "Because, because he was a big old hairy dog...and he was always on the phone during the session."

"During your meetings?"

"That's right. Big old smelly dog didn't care, didn't care that it was my time." Then he started forcing out some belly laughs.

"So...so why did you go to him?" I said.

"'Cause my mommy told me to," he sing-songed. "Na-than, did you see Dr. Ep-stein? Did-ja? Did-ja?" I could see he was starting to get wound up again.

"So Nathan," I said, sharply, "are you telling me you didn't exactly see Dr. Epstein on a voluntary basis?"

"That's rrrrrright sirrr—you're sooooo rrrrright sir."

"I guess you could say it bothered you to be seeing Dr. Epstein, is that right?"

"Yep."

"That you even hated going to see him?"

"Yep."

"And must not altogether be missing him?"

"Nope."

The room became real quiet, except for the flow of traffic off the Brooklyn Bridge and a few drops of rain dinging on the air-conditioner in the window. I thought to myself: This guy, a killer? No, I don't think so, wouldn't hurt a fly. Still, I had to pursue this.

"Nathan," I said, "you know, I've got to ask you something now, and I want you to think real carefully. I want to know, did you think about, or feel that you wanted to hurt old Dr. Epstein? I mean sometimes patients get these ideas, you know?"

"Patients think about that?"

"Sure they do. It's, uh, not necessarily abnormal. Did you ever get these ideas?"

He gave me that weird smile again. "I used to want to beat up his furniture," he said. "I hated that mirror he had in the waiting room. I used to think I'd like to smash it right over his desk. Just smash it up and walk out, yeah."

He seemed to get excited about this. He licked his lips a few times and grabbed his crotch.

"Just smash it right up, huh?" I said.

"Yeah, just smash it into a million fucking pieces," he shouted. "Just shatter the fucking thing, and shatter his fucking ass too, fucking fat, smelly dog."

He started to roll into high gear again, this time with a twisted, angry face, and bits of foam building at the corners of his mouth.

"Nathan," I said.

"Fuck you."

"Nathan," I said, louder this time.

"What?"

"Did you ever do anything like that in Dr. Epstein's office? Did you ever break or hurt anything...or anybody?"

He paused. "Nope."

"No?"

"Nope."

"You're sure nothing like that ever happened in Epstein's office?" I said. "I mean, when you were there?"

"Never. Never saw nothing, never did nothing."

"Nothing?"

"Nothing."

Now his words didn't assure me and his face looked crazy as hell. I could imagine him going after Epstein, just taking him out in some boiled-over resentful, psychotic rage. Maybe even under the command of some voice inside his head. But just as I was convinced that Volknick was a murderer his face smoothed out and softened and he looked like he could even cry.

"Dr.?" he whispered. "Can I get a glass of water?"

"Huh? Oh yeah, sure, Nathan, sure. Hold on."

I stepped out of the office to fill up a cup at the cooler. I passed Moore, who was still on the phone.

"Got a little noisy in there, Dr. Toricelli," said Moore. "Everything all right."

"Oh yeah, but everything's fine, really."

I went back in and handed Volknick the water, and sat back and watched him gulp it down greedily with both hands around the cup.

When he finished he said: "Thanks, doctor. Do we have much more to talk about now?"

"No, I don't think so, Nathan. But, I appreciate you coming by."

"Oh, it's nothing," he said. "I got nothing to do anyway. Hey, uh, are you going to be my new doctor?"

"Me? Oh no, no, Nathan. I'm just here helping out the police, that's all. I'm a consultant."

"That's too bad," he smiled, "I like you."

"Thanks. It's been a real pleasure meeting you."

"I hope we can see each other again," he grinned. "I want you to be my friend." He looked like some lost puppy. "I think you could be a good friend."

"Thanks, Nathan. Look, feel free to call me if you have any questions about our meeting today."

"Doctor," he said, all of a sudden real serious, "can you promise me something?"

"What's that?"

"Can you promise me you won't hurt me?"

"That I won't hurt you?"

"Yes. That you won't try to harm me."

"Uh...yeah sure, Nathan, I can promise you that. I promise you, I won't harm you, or hurt you in any way."

"Thanks, doctor," he said, with this weird, crooked smile on his face. "Now I know I can trust you."

"That's good," I said, "that's good." And as I spoke these words, all the memories of Wilcox, both at Doboy and down at Pershing, came stampeding across my brain.

"So," I went on, "that sounds like a good place to end our meeting here today."

"That's okay by me, doctor, I'm ready to go now."

We stood up to shake hands and I saw him back to the waiting room. On the way back I thought; poor guy, must be giving it everything he's got to hold it together. I sat down by Moore's desk and started flipping through her manual. I didn't know exactly what to think about Volknick, but I guess I had some half-assed idea I'd find an answer in those pages. I started plowing through a lot of jargon that read like: "note the range of affect and its convergence with verbal content. Take special note of guardedness as well as any exacerbation of an underlying formal thought disorder, both indications of increased interpersonal stress." Pretty much as I expected, I thought to myself, a lot of technical bullshit that's not worth squat in the real world.

Just then, Moore came back in and sat down by the desk.

"I wasn't sure you were going to manage Mr. Volknick," she said with this coy little smile.

"How do you mean?"

"He was obviously quite agitated. We could hear him half-way down the hall."

"He wasn't so bad," I said, "all in all I'd say he's going to be easier to figure than Ms. Frontenac."

"What is that supposed to mean?"

"Oh yeah," I said, "I didn't have time to tell you. I ended up interviewing Ms. Frontenac."

"But I told you specifically to cancel her appointment. You have absolutely no authority to interview patients without my supervision."

"Well, she got here before we could cancel," I said, "and she was pretty insistent about getting interviewed now."

"I see. Tell me, Dr. Toricelli, who is running this investigation: me or Dr. Epstein's patients?"

"Well, I don't think it did any harm."

"You don't, do you?" she sneered. "Well I will be the judge of that—after I read a full, properly organized report on what transpired."

"I'll get it to you tomorrow."

"No, you'll get it to me today. Now what did you learn from Mr. Volknick?"

"Bottom line?" I said. "He had the usual over-priced appointment with Dr. Epstein, on orders from his mother."

"What about afterward, Dr. Toricelli?"

"What do you mean?"

"Af-ter-ward, his activities subsequent to the meeting with Dr. Epstein."

"Not sure what you mean," I said.

"Do you mean to tell me you didn't get the details of his behavior after his appointment?"

"No."

"Did you fail to do that with Ms. Frontenac as well?"

"Ask her what she did after the appointment? Don't believe I did."

"But you read the manual, didn't you, Toricelli? Certainly you read the sections on 'Special Points in Taking the History'. And you must have read under 'Information Protocols' that you should already have reviewed existing information from preliminary contacts with the patients."

"I don't exactly recall those items."

"Dr. Toricelli, I can understand, all too well, the depth and breadth of your...well let's be kind and call it inexperience. I can even accept your difficulty in orienting to this job, because it often happens at the beginning of a new task, that people, even good people, will fumble a bit. But what you have done, to have not followed the most fundamental procedures, is just sloppy, stupid, arrogant behavior."

"You could look at it that way," I said. "But why don't we get to the point. Is there something you know that I don't know about Volknick?"

She gave me this real narrow-eyed, hateful look. "Dr. Toricelli, I'm going to bring you up to speed on Volknick, only because when I request that you be fired, I will be able to say that I gave you all the help I could. Now, on the afternoon of Dr. Epstein's murder, Mr. Volknick's mother arrived home at 5:30 to find her son in a grossly agitated state. He was mumbling to himself continuously and obviously attending to internal stimuli. He accused his mother of cheating on his father, his dead father, as you'd have known if you'd followed procedure and read the file on him. When his mother asked him to go to his room, he flew into a terrible psychotic rage; breaking furniture, smashing mirrors, destroying art work, running totally wild. His mother fled to the bathroom and locked herself there, while he proceeded to lay waste to six rooms of furniture. He then went to their terrace and started hurling potted plants onto the street below. It was at that point that a neighbor called the police, and he was taken to Manhattan Hospital for rapid tranquilization and a subsequent ten-day stay at the Astor Clinic. He was only discharged two days ago."

"I see," I said.

"But, of course, you didn't review any of this with him, did you?"

"I think you know the answer to that."

"Dr. Toricelli, I could have gotten a better performance today from a second year medical student."

As much as I was hating this bitch, I had to admit this chewing out I was getting was probably more or less well deserved.

Just at that moment, Jake walked in and came over and sat on the desk.

"Four o'clock, buddy boy," he said to me, and ignored Moore, "'bout time to knock off. How'd the day go anyway?"

"Lt. Roma," said Moore, looking up at Jake, "the day actually went quite poorly for your cousin. And I will inform you now that I shall be asking the commissioner for his dismissal and replacement by a faculty member of the Forensic Institute. Your cousin, Lt. Roma, is clearly not up to the task."

"What the hell are you talking about?" said Jake. "We settled this shit yesterday. He's here, he's a goddamn doctor, he worked in a freakin' psychiatric hospital...and...he stays."

"But let's not forget his most important qualification—that he's your cousin. And apparently you have an excess of I.O.U.'s to cash in at the mayor's office."

"That ain't none of your damn business," yelled Jake. Then they just glared at each other and I'd have only been half-surprised if they started swinging at each other.

"Joey," said Jake, without taking his eyes off Moore, "let's get the hell out of here."

"Well, to tell you the truth Jake, I've got a report to write up before I leave today."

"Fuck the report," he said. "I'm the fucking boss here, remember? Now let's go." With his eyes still fixed on Moore, he reached over to grab my arm and started pulling me out of my chair.

"I'll get to that report as soon as I can," I told Moore. I wanted to tell her by tonight, but Jake was already pulling me out the door.

WE TOOK THE elevator down to the lobby, and started walking up Broadway toward Canal St. I asked Jake where the hell we were going.

"Shaugnessy's," he said.

"Yeah, who's that?"

"My favorite doctor, dipshit. He hands out medicine, not grief."

Up another block we walked into a dark, smoky old bar that had somehow survived all the office construction and condo renovations in the neighborhood. The guy behind the bar was actually named Shaughnessy, and he got Jake what he needed in a hurry, a double bourbon on the rocks. Jake told me he'd already knocked back a couple for lunch.

"But now. Joey," he said, "look, it's tea time. So what the hell are you going to have?"

"Gimme a beer," I told him. "Whatever you got on draft."

"Hey, Eddie," Jake yelled to Shaughnessy, "you got any of that yuppie shit microbrewery stuff for my doctor cousin here?"

"Just Bud on tap, Jake," he said.

"Aw now that's a crying shame, Eddie," he said. "I mean that could really heat up business for you, you know? Especially with all these rich assholes moving into the neighborhood. You gotta get a freakin' sushi bar in here too, you know what I mean?"

He was getting more obnoxious by the minute and I figured lunchtime had just been the beginning; he must have been fueling up through most of the afternoon. And who knew how much Valium he'd taken on top of it. He turned to me, real sloppy looking: "So what do you say, Joey, you like your new job as a fucking expert, or what?"

"I'll tell you if I get past tomorrow,"

"Oh my ass, Joey. That bitch hasn't got any pull, you understand? You tell her to go fuck herself, okay? That's the only way she's going to get it anyway."

"You could try treating her with a little more tact. You're just throwing fuel on the fire."

"I ain't got time for that, Joey. And that broad don't know shit from shinola anyway. But the worst thing is, you can't trust her to, uh, cooperate. That's why I got you here, buddy boy."

"Yeah? I thought I was here to make sure Nina didn't kill you."

"Don't bust my balls. I need you, right fucking here, Joey. I can't do this shit right now, see? I got a couple of snakes in the department just waiting to bite me in the ass. You're my fucking handle right now, Joey, *capisce?*"

"Some fucking handle," I said. "You should have seen me today."

"Joey, c'mon. You're a smart son of a bitch, I always knew that. You'll get on top of it."

He kicked back another double, and ordered up a third, and then he started getting into some stupid flirtation routine with a couple of stewardesses at the next table.

"Jake," I said, "you know if you laid off the sauce here you'd have half a chance of getting back on your feet. What do you want to do now, get into more trouble with your wife?"

He was drunk on his ass and wasn't listening to me. I could see the stewardesses were having a harder and harder time trying to be polite.

When he wasn't looking, I dipped my hand into his jacket pocket and pulled out a wad of cash. I went to the bar to pay off Shaughnessy and then hauled Jake's drunk ass out of there.

"Joey," he whined, when we got out to the street, "what the fuck are you doing?"

"Stuffing you into a cab to Grand Central so you can take the fucking train home to your wife."

"Yeah? And what are you going to do?"

"I'll drive the car up later tonight...I got to take care of something on the West Side. Don't wait dinner for me."

"What? You got some broad already, you son of a bitch?"

"None of your business. Now get your ass home and tell your wife you're sorry for all your bullshit, okay? She'll appreciate it."

"Fuck that."

"Hey, you said I'm here to help. So I'm trying to help you, all right?"

"Some fucking help. I didn't even finish my friggin' drink."

I hailed down a cab, pushed him in, and closed the door. As it was pulling away he stuck his head out the window.

"Hey, Joey," he yelled, "don't do anything I wouldn't do."

"Yeah, yeah, you drunk bastard," I said, waving good-bye.

I WALKED BACK to the Police Headquarters parking lot and pulled out in Jake's Oldsmobile station wagon. I started creeping up through the snarled traffic and grid locked intersections along lower Broadway. No, I wasn't going to the West Side, but I didn't want to get into my real plan with Jake, which was basically to take another look at Epstein's place. The fact is, Moore's words had stung me pretty bad and, regardless of her own faults, not to mention that her own interview with Volknick didn't go anywhere, she was right that I'd handled both those interviews like a clod. But now I felt a new determination, even a kind of obsession, to solve this case. It was about doing the right thing, for sure. But it was also about doing things right—competently, completely—and proving to myself that I could do the job I'd been hired to do.

After about an hour's hassle in rush hour, I pulled up in front of Epstein's office, double parked, and put the police I.D. card on the dash. I hoped my doormen buddies would unlock the suite for me, because I didn't have the keys.

But when I got out of the car, I saw through the transom that there was a light on in the suite, and the outside entrance door was slightly ajar. I walked over and opened it, stepped into the little entryway, and then turned the handle of the inside entrance door. It was locked. Then suddenly, from a speaker overhead in the entryway, I heard this high-pitched voice say: "Can I help you?" Whoever it was, he sounded annoyed.

I looked up at the speaker and noticed there was a video monitor lens above it.

"Uh, yes," I said, "Joe Toricelli, Dr. Joe Toricelli here, New York City police department."

"I see," he said, "after I buzz you in, proceed to your left, through the door marked 'Waiting Room—Dr. Roland'."

I entered the main corridor, opened the door into his waiting room, and settled into a soft leather chair. So now I'd get to meet the famous Dr. Roland. I picked up a copy of a news magazine and looked at the mailing label: 'Bertrand Lelan Stewart Roland, M.D.'. So why the hell does he need four names? I started leafing through the magazine pages, and caught a glimpse of a strangely familiar face. He had a scared look in his eyes as he was stepping out of a limo. The caption under the photo read: 'Landsdowne denies rumors of illness'. I hoped to hell he was getting some help.

Just then Roland's office door swung open and a tall, rail-thin woman in her sixties strolled out. She wore a bird's nest of teased out and sprayed-stiff white hair and had a set of toothpaste ad teeth to match.

"Thank you, Dr. Roland," she said. "I shall see you on Monday."

"Four-thirty, sharp," he said, like he was her father.

"Oh, I hope I'll not act out and be tardy," she giggled.

Then Roland turned to me, as if to show her someone else was waiting for him.

"Oh, I'm so sorry," she said to me, breathlessly. "I hope I haven't kept you waiting."

"No problem," I said.

As she walked out I got up and shook hands with Dr. Roland, and told him I was here on the Epstein case.

"Yes, pleased to meet you, Dr. Toricelli," he said. "This is a bit of a surprise of course, but I would like to help in any way I can. Please, come into my office."

If Epstein's office had a warm, cozy feel to it, then Roland's was exactly the opposite: cool, sparse, and edgy. The walls were painted this kind of clinical white and were bare except for a couple of small, abstract prints. In one corner there was this tall metal sculpture which looked like a phoenix, and along the wall was a cold, black leather couch with a stainless-steel frame and a small black cylinder of a pillow at one end. Roland was slightly built and on the short side. He looked to be in his mid-fifties. He was wearing one of these Wall St. power suits that looked like it was too big in the shoulders for him. His face was small and narrow with a pointy little nose and a weak looking chin. Somehow, I could picture him dressed up in a waitress outfit and serving customers in some cheap roadhouse. You'd just have to put a bleach blonde wig over that slicked back, thin black hair of his. He gestured for me to sit down and we settled into some uncomfortable chrome and leather chairs just to the side of his desk.

"So," he began, "any leads in the case, Dr. Toricelli?"

"Not really. We're still in a very preliminary stage, searching for any plausible motivations."

"Any sense of it being connected with the flower shop murder, or the girl in the park?"

"No, no obvious connection."

"Well, that's my hunch, they're all connected. Different methods, of course, but unified by a single pathological motive. You wait and see, some maniac will claim credit for them all. Perhaps he will even get his manifesto published in the *Times*."

"Maybe. By the way, from what I understand you're the guy who actually discovered Dr. Epstein's body. Is that right?"

"Yes it is. And it was really quite awful. I'd just come back that Friday night; I'd been up in Monotoc all week for a conference. The following morning, I came to the office to pick up the mail. It was then that I noticed both his waiting room door and office door ajar. I walked in, slowly, sensing that something was wrong. There he was, lying on the floor. And I'd only spoken with him the previous afternoon, over the phone. It was shocking, quite shocking. Of course I immediately called the police."

"But tell me this, Dr. Roland, do you think it's possible that one of his patients did it?"

"Patients? It's a sexy theory isn't it, Dr Toricelli? But really quite unlikely. Besides, where's your motive?"

"Don't know. Some sort of retribution maybe, for feeling exploited, or betrayed."

"Doctor, please," he laughed, "those issues come up in ninety-five percent of cases. If that were a plausible motivation, half the psychiatrists on this street would have been slain long ago."

"I understand," I said, "but in the case of someone with a psychotic illness, and maybe a doctor-patient relationship gone haywire, that kind of scenario becomes less unlikely, yes?"

"Perhaps. But Dr. Epstein was a very skillful clinician, very intuitive as well as theoretically sophisticated. In his case, such a scenario would be very difficult to imagine."

"But not impossible."

"Yes. Well, this is growing a bit tedious, Dr. Toricelli. What exactly is the point here?"

"I would like to know if you know of any patients of Dr. Epstein who could have possibly, possibly been capable of such an act?"

"I know very little of Dr. Epstein's patients, Dr. Toricelli. We only shared a suite, not a practice."

"But you must have covered for him from time to time, and had some contact with his patients."

"Very little. But, Dr. Toricelli, if you don't mind, I will need to wrap things up here momentarily. I have some phone calls I must return and I'm due at the airport very soon."

"Sure," I said, "but I just wanted to know what you may know about Nathan Volknick. Do you know him?"

"Yes, as a matter of fact I do."

"What do you know about him?"

"Something of his history and illness," he said. "You see, I met with the young man at the request of his mother while he was in the hospital last week. Technically he is now my patient, temporarily, at the request of his family. A very good family, I might add; they live on the next block from me on Sutton Place. I told them I'd extend myself until I find him a new doctor."

"So obviously you know about his behavior on the day Dr. Epstein was murdered."

"Quite well. The boy and his family have even signed a release authorizing me to speak with any investigators."

"And you're not impressed with his behavior? I mean, around the time of Epstein's murder?"

"Oh, I suppose one could build a case, circumstantially, on his recent relapse, as well as the tragic history. But I don't think it would go very far."

"What do you mean by 'tragic history'?" I said.

"Don't you know? I sent over a complete report to your Dr. Moore, just yesterday."

"I haven't seen it."

"Well, then come with me, Dr. Toricelli. As long as you're here I'll let you review the report, but in Dr. Epstein's office please. I really must return my calls before I leave today."

He picked up a manila envelope and led me down the hall to Epstein's office. There was a strange little wiggle to his walk and his frame seemed to rattle around underneath that suit. I noticed that he tried to keep the volume of his voice modulated, like he had to control it from breaking into higher pitches.

He unlocked Epstein's door, flipped on a couple of light switches, which also powered up the video monitor on the desk, and gestured for me to have a seat at his desk.

"Here it is," he handed me the envelope, "read it over and let me know when you're finished. I will be in my office."

I pulled out the report. The history said that Epstein began seeing Volknick almost six years ago, when he was 22. He'd "presented at that time with a several year history of agitation, obsessive-compulsive behavior and paranoid delusions." He'd already had four hospitalizations and was on heavy doses of anti-psychotic medications. The history went on to describe a typical sad case of early onset schizophrenia: relapses, mental deterioration, social isolation, etc. But then there was something strange in the social history. He'd been brought before a juvenile investigative panel at the age of 14 as a possible homicide suspect in connection with his father's death, from a presumed fall from their 15th floor apartment. He was never formally charged, but soon after that, he'd had his first hospitalization. His father's case was eventually seen as an accident or possible suicide—the guy had had a long history of depression—but the family always remained unclear about all the circumstances. Apparently, there was always this shadow of suspicion over Nathan because he'd been with his father at the time of his fall.

I went back over the history of his hospitalizations and saw there'd been a few episodes of violence prior to a couple of admissions. But it only mentioned breaking furniture, nothing about hurting people. At the end of the report there was a copy of Epstein's note on his last meeting with Volknick. It was just a few scribbled lines, describing Volknick as "increasingly agitated" and that he should up his Risperdal two milligrams.

I put the report on Epstein's desk and got up and walked around the office. Let's say Volknick did it, I thought; how would that work? Volknick's out about four forty-five, Epstein's last patient that day. He leaves the office, maybe the suite, and Epstein has time to write a note. Then, shortly after that, because Volknick was back at Sutton Place by five-thirty, he comes back to strangle Epstein. Supposedly, and this I've got to check out, no one else is in the suite; Roland's out, no other patients. So that means Volknick and Epstein are alone. Volknick's a lean, sort of muscular young guy, a head taller and probably a lot more energetic than Epstein. He corners him, scares the shit out of him probably, pulls out the tie and, whammo, strangles the daylights out of him. It's plausible, I thought, it has its own kind of logic: Volknick resents Epstein, and he sees him, in his own paranoid way, as an oppressor. Over time his rage builds up and finally takes over, culminating in this single act of murder. Maybe the same thing he did to his old man fourteen years ago, right? Except now Epstein's the new father figure and he too has to be slain. That explains why he goes berserk when he gets home, because then he's full of all this recharged conflict and guilt. Then, by the time the cops come, he goes totally nuts and represses the whole thing, because it's too traumatic, too heinous to remember. So now, he doesn't even have a conscious memory of what he did. Yeah, you could start to build something on all this, you really could.

I sat back down in Dr. Epstein's chair, trying to imagine what was going through his mind that afternoon. Was he alarmed in his meeting with Volknick, but just kept his note short and simple? Did he watch to see if Volknick left the premises after the appointment and, if so, what did he think when—if—he buzzed him back in? And was he so scared stiff that he couldn't do anything except be totally intimidated by Volknick, just sit there petrified and get strangled?

Then, suddenly, Epstein's office door creaked open, and a woman appeared at the door; fiftyish, long salt and pepper hair, framing a smiling face. She was on the plump side and wore a long black dress.

"Hi," she said, "who are you?"

"Dr. Joe Toricelli," I said, "police department. And who are you?"

"Oh, I'm sorry," she said. "I understand everything now. Please don't mind me. I'm Evelyn Roland, Dr. Roland's wife. Just came by to pick him up, and noticed Horatio's door was open."

"No problem, Mrs. Roland, not at all," I said as I stood and walked over to her. "Pleased to meet you."

"Oh thank you. But please, don't let me bother you. The sooner you find out who killed poor Horatio the better I will sleep. It's such an unspeakable thing, that someone would murder him."

"Did you know him pretty well?"

"Oh yes. For thirty years now, since his days as a resident at the Astor Clinic. That's when Bert...or...Dr. Roland met him as well. They trained together. Bert and I were engaged at the time."

"I see."

"But you know Horatio was such a lovely man. Very deep, very sensitive. Such a natural. And he so cared about his work." She started to cry, first just a sniffle, and then she really started sobbing.

"Looks like you really...admired him," I said.

"Oh yes, I...admired him very much. I..."

"Evelyn?" came a voice from the door down the hall. It was Roland.

Her eyes suddenly widened. "Bert?" she said. "I'm here, in Horatio's office, just having a word with Dr. Tor...Tor..."

"Toricelli," I said.

"Yes, Dr. Toricelli," she said, in this shaky voice. "I..."

"Evelyn, please," he said, as he approached the waiting room door, "I'm really pressed for time here."

She turned to me with this helpless look. "I'm sorry, Dr. Toricelli," she said, "nice to chat with you, but I need to go."

"Sure, sure, I understand."

After she left, I closed the office door and went back to sit in Epstein's chair. 'A lovely man' she'd said, and she was real broken up by his death. I wondered what that was all about. But then, in the next minute, I heard someone shouting, though it was muffled through the door and wall of the suite. I went to open Epstein's office door and the shouting got louder. I crept through the waiting room and down the corridor a little, and the voice, Roland's, and the words became more distinct. He must have been standing just on the other side of the closed door to his waiting room.

"You are as stupid as you are useless," he was saying, "since when does second grade arithmetic stand beyond your grasp? If the plane leaves at 7:30 and I told you I wanted to be at the airport at 7 then what time would you have to..."

"Bert please..." I could hear Mrs. Roland saying.

"Don't interrupt me, you cow," he said. "Now did you or did you not take the Third Avenue Bridge?"

"Bert the traffic..." her voice trailed off.

"I don't want to hear any of your asinine pleading, Evelyn. I am sick and tired of your chronic, terminal stupidity. And...and look at you. Can't you get yourself fixed up? Or is it that you aspire to wrinkled frumphood? Why not at least try some surgery? Pretty soon you'll look like a bag lady in Grand Central."

"Oh Bert..." she said, with this long, pathetic whine.

"Oh spare me the melodrama, Evelyn," he rasped. "Now is the car out front?"

She didn't say anything.

"Is it?" he said again.

"Yes, Bert," she said very softly.

"Then let's get a move on," he bellowed. "Pick up the luggage and make yourself useful."

When I heard the doorknob turn I hightailed it back into Epstein's office, closed the door and sat down in his chair. In the next few seconds I saw Mrs. Roland on the video monitor on Epstein's desk; she was going out the suite entrance, struggling with a suitcase in one hand and a big package in the other. Roland was nowhere to be seen. In a few minutes she returned and then repeated the performance with another two hefty boxes. So this is the good Dr. Roland, I thought to myself, renowned therapist and healer. Kicking his wife around and using her as a mule. Then there was a rap on the door.

"Dr. Toricelli?" said Roland, as he opened the door. "I trust you've had ample time to review the Volknick report?"

Just about," I said.

He walked up to me and stood over me.

"Any questions?" he said. He had this real phony, singsong tone to his voice.

"Well, just wanted to clarify. Dr. Epstein was in the suite alone that Friday afternoon, right? I mean, neither you nor anybody else was in your office, is that right?"

"Right," he said. "Absolutely. I was in Monotoc that week, and didn't return here until late Friday night. No one else was using my office."

"Monotoc?"

"Ah, yes. Lovely spot. Did a five-day workshop there. On Marriage and Commitment."

"No kidding."

"I don't kid, Dr. Toricelli. But look, I've got to close up shop and get to the airport. I'm sure you have things to do as well."

"Yes. Well, thanks for your cooperation," I said, standing up. "And, uh, my regards to your wife. She impressed me as a very nice woman."

"Oh yes, thank you," he said. "You chatted with her briefly, yes?"

"Yes."

"She's quite an angel," he said, and smiled and showed a row of pointy, childlike teeth. "It will be our thirtieth anniversary this October."

"Congratulations."

"What about you, doctor?" he said. "Married?"

"No."

"No? Too busy eh? Or perhaps having too much fun, hm?"

"Just not lucky enough to meet the right girl," I said. "Not yet anyway."

"It has little to do with luck, Dr. Toricelli," he said, and his face darkened. "It has to do with choices, maturity, commitment. Have you read any of my books?"

"No sir. But I'm sure these things are important."

"Indeed they are," he spouted out, "read my books and you will understand just how important they are. But, for now, doctor, I really must close up."

"Yes, of course, thanks again, and if I need to, I'll be in touch."

"Of course you will," he smiled, "and I shall be here. Goodnight now."

"Goodnight," I said, and went out to the car.

I GRABBED A $65 parking ticket off the windshield (didn't they see the police card?) and started crawling through traffic toward the FDR. What was it with this guy Roland, I thought to myself, what is he all about? Egotistical, a hypocrite, a phony, those all seemed right. But what about his relationship with Epstein? Office partners, lifelong colleagues and...what else? Anything? They seemed to be as different as night and day. But could Roland have somehow wanted Epstein dead? But for what? Money, revenge, envy? Yeah, what about envy? His wife sure seemed to like Epstein. Maybe they were having an affair. But, with the way he treats her, why should he give a shit?

And even if he did, the guy's not stupid right? I mean, he didn't just walk into his office on a Friday afternoon and strangle him. Besides, he says he was upstate, in Monotoc all week. But what about the doorman, the Irish guy, Frank; he said he saw Roland take a limo that Friday. Well, maybe he was confused, maybe it wasn't Friday or, maybe it was on Friday but it wasn't Roland. Yeah, he could have thought it was Roland but, who the hell knows, maybe it was some hit man Roland hired. Yeah, and the doorman just thought it was Roland.

All the way up the Deegan, through all the stop and go traffic and hundred-degree heat, I was spinning out a dozen ways to explain how Roland could have done it. Then, I found some old Clifford Brown piece on the radio, some frantic, whirling explosion of some old Tin Pan Alley melody I couldn't place the name of. It got me suddenly happy, and I got psyched with the idea that we didn't have to look any further than Epstein's next-door neighbor to find his killer.

ABOUT HALF AN hour later, when I pulled up into Jake's driveway, his son ran across the lawn to greet me.

"Hi, Uncle Joey," he said. "Want to play some catch?"

"Not tonight, Frankie," I said. "It's already getting dark. Your dad home yet?"

"Yeah," he said, sounding disappointed. "I think he's sleeping."

I walked into the house and Nina came out of the kitchen to greet me.

"Hi, Joey. I didn't expect you home so early. Jake said something about you having a girl on the West Side."

"What?" I said. "No, no...he must have misunderstood."

"Oh that's his specialty, he doesn't understand nothing, especially himself. Anyway, you hungry?"

No, no thanks, Nina. Where's Jake? I've got to talk to him about the Epstein case."

"You're assuming he's interested," she said. "But I can tell you he doesn't have his mind on his work these days. Haven't you noticed?"

I didn't say anything.

"He's only got his mind on himself. Drunk, feeling sorry for himself, paying no attention to his responsibilities. He's just a selfish little boy."

"He'll work it out, Nina, you'll see."

"Nice words, Joey, but you don't believe it anymore than I do."

"No, I'm serious, you'll see. Now where is the big loser, anyway?"

"Sacked out in the den. Go ahead, take a look. Tell him I told you he can start packing anytime he wants."

I walked into the den and found Jake snoring in a rocking chair while a giant TV was spewing out some hyped-up sports report.

"Hey, Jake," I said.

He didn't say anything.

"C'mon, wake up Sleeping Beauty," I said, slapping his face a couple of times. "Time to get with the program."

His lids rolled open to show two bloodshot eyes. He kept on snoring.

"C'mon, get your ass up." I slapped him harder, a few more times.

Suddenly, he sat up in the chair. "What the fuck? What the fuck are you doing?" he yelled.

"C'mon, Jake," I said, "I'm trying to wake you up. We've got to talk. Now."

He rubbed his eyes and looked around the room. "What the hell time is it?"

"I don't know. Eight, eight-thirty maybe. Look, I want to talk to you about the case."

"We ain't got time. We're going to be late for work."

"What? No asshole," I said, "it's eight at night, see? What are you, demented or what?"

"Shit." He looked around the room again. "All right, what? You want to talk to me about the fucking case? Or what?"

"Yes, I want to talk about the fucking case. And this is what I want to say: somehow, some way, Roland's in on it, okay?"

"Roland?"

"Yeah, Roland. Epstein's partner. The guy who found Epstein."

"Yeah, damn it, I know who the hell he is. But why him?"

"'Cause he's sleazy," I said, "and a phony. And he's a son of a bitch to his wife, even though he promotes himself like he's some fucking champion of marriage. Plus he's a cheap bastard, one of the doormen told me."

"Joey," said Jake, rubbing his face, "you're not really impressing me here, you know that? I mean the guy may be an asshole, but that don't add up to murder."

"No, no it doesn't, but there's something real sneaky about this guy. In fact, as I've thought about it more, I think he's trying to implicate Volknick."

"Volknick? Volknick?" he said, like he was trying to remember who he was. "We following up on him?"

"Jake, c'mon now. He was on the interview schedule today."

"Oh yeah...right, right. That's the kid who went nuts the day Epstein was killed."

"Yeah, see," I said, "you're really on top of things, aren't you? But, yeah, I think Roland's trying to implicate him. He told me today he doesn't think one of Epstein's patients did it, but then he hands me this nice juicy report on Volknick. Who, by the way, just happens to now be his patient."

Jake finished rubbing his face and got up and started pacing around the den.

"Wait a minute," he said, "we got witnesses who say Roland was up in New Pawling, at the Monotoc Hotel, all that week and all day that Friday. And his phone records confirm that, including a call he made to

Epstein around five, on the afternoon he got killed. Plus, we got other witnesses who say he took a limo at six that evening, straight from Monotoc, to his club in the city, where he got in around eight. Then he stayed there until two in the morning, for some big dinner celebration."

"Yeah, so maybe that all checks out, but then, maybe he hired a hit man to kill Epstein. There was this limo, see, that the doormen say pulled out from the suite entrance that afternoon. One of them says that was Roland in it. Well maybe, maybe not; but just maybe, there was a hit man in that limo. So, we've got to check things out. Could Roland possibly have paid for any limo service in the city that Friday? Huh?"

"I don't know," said Jake.

"Well c'mon, let's check it out."

"Now wait a goddamn minute, will you, Joey?" he said, getting real red. "This doesn't make any sense. I mean, Roland paying for a limo for a hit man? C'mon. Besides, what the hell do you know about detective work anyway?"

"Hey, I'm just thinking out loud. What are you getting so pissed off about?"

"Nothing, nothing, I'm sorry. Look, I'll even have some guys follow up on it, all right? But now tell me, what about the Volknick guy? You interviewed him today, right?"

"Yeah," I said. "Nice guy really. But awful bad illness. What a life to live, I'll tell you."

"Right, but what about his story. How does it add up?"

"It adds up that he was Epstein's last appointment that Friday. His symptoms were flaring up and Epstein bumped up his medication. Later in the day he went berserk."

"Did he say anything about hurting Epstein?"

"Nothing. I asked him about it and he denied anything like that. And I believe him."

"Why?"

"'Cause I think Roland did it."

"Joey, get off Roland, will you? For now anyway. 'Til we get a chance to check things out."

Jake and I went back and forth that evening about how to conduct the investigation. He was the expert, of course, and I was just an amateur, and as we argued and speculated Jake started to look a little more like his old self. Boastful, take charge, not feeling sorry for himself. I didn't even mind how many times he called me a Cub Scout or told me how full of shit I was.

Part 4

COME THE next morning I got up before everybody else and walked down to the commuter train station. I'd called about an apartment that night and had made arrangements to check it out in the morning. I didn't quite know how things were going to go between Jake and Nina, but I figured I'd stick with my plan and get out of there and rent a little place in the city.

On the train ride in I picked up a copy of the *Register*. The O'Connor story had moved up to the left top of the front page and the headline got me sick when I saw it. "Mother and Son Found Slain near Car Linked to Murder Suspects—Manhunt for Crassidy and Torento Intensifies." The story said the Hendry County, Florida police had found the dead bodies of Russ and Vera, estimated to be at least a week old, lying in the woods near a Toyota station wagon, apparently stolen only a few days ago out of Miami.

"Shit," I said, and it echoed across the empty seats of an empty train car.

The story continued on the inside pages with photos of Russ's and Vera's bodies and a map of the surrounding area in Hendry County. Bad as it felt, I tried to imagine what had led up to the killings. Crassidy must have come to see them as excess baggage or maybe he saw one of them trying to make a getaway, or at least started to get real nervous about it. It must not have helped, when he found out the cops had found Vera's driver's license under the seat of that Chevy in Miami. And he figured she damn well hadn't left it there by accident. But why the hell Hendry County? He must have found a hideout there, I guessed. Someplace where he could sit tight with his hostages before he figured out his next move. But, no matter what the story was, it was hurting me real bad that Russ and Vera were dead. Damn, somehow I should have handled things differently, I thought. Me and my bullshit story to Crassidy about how I was going to buy his coke. I should have just figured on a way to bust that evil bastard's head as soon as he'd made his return that stormy night. Too late for all that now. Now, somehow, I'd have to find a way to catch Crassidy. But what the hell could I do?

The train rattled past the littered scrub and shattered blocks of the

South Bronx and rocked over the Harlem River Bridge into 125th Street station. It slowed to a stop past posters of Broadway shows and a few people on the platform waiting for the northbound train. A couple of them had their noses in the *Post* or the *News* and I tried to make out what headline on me and Crassidy they'd cooked up. But all I could make out was the back page sports headline in the *News*, something about "Atlanta Tramples Mets".

The train pulled out and down into the tunnel toward Grand Central, and I had some crazy wish that it would just keep burrowing deeper and deeper into the darkness and depth of the earth, and leave everything above sealed off and forgotten in another world. Poor Russ and Vera, I thought. Especially Russ, he was a real good kid. I'd take revenge on Crassidy, somehow I would.

I got off the train and made my way into the Terminal hall. Past coffee shops, bank machines and plenty of newsstands. There were piles of tabloids just delivered and still bundled up on the floor. Again, I saw the headline in the *News*, there on the back, on the sports page, "Atlanta Tramples Mets."

That's when it hit me, something clicked in me with this "Atlanta Tramples..." phrase. Crassidy, I now remembered, had once told me—when was it? —Maybe a few months ago, about some "old lady" he had around Ft. Myers. "Samantha Ann Hample from Atlanta"—that was it.

A waitress, I believe he'd said, who "did all kinds of dirty, sweet things" to him whenever he was up that way. They'd known each other for years and Crassidy had said, yeah, now I remembered clearly; he was drunk at Vera's bar and in a weird sentimental mood. He'd said she was the only girl he'd thought about marrying and maybe he even would someday. I was thinking to myself at the time: what kind of tramp would marry Crassidy?

So now, all of a sudden, I was charged up. Maybe, just maybe, I had a way of nabbing Crassidy. I had to find a phone and get her number, quick as I could. I went over to a bank of pay phones in the back of the station and called up Ft. Myers info.

"I'm looking for the number of Samantha Ann Hample," I said, "H-A-M-P-L-E."

"Don't have a Samantha with that spelling sir in Ft. Myers," said the operator, "only have a Theodore Hample on Bayshore Rd."

"No? Well then try H-A-M-P-E-L."

"There's an initial S. Hampel in Edison."

"Just 'S'?"

"That's all sir."

"And where's Edison?" I said. "That near Ft. Myers?"

"In the area, in Lee County."

"I see, uh—okay, give me the number and address please."

I jotted down the number and address: 1671 Flora Acres Drive.

"And say, uh, operator; you have any idea, I mean, what kind of neighborhood that is?"

She laughed. "No, I don't."

"No? I mean, it's a little town, I imagine?"

"Oh, I guess. With a big trailer park. Believe they call it Flora Acres."

"Yeah? That right? Thanks, thank you, operator."

Now for the set up, I thought. I hoped to hell this was Samantha Ann Hampel's place; anyway, I had to take the chance.

I called up the Florida State Police in Ft. Myers.

"Cranston," a man's voice answered.

"Yessir," I said. "This the Florida State Police?"

"Yes it is."

Well sir, "I said," I'm awful nervous about this but I'm going to go ahead and tell you anyway I believe I seen that Crassidy fellow everybody's talkin' about, you know, the one murderin' all those folks, just like they done said on *America's Most Wanted* on the TV?"

"Yeah, I know."

"Well I believe I seen him," I said, "right...right here in Edison."

"In Edison?"

"Yessir. That's, well that's where I live you see. But I ain't lookin' to get mixed up in all this. And I ain't lookin' for no reward."

"Where you seen him in Edison?" he said.

"At the big trailer park here sir. I...I was visiting there just last night. They call it Flora Acres. I believe I done seen him, at number 1671 Flora Acres Drive."

"You say anything to him?" he asked.

"No sir, just seen him walking into the trailer with a woman. Anyway sir, I...I got to go...but I'm telling you, I believe that's your man, right here in Edison."

"Uh-huh," he said, "and what's your name, buddy?"

"Oh...well...that's confidential officer," I said. "And...anyway...I got to go..."

I slammed down the phone and walked real quickly out to Forty-Second St. It scared the shit out of me, that there was any chance they could identify me. But how? Caller I.D., maybe? Well, forget about it, I thought, it's pretty near impossible.

I GRABBED A cab downtown and tried to catch my breath. All right, all right, I told myself, there's no way they're going to find you, so quit panicking. But I'd be damned if they wouldn't find Crassidy.

We stopped at a light and the cabbie turned to look at me. "What address you say sir?" he asked.

"904 ½ West Fifth St.," I said. "You know where that is?"

"Yes, of course sir," he said. "No problem."

When we got below 14th St., he took a right on Greenwich Ave., and then we proceeded to drive around in different circles through the West Village for the next fifteen minutes. All the time, trying to find the address on West Fifth. He kept telling me in some kind of accent that he knew exactly where it was. But by the time we passed the Pequod Inn for the third time I said, "Hey, stop, okay? I'm getting out here." I threw him a ten-dollar bill and got out and started to walk down Oliver Street.

I ran into a heavy set guy about halfway down the block and asked him if he knew where the address was.

"Oh sure," he boomed, in a voice I thought I'd heard on TV an awful lot, "just around the corner there, past the hardware store."

Just around the corner I found 904 ½ West Fifth, one of a little row of old townhouses that'd been broken up into little apartments. I walked up the stoop and rang bell #1, and the landlady came out the front door, a short, squat old Italian lady with a stern, kind of wary look on her face.

"Hi," I said. "I'm Joe Toricelli."

"Yeah, you're late," she said. "I said eight o'clock. I got to go to work this morning. Don't you?"

"Sure," I said looking at my watch. It was 8:15. "I'm sorry Mrs...."

"D'Angelo," she said.

"Right," I said, "pleased to..."

"Here's the key," she said, "third floor, rear, number 3-B. Take a look and be back in five minutes."

"Sure thing, thank you," I said. "Thanks very much."

I bounded up the stairs and unlocked the door. The minute I walked in, something felt pretty good about the place. It had two windows that looked out over a garden, and dark brick walls and a fireplace and a real cozy, kind of closed in feeling. It was barely big enough to hold the few pieces of furniture in it; a sagging, single bed, a cheap dinette set and a chest of drawers stuffed in a corner. Near the bathroom door was a tiny stove and refrigerator.

A good place to hide, I thought, from everything and everybody in the outside world. And maybe from whatever demons I've got inside of me.

I ran back down the stairs and knocked on Mrs. D'Angelo's door."

"I'll take it," I said.

"It's by the month," she said, "like I already told you. You give me a month's rent now and a month's deposit. That's going to be two thousand all together."

"You want to say fifteen hundred?"

"No, I don't. I want to say two thousand and that's already below the market. It's furnished, didn't you notice."

"So it is," I said, "I almost forgot." I forked over the two grand, which was the better part of a "cash advance" Jake had given me yesterday.

"Here's all the keys," she said. "You got two nice girls from NYU on the second floor, and a real weirdo next to you. But he's quiet. Now what'd you say you do?"

"I'm a doctor."

"You going to use the place for monkey business?"

"What? Oh no, no. I'm going to be living here, temporarily of course, 'til I find a place."

She looked at me like I was full of shit.

"I like it quiet here," she said. "No girlfriends coming in and out. You hear me?"

"Please, Mrs. D'Angelo," I said, "I'm telling you no monkey business. I'll be living like...well like a monk, you'll see. Like a monk, without a peep."

She ignored what I said and pointed out the keys to me. "That key is for the outside door, and you got a top and bottom lock on your door. See?"

"Perfect," I said, "and you know what? You won't even know I'm living here."

"Good," she said. Then she turned back into her apartment and closed the door.

I went back upstairs to my new pad. Good place, I said to myself, good place. But then I realized there was no phone. Well, maybe it's all for the better. But nevertheless, I wanted to call Jake and tell him we should meet by noon to go over any new details in the case. I went outside to the corner pay phone and left a message on his voice mail. When I got back I saw I'd forgotten my key, and was locked out of the front door.

"Shit," I said, and turned the knob but the door wasn't going to budge. I went to ring buzzer #2, hoping the young ladies would be up. But there was no answer after several times. Okay, I thought, let's try the so-called weirdo in #3-A. After I rang a few times an annoyed, bitchy voice crackled over the tinny speaker by the door.

"What is it?" he said.

"Hi, good morning. I'm Joe Toricelli, new guy in the house. Left my keys upstairs, could you please buzz me in?"

"You what? Oh never mind, I don't believe this."

Then it was quiet.

"Hello? Hello?" I said into the little speaker. Momentarily, through the front door window, I saw a short, overweight Asian guy in a long turquoise robe padding barefoot down the inside staircase. As he opened the door I saw he had a kind of girlish movie star face, covered with a three-day stubble of black beard. He had a smooth shaven head and a pair of real sleepy looking eyelids.

"I really wish you wouldn't do that again," he scolded me. "I really can't be taking responsibility for your relationship with your keys, you know?"

"Sure, I understand," I said.

"Oh shit," he sort of hissed. "What time is it anyway?"

"About a quarter to nine," I said.

"Oh, that is un-godly," he whined. "I just got in at seven. Please, please, please don't ever do that again...what's your name anyway?"

"Joe, Joe Toricelli."

"Yeah well, Joe, you seem like a nice guy, and I don't want us to get off on the wrong foot. But, you know, waking me up like this is a real drag."

"I'm sorry," I said, "by the way, what's your name?"

"Jonah," he said, "but everybody calls me Jackie, Jackie Fearington."

"Nice to meet you Jackie," I said, "don't worry, this won't happen again."

We climbed up the stairs and I could hear a TV news show blaring from his apartment.

"Tell me if the TV's too loud," he said, "I can't sleep unless the TV is on." Then he started laughing, in this weird series of short, exhalatory bursts, like he was struggling to cough something up. "The news is especially sedating," he said, "especially empty celebrity gossip."

"Guess I never looked at it quite that way," I said, as we got up to our floor.

"Well try it," he said, "and...aggh—!" he suddenly yelled, as he tripped over his dog, a skinny, nervous-looking Chihuahua.

"Darlene," he said, "be careful, girl, will you?"

Darlene scampered down the stairs, toward the front door. A little bell around her neck tinkled as she ran.

"Tch. Excuse me," he said, and ran down after her. "Darlene, baby, you come back here."

I peeked into Jackie's door and listened to the TV news. Some stuff about hurricane clean up in the Carolinas and then, yes, there it was, the O'Connor case. There was a picture of the stolen Toyota they'd found in Hendry County, and a recent photo of Russ and Vera.

Jackie came back up cradling Darlene.

"Well, c'mon in if you want to watch," he said, "let's do the neighborly thing and have a cup of coffee. I might as well forget about sleep at this point."

As we walked into his apartment, a studio like mine, the TV flashed a photo of Francis O'Connor.

"Oh look," said Jackie, "there they go again with poor little Francis."

"Who's that?" I said.

"O'Connor," he said. "Francis O'Connor, may he rest in peace."

"Yeah? What'd he...get killed or something?"

"You've got to be kidding," he said, looking me up and down. "He was shot last week by two guys near Key West. Surely wherever you've come from they have TV." Then he did his laugh again.

"That they do," I said. "I just don't watch much."

"Well, I will tell you all about Francis in a minute," he said. "But tell me, where are you from?"

"Georgia," I said, "just outside of Brunswick, Georgia."

"Is that so?" he sounded surprised. "You don't look like a Georgia boy."

"Well, I'm originally from New York," I said, "but that's where I've been for awhile."

"Yeah, fine," he seemed to sense I didn't want to go into more details. "Well, anyway, Savannah's a beautiful city."

"Sure it is," I said, "gorgeous."

"Well," he said, "let me fix us up some Joe."

He went to the sink to rinse out a couple of grimy mugs and then placed them on a table covered with papers, medicine bottles, cigarette butts, half-empty glasses of whatever, and a bunch of books on travel.

"French Columbian okay?" he asked, while he went over to rummage through a cabinet.

"Fine," I said.

He started fiddling around with the coffee maker, which looked like it hadn't been cleaned in years.

"So," he said, "you haven't followed the O'Connor case, huh?"

"Not really."

"Well, you know, I'm a bit of an insider on this story."

"Yeah?" I said, "how's that?"

"I'm a friend of the family, sort of. I went to Yale with Bob O'Connor, Francis' older brother. God, that was eight years ago now. But even then it was a 'family issue', as they say."

"What was?"

"Trying to keep poor Francis in the closet. I mean, can you imagine it, a gay member of the O'Connor-Morrison clan. Is America really ready for that?"

"I don't know," I said. "What's the big deal?"

"Well, let me tell you, honey, if it was my family or...your family—well nobody is going to get too upset. But here you're talking about someone who is part of a national monument. Get it?"

I just shrugged.

"Well anyway, Francis had been depressed for years. From what Bob told me, he just hated himself. The family sent him to all kinds of famous shrinks. You know, no one wanted to accept it, especially not his father."

"That's too bad," I said.

"Francis got more and more careless with himself. He always seemed to be caught up in the wrong place at the wrong time with the worst kind of people. Bob told me he had this thing for very macho criminal, ex-convict types."

"Is that so?" I said.

"Oh sure," he said. "That's why it's so obvious, so predictable, his murder, I mean. Sooner or later Francis was going to get hurt, playing so rough with the big bad boys."

After the coffee was made, we sat down at his little table and sipped some. It actually didn't taste half bad. Jackie chattered on about his life while I kept one eye on the TV. I was hoping for some fast-breaking story from Edison, but nothing else came up about the O'Connor case. Meanwhile I got the big picture of Jackie's life since college, basically being a waiter and an unemployed actor for the whole time, dabbling in theater courses and astrology and getting money from his family. He said he was looking for a "serious' relationship", but he spent huge amounts of time hanging out in the local gay bars in the neighborhood. From what I could gather, he was in some kind of psychodrama therapy, and went to weekly meetings with an astrologer.

As we talked, I felt some pressure to try to knit together some kind of story about myself. I managed to shape up an account of the last seven years where I'd been studying psychiatry, doing forensic work and then free-lancing as a consultant. In fact, the more I told the story and embellished it here and there, the more comfortable I felt with it. At any rate, he didn't have any comments about me, until I told him I had to go check on some calls and get going down to police headquarters. As I stood up to leave, he said: "Joe, tell me something, when is your birthday?"

"November 10th."

"That's it," he smiled, "that explains it. You're a Scorpio."

"Yeah? So what?"

"Secrets Joe. Lots of secrets, and guilt."

"What are you talking about?"

"You're carrying around sooo much Joe, believe me, I know that. A lot of secrets. But be careful, Joe, it can all catch up with you."

"Yeah?" I laughed, maybe a little too loud. "So you got any predictions for me?"

"It's not a joke, Joe. You're going through a very dangerous period right now and...."

"Now wait a minute, how do you know what I'm going through?"

"You don't have to get testy," he said. "I just feel it, that's all. It's a very dangerous period for you and, frankly, things could get a whole lot worse."

"Gee, thanks a lot."

"It can all catch up with you."

"All right, already," I said. "You already said that."

"I'm just telling you what I sense, Joseph. No need to take things out on the messenger."

"Yeah, right, okay. Anyway, I've really got to get going, got to check on some calls. So I'll catch you later."

"Fine," he said. "Don't forget your keys now."

"Yeah, thanks. Good-bye."

I WALKED DOWN to the corner phone again and rang up Jake. It was after twelve by now and I figured he must be in. When he picked up, I said, "Hello, Jake? It's Joey."

"Yeah Joey, how you doin'? You see that place this morning?"

"Yeah yeah, I did. It's a great place. I took it. But look, anything happening down there today?"

"Like I told you, we're going to follow up on the questions about Roland. Otherwise, you can just hang loose today."

"I'll get those reports done today, then."

"Oh yeah," he said, "that's right. Moore's already bitching about it. Hey look, I'll fax you the forms today, you don't even need to come in to work on it."

"All right, I'll get back to you with a fax number, and I'll give you a call at the end of the day."

"You got it."

I arranged to get the forms in a little while and went back to my new pad to work on the reports. Every so often, I'd go out to the landing and listen to Jackie's TV. He kept it on the all news station but I didn't hear any news story about Crassidy getting busted. Putting things into Moore's format was pretty damn dry and tedious stuff, and after I finished one of the write-ups I lay down on the bed and dozed off. A while later I woke up in the middle of a nightmare. I mean I woke up sitting up in bed yelling "get out, get out."

In the nightmare Jackie's standing at the foot of the bed, dressed in his turquoise robe and the whole room is in flames around him. And he's repeating, over and over again, "No need to take it out on the messenger Joseph, no need to take it out on the messenger."

I got up from the bed and went to splash my face in the bathroom.

"Fucking weirdo," I said to myself, "just like the landlady said." I looked at my watch, it was almost five. I ran down to the corner phone again and called Jake, to see if he'd come up with anything. He wasn't there and I left a quick message on his tape that I'd try to call him at home.

On the way back I stopped by a TV store display window and watched the news program they had going on all the screens. There was something about a terrorist bombing in Jerusalem and then a photo of the O'Connor kid flashed up and a rehash of stuff about Russ and Vera.

I was about to turn away when I saw—whammo—I'd finally hit pay dirt. There he was, Horace Crassidy, looking very seriously bewildered, being led in handcuffs into the Lee County Prison. Following him was a real trashy, ugly fat woman, "Samantha Hampel," as the title at the bottom of the screen indicated, also in cuffs and surrounded by some real stern looking state police.

I did it, I thought, I'd really gotten him busted. It all worked.

"Now you'll fry, you son of a bitch," I muttered, "and find your special little place in Hell."

Then the TV switched to a commercial. I walked back up to my place and Jackie came out to the landing as I was unlocking my door.

"Got your keys," he teased.

"Got my keys," I said. Then I heard something about a "special report" on the O'Connor case coming from his TV.

"Something happening with that case you told me about?" I asked.

"Oh yeah, yeah. They caught one of the guys today."

"No kidding?"

"Sure," he said, "here, let's go take a look."

We stepped into Jackie's place and on the TV. I saw an earnest-looking sexpot of a young woman standing with a VitaCom microphone in front of a pink and turquoise trailer. She was saying:

"Detectives from the Florida State Police, working in close cooperation with confidential sources, followed a complicated trail of evidence that finally led here, to this mobile home at 1671 Flora Acres Dr., the home of Horace Crassidy's secret fiancée, Samantha Ann Hampel."

"You should see what she looks like," said Jackie, "if she was my fiancée, I'd keep it a secret too."

Then they switched to the same video footage I'd seen just a few minutes ago in the store window.

"See, there she is," said Jackie.

Then they showed some footage of a reporter shoving a microphone under Crassidy's nose while he was being led to jail. At first he gave the guy a real nasty look, then he seemed to crowd in closer toward his police escorts. He reminded me of a freshly caught wild animal, snarling and shaking with defiance and terror.

"Well," I said to Jackie, "they bagged the beast then, didn't they."

"One of them," he said. "They still haven't found the other one, Torento. But I have a feeling they will very soon."

"Yeah? Why do you say that?"

"Just a feeling. I think it will happen in the next few days."

I felt myself getting all hollow and cold inside.

"Well, we'll see," I said. "Anyway, I've got to get back to some paperwork."

"Oh, by the way Joe, don't be frightened if you hear any noises coming from your fireplace."

"What do you mean?" I said.

"Sometimes you'll hear a soft, sighing sound from your fireplace, but don't let it scare you."

"Yeah. I doubt it will. But what is it, the wind or something?"

"Oh no Joe," he said, "it's a ghost."

"A ghost?"

"Sure. There's a ghost in the house. She lives on the top floor here. Sometimes she's in my place, sometimes in yours, she wanders around a lot."

"What are you talking about?"

"You don't believe me," he laughed, "but you'll see. Back in the 1850's some time after this house was built, there was an asylum for insane women just across the street, where that French restaurant is now. Look."

He pointed out through his window, across the street, where people were lined up, waiting to get into this dark hole in the wall with a black awning over it.

"Yeah, I see," I said.

"There was a young woman living there then, Ellen May Stanton, who had been put there by her family when she was 16. It was after she had miscarried a baby conceived out of wedlock, by a boy who died soon after, in the Mexican War."

"Okay." I was trying to hurry him along because he was getting on my nerves.

"She stayed there a few years, hardly eating, never talking to anyone, spending hours gazing out her window, on the third floor, and into the windows right here."

"Why was she doing this?" I said.

"For a long time no one knew. They just thought she was in some hysterical trance. But then someone, maybe an assistant or whatever they called them then, noticed she was interested in the children that lived in this house. A butcher and his family had the house at the time and the youngest children slept on the third floor."

"So right here," I said.

"And right there in your place."

"Okay."

"Well, one day in April, just out of the blue it seemed, she managed to walk out the front door of the asylum. She crossed the street and began playing with the butcher's children, right on the front steps down there. Someone from the asylum noticed her out there and ran to bring her back. She became frightened and ran into the home and up the stairs, to what is now your apartment. Someone told the butcher what was going on and, in a rage and a panic, he came running home and ran up to your room. He found Miss Stanton by the back window holding his youngest child, only a year old. He struggled with her, grabbed the child from her, and then knocked her against the wall and down to the floor. She hit her head against the fireplace mantle on the way down and was dead when she hit the floor."

"And her ghost is still with us?" I said. "Is that what you're telling me?"

"Of course. But don't listen to me, just listen to your fireplace."

"Whatever. See you later."

That night I finished up my other report and sacked out pretty early. I lay in bed and found myself listening for sounds coming from the fireplace.

What, am I crazy, I thought to myself. I mean Jackie's not a bad guy, but definitely a little nuts. I tried to put him and his whacko zodiac charts and ghost stories out of my mind, especially his bullshit about how my secrets could all catch up with me. I tossed and turned for quite awhile before I finally fell asleep.

During the night I had this dream about Wilcox. He came to me, right out of the little fireplace in the room.

"Hey doc," he said, standing by the mantle, "looks like you're trying to put things back together with yourself."

"Wilcox," I said, real surprised. "Thank God, you're...you're not brain dead."

"Oh I'm dead all right, doc, one hundred percent. Look here." He floated over toward the dinette set and turned on the light. He was nearly transparent and only his face and head were distinct in the light.

"Son of a gun," I said.

"Just paying you a little visit doc, just like you done with me. It's real good where I come from, believe me."

"But..." I began to say something, but he interrupted.

"Just got a minute doc," he said, "just wanted to tell you, I heard everything you told me back at the hospital. And I got some advice for you. You got to stay on the Epstein case, keep your nose to it doc, and don't think too much about what's running up behind you."

"Wilcox," I called, "but why do you...?"

But he'd already disappeared.

"Wilcox," I yelled, and woke myself up yelling his name again. I sat up in bed and looked around the room.

"Keep your nose to it," I whispered to myself, "and don't think too much...about what's...running behind you."

Then I lay back down and fell back to sleep. When I woke up next morning sunlight was flooding in through the windows and my head felt clear and steady. I didn't remember my dream until I looked at the fireplace again, and then I smiled to think this could be some site of ghostly visitation, whether from Ellen May Stanton or old Abner Wilcox. But it was a dream, I told myself, just a dream. The seeds of which got planted by Jackie's spook story. So how come I felt like it had really been Wilcox who had been here last night? Ah, put it aside, I told myself, forget about it.

WITH THAT, I jumped out of bed, dressed, grabbed my reports, and went out to give Jake a call up in Yonkers. I wanted to see if he'd gotten anything interesting on Roland, but all he said was none of his guys had gotten back with him yet. At any rate, we agreed we'd meet down at headquarters later in the day.

I started walking down Seventh Avenue, and then zigzagged my way south and east, toward police headquarters.

On the way, I picked up a copy of the *Herald* at a newsstand in Chinatown. The headline knocked the wind out of me. It said: "Crassidy to Police: I Didn't Do It—Torento Did." You got to be shitting me, I thought, and started to read the story as I walked down the street.

"Hey, are you paying me for that, mister?" said the Indian guy inside the stand.

"Oh yeah, sorry," I said, and tossed him some change and got my head back into the paper.

The article said that Crassidy, with the advice of his lawyer in Miami, would soon be putting out a statement "proving his innocence". In it, he would "describe in detail" how he'd witnessed Torento murder

Russ and Vera Parish, as well as Francis O'Connor. And, that he'd tell all about his "amazing escape" from "Torento's hideout" in Hendry County.

The story was so absurd, that I really had to laugh. And, I said to myself, you're going to need to get yourself some more lawyers, you son of a bitch. Like the kind who specialize in appeals from death row. Then I threw the paper in the garbage, and went on my way downtown.

When I arrived at the police building, I took the elevator up to the tenth floor, and headed over to Moore's office to drop off the reports.

"Morning," I said to her, as I walked through her door, "here are the summaries on Frontenac and Volknick."

"Thank you," she said, "just put them on the desk here."

"Okay."

"And by the way Dr. Toricelli," she said, sounding a little softer than usual. "I'm not against giving you the benefit of the doubt, I mean, I think that you're probably trying your best here on this case..."

"Gee thanks," I said.

"But nevertheless, I must tell you I have been speaking with the Commissioner's office, and in all likelihood, you will be replaced next week by a Forensic Institute faculty member. Regardless of what your cousin says."

"That's too bad," I said. "It looks like you really don't want to give me a chance, huh?"

"Well, I'm surprised you'd put it that way Dr. Toricelli," she said. "Professional decisions are made in a professional context. It has nothing to do with giving you a chance. It's just that you simply don't have the qualifications for this job."

"Right," I said, and then sat down by her desk.

"But as long as I'm still here, I'd like to go over a couple of things with you."

She didn't say anything so I figured I might as well keep on talking.

"I had an opportunity," I told her, "courtesy of Dr. Roland, to review the report he sent out on Nathan Volknick. Obviously, the whole picture is suggestive of Volknick being Epstein's killer. And, certainly we ought to get more information from Volknick about the events that Friday afternoon. But what really struck me more than reading the report itself was the guy who wrote it, Dr. Roland."

"And when exactly did you meet Dr. Roland?" she asked.

"The other night," I said, "at his office. I was just on my way home and...."

"Dr. Toricelli," she said. "I've already warned you about going beyond the boundaries of your role, haven't I?"

"You have," I said, "but this was fortuitous, see? I wasn't even expecting to see him, and...."

"Yes, I'm sure it was an accident," she said, "but at any rate, why don't you get to the point and tell me about your impression of Dr. Roland."

"Sure, sure," I said. "Fine. There's something about him that's phony...real phony and suspicious. Bottom line is, I think he's deliberately trying to implicate Volknick in Epstein's murder, frame him, so to speak. And as his new doctor, temporarily so he says, he's in a position to really manipulate the poor guy. I think..."

"Now wait a minute, Dr. Toricelli," she said. "Do you really have any idea about what you are saying?"

"Yeah, I do. I'm saying Roland is a plausible suspect, and he's got to be checked out real carefully. I don't trust the guy."

After I said this she started laughing. Laughing at me, like I was some babbling moron.

"So what's so funny?" I said.

"What's so funny?" she said, trying to keep a straight face. "What's so funny, or more precisely, so ironic, Dr. Toricelli? Quite simply, that we are learning much more about you this morning, than we are about any potential murder suspects."

"Yeah, what's that supposed to mean?"

"It means, Dr. Toricelli, that Dr. Roland is a man of impeccable character and reputation. He was one of my supervisors during my analytic training, so I am speaking from personal experience. And the idea of him being a murderer, or even calling him—what did you say, a phony? —is completely outrageous. It shows just how poor your judgment is."

"How poor my judgment is? Well, maybe you should look at your own judgment, and whether or not it's getting affected by a conflict of interest. Because as far as I'm concerned, Roland's a suspect until proven otherwise."

This seemed to ruffle her, but just for a second.

"I will consider whether I have a conflict of interest," she said, "if and when any plausible evidence is brought up to suggest that Dr. Roland could be a suspect. But for now," and then her voice started to rise, "I'm going to focus my attention on a young man who has a known history of violence, who has a chronic psychotic illness, and who had the last known contact with Dr. Epstein. Is that all right with you, Dr. Volknick?"

"Dr. who?" I said.

"I mean Dr. Toricelli," she said, and her beautiful white skin suddenly glowed red.

"Interesting slip," I said, smiling. "What comes to mind?"

"Perhaps I see you and Nathan Volknick as similar," she said, without missing a beat, "confused boys with hostile transferences toward established, well-respected men."

"Well don't be too quick to go to the bank with that," I said, "until we see what checks out, and what doesn't, with old Dr. Roland."

"Whatever, Dr. Toricelli," she said, taking a deep breath. "You know, I really think we've had enough bantering here for one day. We have important business to attend to. For one thing, Nathan Volknick and his mother are due in at eleven for another interview. I'm going to take some time now to review your summaries. I will expect you at the interviews for note taking."

"Sure," I said, and thought to myself maybe she'd like me to conduct the interview as well, seeing as she's scared shitless of Volknick.

I left her with the reports, and went downstairs to grab some coffee. Then I went over to Jake's office to see if he'd dug up anything yet on Roland. But he wasn't there so I scribbled him a note that I'd be at Moore's office this afternoon.

Then I went back to hang out outside of Moore's office, and got into shooting the breeze with the two secretaries there for a while. Pretty soon, the conversation turned to Dr. Moore.

"The only time she sounds nice is when she talks to her cat," said Marisol.

"Her cat?" I said.

"Yeah, it was at the vet's yesterday, and she told the nurse to put it on the phone. 'Hi sweetie', she says, 'momma's going to be with you very soon.'"

At this, they both broke up laughing.

"I'm glad to hear she's nice to somebody," I said.

Then Moore's office door swung open, and she popped her head out.

"Dr. Toricelli," she said. "May I speak with you in my office, please?"

Marisol gave me a look, as if to say "Here's more trouble, guy."

"I have some comments to make about these reports," she said. "To begin with, your write-up on Volknick only strengthens the evidence against him. It therefore looks all the more odd that you'd in any way want to implicate Dr. Roland in Dr. Epstein's murder."

"So be it," I said. "Anything else you want to say?"

"Well it appears from your description that Ms. Frontenac is probably borderline and has significant dissociative episodes. So why didn't you pursue this in the interview and make it more clear in your formulation?"

"I didn't feel comfortable pressing her further in the interview," I said, "and I don't like to use all that diagnostic jargon." Especially when I don't know it, I thought to myself.

"Weak excuses Dr. Toricelli. You must follow up with her, for the sake of completeness, if nothing else. But in any case, the evidence against Volknick is quite powerful, overwhelming really."

"Well now wait just a second," I said. "I mean in addition to Ms. Frontenac, who by the way, being a head taller and a few decades younger than Epstein, at least had the capability of killing him, Dr. Epstein had other appointments that afternoon. Aren't those people being investigated? Or are we just trying to rush in and nail Volknick as quick as possible?"

"No one is rushing to do any such thing. First of all, we now have confirmed statements, from three interviewers, all prominent Wall St. professionals, that Ms. Frontenac was on a yacht in Westport, from two o'clock on the Friday of Dr. Epstein's death, through the following Sunday evening. Secondly, his three other appointments that day were a telephone consultation, an eight-year-old child, and a wheelchair-bound woman recovering from a stroke. All three of them have already been interviewed and need no further follow-up. Unless of course, you have any other questions about them." The last part she said real sarcastically.

"So it looks to me like you've all but pinned this on Volknick," I said. "Am I right?"

"I will let the evidence speak for itself, Dr. Toricelli, and I suggest you do the same."

I didn't have anything else to say, and in a minute her phone rang and, after she answered it, she waved me out of the office while she took a "confidential" call. I went down to the corner deli and grabbed an egg sandwich. On the way back to her office, I passed Nathan Volknick and his mother sitting together in the waiting area. He didn't see me and I didn't say anything to him as I passed. But I had a real bad sinking feeling in my gut as I came back into Moore's office.

"Mr. Volknick and his mother are here," she announced to me. "We will start with Mr. Volknick, and call in his mother afterward. Will you get him please?"

I went out and got Volknick. He shambled in behind me and fell into a chair opposite Moore at her desk. I pulled up a seat off to one side of Moore.

"Hello, Mr. Volknick," she said, "how are you today?"

He looked down, and mumbled something.

"I'm sorry, I didn't hear you," she said.

He just continued looking down at the floor, and several seconds of silence passed.

"Mr. Volknick," I said. "How are you doing today?"

"Okay," he whispered.

"Good, good," I said. "Any thoughts or questions about our last conversation?"

"No."

"I see. How have you been feeling these last couple of days?"

He didn't say anything.

Then Moore cleared her throat. "Mr. Volknick," she said, "is there something wrong today?"

"I don't know," he said. "Can my mother come in?"

"We're going to ask her in very soon," she said. "But first I wanted to discuss some of the issues you and Dr. Toricelli had gone over."

"Oh."

"I wanted to understand, Mr. Volknick, how you felt during your last appointment with Dr. Epstein."

"Fine."

"Fine?" Well that puzzles me a little bit, because Dr. Epstein's note indicated that you were feeling quite agitated that day, and that he'd advised you to increase the dose of your Risperdal. Do you remember that?"

"Oh yeah," he said.

"And do you remember anything else from that day?" she said. "Anything Dr. Epstein said?"

"We have to stop now," he smiled. "He always said that."

"Yes, yes," she said, "and anything else?"

"He said 'Thank you' when I gave him the check."

"Uh-huh, and what about after the meeting ended, Mr. Volknick, do you remember what you did next?"

"I don't remember," he said.

"Well, try your best. For instance, did you go straight home? Did you go somewhere else?"

"I went straight home."

"Directly after leaving your appointment with Dr. Epstein?"

"I went straight home," he repeated.

"I see," she said. "Now, we all know you became very upset in your house that afternoon, didn't you? You tried..."

"I don't want to talk about it," he interrupted, in a real tense voice. Up to now he'd been pretty emotionless, but now he was getting his back up.

"Uh-huh," said Moore. "It sounds like that is an upsetting issue for you..."

"I don't want to talk about it," he said again, real loud. Then he suddenly stood up from his chair and started shouting over and over again, "I don't...I don't...I don't...I don't...I don't..."

Moore started looking real alarmed. I tried to jump in.

"Mr. Volknick," I said, "it's okay. It's okay...really, you don't have to talk about it. No one's going to make you."

"I don't need you to tell me that," he shouted at me. His nose and lips were quivering with this bizarre expression of defiance.

"No, of course..." I said.

"I'm not talking about anything, anymore," he said. "I...I want my mother right now."

"And I shall get her, right now," said Moore, and she was out the door and back in with Mrs. Volknick just as I was sliding another chair up to the desk.

"Mrs. Volknick," said Moore, introducing me, "this is my assistant, Dr. Toricelli."

"Nice to meet you," I said. "You can have a seat here next to Nathan."

"Thank you," she said, in a hint of a Southern accent. "I do hope everything is all right."

"Everything's fine," I said, trying to reassure her.

Mrs. Volknick was a short, slightly built woman, maybe around sixty, with white hair cut in a sort of pixie style. She wore a simple black skirt with a purple blouse. She looked around the room in short little bursts, like she was some nervous little bird.

"Mrs. Volknick," Moore began, "we're very grateful to you for coming to see us today with your son. As you know, we are continuing to piece together the events and circumstances surrounding Dr. Epstein's death."

"Yes I know," she said, "and I do hope you're investigating the possibility of suicide."

"We have considered that," Moore smiled, "but it is quite unlikely, given the manner of the strangulation."

"I don't really know how you tell such things," said Mrs. Volknick, "but I do know that Dr. Epstein was a very, very depressed man. Things had really gone down the tubes in his marriage, and he looked just awful the last time I saw him. It was a month ago, on the street, after one of Nathan's appointments." She turned to Volknick. "Isn't that right, honey?"

"Yep," he said.

"What was going on with Dr. Epstein's marriage?" I asked.

"Dr. Toricelli," said Moore, obviously annoyed, "why don't we save that for now. I have some questions I would like to ask Mrs. Volknick."

"Well of course, my word yes," said Mrs. Volknick, in this tone of deference toward Moore.

"Now Mrs. Volknick," said Moore, "I know this is difficult for both you and your son. But I would like you to tell me what you remember about Nathan's behavior, when he returned home from his last appointment with Dr. Epstein."

"Well, as you know," she said, turning to her son, "Nathan was very, very upset. And I was very worried, both for Nathan...and for myself. You were just a mess, weren't you honey?"

"No comment," he said, in a real flat tone.

"The house was just turned upside down," she said, "and Nathan was in such a state, well, nobody could talk to him. And you know, normally he's such a sweet boy. But that day, well he just wasn't himself."

"Who was I, mother?" said Volknick.

"Oh Nathan, you know what I mean," she said. "But Dr. Moore, it was simply terrifying, the way he was breaking things, throwing things, and just running amok. I finally had to run and lock myself in the bathroom."

"And then the police came," said Volknick, like he was suddenly giving some dramatic narrative.

"Yes, yes, that's right," said his mother, "just a short while later."

"And they came, boldly, heroically to your rescue, didn't they mother?"

"They were very good," said his mother, "very calm, and very professional."

"New York's finest, definitely the finest," said Volknick, with this smirk on his face.

"There were four officers in all..." said his mother.

"And one of them called me a cocksucker," Volknick announced.

"Oh honey," said his mother, "no one said any such thing."

"He called me a cocksucker," Volknick repeated, rising from his chair, "'you crazy fucking cocksucker', that's what he said."

"Nathan!" his mother shouted, "hush now."

"'He's dangerous', they said," Volknick roared, "and he's got a record, he's a murderer!"

"Nathan, honey. Nobody said any such thing."

"You don't know what they said," he shouted. Now he was standing over her, with spit flying from his mouth, "you couldn't hear them. Not from where *you* were hiding."

"Nathan, honey..." she pleaded, and turned to us for help.

"Say Nathan," I said, "why don't you and I take a walk out to the hall. It'll give you a chance to cool down a little."

"Fuck you," he said, "I ain't going nowhere with you, coach."

"Nathan..." his mother repeated.

"And fuck you too," he told his mother. And then, very suddenly, very strangely, he switched; from this scary threatening belligerent attitude, to this real obsequious, even timid demeanor. "I will be waiting for you outside mother," he said softly. And then he walked out the door.

His mother knitted her eyebrows and gave me and Moore an apologetic smile.

"He's going to be fine," she said, "don't you folks worry now."

Nonetheless I went out to see where Nathan was, and was relieved to find him sitting quietly in a chair. I didn't say anything to him, and returned to the office. Mrs. Volknick was going on with her description of that Friday afternoon.

"It was awful," she was saying, "they took him away in a terrible state. He was mumbling all kinds of things, things about his father, using awful, awful language."

"Do you remember anything else he said?" asked Moore. "Perhaps in some way referring to Dr. Epstein?"

"To Dr...oh my no...why?"

"Well, he had left his office only an hour or so before," she said, "and perhaps..."

"Dr. Moore," said Mrs. Volknick, with a gasp, "I do hope you aren't trying to connect my Nathan with Dr. Epstein's death. That, that would be impossible. He liked Dr. Epstein very much."

"He felt an attachment to Dr. Epstein, did he?" said Moore.

"Well of course he did," she said, sounding more and more defensive. "He saw him every week and...and...why he was the only person he truly, truly trusted. Now that's a fact."

"I see," said Moore.

"He wouldn't lay a finger on Dr. Epstein," she cried, "nor anyone else for that matter."

"Of course he wouldn't," said Moore, in this real patronizing way, "and, tell me, how has Nathan been since he's come home from the hospital?"

"He's feeling better and better, thank heavens. Dr. Roland, bless his heart, is continuing to take care of him, for now anyway."

"And how exactly did Dr. Roland get involved?" I asked.

"Well it was on Dr. Epstein's telephone message," she said, "that Dr. Roland would be covering his practice for the weekend. So when Nathan got sick that Friday, well we called him right away."

"I believe it was quite common for Dr. Roland to cover for Dr. Epstein on certain weekends," said Moore to me.

"Oh, I believe that's so," said Mrs. Volknick. "And he's such a nice man. Thank God, he knew just what to do when Nathan got to the hospital. He arranged for him to get two shock treatments right away."

"Shock treatments?" I asked.

"Yes, yes," said Mrs. Volknick, "that works best for Nathan when he's like he was. He can get terrible allergic reactions to high doses of medications. One time he almost died."

"Is that right?" I said.

Moore sighed impatiently. "Dr. Toricelli, as I'm sure you know, electro-convulsive therapy is a safe, reliable treatment for psychotic agitation. For Mr. Volknick it is the treatment of choice, with his history of neuroleptic malignant syndrome."

"Yes," said Mrs. Volknick, "that's what they called it, when he had that allergic reaction. Of course the shock treatments have their side effects too. They get his memory a little fuzzy."

"Hmm...mmm," said Moore, "and while he was in the hospital, Mrs. Volknick, did he say anything about Dr. Epstein to you?"

"No. No, not at all, Dr. Moore. He was too upset to talk about, to talk about anything, really. But please Dr. Moore, there is absolutely no connection, no connection at all, between my son and Dr. Epstein's murder, or death, or suicide, or whatever in heaven's name it was."

"I understand your position clearly, Mrs. Volknick," said Moore, "we are simply exploring all events...and relationships...anything that may be relevant around the time of Dr. Epstein's death."

"Well I suppose you must," said Mrs. Volknick, beginning to cry, "but...but, oh Lord help me with this boy, oh Lord please, please, help me with this boy." Then she broke down and sobbed real hard.

Moore and I sat there in silence for a while, and just listened. When she pretty much settled down, Moore spoke. "I think we will stop for now," she said. "Dr. Toricelli, why don't you accompany Mrs. Volknick back to the waiting area, and have her rejoin her son."

Mrs. Volknick wiped her eyes, and rose to walk with me out the door.

"Doctor," she said to me, "please don't ignore the possibility of suicide. Dr. Epstein was very, very depressed."

"You mentioned it had to do with his marriage," I said, as we walked toward the door.

"Yes, yes," she said, and her voice lowered toward a whisper, "don't you know the details?"

"No."

She stopped before we opened the door to walk out.

"His wife is a lesbian," she said, "everyone suspected it for years."

"No kidding," I said.

"And so it was no surprise to hear, I suppose about three months ago, that she was divorcing him, and moving in with her girlfriend. He was just...humiliated...devastated."

"I see," I said. "Well, I will review the medical examiner's report, but you understand they've apparently already ruled out suicide."

"I'm only telling you what I know doctor," she said, and started to cry again, "and I know my boy had nothing to do with it."

"I understand," I said, as we opened the door and started walking down the hall. "I don't think your son had anything to do with it, either."

"You don't?"

"No. I don't," I said. "Now go on home and don't worry about it, we'll get to the truth of the matter."

"Thank you doctor," she said, "you're a very kind man."

I said good-bye to her and walked back into the office and sat down across from Moore. She was writing some notes and, without looking up, she asked me, "What happened out there?"

"Nothing, really," I said. "She just went on about the suicide angle, and how Epstein's wife left him for a woman."

"Totally irrelevant," said Moore, as she continued to scribble away.

"Probably," I said, "but you know she's all worried we're going to finger Nathan. So I told her I didn't think he had anything to do with it."

Moore looked up from her papers, with this real pinched expression on her face. "You told her what?" she said.

"I think you heard me."

"Dr Toricelli, you are neither her psychiatrist nor her friend. You are, at least for today, a police investigator and you have no business reassuring her about anything, or telling her whatever your...your opinion may be regarding her son."

"The woman was obviously in pain, and she's not stupid. She sees how you're trying to put together some bullshit case against her son."

"Dr. Toricelli," she sneered, "you are totally inappropriate."

"I don't care what you call it. This kid's not playing with a full deck. His brain's half-rattled from electricity, and who the hell knows what he can even remember from two weeks ago..."

"He received two unilateral treatments," she said, interrupting me, "and if you review any basic textbook on it, you will find that it is highly unlikely that that would seriously affect his memory."

"You don't know what it did to him, unless you test him; plus, he got the treatment from that creep Roland, so who the hell knows what really happened?"

"Dr. Toricelli," she said, with her black eyes fixed on me, "you are completely inappropriate, and more...more than that, you are seriously disturbed."

"And that's coming from a shrink Joey," I suddenly heard Jake's voice behind me, "so you better take it seriously."

I turned around, and saw Jake standing in the doorway.

"On the other hand," he went on "I heard somewhere that seventy-five percent of shrinks are crazier than their patients. So maybe, well maybe, you ought to just try to ignore her diagnosis and sort of like Rodney King once said, just learn to get along with her."

"Lt. Roma," said Moore, trying to calm down a little bit, "apart from the attempt to add some levity to our day, is there any particular reason you've come by here?"

"But of course there is," he said, as he came in and settled into the seat next to me, "I wanted to give you all the lowdown on the good Dr. Roland."

"Good," I said, "so let's hear it."

"Well, you're going to have to shelf your big ideas about Roland being a suspect, Joey," he said.

"An absurd idea to begin with," said Moore.

"Well, let's not be too tough on our boy," said Jake. "I mean, this doorman who says he saw Roland get in a limo that Friday, afternoon, he almost had me convinced too. But as it turns out, this guy's memory is real shaky, probably on account of the way he's boozing it up most of the time. So yeah, Roland takes a limo to his office one afternoon that week, Imperial Limo of Brooklyn to be exact, but it's on the Wednesday afternoon before, not the Friday that Epstein was killed. He came back to the city from Monotoc for a few hours on Wednesday to take care of some business, that's all."

"But what about when he came back from Monotoc that Friday" I said, "maybe he took a limo by the office then."

"He did come back to the city by limo on Friday," said Jake, "but it was in the evening, around nine, and he went straight to his club. Not to the office."

"You're sure?" I asked.

"We got it right from the limo driver," said Jake, "and besides, now that the rummy doorman's straightened out his story, nobody else at the building is saying they saw Roland in any limo that Friday."

"And you're sure of Roland's whereabouts all that Friday?" I asked.

"Let me put it this way," said Jake, "between what the limo driver said, the phone records Roland's given us, and all the people who saw Roland at the conference, all day Friday in Monotoc mind you, there's no way he could have been in Epstein's office around the time our victim met the grim reaper. Okay?"

"So he still could have hired a hit man," I said.

"Joey, c'mon now," said Jake, "you got some kind of hard-on about this guy..." Then he turned to Moore for a second—"excuse my French, there, doctor—about this guy attempting to kill Epstein. I mean, for what? They've been close colleagues for twenty-five years; Roland's a rich, successful doctor, and we got no sign that they had anything against each other. So, I mean, where are you going with this Joey?"

"Lt. Roma," said Moore, "if I may interrupt. As much as I appreciate your attempts at giving Dr. Toricelli a little reality check here, it is sorely needed to be sure, I think it is imperative that we pursue Nathan Volknick for further questioning. He was really quite agitated and defensive today regarding Dr. Epstein's death."

"Right, right," said Jake, "we got to follow up with him, right Joey?"

"Yeah," I said, "we'll follow up. But look, if there's nothing else going on here today, I'm going to head out. I'll give you a call later, Jake."

I WALKED BACK up to the Village and tried to hash things out. Maybe Jake was right, I thought, maybe I was going a little nuts about Roland. The fact is, being a sleazeball and a phony doesn't necessarily add up to being a killer. And like Jake said, what could be his motive, anyway? Nothing I could put my finger on, and certainly nothing as obvious as Volknick's craziness. I guess anybody with any sense has got to look at that kid's behavior and come away with a strong suspicion that he killed Epstein. So what am I trying to defend him for? What am I still on a guilt trip about Wilcox? And so now I've got to be the champion defender of every crazy patient? I walked on and, as I turned the corner of Oliver onto Fifth, I saw Jackie sitting on the front stoop. He was drinking iced tea and smoking a cigarette in the afternoon heat.

"How are you, Joe?" he said, when he saw me approaching.

"Just fine."

"Doesn't look that way, Joe. It looks like you've got a lot on your mind."

"Is that so?

"Oh, definitely, and we already know this isn't a good time for you. I really think the next few weeks are going to be a real struggle for you, a real test."

"Yeah, you've already pretty much indicated that," I said, "so then what happens after that?"

"I can't say, not right now anyway."

I stepped up past him to open the front door, with this real strong desire to get away from him, and all his omens. But he was a real sticky conversationalist.

"Did you read about the O'Connor case in the *Herald*?" he said, "Crassidy's going to come out with a statement."

"I saw something about it."

"And, of course, he says he is innocent. It was really his friend Torento who did it."

"Well, I'm sure that won't hold up for very long," I said, "anyway, I need to head upstairs."

"I'll go with you, I left my cigarette pack on the TV."

As we climbed up to the third floor, I heard a news story blaring from Jackie's TV. The announcer was saying: "We now go to Miami, with a live report on captured O'Connor murder suspect, Horace Crassidy."

"Oh, let's look for a minute," said Jackie. We both stepped into the apartment and, on the TV screen, there was a reporter from VitaCom interviewing Crassidy's lawyer, a dark-looking guy with a Greek last name, Moristopolous.

"And so," the reporter was saying, "you will be requesting a dismissal of all charges?"

"That is correct," said the lawyer "the allegations against my client are groundless and outrageous. We should be concentrating all our police resources on the capture of the real killer, Joseph Torento. My client has pledged his full cooperation in helping the police to find Mr. Torento."

"And does he have any idea where he is hiding?" asked the reporter.

"He believes he is probably bound for, or in, Mexico at this time. My client and I have urged the FBI to coordinate a manhunt with Mexican authorities immediately. I can promise you that when Joseph Torento is captured, any lingering doubts about my client's innocence will evaporate."

"And what if Joseph Torento isn't found?" asked the reporter.

"We are not considering that as an option," said Moristopolous "we firmly believe he will be captured and justice will be done, both for my client, as well or for the grieving family of young Francis O'Connor."

"Thank you, sir," said the reporter, as the camera closed in on him "that was John Moristopolous, defense attorney for captured murder suspect Horace Crassidy." Then the picture flashed to a toothpaste commercial.

"It all sounds pretty bogus to me," I told Jackie, "even if they find Torento, which I doubt they will, it's not going to help Crassidy's case."

"Oh they will find Torento," said Jackie, "that I know."

"Yeah?" I said, laughing "and how do you figure that?"

"I saw something, this morning, when I was time surfing."

"Time surfing?"

"Yes. I caught a wave that pulled me into the fall sometime. I saw this man Crassidy face to face with Torento, and they seemed to be in some kind of duel."

"In a duel?" I asked, trying to keep my attitude real casual "so what happened?"

But Jackie said he couldn't see anything more, because Mrs. D'Angelo had knocked on his door, and told him the neighbors were complaining about his yapping dog. I didn't really believe any of this supernatural stuff of Jackie's or so I told myself, anyway, but I had to admit he'd gotten me a little nervous. So I ended up spending the next couple of hours listening to his theories on astrology, and time travel, and "paranormal phenomena", as he put it. Maybe I was hoping to get some kind of sign that Joe Torento really wouldn't get nailed, but mainly I felt like he was just leading me through a thicket of weird, half-baked ideas that didn't add up to anything more than some kind of crackpot, half-paranoid metaphysics. By the time it got to be five or so I asked Jackie if I could use his phone. I wanted to call Jake, and maybe grab a beer with him before he went home. But when I got him on the phone he said nothing doing, he had to go straight home or Nina was going to brain him. But, before he hung up, he told me a guy named Tim had called up in Yonkers, and had left his cell phone number and wanted me to call him as soon as possible.

I scribbled it down real quick and then hung up with Jake. Strange, it must be Landsdowne, I thought, whom I really didn't expect to hear from again. But there he was. Well, what the hell, I figured, give him a call and see what's going on.

"Hey Jackie," I said, "you don't mind if I make another call, do you?"

"Help yourself."

So I dialed up the cell phone number, and it rang once before somebody answered.

"Hello."

"Hello," I said, "this is Dr. Toricelli, returning..."

"Yes, doctor, thank you," said Landsdowne, "of course...you remember our meeting at Pershing, don't you?"

"Sure I do. How have you been?"

"Dreadful, that's why I called," he said, "I want to meet with you, this evening, about seven. It's very, very important. I hope you can do it."

"Well...uh...yeah, sure I can do it."

"I will be in my car. So where should I pick you up? In Yonkers?"

"Well, no, I'm not in Yonkers now," I said, "I'm staying in Manhattan. You could come by my place and...."

"No doctor, I'd rather not. But perhaps there is a street corner nearby, but not in front of your apartment, where you could step into my car without anyone who knows you seeing you."

"Well, let's see," I said, and a certain corner, not too far away, popped into my head, "what about...Carmine and Bedford, think you can find that?"

"Certainly my driver will find it, doctor. Can we make it at seven?"

"I don't see why not, see you at seven."

After I hung up, Jackie said, "Sounds like you've got a little rendezvous."

"Not exactly, just a little business, that's all. Catch you later."

I WENT OUT to grab a bite to eat and got down to the corner of Carmine and Bedford a few minutes early. At exactly seven, a stretch white Lincoln Town Car pulled up in front of me, the back door opened and Landsdowne said, "Good evening, doctor, please get in."

I climbed in and settled into a soft leather seat across from him. He had a glass of whiskey in one hand and a cigarette in the other. His eyes were real puffy and his precision cut white hair was slightly flattened on one side, like he'd been recently sleeping on it and forgot to comb it again. Before I could ask him how he was doing, he started right in.

"Thank you for coming, doctor," he said "I know how valuable your time is, so I'll get right to the point. The fact is, I didn't call a doctor at Pershing, and you did me no particular favor last week."

"How do you mean?"

"I mean, I should have killed myself. My position is absolutely impossible. I suppose I've already told you as much. I can choose to be the property of blackmailers, or I can watch while they destroy me, my family, my career, and, well, who knows?"

I looked behind him for a second, to see if the driver could hear.

"Don't worry, doctor," said Landsdowne, "he can't hear anything back here. This is between you and me. Period."

"Okay, but so far I'm pretty much in the dark as to the specifics of your situation."

"Then I will enlighten you," he said, and gulped down some whiskey and loudly cleared his throat. "I suppose two words can sum it up, doctor," he said, "somewhat alliteratively, pornography and prostitutes. One always leads to the other, and vice-versa. Been a problem for me for years, doctor, since boarding school days. It began innocuously enough, with a normal teenage boy's fascination with girlie magazines. But it progressed both rapidly and obsessively, I suppose you could say, to hours spent in bookstores, topless bars, peepshows and movie houses. And despite my having a sweetheart from the time I was eighteen, indeed, the very woman to whom I've been married for over forty years, I have always required the companionship and services of whores. And I mean all manner of whores, doctor, from icy-hearted six hundred dollar an hour call girls, to cheap five-dollar a blowjob streetwalkers. It is only when I am with these women that I can feel...fully alive. Well, I'm sure you get the idea, doctor. Drink, by the way?"

"Don't mind if I do. I'll have whatever you're having."

He poured me a half-tumbler of scotch, straight up.

"So, there you have it," he said, laughing "there it is right in front of you, the darkness that dwells in the heart of Timothy Landsdowne; attorney, lobbyist, former senator, and now advisor to the President. For years I've lost sleep imagining nightmare scenarios of public scandal and ruin. And I think I've become as addicted to worrying as I have to my...vices. But what I've got on my hands now, doctor, actually surpasses even the worst fears I ever nurtured."

He poured himself another drink and lit one cigarette from the other.

"This current...crisis, doctor, it all started on one of my whore shopping excursions about a year ago. I met a most exquisite young...lady, a Colombian girl. She was dark and chatty and stupid and mean, my favorite combination, actually. Very soon she became my favorite playmate, sharing my taste for violence and pain and...degradation. And, what enriched the mix to absolutely gloriously intoxicating levels was the added participation of her slutty, pouting thirteen-year-old daughter who was taking right after mama. Are you disgusted enough, doctor?"

"Go on," I said, sipping my drink.

He took another mouthful of whiskey, and continued.

"I was in my own sort of dark paradise, doctor, and if that was all there was to it, I'd certainly have no need of your services. But then, you see, a problem arose. It turned out these two soiled little wenches had been having me taped, audio and video to boot, during our nasty little play sessions."

"How did you find that out?"

"Because I was approached, by a dapper, grinning rat-faced man named Jorge, one day at her—Giselle's—apartment. Everything was made clear to me at that point; what they had on me, and what I must do to prevent my public demise." He gulped down his new drink.

"So what was it you had to do?"

"Oh, something quite simple," he said, with his voice shaking, "actually, quite diabolically simple." He paused, and poured himself another drink.

"You see, doctor," he went on "all I had to do was tape the

President."

"Tape the President?"

"That's right, simply tape record the President, via the equipment with which they custom-wired me."

"But when? On what occasion, or occasions?"

"On what occasions, doctor? Well now that is very simple to answer. On all occasions. On all occasions that I am present with the President."

"Every time you're with him?"

"That's right, doctor. And Jorge, and more importantly, the people for whom he is working, know that I am with the President quite a lot. They expect at least ten hours of taped conversation each week."

"But who are these people?"

"That I cannot say for sure, doctor. I've used certain...intelligence channels, as discreetly as possible, to try to find out who Jorge is, and with whom he is connected."

"And?"

"I haven't been able to come up with anything tangible. There may, possibly, be ties to Latin American banking interests. Perhaps in Brazil, and Argentina."

"But what do they want?" I asked.

"Well, that too I'm not exactly clear on," he said, "perhaps they have a...strategy if you will...of taking in regular deposits of confidential information on the President. With the expectation that, over time, these deposits will accrue in value. Isn't that something you'd expect from bankers? His face was getting real rubbery and he looked like he was on the verge of crying and laughing at the same time.

"So how long have you been...cooperating with them?"

"Three weeks."

"And do you think they've got any stuff they can damage him, or the country, with?"

"Probably...not. Not yet, anyway."

"So you've got one simple choice, then," I said, "you've got to stop cooperating with them. Like now. Like yesterday."

As I said this, he gave me this look, like I was being real naive.

"It's that simple, is it, doctor?" he said. "And set up myself, and my family, for public disgrace? Now, I ask you, doctor, don't you see the true beauty in the suicide option?"

"Well, I'll grant you," I said, "you could make a real good case for it."

"Of course you could. And imagine all the trouble I'd save," he said, with this real nervous laugh "loss of my job, humiliation in the press, prosecution for statutory rape and, well, if those tapes of the

President ever leak, charges of being a traitor to my country."

"Some pretty bad hits, to say the least."

"'Hits,' doctor?" he cried, "this...this is absolute devastation. Do you understand that?"

"Yeah, you're right," I said, "devastation, of your life as you've known it. But, when you get a chance to sober up, I'd like you to sit back and think about this: maybe that's not such a bad thing."

"I...I don't understand."

"Well, let's take the worst case scenario, that all this stuff blows up on you, and leaves you in ruins. Now maybe...just maybe...it'll give you a chance to start over. I'm not talking about career-wise now, obviously. I'm talking about starting over from the inside. And making a new path for yourself."

"Doctor," he said, "with all due respect, this sort of...spiritual guidance from you...is all well and good, in theory. But I need something more practical, you see. I need to know if there is a way out of this mess. Doctor...let's be frank...I want to know if you can assign me some sort of diagnosis. Something...something I can use to mount a defense. I..."

"I don't think anything like that is going to fly," I said, interrupting him "but it sure tells me how desperate you are."

"'Desperate' doesn't begin to describe it."

"Well, look," I said, "for today, why don't you sober up and think about what I said, I mean that 'devastation,' so to speak, may not be as bad as it sounds."

"That's it, doctor? That's your prescription?"

"Yeah. That's a good way to look at it. It's your prescription. And don't do any more taping."

"I won't. And...well...when...when can I call you again?" he stammered.

"I'll call you," I told him, "Monday, around three or so. Meantime, you've got to hang in there, follow my advice, and think about what I said."

"I...I will, doctor," he said, "I will."

By the time we were ending our conversation we were up by Grand Central, and Landsdowne suddenly got a phone call, reminding him he was due at a diplomatic reception at the Waldorf at eight. So he stopped the car, and we shook hands, and he let me out at Forty-second Street. Before I left the car, I repeated to him my promise, that I'd call him on Monday.

THEN I STARTED walking south down Park, turning over in my head all the sordid, pathetic details of Landsdowne's story. Maybe he really ought to kill himself, I thought. I mean, I seriously doubted the world, not to mention national security, would be worse off without him. And, who knows? Maybe he'd even do it before I called him. Could that even be what I was hoping for?

But no, as I thought about it more, no, it wasn't what I was hoping for. Because, somehow—call me nuts if you want—I kind of liked the guy and cared about him, too. Yeah, despite being a drunk, traitorous, cowardly, pervert, I had to say I liked the guy, and really wanted to help him. Maybe it was because I thought I knew a little something about how you could get caught up in a web of evil, and not seem to see your way out. Except for me, at least so far, I had buried the sins, real and alleged, of Joseph Torento. But it didn't look like Landsdowne was going to be as lucky. And what about that stuff I'd told him, that out of the ruins he could begin a new path? Easy for me to say, I guess, but did I really believe it? I mean, if I really believed it, why would I have chosen to be on the lam from my own past? Well, don't think too much about it, I thought, just help the guy to get through what he has to get through. And keep your nose to the Epstein case, just like Wilcox told me in the dream. Keep your nose to it, and don't think too much about what's running up behind you.

As I walked down the street, I looked at my watch. It was a quarter after eight on a Saturday night. And where was I? Park Avenue South and Twenty-second Street. Just then, the words "Club Daylight" flashed through my mind. I reached for my wallet and pulled out the card Ms. Frontenac had given me. There was the address: 4747 East 18th Street, not far from here at all. So, I thought: why not? Ms. Frontenac had invited me, and, as far as I was concerned, she hadn't been erased from the suspect list. Moore was all ready to hang Volknick, and Jake was still too beaten down to take any real charge of the case. So I figured that left it up to me to turn over all the stones. Or at least try to.

The club ended up being just a few blocks from Gramercy Park. I first caught sight of it when I turned the corner and saw a long blue and white awning with the words "Club Daylight," followed by the flat profile of a jackal's head. As I approached the entrance, I saw a handful of beefy-looking thugs wrapped in white shirts and black tuxes, standing around the front door. They had grim, hard, faces and short necks and looked kind of sullen and bored, while they were drifting through the calm of early evening. I went up to one of them, who was about six-six, with a crew cut and three gold rings hanging from his right ear.

"How ya' doing?" I asked, "anything going on inside yet?"

His eyelids lowered as he geared up to acknowledge me. "There is always something going on inside, sir," he said, in some kind of foreign accent, "twenty-four hours a day."

"Well that's a comfort to know," I said, "and, by the way, do you know if a Ms. Frontenac is working here tonight?"

"Maybe, sir. But who are you?"

"My name's Joe. Joe Toricelli."

"And you are her friend?"

"Well, sort of; more like an acquaintance, actually."

He gave a big yawn, before he spoke again.

"You pay at the window if you want to go in," he said, "she is here tonight."

I went over to the window, forked over thirty bucks and got a stamp on my hand, and walked inside to a huge, dark lounge with a glittering stage to one side. There were flickering lights along the walls and ceiling of the room, and thumping disco music was coming from all around. With all the racket, I got a first impression that the place was really hopping. But as I looked around, the tables were empty, except for two guys sitting and talking to a homely cigarette girl standing by them in a bikini costume. I walked across the room to the long metal bar, and ordered up a double scotch, straight up. The bartender reminded me of the big guy by the front door, except his eyes were narrower and he was sporting a bit of an overhanging forehead. After he handed me my drink, I took a few sips and leaned back against the bar. A while passed and, little by little, a few groups of guys—two, three, four at a time -started to come into the room. Middle-aged guys for the most part, with maybe a few younger tourist-types and college kids thrown in. Then some real knockout women started to come out from a door at the side of the stage; tall, big-breasted and long-legged, smiling and strutting and wiggling and teasing. And all these guys in the audience were suddenly captivated and awestruck. They turned into eager, anxious prey; hypnotized by all the lovely flesh, and rapidly weakening in the swelling blood flow of booze and testosterone. The women spread out all over the room, flouncing in and out of every little corner of the place, and chatted it up with their smiling, panting, over-steamed clientele They were all dressed up the same way; in these skimpy, dark gray bikinis with long black gloves and black stiletto high heels. On the side of each bikini bottom was the club's logo, this flat profile of a jackal's head.

Approaching a table just in front of me, full with a bunch of gawking out-of-towners, was this pouting, lavender-lipped young lady with short black hair and a tongue pierced with a silver rivet. Two of the guys at the table, a big blonde kid wearing a "Planet Hollywood" cap and a skinny, greasy-haired geek in a plaid jacket, were falling all over themselves asking the girl to dance. She just laughed and then sat down next to the geeky kid and asked if anyone had a cigarette. The blonde kid was the first to offer, and you could see the looks of fascination and envy on all the other guys' faces as he lit her smoke.

Then suddenly, the stage lit up and the music shifted from the mechanical disco shit overhead, to some Broadway show tune on big speakers near the stage. Then this beautiful, bikini-clad woman with a long, thick mane of black hair, came sashaying out, threw off her top and began dancing around a pole placed just at the front edge of the stage. She'd tease it and bump it and wrap her legs around it, and just about every guy in the room was totally plugged into what was happening up there. But, meanwhile, the geeky guy slinked closer to the girl with the pierced tongue, and one of his hands kept going deeper and deeper into his pants pocket. She messed up his hair and grabbed both his ears and threw back her head and laughed real loud. Then she rose up in front of him and started up with her own sort of bumps and thrusts and gyrations; snaking up close to him and backing away and teasing him to come to her. She worked him up into a real fever and by the time the music ended he was stuffing twenties into her panties and begging her for more.

I turned back to the bar and ordered myself another double. I was starting to get a little buzzed and could feel myself warming up to this joint more than I wanted to admit. I watched a few more girls come on stage and saw the place filling up more and more. It started to get real crowded around the bar, and I was getting jostled back-and-forth just trying to sit on my stool. Then some guy from Buffalo pushed into me and tried to strike up a conversation. He was right in my face and really stinking of booze.

"Hey!" he yelled at me "ain't I seen you here before?"

"No," I said, "it's my first time here."

"No, now wait a minute, you're in sales, right? For Metropolitan Life."

"No," I said, "you've got the wrong guy."

"Yeah? So what do you do anyway?"

"Doctor. On the job right now, doing research."

His eyes got real big. "Yeah?" he said, starting to yuck it up. "Well, look, doc, it's a dirty job, right? But somebody's got to do it."

"Yeah, right," I said and turned away from him. And that's when I first caught sight of Ms. Frontenac. She came out from a door at the side of the stage, and started making her way across the room. She was dressed in a long, low-cut black gown, which became translucent with backlighting, and showed her long, bikini-laced figure underneath. She was smoking an extra-long cigarette and was slowly slinking her way through the crowd. As she passed she became more and more the center of attention and, it was obvious, that among all the women in this joint, she was the most special. And to whom was she going to grant the privilege of her closeness, if not her attention? Everyone, including me seemed to wonder about this, while she floated through the room. As the lights flashed across her high cheekbones and full lips, I felt my own whiskey-infused plasma beginning to boil. I wanted to run over to her and yank her out of this sweating, pulsating vinyl-lined inferno; and then I wanted to grab her and possess her and fuck her into some kind of extravaganza of soaking wet and endless moaning sexual ecstasy. Just at that very moment she looked straight at me and flashed a smile.

"Get a hold of yourself, Casanova," I told myself. Then I waved to her as she made her way to a group of guys just a couple of tables away from me.

"Will you get me a champagne, darling?" she called out to me. "I will come to you in a moment."

"Beautiful," I said, and turned to the bartender. "One glass of champagne," I told him, "and give me a seltzer with lime on the rocks."

"You won't drink champagne with the lady?" he said in this gruff foreign accent.

"I need to keep my balance with the lady," I said, smiling. Then he seemed to mumble something.

"What'd you say?" I asked him.

"I say sir, never trust the man who smiles too much; that is what they say where I come from."

"Yeah? And where's that you come from?"

But he ignored my question and continued, "Because the man who smiles too much, he is hiding something dangerous."

"Yeah?" I laughed. "Well I'll try to remember that." But who is this creep? I wondered about that, as he set the drinks down on the bar.

"And you are a friend of the lady?" he asked, staring at me.

"Yeah, you might say that."

"Yes? But you did not meet her here."

"No," I said, "but how's that any of your..."

"Ah, hello, doctor," said Ms. Frontenac, coming up beside me and taking a seat. I turned my head and found her even more ravishing close up than my steamy little mind could have imagined. She gave a little smile and a nod to the bartender, as if to say "He's okay, don't worry."

"I'm so glad you took my invitation," she said, "did you know I was here tonight?"

"No. I just happened to be passing through the neighborhood, with a little time on my hands."

"Saturday night and no place for you to go, hmmm?" she teased, "and can you give me a light?" She pulled out another long cigarette and I grabbed some matches from the bar. "So tell me, doctor," she said, her voice now getting deep and serious, "what are your impressions of such a place?"

"Impressions? Well, I'll let you know. They're shaping up little by little."

She laughed at this and sipped her champagne. "Oh doctor, you don't have to be a psychiatrist all the time. Can't you just answer a question directly, or do they train you to never do such a thing?"

"Yeah, it's from very rigorous training," I said. "Never answer a question directly. If you do, the patient loses interest in you."

She giggled and sipped her drink and drew up real close to me. Her lips were full and damp with champagne, and were almost touching mine.

"And you must be good at keeping secrets, yes doctor?" she whispered. "No gossiping allowed." Then she brought her hand up behind my neck and pulled me to her lips and kissed me real hard. I was too wired and way too horny to want to wonder what the hell was going on. Just enjoy it, right? But no, I had to wonder anyway. What was with this sudden burst of affection? I mean, I'd like to believe I'm a real turn-on for her. But I had a feeling this was all for show, only I didn't know who the intended audience was.

"That was pretty tasty," I said, as she slowly pulled away. "One more like that and I'm going to forget all about being here on police business."

She laughed and gently bit her velvety tongue. Out of the corner of my eye I saw the bartender wipe nothing in particular from his mouth, and look at me like he was trying to measure something.

"Such an unpleasant business, isn't it, doctor?" she said. "So serious, this police business." She took my chin in her hands. "But go on, doctor, please ask me anything you wish."

She was putting a spell on me and everything inside me wanted to give in. But I have to say, I surprised myself.

"Ms. Frontenac," I said, backing away from her a little. "There are some things I wanted to ask you; specifically about that Friday, of Dr. Epstein's death."

"Yes doctor," she sighed. "I supposed you must ask what you must ask. So go ahead."

"First of all, do you remember seeing any other people in the office suite that day; like, on your way in or out?"

She took my hands into hers and shivered for a second.

"Let me think, doctor. Usually, if I have a Friday appointment, I see this one boy...in the waiting room...but no, not that day."

"Not that day?" I said, "and who...?"

"Ah, I remember now. Of course. I saw Dr. Epstein at noon that day, instead of three-thirty. Because I was invited to a yacht in Westport for the weekend."

"I see. So that wasn't your usual time?"

"No, doctor, it wasn't. Usually, if I come on Friday, it is three-thirty to four-fifteen. That is when I will see this very strange boy, Nathan is his name."

"Nathan Volknick?" I asked.

"Yes, yes, that's his name," she said, laughing. "I often will see him when I come out of Dr. Epstein's office, and often I will see him when I come in too."

"When you come in?"

"Yes," she said, smiling "sometimes he stays in the waiting room all afternoon, just waiting for his appointment. He told me once that his meeting with Dr. Epstein is the only thing he has to do all day, so he likes to come in early and watch the people come in and out of his office. It is sad, isn't it? He reminds me of a little lost puppy."

"Uh-huh. So you and Nathan would have a chance to talk from time to time?"

"Oh, yes. He is a very shy boy, of course. But if he comes to trust you, he will talk and talk."

"Is that right? Like about what?"

"Oh, I don't know," she said, sipping her champagne, "many things."

"Did he ever talk about Dr. Epstein?"

"Oh, all the time," she said, laughing.

"Yeah? And what sort of things would he say?"

"Oh, doctor," she said, shaking her head and slipping her tongue between her teeth, in this real teasing way, "I don't think you really want to know, now, do you?"

"Yeah, I do. So why don't you dangle a little tidbit in front of me, okay?"

When I said this, she got a real kick out of it, and started laughing real loud. I took a sip of my seltzer and lime and waited until she settled down.

"Frankly," I said, "I didn't think it was such a funny line."

"Oh, I'm sorry, doctor," she said, still giggling a little bit. "It's just that when you said 'dangle,' I suddenly remembered a dream that Nathan told me. It was about Dr. Epstein."

"Beautiful," I said, "I said the magic word. That means you've got to tell me the dream."

"Magic word, doctor?"

"That's right, It's from an old TV show...way before your time. Mine too, for that matter. But anyway, tell me about the dream."

"Okay, doctor," she said, lighting up another long cigarette "but I hope you will keep it confidential. He is a very sweet boy and he trusts me very much, I think."

"I'll treat it discreetly, that I can promise you."

"All right," she said, "I will tell you his dream. As it begins, he is sitting in Dr. Epstein's waiting room, and it is several minutes past the time of his appointment. Dr. Epstein is never late, so Nathan is wondering why he has not yet come to open his door. As more time passes, he becomes more nervous and gets up to knock on Dr. Epstein's door. But no one answers. So he knocks again, very hard. But still, no one answers." Here she paused to sip more champagne and showed me this big, sexy smile.

"So what do you think, doctor?" she said. "What will happen next?"

"I really don't want to guess," I said, "so go ahead, tell me the rest."

"Well, after no one answers the second time, Nathan becomes more nervous, and angry as well. He shouts out Dr. Epstein's name, but still, no one answers. At this point he decides he must go into the office, so he turns the doorknob and opens the door. And what does he find there? What do you think, doctor?"

"Like I told you," I said, "I don't want to speculate."

"Oh, you're no fun at all, doctor," she pouted, "you know that? But, anyway, when Nathan finally opens the door, what he sees horrifies him. I mean, absolutely horrifies him. There, hanging by a rope from the ceiling, there is his beloved Dr. Epstein."

"You mean Dr. Epstein has hung himself?"

"Yes doctor, that's right. And our Nathan, our sweet Nathan, turns to him to see if perhaps he is still alive. He runs to him and lifts him down from his noose and lays him out on the couch and tries to revive him and...and...."

"And what?"

"And he sees it is of no use. It is too late, because Dr. Epstein is dead...thoroughly, thoroughly dead. Nathan is shocked, and terribly frightened as well, and runs for the door to tell someone, anyone, what has happened. But, just before he reaches the door, he hears Dr. Epstein call out his name, quite sternly, and with great authority. He calls to him, from where he is lying on the couch.

'Nathan!' he shouts, 'just where do you think you are going?'

'To...to tell someone, Dr. Epstein, that you are dead. I thought you were dead.'

'I am dead, Nathan,' Dr. Epstein says, 'but that is quite beside the point. It seems to me you are forgetting something.'

'What, Dr. Epstein?' says Nathan 'what am I forgetting?'

'Why the check, of course,' says Dr. Epstein 'you mustn't forget to pay me.'

'But, Dr. Epstein,' cries Nathan 'you are dead. How can it be fair of you to charge me?'

'That is self-evident, Nathan,' he says 'I am here for our meeting. If you choose to leave early, you are still liable for the payment.'

'But you're dead!' he shouts.

'That is irrelevant,' says Dr. Epstein 'the rules still remain in effect.'

When he says these words, poor little Nathan flies into a terrible rage and runs to Dr. Epstein and stuffs a pillow over his face. 'Die, you greedy old turd!' he shouts to him between his clenched teeth, 'Die! Die! Die!'"

As Ms. Frontenac finished her story, her eyes grew wide and wild looking and her face drew closer and closer to mine.

"Ms. Frontenac," I said, backing away again and trying to keep some decent distance between us. "You're telling me Nathan actually had this dream, and told you about it in the waiting room?"

"Yes, doctor, of course. It was about three weeks ago, I think."

"Three weeks ago?" I said, "so, you're telling me it was about a week and a half before Dr. Epstein was killed?"

"Yes. I suppose that is right. But so what? You don't think it means anything, do you?"

"I don't know," I said, "but let me ask you this: Did Nathan ever tell you any other dreams, violent dreams...or thoughts, he had about Dr. Epstein?"

"No, not at all, doctor," she said, laughing, "but certainly you don't suspect this boy killed Dr. Epstein, do you?"

"In theory, at least, everybody who was there that day is a suspect."

"I see," she said, teasing me, "well, then, I must be a suspect as well." Then she stood up and put her hands on my cheeks. "Well, I must go to work now, darling," she whispered, "you will stay here and we shall talk more after the show."

Then she turned and swayed back through the hungry, horny crowd, and disappeared through the stage door. She'd left me mainly aching to fuck her, but also half-believing and half- bewildered by her story about Volknick's dream. I finished off my seltzer and tried to sort out my thoughts when suddenly, the not so friendly bartender got into my face.

"You want to pay up now, my friend?" he said, without asking if I wanted another drink. He was looking more surly by the second and I had the distinct impression I'd worn out my welcome at his bar.

"Do I have to?" I said, real annoyed "this minute?"

"Only if you like to keep your bones in the right place," he grinned, and showed me a mouthful of gold teeth.

"What's that supposed to mean?"

"Just a joke, my friend," he said, "I am kidding, of course."

"Yeah, real funny," I said, and pulled out twenty bucks and stuffed it in his paw. "Keep the change," I told him "and put it toward tuition for charm school."

Then I turned my back to him and waited for Ms. Frontenac to come out on stage. What was the problem with this cave man, I thought. Maybe he's some beast secret admirer of Ms. Frontenac, who's roiling at the sight of her flirting with me. Or maybe this is what passes for barkeeping bonhomie in whatever country he crawled out of.

The feeling that I wasn't particularly liked around there didn't get any better, when a big goon in black tie seemed to station himself in front of me, just as the lights went on and Ms. Frontenac appeared on stage. He had me sort of crowded against the bar while I stood up to watch her perform. But crowded or not, I could see she put on one hell of a show, kicking and bumping and spinning under the stage lights, 'till she heated up that crowd into some kind of hooting, hollering, squealing frenzy. Unbelievable, I told myself, and tried my best to put a lid on any ideas I had of going home with her tonight.

At the close of the show she took a long bow and gave the crowd that smile of hers, that mischievous, sexy smile where she presses her tongue between her teeth. A little while after the show ended, she came back to the bar. She gave a sort of worried look to the big goon still standing next to me, and then grabbed my hand and said,

"Darling, I want to take you out for a drink."

"Fine with me," I said, as she led me away from the bar, "and tell me something, is the bartender and the staff here always so pleasant, or am I getting singled out for special treatment?"

"Oh, don't worry," she said, "it's nothing. They get very nervous and protective of me when they see men friends coming to visit me."

"Why is that?"

"Sometimes they behave very badly with me," she said, laughing "and they are asked, or must be...forced, to leave. But it's nothing important, darling, and nothing I care to talk about anymore."

SHE TOOK ME to her dressing room, and told me to have a seat while she got herself ready. She slipped into a tight-fitting short black dress, brushed her hair and put on fresh lipstick. Then she took a bottle of pills out of her dressing table drawer and asked me to fetch a cup of water from the bathroom. She swallowed two pills with a gulp of water, put the bottle on her table, and told me she had to go "to the little girls' room" for a minute. When she went into the bathroom, I took a look at the bottle of pills. It said "Zyprexa 2.5 mg., take three times a day as needed,

Dr. Epstein." That's medication for people who get psychotic, I thought, or at least somewhere around the borderline. And isn't that what Moore said, something about borderline? So does that apply to Ms. Frontenac? I wondered. Well, as a matter of fact, there was something weird, or maybe it was just phony, or empty, about her. I mean, a couple of times when I looked in her eyes, I got a spooky feeling; like there wasn't anybody at home in there. Like she was just some kind of animated, gorgeous, wind-up mannequin. When I heard the bathroom doorknob turn, I put the bottle back down and stood by the table. She smiled without looking at me as she came out, like maybe she knew what I saw and what I was thinking about.

"And so, darling," she said, holding out a cigarette, "will you give me a light?"

I studied her face as I brought the lit match to the tip of her cigarette. Her skin looked soft and creamy and yet, I felt like if I touched it, it would feel as hard and cold as a beautiful round stone washed up on the shore.

"And have you diagnosed me yet?" she teased, and then blew some smoke across my face.

"I haven't thought about it enough yet. But I'll let you know."

"I'm not so sure you haven't thought about it enough. You are thinking all the time, I see that."

"Oh yeah? And what else do you see?"

She laughed and said, "I will keep that a secret for now, doctor." Then she looked at my watch. "But we must go now, darling. I want to take you to Bar Fifty-eight. Have you been?"

"No. I really don't get around much anymore."

"Tsk tsk. Poor, poor man. Poor, boring man. Now come with me. Let's go."

WE MADE OUR way out of the club and stepped outside into the soft glow of light and balmy night air. We took a cab uptown, and in several minutes we pulled up to a crowd huddled around a purple rope fence and dark metal door. There was a pale-looking kid with a shaved head and dark glasses checking names on a clipboard, and giving the nod here and there to a few heads from the herd. We squeezed our way through the press of bodies and the clipboard kid immediately recognized Ms. Frontenac and let us in. We went through the door and made our way down a long flight of stairs and into the entrance of an enormous lounge. It was dimly lit and smoky, and had couches and big chairs and coffee tables spread out all around. It was full of girls who had to be from the pages of fashion magazines, and guys who looked like actors or Wall Street prick types. On one couch there was an old geezer who looked like Ben Franklin, sitting between a couple of deep-tanned blonde Amazons, who were stroking his long gray hair and whispering and giggling into his ears.

"You must get me a drink, darling," said Ms. Frontenac, leaning into me and rocking to the blare of sixties R&B that filled up the room. "I want a martini, very dry, no olive."

"Sounds good," I said, eyeing the bar, "I'll be back in a flash, okay?"

"Of course, darling," she said, "I will be waiting for you over there." She pointed over to an empty couch, just across the coffee table from Ben Franklin and company. She gave a weak little smile and looked just slightly spent. I figured that dose of Zyprexa must have just kicked in. I went to fight my way through a phalanx of sneering, morphine-riddled models and joined the thirsty, baying pack around the bar. After a lot of shouting and money waving, I got Ms. Frontenac's martini and a seltzer and lime for me. I could feel a real beast of a headache brewing from whatever rotgut that ape at Daylight had served me, and I wanted to negotiate the rest of the evening without booze and with at least half a brain on line. When I returned to Ms. Frontenac, she looked distracted and sad and was gazing into the crowd and twirling her hair with one hand.

"There you are, darling," she said, "and I thought you'd gone off with someone else."

"No way. But they need a crowd control detachment around that bar."

I settled in next to her and handed her her drink.

"I'm sure you were very brave," she laughed, and raised her glass. "And now we will toast: To your success, to your brilliant success in solving the murder case of Dr. Epstein."

Then she took a sip of her martini and gave me another high voltage kiss on the mouth. When she finished, she pulled back, and looked me over, real seriously.

"What's the matter?" she asked "didn't you enjoy it?"

"Enjoying it's no problem," I said, "understanding it, that's something else."

"Oh, please doctor, you take things so seriously. Don't be so boring." She laughed and took another hit of her martini. Meanwhile, one of Ben Franklin's girls stood up unsteadily and crashed a bunch of glasses from the coffee table onto the floor. Ms. Frontenac suddenly got this real jolted look on her face and started looking all around the room, like she was listening very closely to something.

"Ms. Frontenac," I said, "you okay?"

She looked at me, startled, and didn't seem to recognize me.

"You okay?" I said again.

But she was way off in some other world, and I figured the best thing to do was just to sit back and watch her. Her eyes started to follow something along the far wall and her face got sort of smaller and round-eyed and childlike. She looked back at me, with this kind of shy and inquisitive expression, like she wanted something from me. I felt, strangely, like I was her big brother or, maybe even her father, or something. Then she stopped looking at me and went back inside herself again. She seemed to be listening to something, or somebody, with whom she didn't agree. After a while she reached for her drink. As she brought it to her lips she stopped to examine it, and frowned. Then she said,

"Now, that doesn't look very appetizing, does it?"

"Why do you say that?" I asked.

She giggled. "Well, what is it, anyway?"

"What do you mean, 'what is it?'"

"Just that," she said, "what is it?"

I could see she was serious and I started to feel a little spooked.

"It's a martini," I said. "You ordered it, remember?"

She looked away from me and said, "That's a strange thing for you to say, isn't it?"

"I don't think so. Don't you remember saying, just a little while ago, 'darling, get me a martini, very dry, no olive'?"

She got a big kick out of my impersonation of her and laughed and laughed, way too hard.

"Oh, doctor," she said, composing herself again. "I remember everything now, everything, darling; believe me."

I took a long drink of seltzer and put the glass down on the table.

"Tell me, honestly Ms. Frontenac," I said, "are you feeling all right tonight?"

She gave a little wince, but in a flash was smiling. "I think so, doctor," she teased "do I not look so good?"

"You look magnificent, believe me, But you seem to get real preoccupied...with stuff going on inside your head."

"I really don't know what you mean."

"Well, I think you do. I think that's why you're taking the Zyprexa, to quiet down whatever's going on inside your head."

"I thought you saw the bottle. Anyway, it helps me to relax, doctor, and to get through my work."

"And does it help you when you hear some sudden noise, like glasses breaking, for instance?"

She just sipped her drink and didn't say anything.

"You seemed to go off into some other world there," I said "when those glasses broke."

"You're really quite dramatic, doctor, and these matters are...were for Dr. Epstein and I to discuss. They do not concern you in any way."

"Maybe, maybe not. But tell me, what did he tell you the Zyprexa was for?"

"It's really not your business, Dr. Toricelli. But, I will tell you something. Dr. Epstein helped me to face myself and to live with myself. That can be very difficult. And many times Dr. Epstein made me angry because he would force me to face things I did not want to face. He could be very difficult sometimes. And sometimes...very cruel."

"What do you mean 'cruel'?"

"It's not important, doctor, not to you." She lit up a cigarette. "And now all that is left of him is a little bottle of pills." She smiled almost as if this gave her some satisfaction.

"You don't seem so broken up by his death right now," I said.

"'If you die, I will be sad for a while,'" she started to recite "'but then I will get on with my life and you will be dead.' That is what he said to me after I did this." She put out her wrists and showed me several old slit marks on both of them.

"I was very angry at him when he first said that," she said. "Now it seems to be a very reasonable attitude. He never expected the shoe would be on the other foot. He shouldn't have underestimated his enemies."

"He had enemies?"

"Oh, I think he did," she said, "and I think he knew just who they were."

"So, who?" I asked. "Who were his enemies?"

She looked at me and laughed. "Such an interesting question, doctor, isn't it? Well, I do not know, but I am very confident you will find out." Then she said, "I must not be late for my show. Right after, I must leave to perform at a private party."

WE GOT UP AND pushed our way back through the crowd, climbed up the stairs and walked out to the street to catch a cab. She seemed caught up in her own thoughts on the ride back and, even though I thought pressing her further wasn't going to pay off, I felt I had to anyway.

"You know, it's hard for me to imagine a guy like Dr. Epstein having enemies," I told her, "I mean, real enemies, people willing to murder him."

"Don't be so naive, doctor. Bad people are everywhere. And in everyone there is badness."

"Yeah? Tell me more.

"There is nothing more to tell, doctor. And nothing more to analyze. Some things are just true, that's all."

The cab pulled up under the brightly lit marquee of Club Daylight and, suddenly, her face looked very hard in the sharp light and shadows.

"It's not necessary for you to get out with me," she said. "I'm...okay. And I'll be very busy in a few minutes."

"I'll escort you in anyway," I said, "it's no problem."

We climbed out of the cab and, as we walked to the door she turned to me and said, "Of course I will need a new doctor now, Dr. Toricelli. Do you have any suggestions?"

"Well, I really wouldn't know, I'm new in town and...."

"I think I will get a consultation with Dr. Roland," she said, interrupting me. "I have heard he is a very good doctor. You have met him, haven't you?"

"Yes. Yes I have.

"And what do you think, is he good?"

"He, uh, he seems to be clever enough."

She laughed at this. "You don't like him, do you, doctor? But be careful. He is rich and famous...and much more powerful than you."

"What's that supposed to mean?" I said, sounding sort of peeved.

"Now don't be envious of such a powerful man," she laughed as we approached the door.

"What makes you think I'm...?"

But then I heard someone say: "Sorry sir," in a foreign accent, just behind me, and I felt a meaty hand press down on my shoulder.

"I really have no more time to talk to you tonight, doctor," said Ms. Frontenac, as she walked through the door. "Come again tomorrow night. Goodbye."

I turned around and looked up, way up, to a seven-foot tall crew cut goon with a massive, jutting jaw.

"So what's the problem?" I asked him.

"It is sold out sir, no one else is allowed to enter."

"But I already paid," I said, "see, I got a stamp on my hand that's supposed to be good all night."

"Sorry sir, it is full. Perhaps you can get a refund at the window."

"But I already paid," I said again, "get it? So I'm already counted in and...."

"I am very sorry, sir. We have orders from the Fire Department. No one else may enter. Now, if you will please step away from the door."

I figured this had to be bullshit, and that this gorilla just didn't want to let me back in. I guessed because I'd been tagged as one of Ms. Frontenac's troublemaking "men friends."

"All right, fine," I said, stepping away from the door. "Now, let me speak to the manager."

He smiled and laughed like some goofball Frankenstein. "I am acting as manager, sir," he said, "so please, sir, see about a refund and have a good night."

Well, I thought about making a stink, just to get myself back into the dump. But then, I figured, for what? Ms. Frontenac said she couldn't talk to me anymore tonight, and I'd see her again tomorrow anyway.

So I decided to take the refund, and grabbed a cab back home and hit the sack. Yeah, I'll be back at Daylight tomorrow night, I thought, as I was falling asleep. And maybe then she'll be willing to speculate more about Dr. Epstein's supposed enemies. And there's no way anybody there is going to pull any "Fire Department" bullshit on me again.

Part 5

I GOT UP THE next morning pretty early and shuffled out to get breakfast at a little greasy spoon on Hudson. The events of the previous night were going round and round in my head. I settled in at a corner table and ordered a black coffee and two poached eggs from this bald waiter with a long, gray ponytail. A huge black cat prowled around the joint and then decided to jump up on my table. While I scratched his head and down under his neck I tried to figure out what had gone down with Ms. Frontenac last night. I'm no expert at diagnosis, but it didn't take a genius to see she was over the edge from garden-variety neurotic. I guessed, at the least, like Moore had said, some kind of dissociative disorder, or borderline or, who the hell knows, multiple personality. I mean, she'd done some kind of channel switching back there at Bar Fifty-eight, kind of like the first time I'd interviewed her. Her tone of voice had changed, and so had her eyes, her face, and her whole demeanor. Man, it was strange to watch. And what about that dream of Volknick's she'd told me about? Was that for real, or was she just playing with me? Or worse yet, was she somehow trying to set Volknick up? I'd be damned if I knew. Anymore than I knew what her flirtations meant, what that stuff about Epstein's "enemies" was about, or exactly why those goons at Daylight didn't want me hanging around that dump.

Yeah, questions for sure. All kinds of questions. And questions I figured had to be answered, before there was going to be any rush by Jake and Dr. Moore to hang the rap on Nathan Volknick.

The waiter came by with my breakfast and started putting stuff down on the table. The coffee smelled like dishwater and the eggs had been fried and laid on two pieces of burnt white toast.

"Hey, waiter," I said, "this isn't what I ordered."

"What do you mean?" he asked, with a cigarette hanging from his mouth.

"I said 'poached,' not fried," I told him, "and this coffee's undrinkable."

He looked down at the food and his cigarette ash fell into the coffee.

"Hey Jerry!" he yelled, "now the man says he wants poached...two poached..."

"On whole wheat," I said.

"On whole wheat!"

"And another coffee."

"It's coming up," he said, "right away."

He turned and walked away and left the stuff sitting in front of me. Pretty soon the cat began sniffing around the eggs and started nibbling away.

"Enjoy," I said, and reached over to the next table to grab somebody's discarded *Daily Bulletin.* The front page showed the mayor going ballistic over the return of drug dealers in Washington Square, and on page three there was an article on the O'Connor case. It said Crassidy was continuing to move to have all charges dismissed and his lawyer was quoted as saying: "We have overwhelming evidence against Joseph Torento, the real killer. Once he is captured, whether it is in Mexico, Florida, or somewhere along the Gulf Coast, I assure you that justice will be done."

As I finished reading the article, I could see it was getting harder and harder for me to feel that I'd ever been Joseph Torento. It all seemed too long ago and way too far away. And too distorted to even recognize anymore. I only hoped that Crassidy and his hired gun wouldn't really be able to bullshit his butt out of jail. More outrageous things have happened, I thought, but no, that'd be impossible. And anyway, I had plenty to worry about right in front of me, with this Epstein case.

The waiter brought over my new coffee and eggs and me and the cat chowed down on our breakfasts together. The toast was still burnt and the coffee was rotten, but at least the eggs were poached, sort of. When I finished I threw a few bucks on the table and got up to leave.

"You come on back now," said the waiter, in this fake Southern accent. "You hear?"

"Oh, I hear all right," I said, "and I'll give it some real serious thought."

I WALKED DOWN Fourteenth Street and hopped the uptown Lex at Union Square. I figured I had nothing else to do, so why not hang out a little around Epstein's suite? I had no particular purpose in mind, except to get a little more of a feel for the place, and to see what my imagination could come up with. I got off at Eighty-sixth Street and walked over to the empty, scrubbed-up fifteen-story ravine of Park Avenue. Most people had taken off for the weekend and I wasn't sure what I was going to find at Epstein's building, except for a locked door and a couple of bored doormen.

So when I got there, I was kind of surprised to see a light on through the transom over the suite entrance. Roland again? I wondered. But no, he must be out in the Hamptons today. I went to push the outside door open, slowly, and saw that the inside door was wide open, as well as the door to Epstein's waiting room at the end of the hall. As I walked down toward the waiting room, I called out: "Hello?"

"Yes, who is it?" came this kind of high-pitched man's voice from inside Epstein's office.

"I'm Dr. Toricelli," I said, as I got to the waiting room, and saw Epstein's door was open. "Police Department."

"Well, come in," said the voice.

When I stepped into the office, I saw a twenty-something guy sitting at Epstein's desk. He was slightly built and balding and dressed in blue jeans and a white shirt. He had a smile that reminded me of Epstein's from a photo I'd seen on the back cover of one of his books.

"So," he said sarcastically, "are you a real, honest-to-God medical sleuth?"

"I'm investigating the death of Dr. Epstein," I said. "Who are you?"

"Dr. Epstein, Jr.," he smirked. "Can't you tell?"

"As a matter of fact, there's a real family resemblance, very striking."

"My, you guys are observant," he said, "but tell me, do you actually solve crimes?"

"We're trying. And, by the way, sorry about your father."

"Why?" You didn't know him. And if you did, 'sorry' may not quite capture your sentiments."

"Yeah? Why do you say that?"

"Well, I'll let you come to your own conclusions. But I can tell you this; he had no friends. He was cold and remote. There was really nothing to like about him."

"Uh-huh. And what about enemies? Did he have any?"

"Enemies? Well, frankly, Dr. Toricelli, I don't think anyone gave a damn."

"I see," I said, looking over at a pile of charts stacked on the desk. "Not even his patients?"

"I doubt it. Patients are patients and they come and go."

"So, if I may ask. What's with all the charts here?"

"Just going through some final notes," he said, "on some cases my father was following for a paper he was writing. Or, I should say, that I was writing."

"What do you mean?"

"Just that it was going to be his paper, but I was writing it. You see he was a lousy writer and didn't know squat about current diagnostic terminology. So he'd exploit my brain at will. I'm a third year resident at Manhattan Hospital."

"In psychiatry?"

"Well, what do you think? But not his brand of Freudian voodoo. Molecular psychiatry is where it's at. It's blown everything else out of the water."

"No kidding," I said, "does that mean you don't need to talk to patients anymore?"

"Oh give me a break with that sentimental bullshit. People want to get better, not spend all their time and money on half-assed rented friends."

"Is that what your old man was?"

"He was one of the better half-asses. But, hey look, Dr...."

"Toricelli."

"Right, I'm out of here in about five minutes. I've got to go get the mail from the doorman, so any other questions?"

"Well why don't you go get the mail, and I'll wait here and see if I can think of anything else."

"Knock yourself out," he said, and walked out the door.

The second he left I hopped over to that stack of charts to see if there was anything on Frontenac in there. Sure enough, a couple of folders from the bottom, I found her name. I slid it out real carefully, opened it up, and began scanning. From what I could gather, he'd been seeing her for over a year but there wasn't really a hell of a lot to read. There was a short intake note that said, "twenty-three-year-old single white female, Belgian born...family history non-contributory...rule out anxiety disorder." Then a bunch of dates of office visits with a few comments to the effect of 'stable' or 'full affect,' or 'no psychotic symptoms.' There was a list of medications, but no other detailed notations. Now, I knew that psychiatrists often put little down in the chart about what was actually talked about in therapy, but I would have expected Epstein to have written more than this. So, I had to wonder if something was missing, that is, had been lifted from the chart. In another minute I heard the front door open, so I folded up the chart and slipped it back into the pile.

Epstein's kid walked back into the office carrying a huge bundle of mail.

"Junk, that's all it is," he said, as he dropped it on the desk. "Look at these psychoanalytic journals. I really can't believe grown men are still writing this shit. Psychobabble disguised as pseudo-science. Anyway, did you come up with any other questions, Dr. Detective Toricelli?"

"Well, actually, I was wondering; who's taking over all the stuff here...you know—bills, charts, correspondence, etc.?"

"You're looking at him, doc," he said,"and the sooner I close down this shop, the better. This is one major pain in the ass."

"So, uh, anybody who wants any access to any records, all that stuff, they've got to go through you, right?"

"I'm the man, Stan. Put it in writing and I'll get back to you...within ten business days if you're lucky."

"Patients' been calling to get their records transferred to new doctors?"

"Well, come to think of it, only one request so far, from Dr. Pinhead down the hall."

"Who?" I asked, "you mean Roland?"

"Precisely."

"That must have been for Volknick."

"Right again, doctor. You really are on top of this, aren't you?"

"How about anything for a Ms. Frontenac?"

" Frontenac? No. But an interesting name...like the hotel in Quebec, yes? But no, that one doesn't ring a bell. But, look, Dr. Toricelli, I really do have to go."

"One other thing, why'd you call Roland 'pinhead'?"

"Consider it shorthand. Because I don't have time to fully describe how and why he is of absolutely no worthwhile consequence."

"I take it you don't like the guy."

"And what is there to like about a suburban shaman pushing a sermon of rich green lawns, blinding bright futures and every sap having 'empowerment' and 'self-esteem' as a birthright? He's a charlatan's charlatan, selling the snake oil of American-brand delusions of grandeur to an army of fattened brain-dead, frightened, lonely women. And, of course, all of his books are bestsellers."

"Can you recommend any favorite titles?" I said, smiling.

"I really must refer you to his entire oeuvre, which you will soon be able to pick over on the swelling trash heap of popular culture. None of it will be fit for composting or landfill, come to think of it. As a highly toxic, non-biodegradable material it will need to be specially containerized and stored in subterranean vaults."

"You think it's that dangerous, huh?"

"As dangerous as the words of any clever cynic ready to exploit the public's appetite for secular psycho-sloganeering."

"And what about the man himself," I asked, "you think he's dangerous?"

"Dangerous? How do you mean 'dangerous'?"

"Well, for instance, let's say, dangerous enough to commit murder."

At this, he laughed and laughed; a nervous, silly, high-pitched teeth shattering laugh.

"Roland as murderer," he tried to say between gasps. "I love it. The culmination of a brilliant career in quackery. But how do we go about framing this juggernaut of Manifest Destinizing junk? We need a motive, yes? But what, what?"

"Money maybe," I said, "or envy. Payback for some perceived injustice."

"Payback, that's it," he shouted, "payback from the cuckold...but no, no," he suddenly got downcast "forget it."

"'Cuckold'? What are you talking about?"

He didn't say anything.

"What's the matter?" I asked, "I thought you were having fun."

"I'm running way off schedule, Dr. Toricelli. Let's pick it up another time."

"Hold on a second, there, Junior. And by the way, what is your name anyway?"

"Call me Chuck."

"Okay, Chuck. Now seriously, what's this cuckold stuff all about?"

He sighed in this real exaggerated way.

"All right, copper," he said, "I'll spill the beans. Family secrets really, and not at all relevant, but I'll let your keen mind be the judge of that. My father, whom I promised never to talk about this with anyone, had a twenty-year love affair going with Mrs. Dr. Happy-Quack, Evelyn Roland."

"Is that right?" I said, "I met her, briefly."

"She's a real dish, isn't she? But seriously, I think she was the only person who genuinely liked my father. She seemed to see idealism and dedication where others only saw pedantry and pomposity."

"She did speak well of him when I met her."

"I'm sure she did. He, on the other hand, seemed to just feed off of her admiration. There wasn't much else she had to offer him, or anybody. Roland had thrown her away like a grimy dishrag long before she hooked up with my father."

"Did Roland know about the two of them?"

He laughed. "Please, Toricelli, Dr. Roland is not a moron, only a charlatan. And, frankly, Roland was very happy about it. He could freely indulge his appetite for bimbos without having to feel like he was leaving the old bag abandoned. No, if we're going to frame Roland, we're going to have to do better than trying to convince people he was a jealous husband."

"So what else, then? Joking aside, any possible murder motive you could attribute to Roland?"

"Not really."

"What about money?" I asked "any angle there?"

"For Dr. Croesus Roland? I really doubt he needs to kill for money. But really Toricelli, with all due respect to New York's finest, don't you have any better ideas than thinking that Roland killed my father?"

"You wouldn't put him on any list of plausible suspects?"

"No I wouldn't," he said, "strutting ass and mega-quack though he is, his own self-interest favored my father staying alive. The affair kept his wife off his back. And he drew off his perceived affiliation with my father to create a veneer of academic-psychoanalytic respectability. He had no conceivable reason to want my father dead."

"I see what you're saying," I said, and imagined a noose tightening around Volknick's neck.

"And another thing about money; with my father dead, Roland gains absolutely nothing. I now inherit my father's share of his suite. No, Dr. Toricelli, the only killing Roland has made is in the marketplace of bad taste. Just look at this mass-produced gobbledygook." He pointed to a row of Roland's books along a shelf in Epstein's bookcase. "Doesn't it make you want to throw up?"

Just then the phone rang, and he reached over to pick it up.

"Hello? Miriam, hi," he said, and then turned to me. "Be with you in just a minute."

While he was chatting on the phone I walked over to the bookcase and browsed over Roland's titles: *Ten Steps to Inner Beauty; You Can Save Your Marriage, Act Now; Rebirth, A Survival Guide to Divorce*; The *Secret Lives of Women We Call Beautiful*; and *Straight Talk from Supermodels, Beauty Isn't Everything.* I pulled the *Save Your Marriage*...book down from the shelf. The back cover displayed gaga clichés of praise from different celebrities and TV talk-show types. Winona Humphrey, some daytime talk show hostess, was quoted saying, "I would like every man in America who calls himself a husband to read this book."

As I started leafing through the opening pages, Chuck Epstein hung up the phone.

"That was my girlfriend, Toricelli," he said, "I've got to go."

I looked up from the book. "I see he dedicated this one to his wife."

"Huh? Oh yeah, it's nauseating, isn't it? But the title's the thing, see? You target a market segment, which is desperate enough to believe there is someone out there, someone who actually has a map to get you through your own morass, and who'll even take you to the mountaintop, to boot. Good old-fashioned huckstering, disguised as medical expertise."

Then a voice came from the waiting room.

"Do I hear another critique of the esteemed Dr. Roland?"

We both turned our heads and, in the doorway, there stood a short, mannish looking woman with close-cropped hair and a long, bulbous nose. Her hands were dug into her blue jean pockets and she spoke in what sounded like a nineteen-thirties upper crust New York accent.

"Yes you do mother," said Chuck "and how long have you been eavesdropping?"

She smiled in a way that reminded me of a wharf rat.

"I wouldn't call it that when the door is open and your voice practically carries to the street," she said. Then she looked at me and wrinkled her nose. "And who are you?"

"Joe Toricelli. Dr. Toricelli, medical consultant, police department."

"Oh, well that's nice," she said, walking toward us. "I'm Frieda, Dr. Epstein's widow."

"Nice to meet you, ma'am," I said.

"Yes, I'm sure. And how is your investigation going?" She said this in a real acid tone.

"It's...developing," I said, "little by little."

As she stood next to me, I could see her eyeballs didn't line up exactly straight.

"It is developing very little by very little if you ask me," she said. "I was called by a lieutenant...Roma, I believe he called himself; he sounded half-drunk on the telephone...about ten days ago. He asked me a couple of positively idiotic questions, if Horatio had ever beaten me or some such nonsense. And I've heard nothing from the police ever since, absolutely nothing. Until now, that is."

"I see," I said, "then I think the department's been remiss. But if I may ask you now ma'am, how were things going between you and Dr. Epstein?"

"Well, now that's a rather complicated issue Dr. Toricelli. Of course, you know we were in the middle of a divorce, made all the worse by his pigheadedness," she turned and flashed an angry glance at Chuck before she went on. "He was absolutely uncompromising, you see, and there was no end to what he demanded of me."

"I don't think we need to go into that here, mother," said Chuck.

"Why not?" she said. "If we're looking for motives for murder, I certainly had one. He wanted to suck me dry. You see I was the real breadwinner in the family, Dr. Toricelli. And I gave the family, the children, every blessed thing they wanted."

"What kind of work do you do?" I asked.

"Real estate," she said, "for the best and the brightest on the Upper East Side."

"Sounds impressive," I said.

"So I brought in the lion's share of income, which only fed Horatio's childish attitude that he was somehow 'above' money in his practice. He was so full of pronouncements of self-importance; he was a windbag with a messiah complex. That you can see in his books, which are unreadable and devoid of any common sense. In addition, he was socially awkward, poorly dressed and...and utterly unable to negotiate the simplest turns and hazards on life's road."

"Thank you, mother," said Chuck "for your very moving eulogy. But tell me, is there anything good we can say about father?"

She paused for a moment. "Well, let's see, he was quite sad most of the time, depressed really. And I think this allowed him to help his patients; they probably felt he really understood them. But, on a more useful note, I'll tell you something else Dr. Toricelli. This self-importance of his, and his depression; well, my feeling is, it points directly to death by suicide."

"Mother, that's ridiculous," said Chuck.

"Why do you say that, Mrs. Epstein?" I asked.

"Because, Dr. Toricelli, Horatio spoke of suicide often. He would complain of a terrible feeling of emptiness, which was unrelieved by twenty years of analysis and every pill in the Physician's Desk Reference. I think the rejection by me—you see, he had the highest respect for me and was utterly attached to me—was just too humiliating for him to bear."

"But with all due respect, Mrs. Epstein," I said, "didn't he have anyone else he could...turn to?"

She looked at her son before she spoke. "If you mean Evelyn Roland, Dr. Toricelli, forget it. She was his little rag doll and nothing more."

"I see, but as far as I know, Mrs. Epstein, the Medical Examiner has ruled out suicide."

"Yes, I know," she said. "And competence runs very high in the government, doesn't it, Dr. Toricelli?"

"Be that as it may, Mrs. Epstein, I'd like to ask you something else. Was there any contact between your husband and your...companion?"

At this, Chuck gave off his high-pitched cackle. "Talk about motives for murder," he said. "Now there's a doozie!"

"Oh that's ridiculous," his mother snapped. "Mabel was in England at the time of your father's death."

"I'd double-check that one, Toricelli," said Chuck. "Now there is someone whom I could work very hard to help you frame."

"Oh Chuck, grow up," his mother said.

"Imagine, Toricelli," Chuck went on "Mabel is sleeping with my mother while she's in therapy with my father, to talk about alleged incest with her brother and a fear of men."

"It was a very confused time for her," his mother said.

"Confused, bullshit," said Chuck. "She's an evil, manipulative bitch."

"She was a patient of his at the time we met," Mrs. Epstein said to me calmly. "She knew I was Horatio's wife but I didn't know she was his patient. He was trying to cure her of 'phallic narcissism' or some such nonsense."

"She is quite a dick, Toricelli, believe me," said Chuck.

"At any rate," said Mrs. Epstein "she was, in Horatio's words, a 'treatment failure', thank goodness. Mabel confessed to me after our first year together that she was being treated by Horatio, and we both decided to tell him about it. He felt shocked, humiliated, betrayed and suicidal. That is now a year ago, and he began divorce proceedings very soon thereafter."

"And what is Mabel's attitude toward Dr. Epstein these days?" I asked.

"I can assure you she harbors no resentment toward him, Dr. Toricelli. She saw him rather...as a kind of sad...joke."

"A joke, huh?" said Chuck. "Well I will personally strangle her if she ever steps across the threshold of our apartment."

"Now, Chuck, death threats in front of the police are not wise at all, are they Dr. Toricelli?"

"Right," I said, "and you say Mabel was in England at the time of your husband's death?"

"Absolutely," she said, "she only returned five days ago." Then she looked down at her watch. "Well, Chuck," she said, "we are now at least half an hour over our departure time for Easthampton, and I'm double-parked out front."

"Just one more thing, Mrs. Epstein," I said, "before you go. Did you ever have any contact with any of your husband's other patients?"

"Absolutely not," she said, "that was a boundary I never crossed, at least not in any deliberate or premeditated way."

"What about Ms. Frontenac?" I asked. "Wilhelmina Frontenac, does that name sound familiar?"

"No, no it doesn't," she said, "but it's a rather strange and flamboyant name, if you ask me. Now, Dr. Toricelli, I really must go."

"Yes, of course," I said.

"Chuck?" she said, "shall we get on with it?"

"Coming mother," he whined, sarcastically.

"Goodbye, Dr. Toricelli," said Mrs. Epstein "and I do hope you will not dismiss the possibility of suicide."

"I'll try to keep all options open. And thank you, thank you both for your time."

"Not at all," said Chuck. "Now if you'll excuse us, I need a little 'man to man' with my mother before we go."

"Goodbye," I said, and left them in the office and headed down Park.

SO WHAT WAS I to make of my little visit, I thought, as I walked back to the subway. Epstein wasn't exactly the esteemed patriarch of his household, but, on the other hand, I sure didn't hear anything from his son or wife that sounded like a motive for murder. And as for suicide, well, Mrs. Epstein sure favored this idea, as did Mrs. Volknick. And I supposed you could put together some kind of circumstantial argument for it, but my gut told me that's not what happened. And the Medical Examiner didn't think so either.

As far as my suspicions about Roland went, the Epstein kid had really put a damper on that. The way it looked, not only didn't Roland have a reason to kill Epstein, but he actually had an incentive to keep him alive, for his wife's, and indirectly, his own sake. So, so much for my screwy ideas about Roland knocking off Epstein. Who knows, maybe I even do have some kind of unconscious resentment toward, or envy of, the guy.

I guess the only thing that struck me as suspicious, from the whole visit there, was that chart of Ms. Frontenac's. Something about it just didn't look right. Despite the general sparseness of psychiatric charts, that one looked just a little too light. But who could have messed with it, Epstein's kid? And why, what's he got to hide? Ah, maybe there're just some pages that got accidentally mis-filed, I thought, and I'm just making a mountain out of a molehill. As I was turning these ideas over in my head, I passed a payphone and got a notion to call Ms. Frontenac. Whether or not her chart had been messed with, she still looked to me like a wild card in this game, and I wanted to see if maybe I could meet with her someplace this afternoon, someplace other than at that Daylight dive. So I called her up and let the phone ring over and over again, but there wasn't any answer. Shouldn't she be home, I thought? Or maybe she's bedded down in some Cro-Magnon bonehead's pad for the day. I hung up and walked on, and, just before I headed down the subway steps I passed one of these giant book supermarkets on the corner. I figured I'd go in and see if I could find a couple of Epstein's books. Maybe there was something in them, something or somebody he'd written about, that'd give me some clue as to why somebody would want to kill the guy.

I went over to the Psychology section and looked up and down all the shelves for his stuff. But there was nothing. Well, I figured, the guy's probably too esoteric, and obscure, for this joint. What I couldn't miss, though, was a life-size, stand-up, cardboard picture of Dr. Bertrand Roland, just to the side of a five-foot high stack display of his new tome, *Beautiful Outside, Ugly Inside: Men, Women, Beauty and Self-esteem.* I didn't remember seeing this one on Epstein's shelf. I pulled a copy off the stack while I looked over Roland's face in the cardboard picture. It seemed to me like he was smirking at all the bookworms and cappuccino guzzlers walking by, ready to con them into taking a sample swig of his latest elixir.

I read over the back cover of the book, again filled with the usual blurbs of admiration from famous people. They were doing somersaults for their healer and high priest in the Armani suit. One of the ones I remember was from Jerry Nesty, some host of one of those punch-in-the-nose, dirty laundry type TV talk shows. He said: "He'll change the way you see yourself—your mind, your body, your life—forever. Presto-change-o shazam! Read it guys, read it gals, and then ask yourself: who do you really see there in the mirror?"

The book was split up into different sections--surface beauty, emotional beauty, beauty and the true self, and so on. Then there was a big photo section in the middle, showing Roland on TV programs or giving his *True Beauty, True Self Seminars* to "men and women from all over the world." Or at least from those parts of the world where they could afford to pay out the five grand per one week fee. This, for going "on a very personal, very person-intensive inner journey with Dr. Roland." There were also a bunch of pictures of Roland, and these gorgeous looking women, in and around this big classical style hotel, which looked vaguely familiar to me. A photo caption read: "Seminar for New York Fashion Models, at the Grand Caribbean Hotel in St. Francis, B.V.I." Yeah, I remembered that hotel, all right. I stayed there for a month, about four years ago now, after that coke deal I did in San Juan. The day after I checked out, the place got leveled by a river of lava in that big volcanic eruption they had. Hundreds of people died and I knew I was one lucky S.O.B. to get out when I did. From what I heard they now rebuilt the place, in the form of two twin glass and steel towers.

But then, in the middle of my reminiscing, something strange caught my eye. It was in one of those pictures in the photo section with one of the faces, in a row of twelve young women with Roland in the center. There was one woman standing three heads to the right of Roland, her hair was pulled back under a bandana and she wore big flashy sunglasses and she was smiling this weird little smile. A smile where she sticks out her tongue a little bit, right between her teeth. Just like I'd seen Ms. Frontenac do. I studied what I could make out of the woman's face and, asked myself: Was that Ms. Frontenac? I looked over all the picture captions real carefully, but there weren't any names given. Then I turned to scan the chapter on these *True Beauty, True Self Seminars*. The description read: "twelve intensive group and individual treatment sessions with Dr. Roland, with unlimited follow-up treatment arranged for additional fees". Now if that is Ms. Frontenac in the picture, I thought, it means she's already had lots of contact with Dr. Roland. But yet she'd told me, just before she went back in the club last night, that she'd like to arrange a consultation with him. That she'd heard, yeah, *heard*, he was very good. She was talking, obviously, like she'd never really met the guy before, not for any kind of therapy anyway. But if she had met him before, and even been a kind of patient of his, why wouldn't she have said so? Why would she volunteer, and even seem to tease me, with misleading statements?

And, if she had been in that St. Francis seminar with Roland, which had to be four years ago or more, and she had the option of follow-up treatment with him, why would she have gone into therapy with Epstein? Which began well over a year ago.

I looked down at the photo again, at what I could make out of her face and, again, at that smile. That smile. Yeah, that was definitely Ms. Frontenac's smile, it had to be.

I closed the book and went out to the checkout counter to buy it. Then I walked outside and went to the nearest payphone to call Jake. I had to talk to him about this as soon as possible.

"Jake," I said, when he answered the phone. "It's Joey. How are you doing?"

"Hey Joey, all right. So what's up?"

"I wanted to talk to you about something with the Epstein case."

"So go ahead," he said, "but make it quick. We're headed out the door in a second, to see Nina's folks up in Bridgeport."

"Okay, I'll be quick. Just tell me something, do you have any information about Dr. Roland ever treating Epstein's patient, Ms. Frontenac?"

"No, no I don't. Why?"

"Because, unless I'm totally nuts, there's a picture of her in Roland's new book, as a participant in one of his seminars."

"Yeah?" he said, and then cupped his hand over the phone and yelled at one of his kids. "Okay, I'm back now Joey," he said, "sorry. So you were saying something about her in a seminar?"

"That's right, in one of Roland's..."

"Okay, fine," he said, interrupting me, "so what's the big deal if she was?"

"It doesn't add up. 'Cause what she told me last night, more or less, is that she never got any treatment from Dr. Roland, okay? But here she is in one of his seminars, and had the option for follow-up treatment with him. But yet she was seeing Epstein, right? The whole thing looks weird."

"I don't know, *Keemosabie*, the only thing that looks a little weird to me, is that you were with her last night. What's up with that?"

"Nothing, nothing. I just went to see her at her...dance club, where she works, that's all."

"Oh yeah?" he said, his voice getting low, "and how is she, pretty hot?"

"Aw, c'mon Jake. Stick to the fucking point, will you?"

"Joey, as far as I can tell, there ain't no fucking point, all right? So she went to one of Roland's classes. Big deal. Then she sees Epstein; so maybe Roland referred her. Big deal. Now look, I got to go..."

"Jake, somebody could be trying to hide something here. Don't you see that?"

"Look, Joey," he said, sounding real sharp, "I ain't got time right now for any conspiracy theories, all right? I'm trying to get out of the goddamn doghouse with Nina and make it through the fucking day without a drink, all right? Those are my fucking goals for today, see? Now you want to check some things out on Monday, fine. But I don't want to be bothered with this happy horseshit right now."

"All right. You leave it alone for today. Meantime, I'll see what more I can find..."

"Let me be the cop, Joey. Okay? You're just a medical consultant, remember? Now why don't you go relax a little bit with your girlfriend on the West Side?"

"I don't have any girlfriend on the West Side."

"Well go fucking find one then, will you? And put a lid on this bullshit 'til tomorrow. Now is that a deal, or what?"

"All right," I said, "it's a deal. So have a good time in Bridgeport. And give my regards to the family."

"Will do, buddy. See you tomorrow."

"Goodbye."

OKAY, I THOUGHT, as I went down to the platform and hopped on the subway, so Jake's less than impressed with my ideas. He's distracted, he's got his hands full at home, so I'll cut him some slack. It doesn't matter anyway, because I'll speak with Ms. Frontenac today and get the story straight from her. And if there's anything about it I don't like, I'll follow up by questioning Roland on Monday.

I got off the train at Astor Place and headed back to my place on West Fifth. As I climbed up the stairs to my landing, I heard a buzz of news coming from Jackie's TV.

"Mind if I listen in?" I asked, putting my head in his opened door.

"Hi Joe," he said, "not at all. See how the media can just suck you in?"

"Yeah sure," I said, feeling, somehow closer to Joe Torento again. "So, anything new on the O'Connor story?"

"Well, it looks like that man Crassidy says he's going to work with the DA in Miami. It just came over the news a little while ago. He says he wants to help the police find the other guy, Torento."

"Is that right?" I said, laughing "and what's the latest on where Torento might be?"

"In Miami, supposedly hiding out with the Mafia. That's what Crassidy just said in this interview."

"They interviewed Crassidy? Just now?"

"Oh yeah," he said, "live from the Miami jail. They'll probably show excerpts from it again...in fact, look, there it is now."

And there, in fact, it was. The scrubbed-up, slicked-back, clean-shaven image of Horace Crassidy, sitting in a chair in some stark, small office at the Miami jail. He was talking earnestly, sincerely, and even politely to this smooth-voiced, chiseled-cheekbone, blonde, cover girl reporter named Cassandra Framingham, who was sitting in a chair facing him.

As I listened in, she was asking him about his speculation that Joe Torento was now hiding out with the Miami Mafia.

"So it is your opinion," she said, "that Mr. Torento is hiding out in Miami, under the protection of organized crime?"

"Yes, ma'am. That's what I think," said Crassidy. "He's real close to those folks, real close."

"But you had said earlier that his plan was to sail to Mexico, originally with you and Ms. Parish and her son as hostages."

"That's true, but as I got to thinking about it, I think that after what happened there in Hendry County, well, I reckon he run back to Miami, to get help from them Mafia boys."

"I see. Now, Mr. Crassidy, can you tell us how you are trying to make a deal with the district attorney's office, to apparently avoid, or at least postpone, first-degree murder charges being brought against you?"

"Well, ma'am," Crassidy laughed "I ain't exactly trying to make any deal. The way I see it, I'm just telling the truth about what really happened, and folks are willing to listen to me. I'm a witness, not a criminal."

"You lying son of a bitch," I muttered.

"Hush, Joseph, I want you to hear this," said Jackie.

"And what did you tell the police and the district attorney really happened?" Framingham asked, "on the night Francis O'Connor was murdered?"

"Well, it was like this, ma'am; the O'Connor boy, he picked me up in his taxi in Key West right around midnight. I'd had me some liquor that night, yes ma'am, and I was in some real powerful mood for partying. This boy, this Francis, may he rest in peace, was feeling real frisky that night, and it looked like he was looking for some fun too, even though he was at work and all."

"What do you mean 'frisky'?"

"Well ma'am," he said laughing, "he wanted to do some partying, I reckon, and I told him if he wanted to, we could head up by Vera's Place on Crossroads Key, just on the way to the marina where he was supposed to take me."

"The Crossroads Marina?" said Framingham gravely "the very place Mr. O'Connor was murdered?"

"That's right, ma'am," said Crassidy. "So there we went, out to Vera's Place. Now it was pretty late, maybe one, one-thirty, and when we pulled up, I got out of the taxi and went to take a peek inside. When I looked in, there was just Vera Parish and Joe Torento in the place, and when I asked them if they were still open and if I could bring a friend inside, they said 'sure—y'all come on in.' So I went back to the cab. I told Francis he could come on in."

"So Mr. O'Connor was waiting for you in the cab while you first approached the bar."

"That's right, ma'am, and when I told him they were still open and he could come in, he was real happy about it."

"Unbelievable," I said, "this rummy, redneck Neanderthal is trying to cook up an alibi."

"Joseph please, I didn't hear this part before," said Jackie.

"So old Joe Torento gets real interested real quick in Francis," said Crassidy. "He's all excited to sell him a lot of cocaine and, well he thought Francis was real pretty I guess you might say. After we done some drinking, Torento says we should all drive by the back lot at the marina. He says he's got some real good blow, er, cocaine, there and he wants we should all do some."

"So if I understand you correctly, Mr. Crassidy," said Framingham, "Mr. Torento was sexually attracted to Francis O'Connor?"

"Oh, yes, Ms. Framingham, ma'am, as sure as I'm standing here. You see, that's where the trouble started. Torento keeps pushing himself on Francis and Francis tries to be real good-natured about it, probably 'cause he was interested in the cocaine. Anyway, we all got in the taxi and go to the back parking lot of the marina, and Torento goes over to one of the cars there and comes back with a big bag of stuff, maybe half a kilo. He leaves some with me and Vera and then tells Francis he wants to be real private and takes him by the beach, maybe fifty yards away. Well, they go away and, uh...maybe fifteen minutes later Vera and me hear a gunshot and, and Torento's shouting some real bad words. Things you can't say on television."

"How did you react?" said Framingham dramatically "what did you do?"

"Well, ma'am, I immediately went a runnin' over and that's when I seen a most terrible, terrible sight, Lord have mercy." Crassidy's voice started to break. "There he was, that fine young man, Francis O'Connor, alive just a few minutes ago, and now all bloody round his belly and, and just as dead as could be."

"And where was Mr. Torento?"

"Standin' right over him, he was ma'am, sayin' the most terrible curse words, about Francis not wanting to...cooperate with him."

"Cooperate? You mean sexually?"

"That's right, ma'am, oh Lord have mercy," Crassidy began to cry on national TV.

"Never thought you had it in you, Horse," I mumbled under my breath, "you sure missed out on a nice career in politics."

Jackie was teary-eyed himself. "You know, Joseph," he said, "it's so sad. But inevitable. Believe me, if you knew Francis, inevitable. He could be very fickle, very coquettish with these prisoner types."

"Oh, I believe it, all right, Jackie," I said.

Then Framingham started asking about how Torento had kidnapped Crassidy and Vera and Russ.

"So tell us, Mr. Crassidy," she said, "how did this kidnapping develop?"

"Well ma'am, right away that night Torento knew he was in bad trouble," said Crassidy, "so he points his gun at Ms. Parish and me and says we all are goin' back to Vera's Place to talk about what happened tonight. But first he has me carry poor Francis from the beach and lay him down in the front seat of his taxicab. Then we go ahead and walk through the darkness back to Ms. Parish's bar."

"But if Mr. Torento had a car parked in the lot, why didn't he drive back?" said Framingham.

"Well he said it wasn't running, ma'am. But anyway, when we get back to the bar, Torento sits us down at a table and, still while he's waving his gun around and pointing it at us every so often, he tells us what we have to do. It's real simple, he tells us, if we ever say a word about what happened to Francis, then he, or one of his Mafia boys, is going to kill young Russ Parish, Ms. Parish's son. He says little Russ'll get his head blown off with the very same gun Torento's holding in his hand right now. Well, I can guarantee you, ma'am, that kind of talk scared me and Vera so, that we just couldn't go to any police about what happened. We just couldn't.

"So you and Ms. Parish agreed to keep silent," said Framingham "and thereby protect Joseph Torento from the law."

"Well you call it anything you want, ma'am. All we knowed is, Ms. Parish and me, is we wasn't going to put little Russ in no danger."

"And with your promise of silence made, Joseph Torento allowed you to go back to your boat?"

"That he did, Ms. Framingham," said Crassidy. "I walked back to the marina that night, right past the taxi cab where poor Francis was, and out to my boat. And come the next day, I felt so bad, so deeply sorry for poor Francis. But I was just too scared to say anything about it, to the police or anybody else."

"But, by the end of that next day, you, as well as Ms. Parish and her son, were all Joseph Torento's hostages, isn't that right?"

"That it is, ma'am," said Crassidy, "that it is."

"Please tell us how that happened."

"Sure, sure will. It was like this: that next morning I got up and got real busy preparing for that big hurricane. Everybody, including me, was afraid old Amos was going to come right over Crossroads Key. I remember seeing Torento by himself, that morning, down by the marina. Well, we didn't talk much, but I remember real clear how he warned me again not to say nothing about the killing: 'you tell anybody, now, Horse,' he said, 'and little Russ Parish is going to be singin' with the angels, you hear me boy?'"

"But why didn't Vera Parish and her son run away that morning?" asked Framingham "if Torento had left them at home and come to the marina by himself?"

"That's a real good question," said Crassidy "and it sure crossed my own mind. And I can tell you, Vera told me later, after we was all already hostages, that she sure wished she had gone away, when she had the chance. But she was just too damn...excuse me, ma'am...just way too scared to be thinking about that. She was afraid that, well, no matter where they'd run to, Torento'd find them."

"But surely, Mr. Crassidy, she could have called the police and had him arrested that morning. And she and her son could have gone into the protective custody of the police."

"Well, in hindsight, ma'am, that sure would have been better than what happened to them. But she was afraid, Ms. Framingham, just like me, that even if we did get old Joe arrested, and put in prison, and get some kind of police protection; well, sooner or later them Mafia boys would get us. It's what they call a vendetta, ma'am, you understand what that is?"

"Yes I do," said Framingham, "so please, Mr. Crassidy, tell us, how did Joseph Torento come to take you and the Parishes as hostages?"

"Well, what happened was, Torento was getting more and more edgy all day. I know this because I went by the Parishes around three that day, on my way up to Lauderdale, to evacuate from the hurricane. I reckon I just wanted to see that Russ and Vera was all right."

"And was...or, were they all right?" asked Framingham.

"Well it didn't look like there was no harm done to them, but I could see in Ms. Vera's eyes that she was scared. Real scared."

"And did you offer any kind of help to her at that time?"

"No, I didn't, ma'am," said Crassidy "there wasn't really nothin' I could do, 'cept I told her I'd call her back that evening, after I got to Lauderdale."

"But you never arrived in Ft. Lauderdale, did you, Mr. Crassidy?"

"No ma'am, I didn't."

"And why was that?"

"'Cause my van broke down just past Homestead, and the roads was closed goin' up to Lauderdale. You see, that old hurricane decided to take a right, up the East Coast, and roll right close to Lauderdale. So I found me a taxi in Homestead, and headed back down to Crossroads."

"Specifically, to Vera Parish's house, isn't that right?" said Framingham.

"Yeah, that's right, I knew she'd let me ride out the storm at her house. And I figured I could keep an eye on her, and Russ as well."

"In case Joseph Torento tried to harm them?"

"I suppose so, ma'am, I knew he'd be stayin' with them there, that night in the house."

"And when you arrived at Vera Parish's house, what sort of situation did you find there?"

"A most terrible situation," said Crassidy, his voice breaking, "most terrible. Right after Torento let me in, he hit me hard upside my head with his pistol, and then he drug me into the parlor and tied me up good. Just like he'd done with poor little Russ and his mama."

"So all three of you were tied up in the living room, is that right?"

"Yes ma'am, we was. We was all bound and gagged real good. And then Torento watched over us all night, through that terrible howling storm. Then, the next morning he went out for a spell, don't know where to exactly, and left the three of us tied up there. By the afternoon, he come back, looking more and more nervous, and he tells me I got to call up a buddy of mine, Ramon, and tell him to fetch a car for us, and park it out back."

"And did you actually call this friend, Ramon, Mr. Crassidy?"

"Yes I did ma'am. Torento done ungagged me and I gave that boy a call. He came by in about an hour with an old Chevrolet he let me borrow before. He parked it out back of the house, and got a ride back with his girlfriend. He never did come inside the house."

"I see," said Framingham, "and this was the car that Joseph Torento drove to Miami in, with you and the Parishes as hostages?"

"That's right ma'am. What he done was, he stuffed me in the trunk and sat Vera and her boy in the front seat. He told them that if they tried anything funny, he'd shoot 'em both real quick."

"And did he tell you how he planned to use you all as hostages at this time?"

"No he didn't ma'am," said Crassidy, "we didn't know nothin'. He just drove the Chevrolet into Miami, and parked it near some big warehouse by the airport. Then he took us all out and stuffed the three of us into the trunk of this Toyota that was parked nearby. Before he closed the lid, I saw he'd put on a pair of work gloves he'd found somewhere. That's probably why the police can't find none of his prints on that Toyota. Anyway, then he went on driving, at least a couple of hours or so, 'til we got to this place way out in the woods in Hendry County."

"This was a hideout of some sort?" said Framingham.

"I reckon it was. He let us all out of the trunk there, and then he told us he had some kind of plan to get us all on a boat in Tampa and then sail out to Mexico. Then, he said, soon as we landed in Mexico he'd set us free and go on his way."

"Did you believe him?"

"I wanted to, ma'am," said Crassidy, stroking his newly shaven face "but I had this real sick feeling he was just waiting for the right time to kill us. I believe little Russ and Ms. Vera felt the same way."

"Is that why they attempted to escape?"

"Yes ma'am, I believe so. But you see, it was really little Russ, bless his heart, who tried to slip out of there at first. We'd been there 'bout an hour or so, and Torento had untied our feet and put us to work cleaning out a place for us to stay that evening. Meanwhile he was working under the hood of the Toyota fixing some old hose that'd come loose there on the way. Well now, little Russ, being the rambunctious little fellow he was, he seen Torento with his head under the hood there, and he decided he could make a run for it. So, faster'n you could bat an eye he started running away, full speed he did, right straight into the woods."

"And this is when Joseph Torento shot him?"

"Pretty much so ma'am," said Crassidy, wiping a tear from his eye. "He called out once to him to stop. And when he didn't, he shot him twice, clean through his little back."

"Horrible," said Framingham "just horrible. He killed this child in cold blood?"

"That's a fact," said Crassidy, shaking his head and crying real hard. "And when his mama went runnin' after the poor boy, he shot her twice too, and she fell down dead in her tracks."

"What an atrocity," gasped Framingham "how...or what did you do? How did you react?"

"Well, I'll tell you, real honestly now ma'am," said Crassidy trying to regain his composure. "I was so scared and I got so weak in my knees I just dropped right to the ground. Old Joe come out to me and pointed his gun right to my face, he did, and then I thought I was a goner for sure."

"What did he say to you?" said Framingham breathlessly.

"He said 'Horse,'" said Crassidy, with his voice breaking again, "he said, 'Horse, get your sorry ass up so's I can tie you to this here tree.' Well I got up, real slow, mind you, real careful like, and walked over to the tree. Just like he done told me to do. Then he tied me up real fast to it, and gagged me too, and then he told me he'd be back after awhile, said he was going off to figure what all he was going to do next. And then he just walked off, he did, and left the car there too."

"And did he give any hint as to where he was going, or what he would do?"

"No ma'am, he didn't. And...an' when I say this I thank the Lord...that's the last I ever seen of Joe Torento. 'Cause in the three days I stayed tied up to that tree, he never did come back."

"You were tied up for three days?"

"Yes I was, Ms. Framingham, that's a fact. I was weak and thirsty and rained on and just as scared as I could be. I wasn't left with nothin' but my faith, ma'am. And I tell you what. I prayed to the Lord for three days for him to save me, to save my life, and to save me from the evil return of Joe Torento. I prayed for a miracle, ma'am that's what I did. And...and praise Jesus, that's exactly what I got."

"What do you mean?" said Framingham, sounding suddenly skeptical.

"I mean, Ms. Framingham, that the Lord answered my prayers. You see, for three days I slipped and struggled and pulled to get free of them ropes that was tied around me. I knew if somehow I got free, I could find my way out of this mess and sure...sure enough, ma'am, every day I tried, them ropes got a little looser. Yes they did, Ms. Framingham, looser and looser. 'Til by the deepest darkness before the dawn of my fourth day there, halleluja, I'd broken my way free of them. And I left them lying there by the tree just like the police found them.

"Quite amazing," said Framingham "so what, then, did you do?"

"First thing I did was go and check Vera and Russ, may they rest in peace, and I saw they was as dead as could be. Then I run to the Toyota and figured I'd drive away but there wasn't no keys in the transmission. So then I just walked, and run, as fast as I could, down the dirt road we'd come from. I must have walked for hours, right past noon the next day, 'til I hit the hard road we'd come in on. I started walkin' west on it, 'bout a mile or so, before I got to a payphone at a little Seven-Eleven and filling station. I immediately called up Samantha Anne, my fiancée, up near Ft. Myers, and told her where I was and how she had to come get me as soon as she could."

"Did you tell her, or had she heard by that time, that you were considered a murderer and a fugitive from justice?"

"Oh yes, ma'am, yes she heard. But she knowed it couldn't be true and, o' course she promised she'd take me to her trailer and not tell a soul where I was."

"And we understand she cooperated fully with your request, Mr. Crassidy," said Framingham. "But please tell us why you hid at Ms. Hampel's trailer and continued to be a fugitive for four more days? Why didn't you notify the police immediately about what you witnessed instead of waiting until you were arrested on charges of murder?"

"Well, I'll tell you what, Ms. Framingham, when I look back on it now I sure wished I had called the police, 'stead of gettin' arrested and all. But I was so...so discombobulated and so scared of Joe Torento and his Mafia boys; I just couldn't get myself to call the police. It was wrong, now I see that, but I just couldn't do it. Thank the Lord I got me another miracle and God brought the police right to my door."

"Through an anonymous tip, from what we understand."

"Yes ma'am, and I thank whoever that anonymous person was. I thank him or her from the bottom of my heart."

"And thank you, Mr. Horace Crassidy," said Ms. Framingham, smiling "that's really all the time we have. Thank you for your very moving and detailed account of the terrible atrocities committed by Joseph Torento."

"Thank you, Ms. Framingham," said Crassidy, brushing back that telegenic hairdo with one hand. "I thank you for the opportunity to tell my story. And I just want to say one other thing," he said, now looking squarely and sincerely into the camera "and that is that I am so very grateful to be alive, and that I want to do everything I can, for Francis O'Connor and his folks, as well as for Russ and Vera Parish, to make sure Mr. Joseph Torento is captured and brought to justice. We got to do it for all of us, for all of us who believe in law and order in America. We got to bring Joseph Torento, and any Mafia members who's protecting him to swift and furious justice. Amen."

"Thank you," said Cassandra Framingham, now with a big, beaming smile "thank you for your time. This is Cassandra Framingham, VitaCom International News, at the Miami-Coriolis County Jail."

Then they switched to a mouthwash commercial.

"So Joseph," said Jackie, "what did you think?"

"Obvious bullshit, all dressed up to look like it could be news."

"Really? Why do you think it's bullshit?"

"Oh, c'mon," I said, "no one's going to swallow that story. The son of a bitch is totally desperate, so he and his fancy lawyer conned this reporter into giving him an interview."

"Well, I don't see it that way. And, p.s., neither do the O'Connors and the Morrisons. In fact, they showed Francis's father on TV, just a little while ago. By the way, he happens to be president of VitaCom Network. Anyway, he said he really believes in Horace Crassidy."

"What? You've got to be kidding me."

"No, not at all," said Jackie, "he said he was very grateful for his cooperation and really believed it could lead to Torento's capture."

"Now that's got to be the wackiest shit I've heard yet. Isn't it obvious what this guy is? A low-life, con man, cold-blooded motherfucking murderer."

Jackie's eyes got real big when I said this.

"I'm just surprised he could slap together this half-assed story," I said, going on "I really didn't think the guy had half a brain."

"You know, Joseph," said Jackie, looking kind of spooked. "I'm starting to get this feeling you actually know Horace Crassidy."

"Only from the news, Jackie," I said, trying to tone myself down a little, "it does that to you. I mean, don't you feel like you know him yourself?"

He didn't say anything to me, but just looked at me kind of funny, and pinched his lips real tight.

"So anyway," I said, trying to change the subject, "you got something to drink around here? I've just got a bit of a hangover from last night and I'm a little irritable."

"I'll fix you something," he said real slow, "then you'll feel a little more like yourself."

He put together a couple of Bloody Marys for us, and we sat down at his table. I took a few sips of my drink and tried to relax. No use getting all riled up, I told myself. First off, Joey Torento disappeared into a shaving mirror last week; second, sooner or later they're going to get the goods on Crassidy; and third, it's not too smart to be talking to Jackie like you know Crassidy.

"Well," I sighed, "enough talk about the news. But hey, by the way, you familiar at all with this guy's books?" I showed him the copy of

Roland's book that I'd bought.

"Oh sure," he said,"I know about Dr. Roland. He was on the Larry Conn Show just last night, answering questions from the audience about self-empowerment. But you really get the feeling he despises everybody, you know?"

"Yeah? You think so?"

"Oh yeah, definitely. And he probably does very nasty things to little boys in his spare time. No, he's not a nice man. You can tell by the way he blow-dries his hair."

"I hadn't noticed."

"Anyway," said Jackie, "last night he went on about beauty and self-esteem. He had a bunch of models with him. They were awfully cute, made me wish I was a lesbian."

"A lesbian?"

"Never mind. But you know, when I saw him with all those gorgeous girls it got me to thinking..." Then he started laughing in his weird, rasping way.

"Yeah?" It got you to thinking what?"

"Well...that he," he said, as his laughing quieted down "that he, Roland would like to be a girl, a cheap, sexy, vamp of a girl. I think it's why he went into psychiatry, to learn how to hide, or at least control his little secret."

"Maybe. Anything's possible."

"But isn't it true, Joe, that all psychiatrists have some secret craziness?"

"Maybe so. And maybe sometimes not so secret."

"And what's yours, Joe?" he asked, teasing me.

I didn't say anything.

"Oh don't worry," he said, "I'm just kidding. I don't expect you to tell me really."

"Good."

"But I am allowed to guess, aren't I?"

"Yeah, sure. Go ahead."

"Okay," he said, rubbing his hands, "here's your secret: it's a crazy...sort of fantasy...let's see...hmmm...okay...I've got it. You're convinced you're involved in some awful act, something unspeakable, and you're absolutely obsessed with it. Obsessed with both the act...and the fear that, sooner or later, you're going to get caught. So there, what do you think?"

"Not bad," I said, clearing my throat, "not bad..."

"Oh, I think I hit it," he said, with that raspy laugh. "I think I hit a perfect bulls eye."

And I thought to myself, who the hell is this guy?

He offered to fix me another Bloody Mary and I took him up on it right away. Let's get off this subject of my crazy secrets, I told myself. It's not leading anywhere good. So I sipped another cocktail and got the conversation drifting over to things like the landlady, and whatever was going on in the neighborhood. But the whole time, I kept asking myself, does he see something about me, could he think I look like those pictures of Torento? But no, no, I told myself, you're getting paranoid, that's all. You're just caught up in a crazy little stream of conversational coincidences, and nothing more.

So we passed a little more time, and then I told him I was going back to my room, to take a little snooze. When I got into my place, I lay down on the bed and, before I dozed off, I flipped through the pictures in Roland's book some more. There was that photo of...well, it had to be...Frontenac, again. Smiling that smile behind those big, gaudy shades. So just what the hell is she doing there, I thought, and why do I get the feeling that I'm not supposed to know? Well, I'll get to the bottom of it, I figured, as my eyes began to close. In just a couple of hours I will, amid the lights and music and dancing, at the Daylight Club.

I WOKE UP A little before ten, hopped out of bed, and went out to grab a cab to Daylight. When I got there, I stood in line to pay my thirty bucks at the door, and then squeezed my way through the crowd and over to the spot at the bar where I'd last stood with Ms. Frontenac.

I was happy to see there was a different guy tending bar tonight, and I hoped he'd be less of a pain in the ass than his ghoul colleague from yesterday. He was a young guy, with a handsome square-jawed look and a real earnest expression on his face.

"How are you this evening?" he said, as I sat down at the bar.

"Pretty fair," I said, "and yourself?"

"Doing okay. So what'll it be for you tonight?"

"Let me have a martini; and just kind of wave the vermouth bottle over the shaker, okay?"

"Will do."

"And by the way, I hope you're not going to get all riled up if I start shooting the breeze with Ms. Frontenac tonight."

"Who?"

"Ms. Frontenac, she's one of the dancers here. Last night a couple of your fellow workers here were more or less threatening to lean on me, all because she and I were talking, and sort of fooling around with each other."

"Really?" he said, "well, I don't know anything about her, I just started working here three days ago. But, what are you saying, they were threatening you or something?"

"Well, not exactly, but the bartender from last night, bald guy, big forehead, real gruff..."

"Oh, you mean Ara," he said, "yeah, he's a real character."

"Well, as far as I can tell," I said, "the guy really ought to brush up on his manners."

"Oh, I think he's really an okay guy, he and I worked together my first night here. He's just a little rough around the edges, that's all." Then he handed me the martini and went off to serve some other guys at the bar.

I turned around and leaned back against the bar, and took in the action in the place, which was more or less a repeat of the night before. I drank the martini real slow and kept an eye on the time, expecting at any minute to see Ms. Frontenac appear. After well over an hour went by and there wasn't any sign of her, I started to wonder what was going on. I turned around and asked the bartender if he knew who had a schedule of the girls who were supposed to perform tonight.

"I really don't know, sir," he said, "don't know what to tell you."

"Uh-huh. Well, I'll see if I can find out what's happening."

I walked over to the stage door and asked a girl there if she'd seen Ms. Frontenac anywhere.

"Willy?" she said, "she's not in tonight."

"But she's scheduled tonight, isn't she?" I asked.

"She was, but she called in sick today. That's the last thing I heard."

"You know about what time she called?"

"I really don't know. But sorry, I've got to go."

Then she stepped up on stage, to a clapping crowd of panting palookas.

Meanwhile, I went over to a payphone and called up Frontenac's apartment. There wasn't any answer. Then I walked over to the front door, where a guy with long, black hair and a scar on his chin was standing.

"How you doin'?" I asked. "I'm looking for the manager."

"I am the manager, sir," he said, "what can I do for you?"

"I'm looking for a young woman who dances here, Wilhelmina Frontenac."

"She's not here tonight."

"Right, I know. She called in sick. But do you know where she is now, or when she's coming in next?"

"And why do you want to know, sir?" he asked.

"I'm with the police department, the name's Toricelli. She's involved in an investigation I'm conducting."

"I see. Well, I don't know where she is, home I suppose. She is scheduled to come in again on Tuesday."

"This Tuesday?"

"Yes, that's right," he said, "but if I hear from her sooner, I will give you a call."

"Thanks, thanks a lot," I said, "here's my number. Goodbye."

By then it was close to midnight, so I called it a night and went back home.

I GOT DOWN to police headquarters early the next morning, and dropped in to see Jake at his office on the seventh floor. He was at his desk, shuffling through some papers, when I walked in.

"Morning, Jake," I said to him, "have a good Sunday with the family?"

"Eh, not so bad, Joey, you know? No fighting, anyway. And who the hell knows, maybe she'll come around to forgiving me. Sooner or later."

"I hope so," I said, sitting down by his desk, "just don't fuck up again."

"I'm not gonna, chief, not any time soon anyway. So look, what kind of trouble did you get into this weekend?"

"Sorry to disappoint you, but it was just another quiet stretch of celibacy, with a little bit of reading, see?"

Then I showed him Roland's book.

"And let me show you the most interesting part," I said, and flipped to page 168 and pointed out the picture, and the woman in question. "Now tell me that ain't Frontenac," I said to him "right there."

Jake looked it over for a minute. Then he said,

"Jeez, I don't know, Joey. Could be. But come on, with the kerchief and the sunglasses? Who the hell knows? By the way, these are some hot looking babes, aren't they?"

"Never mind that, Lt. Playboy," I said, "now look, I'm telling you, I think that's her, and I think somebody's trying to hide something here. Whether it's just her, or she's in on something with that son of a bitch of Roland, I don't know."

Just then, Moore walked into the office.

"Well, good morning, Lt. Roma," she said, "and good morning Dr. Toricelli. It sounds like we're still obsessed with Dr. Roland, are we?"

"Ah, not really, Dr. Moore," said Jake, "but come over here. We want to show you something."

She walked over and sat on the edge of the desk, and Jake held up the book to her and pointed out the woman in the picture.

"Now tell me something," said Jake, "do you recognize this girl right here, all smiling and happy to be with Dr. Roland?"

Moore looked down and squinted at the picture for a few seconds, then she looked up.

"No," she said, "why?"

Jake looked at me and shrugged. Then I turned to Moore.

"That face doesn't look familiar to you?" I asked her.

"No it doesn't. Now tell me boys, what little game are we playing here this morning?"

"Joey thinks that's Ms. Frontenac in the picture," said Jake.

"Let me see that again," she said, and she looked it over, again, with her eyebrows knitted up real skeptically. "And why would you say such a thing, Dr. Toricelli?" she asked, and lay the book down on the desk.

"It's the smile, see," I said, "what she does with her tongue there. She must have done that ten times on Friday night."

"Friday night?" said Moore, "and how did you see her Friday night?"

"I visited her, where she works, at Club Daylight, for a follow-up interview."

"I see," said Moore, "your dedication to your work is quite admirable."

"Yeah, I think so. I think he's a real trouper," said Jake, laughing, "aren't you, Joey?"

"Yeah, yeah, very funny," I said, "but I'm telling both of you, that's the way she smiles. And I'll tell you something else, she really does have some kind of borderline or dissociative disorder and...."

"Well good for you, Dr. Toricelli," said Moore sarcastically, "it's quite heartening to see that, even with your very limited training and skills, you were able to come up with such an assessment. But really, what is most important to note here, is that it is completely inappropriate for you to be following Dr. Epstein's patients around town and...."

"She invited me there," I said, interrupting her.

"Hah," she laughed at me, and shook her head. "Yes, I'm quite sure she did. But at any rate Dr. Toricelli, this case will be solved with or without your naive, unprofessional, stumblebum approach. Now, if we may get on to more important things right now Lt. Roma. The reason I came by is to tell you we need to coordinate a time to meet again with the Volknicks." Then suddenly her beeper went off and she stopped and scribbled down a number. "I'll return in a moment," she said, "I'll need to take this call privately." Then she got up and walked out and closed the door hard behind her.

"She's a real firecracker, ain't she, Joey?" said Jake.

"Bitch is more like it," I said.

"Maybe, but she's going to help us close in on Volknick."

"You really think he did it, don't you?"

"I just follow the evidence, Joey, and it leads straight to Volknick."

"So seeing as you got this case all but solved, Jake," I said, "you won't mind if I pay a little visit to Dr. Roland and ask him about this picture, right?"

He laughed. "Do what you want," he said, "just don't get him pissed off, all right? We want to maintain good relations with the community, you know?"

I WENT OUT, and hopped on the subway, and in half an hour I was at Roland's door, pressing on the buzzer. I hoped to hell I'd get the chance to surprise him.

All of a sudden I heard his high-pitched voice crack through the intercom.

"Yes?" he said.

"Yeah, Dr. Roland," I said, "Dr. Toricelli here. You got a minute to talk?"

"Right now? I'm really very busy."

"I just need a minute of your time, sir. I've got a couple more questions I need to ask you regarding the murder."

"Don't you people believe in calling first? Don't you know Monday morning is the worst possible time?"

"I understand, and I apologize. I just happened to be in the neighborhood on another call. Now if you could buzz me in sir, I'd be happy to wait until you're free."

"All right," he said, obviously pissed off, and buzzed me in. I went into his waiting room and sat there for a few minutes before he opened his door. Then he just stood there, glanced at his watch, and asked me real coldly,

"Now what can I do for you, Dr. Toricelli?"

I stood up and walked toward him, like I was expecting we'd go into his office. But he just stood there in the doorway, with his arms folded across his chest, and stared at me.

"Well, good morning, Dr. Roland," I said, "I'll try to make this quick because I know you're a busy man."

"Fine, fine, so let's get on with it, then."

"Okay, what I'd like to know is, what you know about Wilhelmina Frontenac. She's one of the patients Dr. Epstein saw on the day he died."

"Frontenac?" he said, with his face kind of squeezed, "don't know that I know anything about her. Don't believe I know who she is."

"Well, she's pretty hard to miss, very tall, maybe six feet, long brown wavy hair. Looks like a model."

He closed his eyes for a second. "Let me think," he said, "yes, yes I do recollect such a woman, now that you described her. She introduced herself to me in the suite entrance, about a month ago, thanking me for some medication I'd renewed over the phone for her, when Dr. Epstein was away. Yes, of course, lovely young woman."

"Okay," I said, "and what about when Dr. Epstein was away; did she ever come to see you for any kind of treatment?"

"No, nothing like that. That sort of situation is quite unusual anyway."

"What about before she ever went into treatment with Dr. Epstein? Could you possibly have treated her prior to Dr. Epstein?"

"What? Now that is a very strange question, Dr. Toricelli. Are you asking me if this woman was ever a patient of mine? Prior to her seeing Dr. Epstein?"

"Yeah, that's right. I'm asking if she was ever a patient, or maybe a seminar participant, of yours. Prior to seeing Dr. Epstein."

"That, that would be absurd," he whined. "First of all, I don't remember her, and secondly: why would a patient of mine, or a seminar participant, who has the option of continued treatment with me, subsequently go see Dr. Epstein for therapy? Why?"

"I don't know," I said, "maybe..."

"Did Ms. Frontenac say she'd once been a patient of mine, or say she'd been in a seminar?"

"No, no she didn't."

"So why the devil are you asking me such questions, Dr. Toricelli? What exactly is this all about?"

"Well, I'll show you, Dr. Roland," I said, and pulled his book out of the bag I was carrying, and flipped to the page with the picture in question, on page 168.

"You see this photo?" I said, pointing it out to him, "with all the girls lined up here with you?"

"Of course," he smiled "and I remember it all so warmly. The seminar I conducted at the Grand Caribbean in St. Francis, several years ago. A truly superlative experience."

"And these were all the participants in the photo here, right?"

Yes, there were twelve in all. That's how it's arranged."

"Now tell me something, who is this young woman right here, smiling and sort of sticking her tongue out?"

He looked at the picture for a few seconds and pursed his lips.

"Yes...well, of course, I remember her. She's a lovely, lovely young woman."

"Right. And who is she?"

"Well, I don't recall her name. Not right off the top of my head. It's been quite some time, you see..."

"She looks to me a whole lot like Ms. Frontenac, especially the way she smiles."

Roland looked up at me, with this real annoyed, contemptuous expression on his face.

"Is that what this is all about, Dr. Toricelli? You have some notion that this young woman in the picture is this Ms. Frontenac?"

"I'm asking if that's possible," I said, "that's all."

"You're asking if it is possible that this young woman in the photo here, with whom I engaged in a very positive therapeutic experience, and have since seen for a few follow-up visits, is the same woman as Ms. Frontenac, Dr. Epstein's patient? And, I presume you are further asking if it is possible that I could have seen this very woman in the suite entrance a month ago, exchanged introductions with her, and that somehow neither of us was able to recognize each other or acknowledge that we'd known one another before? Is that what you're asking could be possible, Dr. Toricelli?"

"I'm only asking..."

"Well I can assure you, Dr. Toricelli," he interrupted, fuming now "that such a situation is absolutely impossible, do you understand? Impossible, absurd, and ridiculous."

"Okay, Dr. Roland, okay. Take it easy. You've made your point real clear. So just do one thing for me now and I'll let you go. I need the name of this woman in the photo."

"Well, as I've indicated, that escapes me at the moment. I have an excellent memory for faces, you see. But names, well sometimes... especially if it's been a few years..."

"I understand, but you've got records, right?"

"Well of course I do, doctor," he said, "but that would be confidential."

"Not really. It says right here in your book that everybody in the pictures signed letters for the use of their images and names. So it doesn't look like anybody's too worried about privacy here."

"Well it would really take some time to go through my files and, besides, if you're so concerned about this Ms. Frontenac, why not question her further about this...idea of yours?"

"I'm having trouble getting hold of her right now," I said.

"Yes, well sooner or later you'll speak with her. And if, after you do, my records seem relevant, I'll be happy to cooperate further. Now if you'll excuse me..."

"Dr. Roland...I'd really appreciate your cooperation right now. Whatever information you have on this woman will help to guide me in my questioning of Ms. Frontenac."

He heaved a big sigh and gave me this exasperated look, as if to say he considered me a royal pain in the ass. I didn't care.

"You know, this really is quite out of the ordinary, doctor. It's disruptive as a matter of fact."

"I understand, but nonetheless, I'd really appreciate your cooperation."

"Yes, you've said that already," he said, clenching his jaw. "All right, step into my office, and I will try to help you."

We went into his office and sat down around his desk. He checked his phone messages and returned several calls while I sat and waited. After twenty or thirty minutes passed he finished talking and stood up from his chair.

"All right, Dr. Toricelli," he said, "let us now make haste to reward your...persistence, and put an end to this matter."

He went over to a big filing cabinet and started flipping through a bunch of folders in the top drawer. After awhile, he closed it up and opened the second drawer. He sort of grumbled to himself impatiently from time to time, as he was searching through his papers. Eventually, as he got toward the back of the second drawer, he said,

"Ah, yes, here it is, this is what I need." He spent a few minutes going through a big folder, and then announced: "Here it is. The woman's name is Jayne LeGrande. I'd just wanted to double-check something. But that is she. Jayne LeGrande."

"Great," I said, "and you've got an address there, too?"

"Well, let's see. I remember she was from Canada but I don't see...ah, I see. She gave her address as the Dyckman Hotel, on Central Park West. That's where she was living at the time our seminar began. And during some follow-up visits as well, I believe. So that's all I have here."

"She didn't give any other address? No permanent address, in a specific city in Canada?"

"No. I believe the Dyckman was her regular address at the time. That is a residential hotel, you understand. And I'm sure if you really wanted to, you could have the Dyckman look at their records for any former or forwarding address they might have on her. Who knows, perhaps she's even moved back to Canada. But, at any rate, doctor, I think I've done all I can for you now."

"Yes, thank you," I said, "for your cooperation. I'd just like to ask you one more thing. Does anything ever go wrong at any of these seminars? I mean, do people ever break down, or go crazy, or anything like that?"

"Crazy? That's rather an imprecise word for a man like you to be using, isn't it? But, as a matter of fact, I have had uniformly positive outcomes at the seminars. And that is the result of not only proper therapeutic techniques, but also of very thorough screening. You don't build a reputation like mine without scrupulous attention to the proper fit between patient and treatment, you see."

"Sure. I see how that makes sense."

"Read my book, Dr. Toricelli, *The Patient is Right, But the Treatment is Wrong*. You may learn something."

"Thanks. I'll keep it in mind."

"Fine," he said, "now I really must get back to my work."

"Certainly. Goodbye, and thanks again."

"He really thinks he's shit on wheels," I muttered to myself, as I walked out the front door and on to Park Avenue. And there's something definitely phony about him, regardless of how his story about this LeGrande woman checks out. And that I wanted checked out today. I'd get Jake to get his boys to do all the necessary research on it right away.

WHEN I GOT BACK to headquarters I found Jake with his feet up on his desk, yapping on the phone to somebody about yesterday's Daily Double at Saratoga.

"Joey, all right," he said as he hung up the phone. "So how pissed off did you get the good Dr. Roland anyway?"

"Not very."

"Yeah, that ain't what I heard from Moore a few minutes ago. She told me he called her up and went bullshit about, what he say? Oh yeah, 'high-handed' police tactics. What'd you do, lean on him pretty bad?"

"Yeah, right," I said, sitting down on the windowsill, "he just didn't like being surprised, that's all."

"So what'd you get from him, anything good?"

"A name," I said, "Jayne LeGrande. He says that's the girl in the picture. She's from somewhere in Canada, supposedly, and she used to live at the Dyckman Hotel. At least, she did four or five years ago. I say we've got to check his story out, completely, and as soon as possible. Like today."

"Well now whoa there, Joey, what's the emergency? I mean, I ain't heard you tell me anything here that's exactly suspicious sounding. You know what I mean?"

"I'll tell you what's suspicious, is the girl in that picture. As far as I'm concerned, that's a picture of Ms. Frontenac until proven otherwise. And if we can't prove it otherwise, then we've got to ask ourselves: what could she have been doing with Roland, why didn't she or Roland say something about it, and how could it be connected to Epstein's murder?"

" You know what?" said Jake, laughing "you're getting way too fancy for me here, you know that? Why are you wanting to go on some wild goose chase when you got Volknick sitting right in front of you?"

"Now that's real convenient, isn't it? Just pin it on Volknick, right? That'll make your job real easy."

"Now wait a second, Joey, that's not the point."

"No? Well maybe it really is the point. Just take the easy way, and don't try to think too much. Shit, thinking too much, that could get to interfere with what's really important, like drinking booze and chasing broads. Right?"

"Hey, you're getting way the fuck out of line here, you know that? Since when do you tell me how to do my fucking job, huh?"

"I'm not telling you how..."

"Don't fuck with me now, Joey. You hear me?"

"Jake, I'm not trying to fuck with you. But let's just not hang Volknick yet, that's all I'm asking you. Not until we've got a chance to check out this LeGrande story."

Jake had gotten real heated up, and he was sitting upright on the edge of his seat, like he could get up at any second and take a swing at me. But then, he took a deep breath and slouched back down again.

"All right, Joey," he said, "we'll check out this friggin' woman. What'd you say her name was?"

"LeGrande. Jayne LeGrande."

"Right. Okay. We'll check her out. Now is that going to keep you happy?"

"Yeah, it will. And if my hunch is crazy, my hunch is crazy. I'll live with it."

As I finished saying this, Moore walked into the office.

"I'm not sure what you're willing to live with, Toricelli," she said, "but it appears that people are finding it quite difficult to live with you."

"What are you talking about?" I said.

"I'm talking about how you're out of control," she said, standing over me. "Who told you to pounce on Dr. Roland and insinuate some sort of clandestine relationship between him and Ms. Frontenac?"

"Nobody told me to," I said, "I thought it up all by myself."

"You're not even embarrassed, are you?" she sneered.

"Why should I be? I'm not afraid of what he thinks about me. Are you?"

"Hey, boys and girls," Jake piped in "let's play nice now, huh? We all got our favorite theories here, 'course some are a little easier to take seriously than others."

Then he smirked at me and said, "Just kidding, Joey."

"But look now," he went on, "Dr. Moore, for instance, has this theory here about a motive for Volknick, and it ain't half-bad."

No one said anything.

"Why don't you tell Joey about your theory, then, Dr. Moore," said

Jake.

"I wouldn't waste my time," she said.

"Up to you," he said, "but I'll tell you what, I'll take a shot at explaining it. It's like this, Joey: Nathan Volknick was there when his old man died, right? Now whether he killed him, or what, nobody could ever say. But what we do know from Dr. Roland's report is that Volknick talked a lot about his father being a weak, little man and how he was the strong one. So now Epstein comes along, and becomes like a father figure to Volknick except he's strong, see? And this gets Volknick real confused; part of him wants a strong father figure and part of him wants to whack Epstein 'cause he wants to be more powerful than him, just like he thinks he was with his old man. It's something like that, right Dr. Moore?"

"That's roughly right, Lt. Roma," she said. "It's a theory based on what Dr. Toricelli might one day read about; an unresolved oedipal complex in chronic schizophrenia."

"I don't buy it," I said. "It's ass-backwards pseudo-Freudian bullshit. And coming out of your mouth, Jake...well, frankly it sounds kinda weird."

"You might consider your own oedipal issues, Dr. Toricelli," said Moore, "in your envy of and preoccupation with Dr. Roland."

"I don't need your curbside psychobabble," I told her. "My old man died in the line of fire, working in this department. I remember him as one hell of a guy and I sure as shit wouldn't compare him with Roland. Sometimes an asshole is just an asshole, Dr. Moore. Think about it."

"You are beyond hope, Toricelli," she said, "I'm only grateful that this investigation will be over soon."

Then she turned and walked out.

Jake shrugged, "So anyway, Joey, we'll check out this LeGrande thing. I promise."

I looked at him real steady. "Jake, you know you sound pretty wacky with this psychological stuff. What the hell's gotten into you?"

"Nothin'. And hey look, what's the difference? There's so much evidence against this Volknick kid anyway."

"Yeah, but Jake, really. What are you doing now, sitting around with Moore and having cozy little chats with her about psychology?"

When I said this, he got real red and turned his eyes away from me.

"So what're you so embarrassed about?" I asked him. But before he could say anything, I already suspected the answer. "Holy shit!" I said, "don't fucking tell me...no, do fucking tell me. Are you fucking her, Jake?"

"Joey, c'mon," he said. But he still couldn't look at me.

"You slimy fucking sick fucking snake!" I said, standing up from the windowsill. "You're fucking her aren't you? You're fucking Moore. And this is how you get it together with Nina, you stupid shit?"

"Joey, c'mon," he said, "lay off, will you? First of all, she, believe it or not, she...she came on to me. It was on Saturday, in the afternoon, we were about the only ones hanging around in the office. She starts...comin' on to me, starts saying something about how, uh, what'd she say, like natural, like primitive I am..."

"She's got that right, 'primitive's' a real good word for you."

"I could see she just wanted me to take her, you know, overpower her, and rape her right here in the goddamn office."

"You could see that, huh?"

"Yes I could. And I could smell it too. And I'm telling you she's hot. She's fucking unbelievable."

"You are one dumb shit, you know that? And your wife's trying to forgive you for—ah, forget about it, Jake, you're fuckin' hopeless. But for Pete's sake, don't let Moore fuck with your mind about this case, will you? Don't buy that psycho-horseshit about Volknick, just 'cause you like her pussy, you know what I'm saying?"

"I know what you're saying, so don't worry about it."

"I'm worried about it," I told him, "real worried about it."

Then he looked down at his watch. "Hey, look," he said, "I got a meeting at one, I got to get out of here."

"Sure you do, you've got to run real fast out of here."

"No really, I do," he said, standing up "and hey, by the way, Nina told me you got a call from that guy Tim again today. Here's his cell phone number." He handed me a slip of paper. "So what's he, your coke dealer?"

"Very funny," I said, "anything to change the subject, right?"

"Fuck no. Anyway, I do gotta run. See you later."

"Stay out of trouble."

"Don't worry, Joey," he said as he walked out the door, "I'm fine. Later."

Crazy, sick son of a bitch, I thought, as he left. But, ultimately, fuck it. It's his problem.

I WENT OVER TO Jake's phone and called Landsdowne and set up a meeting for five o'clock that afternoon. Then I left the office and walked home. When I turned the corner onto my block I saw Jackie sitting on the front stoop, smoking a cigarette and drinking a Coke.

"Beautiful day, isn't it?" he said, when he saw me.

"If you like ninety-five in the shade and lots of mugginess,"

"But look at the light, Joe, the way it plays on the brickwork and fire escapes."

"Yeah, nice," I said, "real nice."

"Hey, by the way, you like lobster?"

"Yeah, sure, why?"

"A friend of mine works at Fulton Street and he dropped off four of them a little while ago. Want to go eat a couple?"

"Sure, thanks. I'm ready when you are."

We went upstairs and started to steam up the lobsters. While they were cooking, we sat at Jackie's table, and he filled me in on the latest on the O'Connor case.

"Believe it or not, the FBI is backing up Crassidy's story about Torento being connected with the Miami Mafia."

"Yeah? What are they doing?" I asked," offering early release to any goombah who'll say he once knew the guy?"

Jackie laughed. "Well, not exactly. But the FBI had this boss, Danny Corona I think his name is, they had his house under video surveillance for the last few months. And they've actually got a tape of Torento driving in and out of his front gate. On the same morning Crassidy said Torento had left them all tied up and went out for awhile."

"Oh shit," I said, feeling my belly go hollow, "that doesn't prove squat. You...you think that proves Torento's guilty?"

"Well, not really, but you really don't have to take it so personally."

"I'm not. I just don't think a videotape of the guy going to some Mafioso's house necessarily tells you anything."

"Well, I think it does. It tells you Crassidy was telling the truth, just as I told you he was. You just don't know these rednecks the way I do, Joseph. I spent a lot of time around them when I was growing up."

"Right. And by the way, what sort of picture did they get of this guy Torento, something like the police composites?"

"Something like that, He had long curly hair and a beard, and was wearing sunglasses."

"Sounds like it's going to be tough to really get an idea of what his face looks like."

"That's true. Except for his nose. He has a very handsome nose. Long and straight. Like yours."

I looked at him real wide-eyed.

"Oh don't worry, darling," he laughed, "I'm not coming on to you. Anyway, I think our lobsters are ready."

We pulled those hot red critters out of their steam bath and cracked them open on his little table. He brought over a bowl of melted butter and a couple of beers and we sat down and started to dig in.

"Oh, I wanted to tell you Joe," he said, as we were eating, "I finished your chart last night."

"Really? And what'd you come up with?"

"It's been a very difficult period for you, at least the last seven years."

"It's had its ups and downs."

"But mostly 'downs' Joseph, aren't I right?"

"Hard to say. But did you get any other angles on the future?"

He paused, "Well, as I said, it's not going to be any day at the beach."

"Yeah, I know. But anything more specific?"

He took a deep breath, and started going on about planets and stars and constellations and alignments, but I got impatient pretty quick and cut him short. I just wanted the bottom line, I told him, that's all. I didn't believe in this shit anyway. Did I?

"You always get so bitchy when we talk about this stuff," he said "but remember, I'm just the messenger. Anyway, the bottom line, as you put it, is that there's a huge concentration of forces working against you right now, at least through the end of the year. And it's absolutely not a good time to be making decisions, it's better to sit back and wait."

"And what if I do have to make decisions?"

"Then it's going to be risky, very risky. You're like a fly caught in a spider's web, and any move you make gets you closer to trouble, closer to getting snatched." He held up a lobster claw and snapped it in the air.

"Real bright tidings there, huh?" I said.

"You shouldn't look at it that way Joseph, as good or bad. It's just information. Try to use it intelligently."

"Whatever," I sighed, and finished off my lobster.

AFTER WE CLEANED up I gave Frontenac's place a call and, predictably, got no answer. I chatted it up with Jackie a little more about this zodiac stuff and then headed down to Carmine and Bedford to meet Landsdowne. It would be one fly in a web meeting another, I figured. His limo was there at five sharp, and when I got in I was surprised to find him smiling. But then I saw he was also three sheets to the wind.

"Hello doctor," he boomed "make yourself comfortable. How about a drink?

"No thanks," I said, trying not to gag at the stench of his breath, "it's really best not to drink on the job."

"Sound policy," he laughed "but I thought we could toast to a job well done."

"How do you mean?"

He took a deep drag off his cigarette and wiped his brow.

"I did a lot of thinking since our last meeting doctor," he began "about history, about politics, about what's important...in the end. I've had an extraordinary ability to manufacture images doctor, illusions if you will. And to hide behind them and do whatever I damn well pleased. But what does that all come down to? Nothing. Nothing I tell you. Nothing but an ability to fool most of the people most of the time, with empty slogans and empty images; fading, vanishing just as quickly as they're spun out."

His voice got a little shaky.

"And where is it all in the end, doctor? When you've come to the end of your time and have to account to...someone...maybe just yourself. What is there then, doctor? Nothing, that's what. It is all vanity, just as the Bible says."

He refilled his tumbler with more Scotch.

"So, in the end there are only a few things of real value, and I can only laugh at myself that it took me so long to see it. Your family, maybe a friend or two, and whatever peace, whatever honesty you can find in your own soul. That's it, everything else is...is bullshit."

He looked at me with tears filling up in his eyes. "Sure you don't want a drink doctor?"

"No thanks. So tell me Mr. Landsdowne, what are you going to do? What, if any, decisions have you made?"

"What am I going to do doctor? Is that what you want to know? Well doctor, I've told my wife about you, and all that we've talked about. She knows everything. And when I see Jorge this week, on Thursday, I'm going to tell him and whoever it may be behind him to go straight to hell. I will then resign my position, and deal with whatever is to come. I am prepared to go to prison, before I will continue to be blackmailed."

"Sounds good," I said.

"It is good. And it's going to hurt terribly, especially when, as I am certain it will happen, my actions are fully exposed. But I will face the cameras and the questions, and the idiotic partisan moral posturing that is sure to follow. Of course, I will be thought of as a total disgrace. But I think I can get through it."

"Do you?"

"I do. Because I'm going to keep my eye on what I hope may be beyond it all, on what I hope will ultimately await me in my future: going back to the family farm, in Indiana. Feeding the cows, and fixing the fences, spending time with my grandchildren, and studiously avoiding any exposure whatsoever to television or newspapers or radio, for at least a hundred years." He let out a big laugh. "So what do you think of that decision doctor? Healthy enough for you?"

"I think it is. And regardless of what the future holds for you, I definitely think you're doing the right thing."

"It's thanks to you doctor that I am. You saved my life twice. First back there at Pershing, with that fool gun, and then again when you showed me there was only one honorable choice to make."

"I'll take credit for the first time," I said,"but I didn't save you the second time, you did. I only reminded you of what you already knew, but had forgotten."

"You know, without being immodest, I'm going to have to agree with you there. It's absolutely staggering what we can forget, and run the risk of never getting back again."

We rode on in silence for a while, along the side streets of the West Village and up through Chelsea, and I had to admit I felt pretty good that I'd helped this guy through the swamp of his own bad choices. Now if I could only help myself do the same, I thought, while the car rolled on. It started to rain, first in little droplets one by one, and then in a steady march which built to a rushing downpour all around us. One of those cloudbursts that pushes away the heavy, lazy heat of a summer's day, at least for a while. Landsdowne looked out the window and smiled.

"It's washed everything very clean, doctor," he said, "that's how it looks to me."

"That's how it looks to me too, sir," I said.

The driver turned south on Seventh Avenue, and we made our way back toward Carmine and Bedford. By the time we pulled up to the corner, the rain had receded and the sun was coming out again.

"Doctor," said Landsdowne, as he grasped my hand, I want to thank you, for everything, from the depths of my soul."

"You're welcome. And good luck to you Mr. Landsdowne. Please call me if you need anything."

"I will. But frankly, I think I've got the worst of it behind me. The decision to come clean was the hardest part. Now I know what I need to do. So, goodbye doctor."

"Goodbye, Mr. Landsdowne," I said, and got out of the car.

I WALKED BACK home, and hung out real peacefully in the apartment that night. I continued to feel good about Landsdowne, and even hoped that his case could somehow be a sign that luck was going to be running my way. Who knows? Maybe I'd even be asking Jackie to take a second look at his zodiac analysis.

Before I went to sleep, I went out to a payphone and tried Frontenac again and, as usual, there wasn't any answer. Strange, I thought, isn't she ever at home? Or is it that she just doesn't feel like picking up the phone? I thought about paying her a visit, but I didn't have her address on me, and the phone company didn't have any listing with her name. Maybe the phone was in a roommate's name or something. Then I called up Club Daylight to see if they'd heard from her. No, they said, but they were expecting her in tomorrow night. And when I asked them for her address, they said they didn't have that information, and wouldn't give it out over the phone even if they did.

So I called up Jake at home and, after he told me he hadn't heard anything yet about the LeGrande woman, I told him I thought it was a little weird that I could never get a hold of Frontenac.

"Joey," he said, "relax will you? Maybe she's at her boyfriend's. You know?"

"Yeah, maybe," I said, "or maybe something's happened to her. Maybe she's even lying dead in her apartment as we speak."

"Aw, jeez, c'mon Joey, save your imagination for writing a book, okay?"

"Yeah, sure, but look, why don't we send somebody to her place from the local precinct all right? Just to check that everything's all right, you know what I mean?"

"All right, all right. I'll get some guys to pull up her address and we'll go check on her. Is that going to make you happy now, Columbo?"

"Yeah, that'll make me real happy."

"Then I'm happy," said Jake, "see you tomorrow sport."

THE NEXT MORNING, I was the first one in the office, and I found a note from Moore to me sitting on the desk. It said:

"Volknick will be interviewed at one today. You are expected to attend."

Oh I'll be there, I said to myself, if for nothing other than to stop you from nailing him to the wall. I made a call to Frontenac from Moore's phone and, again, there was no answer. Then I went over to Jake's office, just as he got in. He looked a little sheepish, the second I laid eyes on him.

"How you doing Joey?" he said kind of cautiously.

"Fine, Jake. But don't worry, I don't want to talk to you any more, about you and Moore."

"What's that supposed to mean?" he said as he sat down at his desk.

"It means what it means. Now tell me something, any news from the precinct about Frontenac?"

"Not that I heard."

"Well...is she all right?"

"I didn't hear nothing," he said, "so, uh...you know...no news is good news, okay?"

"You did call the local precinct last night, right?"

"Yes, yes Joey. Now relax, will you? There ain't nothing wrong going on with her, or we'd have heard something, okay?"

"And what about the LeGrande thing? Do we have any follow-up there?"

"Yeah, as a matter of fact, we do," he said, and reached into his briefcase and tossed a big manila envelope onto his desk. "I just picked this up on the way up here this morning, from the guy who talked to her last night. Read it over Sherlock, we did everything you asked us to do."

"Well then tell me," I said, sitting down by his desk, "what'd you do?"

"We talked to the Dyckman Hotel and they dug up this girl LeGrande's address and phone number, her parents' place actually, up in Montreal. We call up there and her mother answers. She says Jayne is still living in Montreal, but she's married now, and her last name is McNeil. So then we call up this Jayne LeGrande McNeil, real nice girl, and she's flabbergasted she's hearing from the police. She settles down when we tell her we just want to know if that's her in the picture in Roland's book. She says yeah, sure that's her and, by the way, she's available for modeling jobs and willing to travel. You believe that? Think the police department can use her Joey? Maybe we can figure some angle where..."

"All right can it," I said. "So you found out that's definitely LeGrande in the picture, with her tongue between her teeth."

"Yes, right Joey. And who the hell else would have thought it was Frontenac besides you? Why are you trying to get fancy when we got a suspect right in front of our noses, huh?"

"But doesn't it bother you that no one's actually told us they've seen or talked to Frontenac, going on three days now...and that it looks like somebody combed through her chart?"

"Her chart?" said Jake, "when did you see her chart?"

"On Sunday, when I was up at Epstein's office, talking to his kid, I took a peek..."

"The kid showed you her chart?"

"Not exactly, he left the room and...."

"Joey, don't do that shit, all right, there's procedures to follow and...so what the hell did you see in there?"

"Nothing. That's the problem. Just a lot of dates of visits and comments like 'stable' or 'full affect,' stuff like that. There ought to be something more, more information, that's what I think."

"Yeah?" he said, "and...."

But before he could finish we were interrupted by the sound of Dr. Moore rapping on the open door.

"Good morning boys," she said, kind of singsong. "Remember,

interview with Volknick at one today."

"Say Madeline," said Jake, "I mean, Dr. Moore, we want to ask you something, about how these uh, psychiatric charts work."

"Yes, and what's that?" she said, as she walked into the room.

"What would you think, just hypothetically that is, if you saw a patient's chart, say they were coming to see somebody for a year or so, and all it had was the dates of the visits and that the patient was stable or something, and not much else. Is that unusual or what?"

"That would depend," she said. "If it were someone primarily in psychotherapy, and they were functioning more or less normally, not being hospitalized, it wouldn't be terribly unusual."

"Like, say for example, Ms. Frontenac?"

"Ms. Frontenac? Well, from what we know of her history; she was in twice a week therapy, had no hospitalizations and no suicide attempts. And from what we can assume about her diagnosis, probable borderline personality disorder; yes, I suppose I could imagine someone maintaining a relatively sparse chart on her."

"Could you imagine it with Epstein?" said Jake.

"Oh most definitely," she said, laughing, "first of all, he hated paperwork. And second, and most importantly, he firmly believed that the official medical record should contain as little personal information about the patient as possible."

"And why is that?" asked Jake.

"For the protection of the patient," said Moore, "just in case the chart got involved in some legal matter, be it civil or criminal. That was the way he practiced."

"I see," said Jake, looking at me and cocking his head "thank you Dr. Moore."

"But just what are we doing all this speculating about, Lt. Roma?" she said, "as far as I know, no one has examined Ms. Frontenac's chart. Unless, of course, someone has broken into Dr. Epstein's office and done so."

Jake kept looking at me and knitting his eyebrows, as if to say "Forget you saw the chart."

"Oh, it's nothing like that," I said, "but you know, I just don't like that for the last three days, I haven't been able to reach Ms. Frontenac. Not at work and not at home."

"And just what is your continuing preoccupation with Ms. Frontenac?" asked Moore "thoroughly...professional, I hope."

"Thoroughly," I said, "I'd be real stupid to mix up sex with doing my job. You know what I mean?"

She just looked down after I said that, and it looked like I'd pretty much slammed down the brakes on any more of her sarcastic conversation. Then Jake mumbled something about a meeting he had to go to, and Moore said she was on her way to the hospital for rounds. Before they ran out, we all agreed we'd be back at one to see Volknick.

I poured myself some lousy-tasting coffee and sat down and looked over the report on Jayne LeGrande. "Jayne McNeil," it said, "age 28, address: 14711 Rue St. Denis, Montreal." Work and home phone numbers followed. Her mother's address, at 102717 Prince Arthur Street, and phone number were also there. They said Ms. McNeil was very cooperative and pleasant on the phone and she confirmed she was the woman in "said photograph." Time of contact was listed as eight thirty-seven last night and it looked like they spent about three minutes with her on the phone. It was a real skimpy report, with no details about how she confirmed that it was her in the picture. All right, I thought to myself, so Jake got one of his flunkies to go through the motions of calling this girl, just to make me happy. So why don't I give her a call, I thought, seeing how she's so cooperative. Maybe I can nose around a little more, and if nothing else, get another angle on how old gasbag Roland operates. So I dialed up her number and I got this real squeaky voice on the other end:

"Hello?" this girl said.

"Yes, hello. May I speak with Jayne McNeil please?"

"This...this is she. Who is this?"

"Joe, uh—Dr. Joe Toricelli, New York City Police Department."

"Ohh," she squeaked. "I talked to one of your men last night."

"Yes, I know."

"I hope he knew I was just kidding about the modeling stuff. I'm a physical therapist now anyway, didn't he tell you?"

"Well no, as a matter of fact..."

"And didn't he tell you my name is LeGrande again, and I'm getting divorced? And that's regardless of what my mother is telling people, about my marriage, or my name."

"Well, I don't need to get into any details about your marital status. But what I was really curious about, Ms. LeGrande, was how exactly you identified your picture, in Dr. Roland's book, for the police."

"Oh, that's easy," she said, giggling, "I have a copy, signed and mailed by Dr. Roland personally. So I just turned to the picture on page 168 and, voila, there I am, three down from the right of him, showing a little bit of tongue."

"Uh-huh," I said, "now let's back up a minute. You said you've got a copy of his book, signed and mailed by him personally?"

"Yes. With a wonderful letter from him, and an invitation to a symposium he'll be conducting next month in Montreal."

"So he definitely knows you're in Montreal? He's got your

address?"

"Oh sure he does," she said, "that's the same thing the officer asked me last night. But Dr. Roland's just so busy, and maybe a little absent-minded, that he must have forgot that he has my current address.

"Right. And uh...you have any kind of regular contact with Dr. Roland?"

"Oh, I wish. But I do get a call from him, at least once a year. And he's wonderful. It's because of him that I have the courage to make major life changes, and major life choices. He taught me to stop running after all my ego-illusions."

"Ego-illusions?"

"Yes, that's part of the False Me, the Me I thought was so wonderful and attractive. But he taught me about my True Beauty, which was hidden and forgotten behind my False Me Mask."

"That was your problem?"

"Oh it was. But you know, there is something about just being around him, Dr. Roland that is. He's so centered, so clear. You'd know what I mean if you spent time with him."

"Yeah, actually I have."

"You have?"

"Oh sure," I said, "just yesterday as a matter of fact."

"Really?" her voice suddenly got even more high-pitched, "and...well, what'd you think?"

"Well, he really seems to believe in the importance of what he's doing."

She giggled again, real nervously. "Oh that's true. And...will you be seeing him again?"

"Yes, yes I will. Shall I give him your regards?"

"Ohhh," she giggled "no...I mean...yes, or whatever. But I've...I've got to get off the phone now officer, or I'll be late to work."

"Sure, sure," I said, "just one more thing. Does the name Wilhelmina Frontenac ring a bell?"

"Wilhelmina...Frontenac? No, no officer...I've never heard that name before."

"You're sure?"

"Oh yes, officer. Now that's the truth, I've never heard that name, honest."

"Okay," I said, "thanks for your time. Goodbye."

I hung up the phone, with this real confused feeling. Okay, I thought, so LeGrande apparently identified herself in the photo. But what did she seem to get so nervous about, when I told her I had seen, and was going to see, Roland? I definitely got these vibes from her that she was hiding something. And then, what about her address, and phone number. Obviously Roland had it, so why didn't he say so yesterday? Was it really just innocent absent-mindedness on his part? Or was he trying to hide something? I had to find out.

My watch said it was five to nine. I didn't know whether Roland would be in his office or not, but I figured I wanted to find out in person, not by chasing him playing telephone tag. So I hopped the uptown express and had my finger on his buzzer by nine-thirty. Popping in on him again was going to piss him off, I knew that, but I needed to see the specific look on his face when he'd explain to me how he couldn't give me the LeGrande girl's address.

No one answered on the intercom, but I saw through the frosted glass that someone was moving around there in the corridor. I rapped on the door a few times and this black woman came out.

"Can I help you?" she said, with some kind of West Indies accent.

"Morning ma'am," I said, "just waiting to see Dr. Roland."

"He's usually not here before ten on Tuesdays, what time is your appointment?"

"Actually for nine-thirty. Okay, if I come in and wait?"

"Okay by me. I'll be finished cleaning momentarily. He should be here very soon, he doesn't like to be late."

"Good," I said, and stepped into the main corridor. She packed her things up and was ready to leave in a couple of minutes.

"You going to be all right here?" she asked me.

"Oh yeah, I'm fine, don't worry. He'll probably be here in a minute."

"Okay. Goodbye now," she said, just a little unsure of herself.

"Yes, goodbye," I said, "thank you."

I watched her close the inside frosted glass door behind her, and saw her shadowy figure disappear through the outside door. I looked at my watch, and saw it was now twenty minutes before ten. This is it, I figured, one golden opportunity to really snoop around the place, all by myself. I went into Roland's waiting room and to his office door and turned the handle. I wasn't surprised to see it was locked. Then I went back to the main corridor and over to the maid's closet, where I'd seen her fumbling around with some keys a minute ago. I opened the closet door and, sure enough, there were two hooks with keys hanging on them. Over one hook it said "Dr. E." and over the other it said "Dr. R."

"Dr. R. it is," I muttered.

I went back and unlocked his door and went over to his desk to flip on the video monitor. In a second there was a picture of the front doorway lit up on the screen. Then I went over to the filing cabinet where I'd seen him get out the folder on LeGrande. The drawers were locked tight and I wasn't going to try to yank them open.

I went back to his desk and opened up the big center drawer. It was cluttered with prescription pads, paper clips, old date books, postage stamps, his passport and all kinds of crap. Underneath a couple of drug company pamphlets I found a bunch of keys. Let's give it a shot, I figured, and went back to the file cabinet and started trying each one. Then I saw somebody open the outside door on the video monitor and I thought I was cooked for sure. But it was just some Chinese kid dropping off menus and I let out a deep breath and felt my heart pounding. I kept trying the keys, there must have been a dozen of them, and finally, I was able to jam one of them in the hole. It wasn't the right key, but for this cheap lock it was close enough, and in a few seconds I'd jiggled it around and unlocked the drawer. I got busy flipping through the row of manila folders inside, with all sorts of stuff written on the labels and none of it in any kind of order I could figure out. There were first drafts of a couple of his books, lecture notes from some class he taught at the medical school, collections of correspondence with publishers, TV producers, and colleagues. Toward the middle of the drawer I found what I was looking for: "St. Francis Seminar. Grand Caribbean Hotel. True Beauty, True Self." The folder was packed with pieces of paper and lots of pictures and I took it over to his desk and spread everything out on it. A long list of names caught my eye and I went down it looking for Frontenac, but she wasn't anywhere there. I did find LeGrande, though, Jayne E., at the time age 22 and—son of a bitch—her mother's address, 102717 Prince Arthur Street, Montreal. He had the mother's phone number too. So much for absentmindedness, I thought, you could have given me that information yesterday. And we wouldn't have had to waste time with the Dyckman Hotel.

I threw a glance at the video monitor, the screen was quiet. I looked at my watch. It was five to ten. A few more minutes was all I had.

I pored over the photographs as fast as I could, all of them with Roland in different poses with his self-esteem seeking lasses. I recognized a few of the pictures from the book, including the "said photograph" on page 168. It was pasted on heavy paper and had the names of the people in it listed with the directions underneath, saying, "left to right." There were twelve women in all and Roland in the center and I could see immediately that something didn't fit. "Jayne LeGrande" was listed three names before Roland, so she should be standing three positions to the left of him. But that wasn't the girl I'd thought was Frontenac, who was three heads to the right of Roland. The name of the girl I thought was Frontenac was listed as Sabrina Briand. I went back to the name and address list and found her there: Sabrina Briand, age 19, address: 267 Corso di Porta Roma, Milan. No phone number. I scribbled down her address real quick, put all of Roland's stuff back, and got the hell out of there. I'd be back to talk to him all right, but I had some research to do, and I wanted to do it in a hurry.

I got a bunch of quarters at a bank around the corner and went to a payphone to call back Jayne LeGrande. She was still home to answer the phone and I figured she couldn't have been in too big a hurry to go to work.

"Hello, Ms. LeGrande," I said.

"Yes?"

"Dr. Toricelli again, NYPD."

"Oh, yes," she squeaked "hello again."

"I've got a problem with that picture on page 168 in Dr. Roland's book. Can you get it? I want to ask you something."

"Wow, you know I'm really in a hurry," she said. "Uh...uh...you know? She was definitely sounding rattled.

"Right, you've got to go to work. But this is just going to take a second. I want you to take a real close look at that picture again."

I heard her breathing into the phone. "Okay, hold on," she said.

After four or five minutes, and half of my quarters, she came back on the phone.

"Sorry," she said, with her voice shaking, "what was the question?"

"You see the picture on page 168? Tell me specifically which one of those women is you, and take your time."

"Uh, let's see," she said, "oh, that's me there, over there on the right..."

"Well—wait a second now," I said, "let's keep it real simple. Okay? Are you on the right half or the left half of the picture?"

She didn't say anything.

"Ms. LeGrande, do you understand my question? Just look at the picture. Are you in the right or left half of that picture?"

"I...I'm in the left half," she said.

"Of course you are, you're in the left half. Your tongue is not between your teeth, is it?"

"Well...I see my tongue there."

"Well, maybe you do," I said, "but it's very different from the girl who is in the *right* half of the picture, three heads from Dr. Roland, isn't it?"

"I...I guess so."

"That's the woman the police are interested in. Do you know her?"

"I...officer I'm very confused," she said, sort of whining, "are you tape recording this?"

"No. Now try to settle down. And just tell me, who is this girl with her tongue between her teeth?"

"Sabrina," she cried "Sabrina...Briand."

"And how well do you know her?"

"Not very. She's a real nut case."

"What do you mean?"

"I...I don't want to talk about her," she was sniffling. "I'm sorry officer, I...I was confused, I made a mistake. I'm not going to be in trouble am I?"

"Look, don't worry about it. But you need to tell me what you know about this Sabrina Briand. It could be very, very important."

"But..."

"Very important," I said, "like a matter of life and death."

"Really?"

"Really. Now do you know where she lives?"

"I...I don't, exactly," she said, "somewhere in New York."

"New York City?"

"I think so, yes."

"When was the last time you talked to her?"

"Um...I don't know. Maybe a year ago?"

"A year ago?"

"Yeah, uh, she called me, just to say, 'hi this is how my life is going,' that kind of thing."

"Well, what...what'd she say, what's she doing?"

She laughed. "She's a dancer. I don't know where, some nightclub...for men."

"Club Daylight?"

"I don't know."

"What does she look like? Describe her for me."

"She's very tall. About six-feet, like me. And she has long, reddish brown hair."

"And her age?"

"Twenty-something, I guess. I don't know exactly."

"Ms. Frontenac," I said, "Wilhelmina Frontenac. Tell me again, think hard, do you know that name?"

"No."

"Never heard it?"

"No."

"Did this Sabrina, did she ever go by any other name?"

This got her tittering.

"What's so funny?" I said.

"It's just...well she claimed, back in St. Francis, that she had seven different personalities and I'll bet every one had a different name, but I don't know any of them officer. And basically, you can't trust anything she says, and not about anyone. I told you she's a nut case."

"Tell me more."

"Well, it's probably confidential but...back in St. Francis when we were all with Dr. Roland, she started to spread a rumor that she and Dr. Roland were sleeping together, isn't that unbelievable?"

"Shocking."

"And that Dr. Roland would dress up in her bikini and beg to be spanked by her, that it was the only way he could, uh...you know..."

"Ejaculate?"

"Exactly."

"And was Dr. Roland aware of these...rumors?"

"Oh, I think he was. But he's such a gentleman, such a wise man, you know? And besides, she was totally crazy, officer. One minute she'd be Miss Prissy, all sweet and nice and the next minute she'd turn on you, just a total bitch, about the littlest thing. Maybe she really did have different personalities, I don't know."

"So I don't guess anyone actually believed these rumors about her and Dr. Roland?"

She laughed. "Not at all. I mean, well you have Dr. Roland and you have this...crazy woman...and, well isn't it obvious who you're going to believe?"

"Right. And what about after St. Francis. Did Ms. Briand have any other contact with Dr. Roland?"

"Not that I know of, officer. But, you know, I don't really know her that well. We spoke on the phone, like I said, maybe once a year. But officer, now I really, really have to go. To work, I mean."

"Yes, of course, Ms. LeGrande. But just one more thing."

"What's that?"

"Did Dr. Roland tell you the police could be calling, to ask you about this photo in the book?"

"Oh no officer," she said, "absolutely not. I'm sure he's too busy for that."

"Did anyone else call you, to warn you that the police would ask about this photo? Like maybe this Sabrina Briand?"

"No officer, no way. And I still don't understand what it's all about. The police just asked if I could answer their questions, they said it would help them in some kind of murder investigation, involving a doctor. I think they said Dr. Roland was...helping them somehow."

"Okay," I said, "thanks Ms. LeGrande. Goodbye."

I WENT BACK to Roland's and rang the buzzer. I figured he'd be back by now, and I was real interested in his recollections of Sabrina Briand, as well as Jayne LeGrande McNeil.

"Yes?" came his voice through the intercom.

"Morning, Dr. Roland," I said, "Dr. Toricelli here. Got two

minutes?"

"I'm sorry I don't, doctor. And I believe you've already been advised about the impropriety of visiting here without notice."

"That I have sir, but I just got off the phone with Jayne LeGrande...McNeil. And it looks like you got things all mixed up in that photo I asked you about."

"What?"

"You made a mistake sir. You mixed up Jayne LeGrand McNeil with Sabrina Briand. Can I come in now?"

There was a very long pause, like he didn't know what to say, or do, next. Then his voice came piercing through the intercom.

"Please have a seat in my waiting area," he said and then he buzzed me in.

He must have kept me sitting there maybe thirty or forty minutes. When he finally did open the door, he looked a little pale and he had kind of a smirk on his face.

"Come in Dr. Toricelli," he said, "and have a seat."

"Thank you."

We entered his office and settled in around his desk.

"Now just what is all this confusion about?" he asked.

"Like I said, Dr. Roland, it looks like you mixed up girls in that photograph."

"Well, let's assume for purposes of discussion, that I did Dr. Toricelli. So what? Isn't this all really much ado about nothing?"

"It could be sir. But why don't you tell me what you know about this Sabrina Briand?"

"Well that would be confidential doctor, I think you're well aware of that. Name and address are the only things I can release at my discretion." Then he handed me a piece of paper with the Milan address I'd seen in his drawer. "I anticipated you'd want this," he said, "so here it is."

"Thanks, but this is an old address. I need her New York address."

"I don't know what you mean," he said.

"Jayne LeGrande McNeil just told me Sabrina Briand lives in New York, so I need her New York address."

"That's the only address I have. Perhaps the phone company, or Ms. McNeil, can help you with Ms. Briand's New York address."

"Uh-huh. But tell me something Dr. Roland; when was the last time you actually talked with this Sabrina Briand?"

"Dr. Toricelli, I have already advised you that any contact I have with patients is completely confidential. Only with the patient's permission, or under subpoena, will I release any information."

"Sure, sure. I understand that. And I certainly respect your adherence to professional ethics. But if you just ran into her, on the street say, or by chance in your office suite entrance, you could tell me that, right?"

"And what is it you're trying to suggest Dr. Toricelli?"

"I'm suggesting that Wilhelmina Frontenac and Sabrina Briand are one and the same person, and you know it."

"That's an absurd statement Dr. Toricelli."

"Do you deny it?"

"I not only deny it," he said, "but I must protest your compelling me to entertain these wild notions of yours."

"They're really not so wild, because according to Ms. McNeil's descriptions of Sabrina Briand, she sounds a lot like Ms. Frontenac. Same height, same color hair, same occupation, about the same age. Maybe even the same psychopathology."

"I see," he said, in this very condescending tone, "I see. And these sorts of clinical and demographic coincidences, they intrigue you do they Dr. Toricelli?"

"Yeah, as a matter of fact they do. Just like the coincidence of you and Jayne McNeil making the same mistake about her position in that photo really intrigues me."

"Dr. Toricelli," he said, now smiling, and shaking his head, "you know I really do admire your investigative zeal. You're quite a hard-working and dedicated...civil servant, I'm sure. But, I would respectfully suggest to you that you are losing your perspective in this case. You seem quite invested in this idea that I am concealing relevant information, and am even orchestrating some sort of cover-up, all around this woman Ms. Frontenac. Now, I will try to cooperate with you to the extent that ethics and common sense allow, doctor, but I would also recommend you re-evaluate how you're approaching this case and the evidence at hand."

"Well, I'll take your thoughts into consideration," I said, "but I'd like to know this: did you have, or arrange, any contact with Jayne LeGrande since I was here yesterday?"

"Contact? No, of course not. Not at all."

"And what about in the recent past, like the last few months, or the last year? Any communication at all?"

"No. Not that I recall, anyway."

"Because she told me that she received a signed copy of your latest book, and a letter from you, in the last few weeks. And that she's talked to you on the phone at least once a year since the St. Francis seminar."

"I see," he said, smiling.

"So how does that square with you denying you have her current address, or even her old address and phone number when she lived with her folks; and also, your not remembering any communication with her?"

"Very simple," he said, laughing, "volume. Do you realize I'm in touch with literally thousands of people each year, by telephone alone? And do you think I am personally addressing and sending out letters and signed copies of my books to additional thousands of people? And, on top of that, keeping personal track of name changes or address changes? Please doctor, I realize you operate in a very different world than I, but let's not be naive, shall we?

"Well, by that argument, it might be possible that Ms. Frontenac, formerly with another name, could have been your patient, and you could have forgotten about it."

"Very faulty logic there, doctor," he said, "first of all, it is one thing to not keep track of names or telephone contacts, but quite another to forget a face. Secondly, even if I did somehow forget her face, why wouldn't she then remind me that she'd once been a patient or seminar participant? And thirdly, as I've already said, why would she be seeing Dr. Epstein instead of me? Now really, Dr. Toricelli, hasn't this gone far enough?"

"Not yet. Because yesterday, when you knew the Dyckman Hotel address on LeGrande wasn't current, you could have referred me to your secretary, or publisher, or whoever tracks this address stuff for you. And they could have given me all the information I needed to contact Ms. LeGrande, immediately. And without police detectives dragging their feet, and going through time-wasting procedures to get old hotel records."

"Well, I really find your comments quite dismaying. I had, and have every reason to believe, that contacting the Dyckman was your easiest and most expeditious route to getting Ms. LeGrande's information. The fact is, most of my demographic information on seminar participants is stored at my office in Easthampton and, what with my secretary there on vacation all week, no one would have retrieved any information for you as quickly as the Dyckman."

"So that means you could have other information on Sabrina Briand there."

"Actually, I couldn't. I double-checked my log here to see if I have other address information stored on her anywhere, and I do not. Now if you will excuse me, I have a brutally busy schedule today and you've already taken up a great deal of my time."

"I understand," I said, "but I'd like to inquire about just one more thing."

"And what is that?"

"Well, I was just wondering, uh...how do you handle it if a patient of yours or, let's say a former patient of yours, one of the girls in your seminars, for instance, starts telling people she's having sex with you?"

"That's a strange question, doctor," he said, clearing his throat and getting kind of stiff.

"Maybe it is strange. But, from what I gathered from Ms. McNeil, it appears there were rumors of you and this Ms. Briand getting it on, so to speak, in St. Francis. And it looks like this Ms. Briand was blabbing about it all over the place during that seminar week."

"I don't know how this gossip got started, but in general, it is not uncommon for some patients to develop certain kinds of fantasies. It's something we all have to live with."

"But if people start believing these stories, say friends, family, even other doctors of the patient, then you've got a real serious problem on your hands wouldn't you say?"

He took a slow breath before he spoke. "Potentially, you could. But fortunately, I've never had to worry about it."

His jaw seemed to tighten and I had a feeling he was forcing himself to keep eye contact, almost like he was watching for my reaction. Could he be scared, I thought, that I was really hitting too close to home?

"Now I must insist that we adjourn, Dr. Toricelli," he said, "and, frankly, I do hope you're generally more efficient about how you spend taxpayer's money.

"We try our best, Dr. Roland. Thank you for your time."

ON THE TRAIN back downtown I put together what I thought I had so far; that Briand had to be Frontenac, that Roland had been screwing her while she was his patient, and that he knocked off Epstein because Epstein had developed a credible case against him. Roland then figured framing Volknick would be a piece of cake, but where he stumbled in his cover-up was when he forgot, or didn't think it mattered, that Frontenac's picture was in his book. And what about Frontenac? Is she still alive, or did Roland figure he had to kill her too? And then there's Jayne LeGrande; did Roland grab her as a decoy, or a stooge or maybe even a fucking accomplice? Who knows? We'd have to see if hers and Roland's phone records matched up anywhere. But basically, everything depended on finding Frontenac or Briand or whatever the hell her name was.

When I got back to Moore's office it was lunchtime and no one was around. I called Frontenac's number and got the predictable no answer. Then I looked through the New York City phone books and found a few Briands. I started calling and got through to a couple of them, but nobody answered to or knew squat about the name Sabrina Briand.

Then I decided to call up the police in Milan, and told them I needed information about this address on Corso di Porta Roma, how I could find out who lived there, and when. They dragged their feet awhile and I had to go through about eighteen levels of bureaucratic ass dragging before I could get my answer. There was no 267 Corso di Porta Roma, they said. "*Non esistente*." Somehow, it didn't surprise me.

Shit, I thought, this case is screwed without Frontenac. Even if we could get a subpoena for all of Roland's files, that son of a bitch must have already covered all his tracks. I looked at my watch, it was a quarter to one. This Volknick interview was coming right up. All right, I figured, just be there, and make sure he doesn't get framed. As soon as it was over I was going to call on Frontenac's apartment personally. Who knew if Jake's guys had really even gone by there to take a look? I wrote down her address from her file, and started flipping through a street atlas to locate exactly where she lived. Then I heard Moore's voice barking orders down the hall.

"Yes, right now, Marisol!" she was saying, "put another chair in the conference room. The Volknicks are here with an attorney."

Then she showed up at the door.

"I received an angry message on my voice mail from Dr. Roland," she said, "you actually had the audacity to barge in on him again?"

"He doesn't like surprises," I said, "it doesn't give him time to cook up a new set of lies."

"I'm not even going to dignify your remarks with a response. Now we're ready to see Mr. Volknick. I hope your presence will be useful, he does seem to have some sort of connection to you."

"Yeah, really? Well that's because I'm the only one around here who's not trying to fry him."

When Moore and I entered the conference room where the interview would be held, Nathan Volknick, his lawyer and his mother were already sitting down along one side of a long table. Volknick had his hair combed back, and was dressed in a dark three-piece suit and looked crazier than usual. His lawyer was a young guy with bushy hair and wire-rimmed glasses and was shuffling through some papers. His mother was just looking straight ahead, kind of sad and somewhere in her own thoughts. Moore and I took up chairs across the table from them and just as we sat down, Jake came in and joined us.

"Good afternoon, Mr. Volknick, Ms. Volknick," Moore said. She looked at his lawyer. "I don't believe we've met."

"Barry Friend, Nathan's attorney," he smiled and then stood up and shook our hands.

We all introduced ourselves and shook hands.

"Now, Mr. Volknick," Moore began "can you tell us your understanding of our meeting today?"

"Yes. You want to keep asking me questions about Dr. Epstein's murder."

"His alleged murder," Friend piped in.

"Yes, that's right, Mr. Volknick" said Moore, "and can you tell me who I am?"

He looked down and didn't say anything for a few seconds. He seemed to be concentrating on something inside his head. Then he looked up at Moore and said, "Could you repeat the question?"

"Yes. Who am I?"

He grinned and put his head down like he was enjoying some private joke. "You're a policewoman," he mumbled "a policewoman doctor."

"Okay," she said, "and who are the men seated with me?"

He looked at me and Jake. "He's a doctor and he's another policeman, a homicide detective."

"Good," said Moore, "and who are you with today?"

"My mother and...and Mr. Friend of the family," he cackled.

"Who is Mr. Friend?" she asked.

He stood up, like he was about to recite a speech.

"Mr. Friend...Mr. Barry Friend, Esquire, is a fine attorney and a very good friend of the family. A fine and foul-weathered friend is Mr. Friend, but he's no fucking friend of mine."

"Nathan!" his mother yelled.

"Foul fucking frizzy weathered hair of the dog, best friend, he is man's best friend, he is Barry Friend, Esquire.

"Nathan, sit down and be quiet," his mother said. Then she turned to us. "Nathan is upset that we brought Mr. Friend with us today," she said, "he feels..."

"I feel nothing, mother," he interrupted "let the hungry parasite feed on the wrinkled, inflamed hide of insinuated criminality."

"What are you talking about Nathan?" his mother asked.

"Nothing." He sat back down. "Mr. Friend can stay. Let's get on with it."

"All right," said Moore, looking a little frazzled. "I believe we have established the purpose of our meeting and identified the participants, now if we..."

"I don't like you," said Volknick, staring at Moore.

"Excuse me?" she said.

"You heard me," he said, "with all due respect, officer, doctor, your attitude sucks."

"I really don't believe this," his mother cried.

"She's haughty," he said, "she is brutalizing me with haughtiness."

"If I could have a word with my client," said Friend.

"I don't want your words," said Volknick, "I will talk to him," he pointed to me "but not to Her Royal Heinous."

Moore sat back in her chair. "Dr. Toricelli," she sighed, "please continue with him.

"Mr. Volknick," I said, "if you don't mind my saying, you seem awful tense today."

He didn't say anything and seemed to drift back into his own world.

"Mr. Volknick?" I said to him again. And then again.

"Yes, doctor," he answered, finally "can you repeat the question?"

"Not a question, exactly. I said you seem to be awful tense today."

"Yes I am."

"Why?"

"I don't know."

"And you seem to be having trouble paying attention."

"Yes I am."

"Why is that?"

"It's the conversation," he said.

"What do you mean?"

"The conversation's very noisy today, very busy."

"What conversation?"

"Inside my head."

"You're hearing voices?" I said.

"Oh yeah. Definitely."

"And what are they saying? Can you say?"

He was quiet.

"Can you say what they're saying?" I said.

He didn't say a word.

"Doctor," said Mr. Friend "I don't see the relevance of probing my client about..."

"I'm not your goddamn client," said Volknick, "so butt out."

Then Volknick turned to me and stared straight into my eyes.

"You, motherfucker," he said, "you killed him."

I just looked at him.

"You killed him," he repeated "you lassoed him and brought him down with nary a grunt."

"You talking to me?" I said.

"I'm talking to me," he said.

"I'm confused, Nathan. What are you saying?"

"I'm saying you...or, I...I brought him down with nary a grunt."

"Brought who down?"

"Dr. Epstein, fool. I brought him down, hard."

"The voices are saying you brought down Dr. Epstein, you lassoed him, you killed him? That's what the voices are saying?"

"Amen," he said, "I do believe we are communicating."

"Mr. Volknick," Moore jumped in "these voices you are hearing, are they...telling the truth?"

"I don't talk to you," he said, and turned to me. "I talk to you."

I hated to do it, but I figured I had to follow up on Moore's questions.

"So what do you say, Nathan?" I said. "What do you have to say about these...hallucinations?"

Friend leaned over to say something to him.

"Get away from me, Mr. Friend," he said. Then he took a deep breath and crossed his arms. "Doctor," he said, "the voices speak the truth. I killed Dr. Epstein."

"You killed Dr. Epstein?"

"I killed Dr. Epstein. Oh yeah."

"Nathan," his mother cried, "you're confused, please."

"I'm not confused," he said, "I killed Dr. Epstein, strangled him with a tie."

"Nathan, you don't even own a tie," his mother said.

"I bought one, that afternoon. From a street vendor."

"But why Nathan?" I said. "Why would you want to kill Dr. Epstein?"

He thought about it a minute. "Because he was there," he said.

"What the hell is that supposed to mean?"

"He was my Everest."

"Nathan, c'mon," I said, "that's crazy."

"Joey," Jake spoke up, "that's enough. Mr. Volknick, are you prepared to sign a statement confessing that you strangled Dr. Epstein on the afternoon of Friday, August 5?"

"Yes, I am," he said real solemnly. "I don't want to keep it inside anymore."

"Nathan," I said, "how exactly did you kill Dr. Epstein?"

"We had our session and he...dismissed me, as usual. I'm his last appointment of the week. The last on his list. I went to the bathroom after he closed his office door. My hands were shaking, for they knew this would be the day of the no good deed. I pulled the tie out of my pocket; it was long and red and satiny and strong. This was the day, this would be the day that I'd been thinking about a long, long time. How to tear him down; how to forever topple the larded monument of Dr. Horatio Epstein. The big barrel-ass philosopher king."

"So then what?" I said, "you said you were in the bathroom...?"

"I was in the toilet, that's right. From the toilet came the assassin. I rolled the tie in my right hand and stuffed it in my pocket. Then I exited the bathroom and tiptoed down the corridor and rapped hard and smartly on his door. I called to him and said I needed another minute of his rare and precious time. I heard him lumber to the door and when he opened it his face told me he didn't want to see me. But his words were all hypocrisy; he said, 'Nathan? Please, come in.'"

"Dr. Epstein was a very kind man, Nathan," his mother cried "he always had time for you."

"He never liked me, and he only wanted his money. He sat his fat ass down by his desk and said 'Nathan, what can I do for you?' and I said 'Dr. Epstein, sit very still, just like that.' He half-closed his eyes and said, 'Nathan what is this all about?' And then I walked around back of him and pulled the tie out. I said, 'I'm taking you home, Dr. Epstein,' and he said 'What?' and I said 'I'm taking you home, Dr. Epstein, where you belong,' and he said 'Nathan?' and began to turn around, but I said 'Whammo, Dr. E. —whammo' and I got him in my red lasso and tightened it and tightened it until I felt him snap. I brought him down with nary a grunt."

Volknick showed his teeth and gave a weird, monotone laugh. Then he looked around the room at each of us.

"With nary a grunt?" I said.

"With nary a grunt," he echoed.

"Just like that?"

"Just like that."

"I think that's some real bullshit, Nathan," I said.

His face got real red.

"You calling me a liar?"

"I'm calling you sick, I'm calling you messed up," I said, "you don't know what the hell you're saying."

Then, very suddenly, he stood up and lunged at me across the table. He knocked me to the floor in my chair and started squeezing down with both hands on my throat. Jake got on top of him but he couldn't pull him off. Moore yelled for help and a few seconds later three big guys came in and helped Jake yank him off of me. After half a minute or so, I stood up real unsteady, and tried to suck in some air. The room was spinning all around and Wilcox's crazed face burned across my brain. I thought I heard Volknick yelling something out in the hall. Little by little, I got things holding still and back in focus and I saw Jake looking at me real wide-eyed and tense.

"You satisfied now, doc?" he said, "or does he need to break your fucking neck, too?"

"He's crazy," I tried to croak.

"Oh I'll grant you that," said Jake, "he's a fucking whacko homicidal maniac."

I looked around the room and whispered: "Where is he?"

"They're taking him downstairs," said Jake. "Moore's going to try to medicate him."

"Shit."

"What, 'shit'?" said Jake "look, Joey, you did good today. You got a goddamn confession out of him, in spite of yourself."

"That was no fucking confession," I tried to yell, but only a whisper came out, "that was crazy, deranged bullshit."

Jake shook his head and laughed. "You're a stubborn son of a bitch ain't you Joey? You do a good job, and then you say it's all bullshit."

"It is."

"Joey, c'mon, think about it now, logically. This Volknick, he's got the means, he's got the opportunity, he's got the fucking motive, and he hands us a fucking confession. Now if he didn't do it I don't know who the hell did?"

"Roland," I whispered.

"Roland? C'mon, you're in dreamland, you know that? You got one goddamn hard-on for this guy. Hey, maybe Moore's right, you got some kind of Epedal complex or something."

"Gimme a break," I said, "will you?"

"A break? No deal pal. As a matter of fact you're going to be working overtime on this case. Didn't you hear that cuckoo clock yelling out in the hall? He said you're the only one he's talking to, from now on. Hey, after this case Joey who knows, we may have a permanent shrink job for you here in the department."

"Oh now that's really fucking thrilling. My fucking dream come true."

"Hey, don't knock it, Joey. What's the matter, you too good for the police department?"

"I don't think I got the temperament for it," I said, starting to get my voice back, "personnel'd screen me out in a heartbeat."

"Hey," said Jake, "that reminds me, I just got a call from personnel. They want to see you, ASAP, something about your fingerprints."

"My fingerprints?"

"Yeah, your fingerprints. There's something screwy with them, they didn't clear NCI."

"What's NCI?"

"The FBI computer, they didn't clear."

"But what fucking fingerprints?" I said. I was trying to act calm, but I was suddenly jittery as hell. "I didn't give no fucking fingerprints."

"Yeah you did."

"What the hell are you talking about?"

"About eight or nine years ago, Joey; when you were going to get that hack license."

"What?"

"'Member, you needed prints to get that taxi driver license, when you drove a cab one summer in med school. So we made up a couple of cards. And I kept one all this time."

"Yeah...but uh, but so what?"

"So I sent it down to personnel, along with, uh...an old passport picture of you, last Thursday. It was to, you know, get all our ducks in a row with your application form."

"My application form?"

"Yeah, your application form."

"But what application form? I didn't fill out any fucking application form, I just signed a couple of tax forms last week."

"Yeah, but that was just part of a whole package, Joey, with lots of forms and shit, which I was kind enough to fill out for you."

"Damn! Why the hell didn't you tell me about that, that you sent all kinds of shit about me down to personnel?"

"Well, I don't know. You were so friggin' nervous that first night you came up, about screening interviews and all that shit, I must have figured: why even mention it? But what's the difference? What...did you get busted for something, or what?"

"No...no!" I yelled.

"So what are you getting so pissed off about? Just go down there and give them some new prints, that's all they want."

I didn't say anything, but Jake could see I was real riled up.

"Look Joey, honest to God, it doesn't matter if you got busted, all right? What was it, DWI? Pot? Don't worry about it, I'll take care of it. It ain't going to matter."

"Did they say what the problem was; I mean did they say anything specifically?"

"I don't know. I just got the message through my secretary. They couldn't process the fingerprint card or something, the prints were too old or weren't good enough. Something like that. And some guy down there's all hyped up about it, so they want the problem straightened out today."

"Today?"

"Yeah, today. So look, let's go downstairs and see how our boy Volknick is doing. Then you go over across the street, Administration Building, ninth floor, and get this fingerprint shit straightened out. All right?"

"All right."

So what else could I say? I felt like a fucking cockroach trying to scramble for cover when the lights get turned on. We went downstairs and paid a visit to Volknick, who was sleeping like a baby after Moore shot him up with some industrial strength tranquilizer. His mother was off in a corner bawling and his lawyer was arguing with the cops about all kinds of violations of his client's rights. Mr. Friend came over to me and tried to get me to put together a statement saying that Volknick had given some kind of sham, delusional confession. I wanted to help out, I really did, but now my mind was really on covering my own ass. I just took his card, told him I'd call him, and walked out of the building and onto the street. I was in a daze. I looked up toward the ninth floor of the administration building across the street. No, I really don't fucking think so, I said to myself.

I TURNED AND walked up through Chinatown and toward the Village, trying to figure out what the hell I was going to do next. Can't do the fingerprints, right? Or can I? But how can I? Of course they're going to match with the prints they got back in Crossroads, and in that old Chevy in Miami. And of course they're going to haul me in and have about two dozen people I.D. me as Joseph Torento. And I've got some real explaining to do as to how my name isn't Joseph Torento and why I didn't come forward a couple of weeks ago. But worst of all, I've got no alibi to account for my whereabouts when Russ and Vera were shot. In fact, I've got nothing at all to challenge Crassidy's story with. Now that's sure some bad luck, I figured, and maybe Jackie really is on to something with that zodiac crap.

I crossed Houston Street against the light and came within maybe two inches of getting flattened by a cab. Strange that it didn't faze me, I thought. But that's how numb I was. When I got back to my place, I lay on the bed and tried to think things through. I was cornered, that was for sure, but I figured I had a couple of defensive moves. One might buy time, and the other might put a crack in Crassidy, and maybe his story.

I went down to a phone booth on Seventh Avenue and called up the Miami Police Department.

"Hello," I said, "please let me speak with the person who's supervising Horace Crassidy, supervising his cooperation with the police."

"Who is this?" they asked.

"An insider," I said, "I got some very hot, very confidential information on Crassidy. So let me speak with the people working with him."

They put me through to the office of Lieutenant Danvers.

"Danvers," he said, when he picked up the phone.

"Hi, uh, Lieutenant Danvers, I understand you're working with Horace Crassidy on the O'Connor investigation."

"That's right. Who's this?"

"An insider. That's all I can say right now. Now look, Crassidy's a worthless, scumbag murderer with a modest talent for bullshit. So far he's fooling you guys into thinking he's some innocent victim."

"Maybe. But what's this all about?"

"Crassidy's bullshit story is based on his assumption that he killed Torento, by drowning him in the cellar of Vera Parish's house back on Wednesday, August 10. What he doesn't know is that Torento survived and has been in hiding ever since."

"How do you know?"

"I got connections, okay? Bottom line is Torento's hiding out...in California...right now."

"Can you prove it?"

"Got no reason to. But I'll tell you what, you give Crassidy this message, from Torento: 'I didn't drown in the cellar that night, asshole. And soon everyone's going to know the truth. You ask him what he thinks of that, hear me? Preferably while he's hooked up to a lie detector. You'll see that son of a bitch shit a brick."

"And you give your friend Torento a message," said Danvers "the sooner he comes forward, the better it'll be for him."

"Torento's not real confident about the criminal justice system just now. But if you can get the truth out of Crassidy; that he shot O'Connor in cold blood, that he kidnapped and killed Russ and Vera after he put Torento in the cellar, that he stole all of Torento's money—not just what he gave him to cover the coke that Vera lost in the hurricane. Yeah, and you make sure you ask him about that too, the coke that Vera lost in the hurricane, when she thought the cops were coming to bust her. If you ask him about all that and he finally tells the truth—well, when Joseph Torento reads about that, he'll be real happy to come forward."

"He'd be a lot wiser to come to us now."

"I don't think so lieutenant."

"Now, look here, buddy you told me a whole lot of things and we're going to have to go back over it real slow now."

"Not too slow lieutenant. I got to get going soon."

I took a few minutes to go through the details again, and was real sure they were trying to pinpoint the whereabouts of this payphone in the meantime. I hung up as quick as I could and drifted into the crowd going up Seventh Avenue. I started to feel a little better, optimistic even, that maybe, just maybe, Crassidy would get just rattled enough when he heard this stuff, that he'd make a mistake, contradict himself somewhere, and then they could move in on him and tear apart his story.

I took a look at my watch, it was a little before five. I figured I'd gotten through today without the personnel stuff. But what about tomorrow? That was going to be sticky, and that's where my second defensive move would come in. I figured I'd stall as long as I could and, if push came to shove, I'd tell them I was resigning my position in protest of the Volknick confession. That might or might not make them go away, depending on exactly what their level of suspicion was about me, but it might buy me more time, to wait and see what would break with Crassidy. And if nothing broke? Well, I didn't want to think about that, not at the moment, anyway.

Part 6

I WALKED up to Times Square and ate at a little greasy spoon on Broadway. The overhead TV didn't say anything new on the evening news. I hung out and drank coffee and tried to get my mind back on the Epstein case. I figured if I didn't find Frontenac soon, and thereby nail Roland, Volknick was as good as fried. I couldn't let that happen, especially seeing as I was the one who got the phony confession out of him. And that was some weird confession. Roland probably hypnotized him for it. But no matter, because I was going to make this one right; for Volknick's sake, for my sake, and somehow for Wilcox's sake as well.

This was the night, Tuesday, that Frontenac was supposed to be back at Club Daylight, and I was either going to see her there or find out where the hell she was. After a pot of bad coffee and some stale lemon meringue pie, I made my way back downtown to the velvet roped entrance of Club Daylight. A big bald-headed goon at the door recognized me right away.

"Good evening sir," he said "good to see you again."

"Evening," I said. I reckoned I was starting to get treated like a regular at this dump.

I went inside and made my way into the big lounge, already half-full of three-piece suits and loud-mouthed out-of-towners, and sat down on a stool by the bar. The same bartender was there as from the first night. His big, over-hanging forehead was glistening under the lights and he gave me a big, gold-toothed grin.

"Hello, old friend," he said in his gruff accent, "how are you tonight?"

"Fine, thanks," I said.

"And you are here to see your friend tonight, yes?"

"That's right. She here?"

"I have not seen her; but she will be here tonight."

"How do you know?"

"Her name is on the stage sign, see?"

I turned around and saw her name written on a program sign to the side of the stage.

"And how about some good whiskey for you tonight?" he asked

me.

"Sure," I said, "what do you have?"

He showed me a bottle of some expensive-looking single malt, and poured me a double.

"This one is on the house, because of the misunderstanding the other night."

"Well, thanks," I said, "thank you."

"When she came back that night, she told me you are absolutely a good man, and very well-behaved."

"Glad to hear it. Cheers."

I raised the glass and took a sip. It was real good stuff.

"And all the best to you," he said, "all the best."

"Thanks. My name's Joe, by the way," I said, and shook hands with him.

"Yes, I am Ara. Good to meet you, Joseph."

"Same here. And tell me something Ara, have you seen Ms. Frontenac since the other night here?"

"No. No I haven't."

"And is she usually pretty good about showing up for work?"

"As far as I know, she is a very dependable girl," he said, smiling, "but now please excuse me, you see I'm getting very busy."

"Sure. But just one more thing Ara. This may sound like kind of a crazy question, but do you know if Ms. Frontenac has ever gone by any other name, like 'Sabrina Briand'?"

"This I don't know Joseph," he said, as he walked away, "but I don't really know the girl very good."

He went over to serve a carload of guys who'd just arrived, and I leaned back against the bar and sipped my drink. I looked around the growing crowd but didn't see Frontenac anyplace. Very dependable girl, I thought, that's what he said. "Well, let's hope you're right Ara", I muttered to myself, and sipped away at my single malt.

Then the stage lights suddenly went on, and the room filled with pounding music and flashing lights. Two girls came whirling out on stage and started doing their thing. Neither of them was Ms. Frontenac.

So I sat and drank, and looked at my watch, and I eventually waited through four more acts, but still there was no sign of Ms. Frontenac. By this time the place was jammed and my buddy behind the bar had given me another double.

"You know about when she's coming on, tonight, Ara?" I asked him.

"I am not sure Joseph, but I suppose very soon."

I hung out for another half an hour or so, but she still didn't show up. So I got up to go find the manager, and felt real sloppy walking through the crowd. It felt like the booze had really caught up with me. I went up to an important-looking guy near the ticket window and asked him where Frontenac was tonight.

"Who?"

"Frontenac. Wilhelmina Frontenac, one of the dancers."

"Not here," he snapped.

"But she's scheduled tonight, right?"

"She canceled."

"When?"

"Couple of hours ago."

"Why?"

"Still sick, that's what she said on the machine. By the way, who are you?"

"Dr. Joe Toricelli, I'm working with the police. And, uh, do you know where she called from?"

"Hey, I don't know doc," he said, "I hardly even know the girl. But uh, you know, I guess she called from home."

"All right," I said, "thanks."

I went over to a payphone and called her at home. As usual, there was no answer. Then I went back to the guy by the ticket window.

"Look," I said, "I know you hardly know the girl, but do you have any idea where else she could be besides at home? Does she have friends or family, or a boyfriend? Anything?"

"I don't know, doc, I really don't know."

"And do you know if anybody else in this place knows anything about her?"

"Not that I know of. But look, what's she in trouble or something?"

"No," I said, "I mean, I don't know."

THAT SETTLED IT, I thought. I checked my pocket to see that I had Frontenac's address: 570 Krueger Place, Brooklyn. I was going to have to pay her a visit, face-to-face. I walked out to 18th Street and took a few deep breaths of fresh air. I was feeling pretty rough in the head, kind of foggy and heavy and slow, and I figured I'd clear up a little on the walk to the subway station. I headed west toward Sixth Avenue, down those blocks with the big loft buildings. It was close to midnight and pretty quiet. I got a little ways down a block between 5th and 6th when I heard something hit the wall next to me, then again and again, like a "ping, ping, ping." I stepped away from the wall and looked up, thinking something was breaking overhead. Then I heard something click up the street and I turned and saw this brick shithouse of a guy with dark glasses walking on the other side, maybe a hundred feet up from me. It looked like he had something in his left hand. He stepped down the curb to cross, but he had to wait for a couple of cabs to go speeding by. I stepped up my pace, keeping an eye on him over my shoulder, and saw him cross diagonally after the cabs went by, and speed up after me. Is this for real? —I thought—is this guy after me? I didn't have to ponder that much further when I saw him raise a gun in both his hands, it looked like it had a silencer attached, and point it straight at my head. You're a fucking dead man, I thought to myself. Get the fuck out of here!

I started running down the block, close as I could to the wall, and dove to the left down a narrow passageway. It was pitch black in front of me, and about ten yards in I fell over some garbage cans and heard a bunch of rats scrambling and squealing around me. He came to the entrance of the passageway, I didn't think he could see me, and started firing bullets that whistled by and ricocheted over my head. I crawled on my belly, quick as I could, deeper into the darkness, hoping I'd find some kind of alleyway or escape route in back of the building. He stopped shooting and started coming after me. I heard him stumble over the garbage cans and figured he fell flat on his face. I sprang up and ran to the end of the building and hung a right into a short, dead-end alleyway, dimly lit by a single bulb over a ground floor window. I grabbed a garbage can, stood up on it, and jumped up to grip the bottom of the fire escape. I figured I had about ten seconds of climbing time before this son of a bitch was going to turn the corner and start putting holes in me.

I hoisted myself up and ran up a few flights before I heard him run into the alleyway. His footsteps stopped suddenly, and then picked up again. It sounded like he was walking around down there, checking in every corner to see where I was. I had stopped on a landing so as not to make any noise, and when I looked down I saw his shadowy form moving around that grimy space, like some dreadful, evil ghost. He started backing away from the building, trying to look up the fire escape for me. I was well above the light bulb and it was too dark for him to see me. But just to be on the safe side, I slowly pressed back against the bars of a big window I was near. As I stepped back I bumped into a big cement flowerpot someone had left on the sill. He heard the noise and shot up at the window, shattering the panes behind the bars. Shit, I thought, I'm going to end up as target practice for this maggot. I reached down real slowly and picked up the flowerpot. I figured if I wasn't lucky enough to smash it on his skull I might at least create enough confusion to go another few flights, which would get me near the roof.

I leaned over and heaved the thing in the general vicinity of his head...at the same time screaming out some bullshit like, "Put up your hands—police!" Then I started hauling ass up the stairs. There was a loud crash, and then I heard him hollering, "You fucking mother fucker,

I kill you, I kill you, you fucking fucker!" More bullets flew by but I scrambled to the top without a scratch. I sprinted across the rooftops toward Sixth Avenue, yanked open the skylight of the building on the corner, and flew down the staircase and out the front door. I jumped into a cab at the corner light, told the driver 570 Krueger Place, Brooklyn, and sat back to catch my breath and double-check that I hadn't been hit. I was all right ballistics-wise, but my head was pounding and I was having trouble focusing on things. I figured my new buddy Ara had slipped me a Mickey just to get even more favorable odds going for the grim reaper in the alleyway. I sure hoped I'd put a good dent in that bastard's skull.

But, I thought, who is it who's really trying to kill me, and why? Is it Roland, paying off goons and hit men to keep me off his trail? I couldn't exactly figure it, but I believed more than ever that Frontenac held the key to everything. The cab bumped along through the tunnel, down the Prospect Expressway and over to Coney Island Avenue. The streets were real quiet, it must have been around one in the morning by this time. When we drove under the El that crossed near the end of Coney Island Avenue, the cab driver told me the 500 block of Krueger Place was just another block away.

"Then I'll get out here," I said.

I PAID THE FARE and hopped out of the cab and over to a little corner deli that was still open. I bought a big cup of coffee there and guzzled it down in one swoop. It actually did straighten me out a little, after the stuff I'd been served at Daylight. Then I went over to Krueger Place and walked down a long, dark block lined with old shabby apartment houses, looking around for Ms. Frontenac's address. You could hear the air conditioners humming in the windows and smell the ocean, which was just a stone's throw away.

I got up to the front door of 570 Krueger Place, a big old gray apartment house built right up to the edge of the boardwalk, and saw the name "Frontenac" listed by the row of doorbell buttons. She was in apartment 5-E. The front door was locked, so I rang her buzzer several times, figuring I'd have to wake up whoever was in there. I waited awhile, got no response from the door buzzer, and rang again real long, a couple of times. Still nothing. I didn't know what the hell was going on but I figured the next step was to get into the building, and into that apartment, one way or another.

I walked back out to the street and around the building, seeing if there was any other way to get in. There were a couple of basement doors in the back, but they were both locked. Then I came back around front, and saw a woman standing by the front door, taking some keys out of her purse. I walked toward her and waited for her to unlock the door. She must have heard me coming and she turned and gave me an uneasy smile.

"Evening," I said.

"Good evening," she said, and seemed to study me.

I gestured for her to go first and then I walked in behind her. She turned at the corridor and I went for the stairs.

"Good night," I told her.

I got up to the fifth floor and found apartment 5-E at the end of the hall. I listened by the door for a few seconds, but there wasn't a sound coming from inside. I rang the bell a couple of times, it clanged real loud. No one came to the door. I tried to peer into the little peephole, just to see if there was any light inside, but I couldn't see a thing. Without really thinking, I put my hand on the doorknob, squeezed it real slowly and started to twist it. It moved and didn't stop 'til I made almost a full turn. I pushed the door a little and didn't feel any resistance. Could it be it's not locked? I pushed a little more and, sure enough, it opened.

I stepped just over the threshold and took a peek inside. It was pretty dark in there, but it looked like the door opened into a small entrance foyer.

"Hello," I said, "hello, Ms. Frontenac?"

No answer.

"Hello, hello. This is Joe Toricelli, police department."

No answer. The place was dead quiet. I took a few steps into the foyer and tried to look around. Straight ahead was a doorway that looked like it opened into a small kitchen. To the left and right were two other doorways.

"Hello," I said again. "Anybody home? This is Joe Toricelli, New York City Police Department."

Not a sound. Nothing but the echoes of my own voice. I felt along the wall and flipped on a light switch. A little nightlight in a socket near the floor went on. There was enough light to see the foyer was empty. I walked to the doorway at the right and looked in. There were a couple of open windows where you could hear the waves breaking on the beach.

"Hello? Anybody home?"

Just my echo again, this time it was louder. I looked around the room, as best I could in the dim light. I couldn't see the outline of any furniture, there weren't any curtains on the windows and the walls and the floor looked bare. I stepped back into the foyer and looked through the doorway on the left. A street light shone through the window and reflected across a bare wooden floor. There was more than enough light to see the room was totally empty. Then I went around the whole place, basically a small one-bedroom apartment, and checked the closets, the bathroom, the little kitchen. The whole place was empty, cleaned out really; no utensils, no toilet paper, no hangers in the closets. Nothing in there but that little nightlight in the hallway.

"So what's going on, Ms. Frontenac?" I muttered, "where the hell are you?"

I LEFT THE APARTMENT and went to sit on a bench on the boardwalk. I tried to think about what to do, who to talk to, where to go look next. But everything was all jumbled up in my mind and my head was starting to pound again. I lay down on the bench to rest a few minutes, and didn't wake up until the sun was coming over the water and shining in my face. It was around seven, and I got up and walked back to the corner by the el. There was a little breakfast place open and I went in and sat down at a table and got some coffee. My head was more or less on straight again and I decided first thing I had to do was call Jake and tell him that Frontenac, for all practical purposes, had disappeared. Then, of course, there was the sticky little matter of the fingerprints. I'd just have to stall him on that, that's all.

I leaned over and picked up a copy of the *Herald* off another table, and saw a police composite of Joe Torento taking up most of the front page. I was still bearded, and the eyes were drawn a lot more accurately. Those renderings are getting closer and closer, I thought to myself. The headline read: "O'Connor Killer Hiding out with New York Mob?"

I turned to the story on the inside pages. It boiled down to this: "undisclosed police sources" told the *Herald* that the Miami cops had gotten "an anonymous message, traced to a Manhattan payphone." The caller said Torento was hiding out in California, and wasn't going to come forward until Crassidy confessed to the crime. But, "according to investigators in Miami," they had "reason to believe that Torento himself had actually made the call, and was being harbored by an organized crime connection in New York." Now what kind of half-assed thinking led them to that conclusion, I thought. A conclusion which, unfortunately for me, was exactly half right. At this rate, I thought, I could well get nailed before I ever find Frontenac, or have a chance to save Volknick's neck.

The waiter came over to pour me more coffee.

"You want something else sir?" he asked.

"No thanks," I said, "that's fine.

He seemed to stare at me for a few seconds, and I wondered what the hell he was looking at. Did I look like Joe Torento in the *Herald* or was I just real wasted looking from the Daylight drinks and sleeping in my clothes on the boardwalk bench?

"Something wrong?" I asked him.

"No, no sir," he said, and walked away.

I went to pour some cream in my coffee and, out of the corner of my eye saw an old lady, a couple of tables away, looking at me. I turned to look straight at her and she looked away.

No way, I thought, no way they could recognize me. Could they? Then I saw a guy at another table, maybe twenty feet away, looking straight at me. He didn't even turn when our eyes met, and I was the one who looked away. What the hell is going on, I thought, do I really look like the guy in the *Herald?* I looked up again. The guy at the table was still staring at me. I'd had it now, with all this attention, I thought. I stood up, threw a couple of bills on the table and started walking out.

As I got near the door, I heard a man's voice call,

"Sir, excuse me sir."

I kept looking straight ahead.

"You sir," he said, "by the door."

No buddy, I thought, you mean out the door.

"Sir," he said again, real loud now. Then I heard him coming after me.

Just as I opened the door he grabbed my arm.

"What do you want?" I said.

It was the waiter.

"Sir," he said, smiling kind of sheepishly, "you don't want any change?"

He held out the money I'd put on the table, a one-dollar bill and a fifty.

"Yeah, right," I shook my head, "thanks, my mistake." I took back the money and gave him a five.

"Keep the change, really appreciate it," I said.

"Thank you sir."

False alarm, I thought, get a grip. I took a quick look over the room. The old lady was sitting at her table sipping her tea and mumbling something to herself. And the guy I thought was staring at me was digging into a couple of big sausages. Neither of them looked like they gave a damn about me. But then all of a sudden, the guy with the sausages looked familiar to me. He was kind of square-headed, with big shoulders, and pretty short looking even though he was sitting down. That's what's-his-name, I thought, the little Russian guy who rescued me at Vera's that's...Gene. For a second I wasn't sure what to do, but I figured no...I've got to talk to him. Yeah, definitely, I've got to talk to him. He could even be my alibi, couldn't he? And maybe help me out of this whole friggin' O'Connor mess. I walked over to him, slowly, kind of double-checking to make sure that was really him. Yeah, yeah, I thought, it's no mirage, that's him. Meanwhile, he was chewing on his sausage and looking away from me. It was like he wanted to avoid me now, like he wished we hadn't seen each other.

I walked over to him while he stuffed a big piece of kielbasa in his mouth.

"Gene?" I said.

He looked up at me, chewing, with no sign that he recognized me.

I sat down across from him.

"Gene, it's me," I said, "Joe, remember? From the basement in Crossroads Key."

He stopped chewing and opened his eyes real wide.

"Yeah, that's right," I said, "you remember me now?"

"Oh my God!" he said, through a mouthful of kielbasa, "it's unbelievable."

"It is unbelievable," I said "what the hell are you doing here anyway?"

"Business," he said, after he swallowed the sausage. "Anya's aunt is owner here, and wants Anya to be new boss, so we came from Philadelphia last week."

"No kidding?"

"No, no kidding," he said, "and so I came to help move her furniture. It doesn't look like she needs me for anything else. But, please Joseph, now I must ask, what the hell are *you* doing here?"

"Well that's a real long story," I said. "But, basically I'm here on a police investigation. Problem of a young lady missing."

"I see," he said, "but, Joseph, there is something I don't understand. You are in very big serious trouble, yes?"

"Well, uh...you could put it that way, if you want to believe the papers."

"You see, in papers, Joseph," he said, "there are so many stories, that you killed many people, yes?"

"Yeah, but those are bullshit stories, Gene. Criminal propaganda from the criminal mind of Horace Crassidy."

"This is what I said Joseph, and it is what Anya said too. It is all bullshit propaganda. But why Joseph? Maybe you were in some trouble with government and now CIA makes this story."

"No, nothing so fancy as that. It's just a lot of confusion, and people being in the wrong place at the wrong time, that's all."

"But this criminal man they have on TV, he tells the police, the journalists you are murderer. And it seems to me many people believes him."

"That's the real son of a bitch who killed everybody. And he's the one who tied me up there in the cellar where you and Anya found me."

"And you are frightened to argue with this man Joseph? Police will not believe you?"

"That's a real long story," I said, "but the bottom line is I decided a while back, that going to the police wasn't going to do me, or anybody else any good..."

"No?"

"No. Unless...unless, that is, you and Anya want to tell the police how you found me. As a matter of fact, that could really help."

"How this could help?" he said, sounding like he doubted it.

"It could support my story. That I was tied up under the house while Crassidy made his getaway. And probably when he killed Vera and Russ, the mother and son he took as hostages."

"But, Joseph, for me to go to police. For many questions. It's...it's not comfortable for me. It is even dangerous. I have already problems with government in this country, and with police. No Joseph, I cannot go to police, it is impossible."

"Impossible?"

"Yes, Joseph. Absolutely impossible."

"That bad, huh?" I said. "Well, maybe on second thought, it's not exactly a guaranteed alibi anyway. The timing's not tight enough, for when you found me and when they estimated Russ and Vera got killed.

"I'm very sorry Joseph," he said, looking real ashamed, "I really am."

"Hey don't worry about it. Look, I'm not exactly in a big hurry to turn myself in, in any case. And besides, I don't think Crassidy's bullshit story can hold up much longer anyway."

He smiled. "Yes Joseph, and believe me, this haircut, this shaving, it's very, very good disguise for you."

"That's good to know, but hey...what about when you were staring at me when I was sitting over there before. You didn't think I looked familiar?"

"What? No, no. I thought you were Ivan—dirty pig who owes me money. You look like him."

"Gee, thanks a lot."

"No, Joseph...you don't understand..."

"Forget it," I said, "I'm just busting your balls."

We had a few laughs and drank some coffee, and I decided to fill him in on the details of the Epstein case, including how I was almost killed and how I'd walked into Frontenac's empty apartment at the edge of Brighton Beach.

"It's strange Joseph," he said, "very strange. It must be somebody is hiding this girl, yes? Or someone has killed her?"

"Maybe. But tell me, what about her name...or names...Frontenac, Briand...are those names you've heard in this neighborhood?"

"No, Joseph. They sound French, yes? Not names for this neighborhood. This is almost one hundred percent Russian neighborhood." Then he looked over at somebody behind me. "Anya," he called, "Anya." He waved to her to come over.

"What is it?" she asked.

"Come here, now. I want you to meet very good, old friend."

She came over and sat down beside Gene.

"So Anya," said Gene, "how do you think he looks?"

Anya examined me for a few seconds, and little by little a smile came to her face.

"So," she said, softly, "our famous friend. You look better shaved and with this haircut."

"Thanks," I said. "Nice to see you again, Anya."

"You didn't tell us what a dangerous man you are in Florida," she said, "you were afraid you could scare us?"

"I didn't know how dangerous I was either. I found out later, in the news, just like you."

"But Anya," said Gene, "Joseph is working on very complicated investigation now, this is the reason he is here."

"Investigation? But what about your own case?"

"I think that's going to take care of itself," I said. "This criminal Crassidy, he's the one who really killed these people, and put me in that cellar. He's got to make a mistake, you wait and see."

"And you are working for police and they don't know who you are?" she asked.

"That's about right."

"It's very strange situation Joseph. Unbelievable."

"I'm having trouble believing it myself, Anya. If I thought it'd go this far, with people actually accepting Crassidy's story, maybe I'd have played it differently and come forward a long time ago. But now...well Gene and I have already talked about it. I'm just going to lay low as long as I can."

"You can hide here," said Gene. "Anya's family can find good room for you."

Anya looked at Gene, as if to say who the hell are you to be making invitations?

"Well, thanks Gene, but let's see how things go for now," I said. "But tell me something Anya, about your family. Do they know this neighborhood pretty well?"

"Yes. My aunt, my cousins, their children. They live in Brighton Beach a long time now."

"Yeah? Well maybe they know something about this girl I'm looking for. She's involved somehow in the murder of her doctor and...she seems to have disappeared."

"What is her name?"

"Frontenac. Wilhelmina Frontenac. Ring a bell?"

"And where is her house?"

"Around the corner. 570 Krueger Place, a big apartment house near the boardwalk."

"Excuse me, Joseph," she said. She turned to Gene and started going on and on with him in Russian. He was nodding his head, at times looking surprised, even worried. I couldn't make out any of it. After a while, I started to lose my patience.

"Hey guys," I said, "what's all the talk about?"

"Joseph," said Anya, turning to me, "speak with me frankly, what do you know about this girl?"

"Not too much, that she's a dancer, at a place called Club Daylight, in Manhattan. That she's used another name in the past, Sabrina Briand. That she's supposedly from Belgium or Italy, or who knows where. And uh, well, she's needed psychiatric treatment."

"Uh-huh, that's all?"

"Yeah, that about wraps it up."

"That's good Joseph. You don't need to know more. You have enough of your own troubles already."

"What's that supposed to mean?"

"You should hide yourself, 'lay low' you said, until they catch this criminal Crassidy in his lies."

"Yeah, fine," I said, "but an innocent man is going to go to prison for the murder of this doctor. And the real killer, and whatever his motivation was, is never going to get found out, until I find Frontenac."

"And is it so important to you?" she asked.

"Yes."

"Why?"

"'Cause I'm in the middle of it, and I've got a chance to do something right. An innocent man is going to go to prison."

She laughed. "You are very naive man, Joseph. You have some silly idealism. Some things are better for you to forget about."

"Anya," an old woman called from the kitchen door, and shouted out something to her in Russian.

"Excuse me," said Anya, getting up, "you may stay here, for now, Joseph. Have some tea...and you will do better if you stop asking questions about this girl."

Gene got up with her. "I have some jewelry business this morning," he said, "in Sheepshead Bay. But stay here Joseph, I will be back."

"But Anya..." I said.

"I will come back to you Joseph," she said, "but first I must help my aunt. You look very hungry. I will send you some breakfast."

They obviously knew something about Frontenac and didn't want to tell. But what? What the hell could be so dangerous that I shouldn't know more about it? I wanted to run back in the kitchen and shake it out of Anya. But...well I can't force the issue, I thought, not just yet anyway, not with the only people I can trust to cover me.

I looked at my watch. It was close to nine. Maybe this morning, I thought, maybe this morning they'll pitch Crassidy my curve ball about Torento crawling out of the basement. And if he freaks about that, I'm home free. It was a real long shot, I knew that, but basically the only bet I could make right now. Meanwhile, Jake had to be shitting a brick about those fingerprints and wondering where the hell I was. But I figured I'd hold off on calling him, at least until I could give him something more about Frontenac.

While I waited for Anya, I got served one helluva breakfast. A huge schnitzel with a fried egg, potatoes, boiled beef, bowls of herring and caviar, a big pot of tea and a half a loaf of heavy, bitter black bread. I ate like a horse and couldn't believe how hungry I was. If I had to hide out from the law, I figured, there'd be a lot worse places than this. As I was just finishing off everything, Anya came back from the kitchen.

"Great breakfast," I said to her, "thanks a lot."

"You need more tea?"

"No thanks. I'm fine for now."

She threw back her hair and sat down across from me.

"It is busy here almost all day," she said, "my uncle was the manager, but he is sick now. My aunt tries, but she is very slow. So it's up to me to be the boss now."

"Like it okay?" I said.

"It's only been a week. But yes, it's okay."

"So look, Anya," I said, "I know you think I ought to keep my nose out of things, but...uh...what gives with this Ms. Frontenac, what is it I shouldn't know?"

She looked around the room for a second and then leaned toward me, speaking softly. "I don't know this girl," she said, "but I heard she moved out very suddenly yesterday afternoon."

"Yesterday afternoon, huh?" I said, and thought about how that coincided real well with me finding out about Sabrina Briand. "So how'd you hear about that?"

"My cousin's husband, he is the super in this building. He was talking about her yesterday."

"So what else did he say?"

"She is crazy and she works in Mafioso club in Manhattan."

"Daylight."

"He didn't say that name. Maybe it is this club."

"So did he say why she moved out? Where she went?"

"He doesn't know. He was angry because they made such trouble for him moving out. Nobody told him, and the neighbors complained about the noise and all the mess."

"Was anybody with her?"

"I remember he said some very bad looking guys took her away. It looked like she didn't want to go. It was real scary."

"Son of a bitch," I said, "but look Anya, I've got to talk with your cousin's husband."

"Joseph, believe me, this is not something you need right now. It's some Russian Mafia thing, you don't need it."

"Look, I'm already a fugitive from the Miami police and the FBI, not to mention a deadbeat with the South Florida Mafia. So what's a little attention from the Russian mob?"

"You think it's a big joke?"

"Might be the best way to look at it, for now. But Anya, let me speak with your cousin's husband."

"He will not tell you more. He will be frightened to say anything to some...stranger."

"So tell him I'm a friend of yours...yours and hers, and I just want to see if there is any way I can get in touch with her. It's very important Anya, you've got to help me out here."

She looked away from me.

"Anya, c'mon. We'll take a little stroll over there right now. We're talking about saving somebody's life here, and solving a murder."

She looked at me for a long time. Then she said, "Naive idealistic man. Come, we go now. And you must not tell him you are with police."

We left the restaurant and walked to the apartment building. By day it looked even more gray and drab than it did at night. It was called the Brightwater. We walked through the front door of the building, which was unlocked during the day, and over to her cousin's family's apartment, which was on the first floor, just off the lobby.

Anya was about to ring the doorbell when a big fat guy with a bald head and a Mets T-shirt opened the door.

"Ah Sergei, good morning," said Anya.

"Yes, good morning," he said, "and looked at her and then at me and then back at her again."

"Sergei," Anya said, "this is Joseph."

We looked at each other and nodded.

"Joseph is a friend of mine, and he is also an acquaintance of this girl, this Miss Frontenac."

"Oh my God," he said, "you don't find her here, she is gone away,

away."

"Yes, yes I heard all about that Sergei," I said, "but what I want to know is, do you have any idea where to?"

"Hah," he laughed, "it is not my business. She just go, that's all."

"But no address of where she's gone to?" I said, "nothing?"

"Hah," he laughed again "she was in very big hurry. No, no address. But look here, what mailman leave with me this morning."

He reached inside his door and pulled a box off a little table.

"It's package," he said, "it's my habit to sign and hold it for her."

"No kidding?" I said, "well, let's take a look at it, where's it from?"

"Moscow. See," he said, and pointed to the return address.

"What's it say?" I said, "I don't read Russian too well."

Anya took a look at it.

"1322 Prospect Mira, Apartment 11-B-L-V," she said.

"And who's the person who sent it?" I asked.

"No name," said Sergei.

"Well let's open it up," I said.

Sergei just shrugged and Anya didn't say anything. I took the box from Sergei and unwrapped it. Inside was a box of Red October chocolates, and a card with a note.

"Anya," I said, "read this please, see who it's from."

"It's a birthday card," she said. "It says: 'My dear kitten, happy birthday and best wishes for all the future. I miss you very much. If you decide to come to Moscow, call me as soon as you arrive. I will be back from dacha on twentieth of August. Love and kisses, Aunt Valentina.'"

"Aunt Valentina, huh?" I said, "and we got a telephone number for this aunt, or a last name?"

Anya shook her head. "No," she said, "that's it."

"And she doesn't use her name anywhere?" I said, "just 'kitten'?"

"The only name I see is Wilhelmina Frontenac on the address."

"This is good firm for making chocolates Joseph," said Sergei "you and Anya should try."

I took one and popped it in my mouth. "Yeah, delicious," I said, "and say, Sergei, did you ever know of Ms. Frontenac being called by another name, such as Sabrina Briand?"

"No Joseph," he said, "I never hear any other name for her and no such name as this Sabrina Briand."

"I see," I said, "by the way, you want a chocolate?"

His mouth opened wide. "Of course," he said and grabbed a handful.

"I guess they're yours now Sergei," I said, and handed him the box. "You signed for them. I just need to write down this address of Aunt Valentina's here."

AFTER I SCRIBBLED it down, we left Sergei to chow down on the birthday present, and walked back toward the restaurant.

"I've got to get to this Aunt Valentina," I told Anya, on the way, "who knows, maybe Ms. Frontenac's in Moscow right now, right at her aunt's place."

"And if she is, so what?" said Anya, "what will you do?"

"I don't know yet, but today's already the twenty-second, so this Aunt Valentina's back from her dacha. I could send her a telegram to call me.

Anya laughed. "And what will it say, that she should call New York police immediately because her niece is a murder suspect?"

"Well, I think we could word it a little more subtly than that."

Anya was quiet for a moment, and then she said, "Probably I can find this Valentina for you, and even find out if she has seen her niece."

"That's great. How?"

Anya looked at her watch. "Now it is six in the evening in Moscow. I may call my sister, who lives maybe twenty minutes from Prospect Mira station. She can go to this woman's home, and say she is an acquaintance of a friend of Ms. Frontenac's in America. She can say she is there to give Ms. Frontenac some message and then she can ask if she has been there, or where she is now."

"Perfect," I said, "and let the message be to call Anya at your number here, if that's okay. I don't exactly want to advertise my whereabouts right now."

"Yes, it's okay Joseph."

"And tell your sister to ask about this other name too, Sabrina Briand."

"I will Joseph."

When we got back to the restaurant, I went to a booth while Anya went to call her sister. It was after ten and I figured Jake must be wondering where the hell I was. This fingerprint thing wasn't going to go away, I thought, but it would sure as hell get a lot less messy if Crassidy would just stumble over his story a little. There was a TV on over the lunch counter and I got up and switched it to the all news station. C'mon, I thought, let's hear something good, like how Crassidy broke down and confessed, and how they'll be seeking the death penalty for him. But there was nothing. Nothing at all about the O'Connor case. Just more than you wanted to know about weather patterns over North America. Then Anya returned from the kitchen, smiling.

"She will go to this woman's house now Joseph, so maybe you will know something very soon."

"Beautiful," I said, "that's just beautiful." I was really beginning to like this girl; those green eyes, that willowy walk, the way she called me 'Joseph'.

"Do you want some tea?" she asked.

"Sure, thank you."

She went to the kitchen and brought back a kettle and poured us a couple of cups. Then she sat down across from me in the booth. The place had quieted down since the breakfast rush and, besides us, there was only the old lady who'd been there since early this morning, still mumbling to herself.

"I really appreciate what you're doing," I said, "you may be saving this guy's, Volknick's his name, you may be saving his life."

"We'll see," she smiled, "but this situation of yours Joseph, it still seems to me, unbelievable, yes?"

"I know what you mean. I still keep thinking I'm going to wake up from a bad dream."

"But how Joseph, can you tell me really, how you are in this situation?"

"I can tell you Anya. And, as a matter of fact, I really want to."

So, I explained everything to her; how my name's really Toricelli, where I came from, how I lost my father and how I was raised. Then what happened with Wilcox, and the whole mean seven-year life of Joe Torento too. Right up to Russ, Vera, Crassidy, the O'Connor murder, the whole bit. And, of course, how I didn't expect the misdeeds, real and alleged, of Joe Torento to ever start shadowing me so close.

"But he is you Joseph," she said. "How can you run away?"

"Good question. I probably should have asked it a long while back. Same way I'm my old man's son, I tried to forget that too, 'cause it hurt too much."

"Strange, strange, man, you are," she said, and poured some more tea in my cup.

"And what about you, how does your life story go? I only got a little sketch back there in Florida."

She laughed, and said, "Not so complicated as yours."

"Well, somehow that doesn't shock me. But still, there must have been a few twists and turns along the way, that got you from Russia to Philadelphia to Brighton Beach."

"And Florida."

"Right. Let's not forget Florida, and the brave deeds of Senya, Anya and Gene."

Again she smiled, and those green eyes of hers really shone. I was really liking this girl, and something warm was dancing inside of me, and whispering to me that she really liked me too.

"Yes. And so Joseph," she said, "as I told you, I came from a city not far from Moscow. It is Yaroslavl. My parents are living there with my brother. I came to this country two years ago. Just before that, I was living in Moscow."

"With your sister?"

"No. She goes to university and lives with another girl."

"I see. So what were you doing in Moscow?"

Again she smiled, but this time a little too much, like she was a little nervous talking about herself. Then she said, "With me Joseph, it happened like this. I lived in Yaroslavl until I was 18. I studied in the business high school and became a secretary for a very rich man. He did business in Moscow and in Yaroslavl. Very soon, he fell in love with me, and he rented for me a very beautiful apartment in the center of Moscow. There I lived almost four years."

"With him?"

"Sometimes. But he traveled and...he had to spend time with his family...his wife, and his children. Also in Moscow."

"I see. So that gets kind of complicated."

"It was very uncomfortable for me. But he gave me good work, a house, and money. And he made plans to marry me."

"Yeah? So what happened?"

She poured herself some more tea, and said, "I will tell you. He began to treat me with anger and...how do you say...he became suspicious of me. He made many accusations, that I had boyfriends to the apartment when he was away. And sometimes he would get drunk...and beat me."

"That's rotten," I said, "and rotten enough to squash any marriage plans, I guess."

She looked down at her teacup. "It became more...more complicated. Because another man, American businessman, fell in love with me. Very nice man. He had an assignment in Moscow for several months. And Andre, this was Russian man, he saw us together one time in a cafe."

"I'm sure that didn't help things."

"He became very angry. Even a little crazy. One minute he says he must marry me, and the next minute he says he will kill me, and then himself."

She took a deep breath, and you could see the whole thing still made her feel really bad.

"I told all of my situation to Stephen, this is American man, and he said that he and I should marry, and we will live in America, in his town of Philadelphia. He was...is...a very nice man, a little like my father, and about the same age. So, a little less than two years ago, I received a visa and came to Philadelphia and married Stephen."

"I see. And, uh...and where's Stephen now?"

"In Philadelphia, living in our house."

"So you divorced or..."

"I am still married...legally. But I do not love him. I never did. He is nice, very nice man. But for me to stay with him, when I do not love him, no it's impossible."

"Well, at least he was your ticket out of Russia," I said, and the second I said it, I really wished I hadn't. She looked at me real hard.

"You can look at it this way if you want," she said, "but I sincerely thought I could love him. No, I did not want to stay in my country. I did not want to be poor, or a slave of some crazy man, it is true. But I thought I could love him, I told myself this when I came to America."

I felt like a real heel. "Things change," I said, "that's for sure. And your heart can't just follow your head."

"This is for sure Joseph, and...maybe I should feel ashamed. That I leave my husband, who is a good man, and come to live here, and look for a new life."

"Does he know you're here?"

"Yes, of course. He calls all the time, and he cries, and he begs me to come back to him."

"Poor guy. But hey, you got to do what you got to do."

She started to cry, just a little, and her face softened and I could clearly see the teenage girl leaving Yaroslavl five or six years ago. I could feel myself warming up to her more and more.

Then her aunt called from the kitchen. "Anya," she said, and something about the "telephone."

"Excuse me," she said, getting up.

"No problem, maybe we'll get some interesting news."

From the kitchen I could hear her speaking in Russian. I could only make out the name "Katerina", her sister's I guessed, and something that sounded like "Frontenac." In a minute, she came back to the booth.

"It's some interesting news for you, Joseph," she said. "It seems this girl Frontenac was visiting her Aunt Valentina, maybe yesterday. But she does not stay there now."

"So where is she?" I asked.

"This aunt would not say. She is very strange old woman and became...suspicious of so many questions. She closed the door very rudely on my sister, and did not take message with phone number."

"And did your sister ask her about this name, Briand?"

"She did not have a chance to."

"Damn it. And can your sister get this aunt's number? Or maybe her last name?"

"My sister said she lives in very old, dirty apartment house, and there was no name on the door."

"What about in the lobby?"

Anya laughed. "You don't know Moscow apartment houses, Joseph. It is the usual case that there are no names. And no lobby."

"Shit. Uh, excuse me Anya...I mean, that's a bad situation. And it's not enough to work with. Maybe I can call the Moscow cops"

"Joseph, please," she said, "for them this will not be serious. And what will you tell them?"

"Yeah, you're right," I said, "I can't even convince my own cop cousin something's wrong, or phony, with Ms. Frontenac."

"And you have your own problems."

"Yeah, don't remind me. I need to just disappear, or else I'm on my way to getting booked."

"You already tried to disappear."

"Right. Bad idea. But hey...wait a second...maybe not such a bad idea."

"What do you mean?"

"I don't know. I don't know exactly what I mean...yet. But look, Anya, you've been...lovely, absolutely lovely."

"Yes?" she smiled.

"Yes, absolutely lovely," I looked into those dreamy, soft green eyes. "But now...I'm going to need to go. I've got to speak with my cousin, the policeman, there's a whole lot of stuff I've got to discuss with him."

"You will be arrested?"

"I don't know. I mean no, I don't think so."

I kissed her lightly on the cheek. "I must go," I said, "I'll let you know what's happening...with all of this."

"Good Joseph. I want to know."

"Goodbye."

I HOPPED ON THE D train back to Manhattan, and tried to figure out what to do next. It'd be afternoon by the time I got back, and Jake was sure to be having a fit about where me and my fingerprints were. I wished to hell something would break with Crassidy, but it wasn't looking good so far. Nonetheless, I had a fallback plan coming together in my head. I hadn't worked out all the details yet, but the basic idea was to light out for Russia. I figured it'd be a good hideout, at least for now, and give me a chance to crack the Epstein case. I got off the subway a couple of blocks from police headquarters, and called Jake on a payphone. Here goes, I thought, let's see how the cookie crumbles.

"Lt. Roma," he answered, already sounding kind of edgy.

"Hello Jake?" I said, "It's Joey."

"Joey? What the fuck is going on with you man? Are you fucking crazy? Where the hell are you?"

"Hey calm down, will you?"

"Calm down? Do you fucking realize what a world of shit I'm in—we're in. You're supposed to have your goddamn prints done. Now what the..."

"Jake, listen to me. It's as good as taken care of, all right? But you've got to know about Frontenac, she's gone man, somebody took her..."

"Joey, I don't want to hear no more shit about that, you hear me? This case is fucking history. We got our guy. Get it?"

"No, I don't get it. You got no evidence that Volknick did it."

"Aw Joey, c'mon now. You know I love you but you're...you're fucking nuts you know that? And...bottom line is...the department's got a bigger hard-on over your fingerprints than this Epstein shit."

"Why? What's the big deal?"

"The big fucking deal is your prints didn't clear, got it? Now I don't know exactly what the fuck is going on, but it's some real serious shit. Somebody thinks you fit the description of some scumbag, who's got an outstanding warrant."

"For what?"

"Murder."

"Aw, that's fucking crazy."

"Joey, get your ass in here."

"Look, I tell you what. I quit. See? I quit. I'm giving notice right now."

"Joey, it don't matter. They want your ass in here. You hear me? Now where the hell are you?"

"Me? I'm here. I mean I'm here on the street."

"Where?"

"Uh, Brooklyn. Court Street. Look, I'll be up, I'll be there. Give me thirty minutes."

"You get here Joey. No more fucking around."

"No more fucking around. You got it. Goodbye."

Yeah goodbye old Jake, old buddy, I thought. I'm real sorry to be doing this to you, but it's going to work out somehow, you just wait and see. I hopped back in the subway and got on an uptown train. I didn't even know where the hell I was going. I just knew it wasn't going to be to the police, or to jail. Got to get the fuck out of here, I kept telling myself. Got to get my ass to Russia. But how? You must need a visa, I thought, but hell, I don't even have my passport. I let it expire a couple of years ago. But even with that stuff somebody, the FBI I guessed, by now could have some kind of shit on Joe Toricelli. And so could

Customs, and the airlines too. No, I figured, they'll nab me before I ever get on the plane. Then it hit me. Yeah, that's it, I thought to myself, that's definitely it. Landsdowne. Fucking Landsdowne. He could do it, or he's got to know somebody who could. I figured I needed a passport with a phony name, and a visa to match, and a lot of cash. That'll get me started. But how could I do it? Tell Landsdowne I'm a fugitive? Ask him to help me make a getaway? And this guy is supposed to be a patient. But breaking medical ethics, that would be only part of it. What about fraud and conspiracy and who the hell knows what else, to add to my problems? But the way I felt at that moment, about to be arrested for three murders, Volknick getting hanged for something he didn't do, and no sign that Crassidy's story was falling apart, I just figured it was too late to start acting reasonably. I got off the train at Grand Central, dug in my pockets for Landsdowne's number, and gave him a call.

"Mr. Landsdowne?" I said.

"Yes? Ah, doctor, it's you."

"How are you?"

"Holding up pretty well doctor. Scared as hell but, somehow—serene."

"And still sticking to your plans?"

"Oh yes. Absolutely."

"Good. Sounds good. I'm happy to hear you're holding steady. But uh, frankly, the reason I called, it's not to find out how you're doing."

"No?"

"No. The fact is I need to meet with you, Mr. Landsdowne, as soon as possible. I need your help."

"Well of course, certainly doctor," he said. "Is...is everything all right?"

"Well, not exactly. There's a certain matter, of some urgency, which I need to discuss with you. Face to face. Privately."

"Absolutely doctor. I'm at the U.N. as we speak. Can I pick you up at that corner...?"

"Carmine and Bedford."

"Yes, of course, Carmine and Bedford. Say at four today?"

"Perfect," I said, "see you then."

I SPENT THE next couple of hours meandering my way downtown, and going over exactly how I was going to present things to Landsdowne. I had a few versions of my story in mind, and I tried to imagine his reaction to each of them. He'd be flabbergasted for sure, I thought. And probably angry, and suspicious, and disappointed and...who knew what else? Every so often in my walking, I'd pass a shop window with TVs on, and I'd look to see if anything was breaking on Crassidy. There was going to be something, I thought, to rescue me from this fugitive mode. But there wasn't. Not a thing. I even called down to the Miami P.D. a couple of times, to ask if they knew of any developments in the case. But no one was saying anything about the investigation.

When four o'clock came around, I was there at our meeting place, and Landsdowne's limo pulled up to the corner right on time. The back door opened, I got in, and we rolled on.

"Good to see you again, doctor," said Landsdowne, "make yourself comfortable, please."

He looked pretty drawn, and more than a little pasty, and just after he'd greeted me he washed down a couple of pills with a mouthful of Scotch.

"Don't worry," he said, as he smacked his lips, "I'm okay. These are just for blood pressure."

"That's good. But take it easy on the booze, that's not going to help the blood pressure."

"Moderation doctor," he said, laughing, "as of today, I'm the very soul of moderation, with a daily limit of no more than two drinks. But now tell me doctor, because I want to help in any way I can, what sort of problem are you having?"

"Yes, thank you, Mr. Landsdowne," I said, and took a deep breath. "I'll try to be brief. The fact is I must get to Russia, specifically Moscow, as soon as possible. My presence there may well save a man's life."

"I see."

"The problem is, I need a passport and visa issued immediately. Right now I have neither."

He laughed. "Consider it done. I can arrange both for you by the end of the day tomorrow. Problem solved, one, two, three. Now have a drink. Scotch?"

"Uh, no thanks. But there's one complication. I want them issued under another name."

"I see. This is for someone else?"

"No, sir. They're for me. But I want...I need to assume another name, another...identity...so to speak."

He sat his drink down on the bar and lit a cigarette. "But why doctor? I don't understand."

"If I go under my own identity, it will endanger me...and my ability to do what I need to do. At this point, I cannot tell you anymore."

He gave me a puzzled look. "Doctor, you saved my life. You're a good man and I trust you...your integrity..." He paused.

"Yes?" I said.

"But this...seems to me...strange."

"It is. But this is the way it has to be, for me to do what I need to do. On that, I guess you're just going to have to trust me."

He didn't say anything, and he looked like he was thinking things over. I decided to pour myself some Scotch after all. I sipped it slowly while we bumped along some side streets through Tribeca. He took another bottle of pills from his pocket and tapped a couple into his hand. He looked at me with a smile.

"Antacids doctor," he said, "I really do have to cut down on the booze. I've made an appointment for tomorrow, to get into a program."

I nodded my approval.

"But you know," he said, "there is no problem in getting those documents for you, any way you want them. But, I just can't imagine what the devil you'd be involved in, for you to make such a request."

"One day I will tell you more about it, that's a promise. But right now the situation is too...delicate. I hope you can accept that as an explanation."

"Ah, doctor," he said, rubbing his eyes, and pausing before he spoke again, "I suppose I've accepted stranger explanations. I...I will take care of things for you, as you wish."

"Excellent. Now I must ask something else of you."

"What's that?" he said, looking suddenly worried.

"I want you to promise me that you'll never talk about this with anyone no matter what. No matter what you may hear about me, no matter what you may read about me."

"But...why...why...doctor. I'm really not following you here."

"I know, I know. And I don't expect you to, for right now, anyway. But, as I said, I'm involved in a very confused situation, and it's possible you may hear or read things about me, which are absolutely not true. You should not believe them, and you must not say anything about me. In return, you have my promise that I will eventually explain it all to you."

His jaw was a little crooked, and his face looked dog-tired and slightly stupid. He opened his mouth to speak but, for a moment, nothing came out. Then, almost whispering, he said, "I don't, I don't understand. I don't seem to understand anything, anymore."

"You will one day, Mr. Landsdowne. I promise you."

He looked at me, squinting through watery, bloodshot eyes, trying, it seemed, to finally size me up.

"You saved my life doctor, you saved my life."

"And now, in a way, I'm asking you to save mine, as well as someone else's."

"I have to trust you, don't I?"

"Yes you do. And I have to trust you too, to keep me safe."

"Then it's done doctor." He raised his glass and I raised mine. "To your good voyage and success," he said, "your secrets are safe with me."

"And to your good voyage as well," I said, "and peace of mind...and soul."

We clinked our glasses and drank. We were both on our way to God knows where, and I really hoped that one day we could sit down together and talk and laugh about how it all worked out.

Before he let me off, near Seventh and Fourteenth Street, he said he'd get everything ready; documents, airline reservations, and necessary cash as well, by noon tomorrow. All I had to do was get a couple of photos taken and drop them off at a place near Wall Street by nine that night. Then I'd pick up everything I needed at the same place tomorrow, and head out to the airport. I did as I was told, and spent that night in a small, fleabag hotel on the Lower East Side.

BY NOON THE next day, I'd picked up the stuff and headed out to Kennedy to take a three o'clock Air Volga flight to Moscow. There'd been nothing new about Crassidy in the news and, so far, nothing about me. I felt really bad about what Jake must have been going through right then and, just before boarding time, I put in a call to him. All I got was his voice mail, and I decided to leave a message:

"Jake, everything's going to be fine," I said, "I promise you. You've got to believe...I didn't do anything wrong, and when I see you next I hope that'll be real clear, to everybody."

I hung up the phone and went to stand in the boarding line. I felt a little nervous when I got there, and figured the cops were probably watching the airports for me by now. But how much could they really monitor? And no one but Landsdowne knew where I was going. In a few minutes, I'd inched my way up to the Customs guys. One was Russian, and the other American. They flipped through my documents and gave me the perfunctory once over.

"First time to Russia?" the American guy said.

"Yep. That's right."

"Business I see, huh?"

"Uh, yeah business," I said, "you got it."

"Well I hope you've got plenty of cash there Mr..." he looked at my passport again "Ellsworth, 'cause they don't take Visa and they don't take American Express."

Then he let out this boisterous laugh, and waved me on.

By the time we'd reached cruising altitude, I'd already drunk a couple of beers, and then I fell asleep through most of the trip. That was fine with me, because I hated to fly. By the time I woke up, we were flying into daybreak, somewhere over Norway, and they were serving breakfast. I chowed down a couple of trays of stale croissants and cold scrambled eggs and then tried to memorize some vocabulary from a Russian phrase book I'd picked up at the airport. I managed to nail down some basic stuff like "Allow me to introduce myself" and "Where is Red Square?" but, beyond that, it was going to be hand signals and charades if no one could speak English.

Part 7

THE CAPTAIN announced the approach into Moscow and pretty soon we lowered down over rolling green plains and birch and pine forests and then touched down on the runway of Sheremetyevo Airport. I made it through the bottleneck of Passport Control without a hitch, and squeezed through the crowds in the dark, low-ceilinged terminal. I ran into a chorus of grizzled old cabbies yelling "Taxee, taxee," and had one of them lead me outside and into the front seat of this banged-up old Moskvich.

"Rus Hotel," I told him "you know it?"

"*Da, da*, Rus," he said "*konyechno*" (of course).

I didn't know squat about places to stay but some guy on the plane, from Murmansk, had told me the Rus was "biggest hotel in Russia and very clean and very cheap." When I got there I saw he'd been right about the cheap part, 50 bucks a night, and the big part, the place was five blocks long and 20 stories high. But it was grimy as hell and when you checked in, the staff had this attitude that you were just one more pain in the ass they were going to have to deal with that day. The desk clerk tossed me my room key without making eye contact, and didn't look too fazed when a couple of roaches went rushing across the counter. When I got up to my room, a filthy little cubicle with a broken TV and a view over Red Square, I spread out a map of the Moscow Metro I'd grabbed in the lobby, and spotted the station on this Aunt Valentina's street, Prospect Mira. It was about five stations and one transfer from the hotel and, I figured, no more than half an hour away.

I went to shave real quick and put on a clean shirt. By this time it was about noon and, I thought to myself: Aunt Valentina, here I come, ready or not. I just hope to hell you speak some English.

I went down and hopped on the Metro, and got lost a couple of times before I finally popped up outside Prospect Mira station. There was a huge, gold-colored crescent-shaped hotel across the street, and the remains of some sprawling park and exhibit of Soviet Economic Achievement behind the station. Crowds of people were milling around domed pavilions with names like "Uzbekistan" and "Electricity" and carrying armfuls of newly bought clothes, all kinds of furniture and boxes with TVs and radios inside. It looked like the whole place had been turned into some kind of shabby shopping bazaar.

I went up to a gawky-looking kid in a tight-fitting cop's uniform and showed him Aunt Valentina's address.

"*Gde?*" I said, "which way?"

"*Ne deleko,*" (not far), he said and pointed out beyond this ten-story curved glass tower with a rocket sitting on top.

I walked east maybe fifteen blocks or so, following the numbers, until I came up to 1322 Prospect Mira, a dense grove of crumbling high-rises surrounded by a lot of overgrown grass and windblown litter. There must have been ten towers in all there, and I'll bet I went into every damn one of them at least once before somebody gave me the right directions to Valentina's apartment.

I took a cramped elevator with the stench of old piss up to the eleventh floor of her building and walked down a dark, gray-tiled corridor until I got to Valentina's door, apartment 11-B-L-V. The door was covered with brown vinyl except for the little peephole in the center.

I rang the bell and waited.

After a few seconds I heard some floorboards creak and then the sound of an old woman's voice.

"*Kto tam?*" (Who's there?), she asked.

"Dr. Joe Toricelli. I'm a friend of...you speak English?"

"A little."

"I'm a friend of your niece, Wilhelmina Frontenac. Is she in?"

"She is not here."

"And do you know where I can find her?"

She opened the door a little, but kept the chain on. The light was kind of dim where she was standing but I could see she was short, wrinkled, and slightly stooped.

"I don't know where she is," she said. Then she looked up at me and squinted. "And how do you know my niece?"

"Met her in New York, during the murder investigation of her doctor. I'm with the police."

"You are police doctor?"

"That's right. Psychiatric consultant."

She unlatched the chain and opened the door. She was all gray-haired and pretty ancient looking, but her eyes were real sharp and bright blue.

"And why you come to me to look for her?" she asked.

"I've got some questions to ask her, about her doctor. She is here in Moscow, isn't she?"

She didn't say anything.

"I assume she is here in Moscow," I said, "because a young lady I know of, came here looking for her the other day, and you told her you'd just seen your niece, the day before.

"She did come to visit me," she said, looking away from me, "but now I don't know where she is nor when she will return."

"Well did she give you any idea where she was going?"

"Nothing. I repeat to you, I don't know where she is." She was starting to get peeved.

"Fine, fine. But let me ask you something else; did your niece ever go by another name, I mean, besides Wilhelmina Frontenac?"

"I don't know what you mean."

"Another name. For instance, did she ever call herself Sabrina...Sabrina Briand?"

"It is unusual question. No, no...I never hear this name."

"Did she ever use any other name, besides her own?"

"No, doctor. No. I never hear another name. And now, I will ask you to excuse me. I am very busy and must prepare to go to my work."

"Yeah, sure, of course. But, uh, if you don't mind, I'd like to get your phone number, just in case anything else comes up."

"Yes, of course." She wrote it down on a scrap of paper and handed it to me. "Valentina Lubimova—130-0000."

"Thanks," I said, "uh, by the way, what kind of work do you do?"

"I am chemist, doctor," she said, smiling a little for the first time "at First Physiological Institute."

"No kidding? What's that, biochemistry?"

"Yes, but please, doctor, I must prepare now."

"Sure, sure. Thanks. Goodbye."

I TOOK THE Metro back to the hotel and ordered a glass of cold vodka, straight up, at one of the bars off the lobby. I was getting stonewalled by Aunt Valentina, that was for sure, and I had to figure a quick way around it. Trouble was, I was flying solo in a country where I had no real contacts and couldn't speak the language. I thought about calling Anya and getting her sister's number, but then I figured it'd be best to keep my whereabouts as quiet as possible. I'll come up with something, I thought.

I sipped the vodka and sat back and tried to relax. Just then this kind of heavy-set blonde in a black dress came up and sat down next to me. She threw her hair back and gave me a big, fake smile and a low, breathy, "Hello." Her lips were bright red and the make-up was real heavy, and you didn't have to be too slick to see this was going to be about business, not romance.

"Hi, how are you doing?" I said.

"My name is Natalia," she said, and went to shake hands with me.

"Nice to meet you," I said, "my name's Joe."

After a few minutes of the predictable small talk and bullshit; life in New York, life in Moscow, how she's a journalist (but out of work), how I'm a businessman just arrived, she got down to the nitty-gritty.

"So, Joseph," she said, "you should buy me a beer and then we will have sex."

"Guess you don't have a lot of time to waste," I said, and signaled the bartender to bring her a beer "so I'll tell you up front I'm not interested."

"Why? You are a healthy young man. Nice, rich too. I will give you a good deal, fifty dollars for one hour."

"Forget it. But look, have a complimentary beer."

"This beer will not feed my son."

She started to lose that phony smile and I figured I'd go ahead and make a donation, just to have her go away. But then an idea occurred to me.

"Tell you what," I said, "you want to make fifty bucks real quick, like in the next ten minutes?"

The corners of her mouth drooped.

"And what is it I must do?" she said.

"It's real simple," I said, and pulled out Aunt Valentina's number. "You just go over to that payphone there, and call this number. When somebody answers, you say you want to speak with Sabrina Briand."

"Sabrina Briand?"

"That's right, Sabrina Briand. You say you're uh...Natalia, a friend of hers from New York and you just came to Moscow and...you're giving her a call, just like you said you would."

"Like I said I would?"

"Yes. See the main thing is, you want to speak directly to Sabrina. So if she's not there, you want to find out when she gets back, all right? And say it all in Russian. Yeah, you're her Russian friend from New York."

"And where is my money?"

"Here," I said, "twenty-five now and twenty-five after you make the call. But no more questions, just go make the call, and tell me exactly what happens."

She went to make the call and was back in a couple of minutes.

"So what happened?" I asked.

"An old woman answered and when I asked for Sabrina she said, 'Sabrina is not at home.'"

"She specifically said 'Sabrina's not at home,'" I said.

"Yes."

"And what else? What else did she say?"

"Not so much. She asked me who I was, and sounded very

suspicious."

"And what'd you say?"

"I said 'I am Natalia from New York'...she said she wanted my number, and when Sabrina returned, she would call me. I said that was okay and I would call back."

"That's it?"

"That's it."

"You didn't ask when she'd return?"

"No, I didn't want to talk more, she was very unpleasant. I made a mistake?"

"No, that's okay. You did good, very good. Here's the other twenty-five. In fact, here...take a fifty."

"Thank you, Joseph," she said, with a big smile, "and tell me, you are absolutely sure you don't want to have sex?"

"Absolutely," I said, getting up to leave. "But look, you're seventy-five bucks ahead and you got the whole afternoon in front of you. Enjoy the beer."

I left the bar and went up to my room to call Valentina. I was betting that a quick confrontation about the Sabrina cover-up would get her rattled enough to start talking. But when I dialed her number all I got was a busy signal. So I tried again in a few minutes and then again, and again—over and over—for maybe twenty minutes. Damn it, I thought, she's probably figured out something's up, and has the phone off the hook. Nothing to do but keep trying, I thought, and if it keeps up much longer, I'll just go pay her another visit.

I paced around the room and started leafing through the local English language daily somebody'd left on the nightstand. I was looking for something about the O'Connor case there, but I saw nothing and it didn't exactly surprise me. But, when I looked through the section called "Events of Interest to the American Community," I saw an entry there that really blew me away. It was an announcement of something that was happening that day, on that very afternoon, as a matter of fact. The item I was looking at read like this: "Friday August 24, Sponsored by the All-Russia Neuro-Psychiatric Confederation: Dr. Bertrand Roland, Kievskaya Hotel, Main Ballroom, 1:00 p.m."

Now that was some kind of a coincidence, I thought. Roland and Ms. Frontenac, a/k/a Sabrina Briand, in Moscow at the exact same time. And I was real interested to see just what the hell Dr. Roland was going to make of it when I asked him about it. I looked at my watch, it was 1:30, and I figured if I left now, I could catch him before the conference was over.

I HOPPED BACK on the Metro and got off at a station a couple of blocks from the Kievskaya Hotel. The hotel itself was nothing fancy, just your basic modern box of a building, but it looked pretty rich sitting next to the weather-beaten Kiev Train Station and the sad and gray folks milling around in front of it. I walked through the doors of the hotel and stepped into a small-time shopping mall out of anywhere, U.S.A. Straight-ahead was the main ballroom, where I was about to catch the last five minutes of the Bertrand Roland Medicine Show.

I went up and stood by the entrance door of the ballroom and saw Roland up on stage behind the podium. He had a slide screen in back of him that showed the different phases of his "Self-Rescue Therapy. An Overall Strategy for Stress Reduction, Time Management and Optimal Enjoyment." The place was pretty packed and it looked to me like at least a few Russian shrinks were gearing up to take care of the problems of the worried well.

"Ladies and gentlemen," Roland was saying "this will conclude my presentation for today. I thank you for your kind attention and I do hope my talk has been of some use to you."

There was a big round of applause for the little man while he stepped back from the podium and a tall, muscular young woman with close-cropped black hair came forward.

"If you would like to speak with Dr. Roland," she said, in a Russian accent, "or get a signed copy of his new book, please come to the West Reception Room."

Most of the crowd got up and moved into the next room, where Roland started shaking hands, answering questions and signing copies of his book. I stayed back on the fringes of the herd, and when things started thinning out a little, I began to move closer to the little group jostling and chattering around Roland.

"Dr. Roland, if you please," I heard this bearded, bald guy with a bow tie say "what is expected length of treatment for stress reduction component of your program?"

"Twice a week for three weeks," said Roland, "if the patient hasn't achieved his goals by then, I'd introduce medication."

"And what about hypnosis?" asked a short, tubby woman in high heels "why you don't say it is important in program?"

"No place for it, in my view," said Roland, "it doesn't empower the patient, just gets him to think he can rely on magic."

"Is an identity issue ever a part of the problem?" I piped up from a few heads back "that is, is there ever a question about who the patient is?"

"I'm not quite sure what you mean," said Roland, and his face tightened a little, "perhaps you could be more specific." He craned his neck and tried to get a full-face view of his questioner. I squeezed in closer and got up face to face with him.

"I mean," I said, "a case where a patient apparently goes by two names, but it's got to be kept a secret, and it's used to hide something...maybe something that's real dirty. Should I get more specific?"

Roland dropped his jaw and turned white. The drink in his left hand started to shake.

"Tor...Toricelli?" he stammered. He puckered up and wrinkled his nose like he'd just smelled something that'd gone bad. "What...what the...what are you doing here?"

"Just happened to be in town to pay a visit to Sabrina Briand...and her Aunt Valentina," I said, "shall I send everyone your regards?"

"You...you what?" he said, breaking into a high pitch, "you're visiting here, in Moscow?"

"That's right. Real small world isn't it? You know, we all ought to get together, tonight as a matter of fact."

Roland jerked his head around the crowd, smiling and laughing real nervously. Then he cleared his throat. "Ladies and gentlemen," he said, "if, if you'd be so kind as to...excuse me a moment. I'd just like to have a chat with my colleague here, Dr. Toricelli. Excuse me, excuse me."

He came over and grabbed me by the arm and took me over by the wall. His drink was sloshing in the glass and spilling over his hand. He took a deep breath and tried to take charge.

"Toricelli," he said, "this...is an outrage. It's harassment, that's what it is, barging in on my conference like this."

"You're scared shitless and we both know it Roland. So why don't you just tell me why you lied about knowing Ms. Frontenac, formerly Sabrina Briand?"

"Lied?"

"Yeah lied. Now look Roland, quit fucking around and come clean on this, will you?"

All the color had left his face and his lips and jaw and pointy little nose were all twitching and trembling.

"You know Toricelli..." he began "you know..."

"Yeah," I said, "come on—what is it that I know?"

"You...you should know, Toricelli," he said in a raspy little whisper, "that...that when you see as many people as I do...you just may not clearly recollect everyone."

"Really? And I thought you had such a great fucking memory for faces."

"Nevertheless, I...I can't clearly remember everyone."

"Yeah but some patients can leave a real lasting impression on you, can't they Roland? Especially ones as...fuckable as Ms. Frontenac."

"That is libelous. It's...slander Toricelli. You're out of control."

"Well then, let's get on the horn and make a complaint to police headquarters right now. You just can't let my irresponsible allegations go unreported now, can you? But the way I see it, you've got one solid motive for murder."

"What are you talking about?"

"You had Epstein knocked off because he was going to turn you in for unethical behavior with Frontenac. Then you tried to hide Frontenac, or Briand...in Moscow, before she could have spilled the beans about everything."

"This...this is madness Toricelli. Do you realize the absurdity...the... the utter irresponsibility of your accusations?"

"I'm going to let the police decide who's crazy here Roland, you or me. I'll be down in the lobby, or wherever the hell the telephones are around here, if you need me."

I turned to walk away.

"Toricelli," Roland shouted "please...I...I'm not finished."

I turned back around. "You got something else to say?"

"I, I do," he said, with this grave look on his face, "a full explanation."

"All right. Let's hear it."

"I only ask...that you give me a moment, to wrap things up here."

He looked toward the people still waiting to get a signed copy of his book.

"Go ahead," I said, "I'll be waiting, right here."

Roland went and finished off the last of his glad-handing and self-promotion, and then we walked over and sat down at a table in the lobby lounge.

"Toricelli," he began "this is more difficult for me than you can possibly imagine. Painful, really. But I'm going to tell you everything I can. Frankly, I never thought things would get this far. It was...a misjudgment on my part and I'll have to take responsibility for that."

"Right. So let's hear it."

"All right," he said, and cleared his throat, "All right, this young woman, Sabrina Briand, it is true, she was once a patient of mine. Several years ago, it was."

"Beginning with the Caribbean seminar?"

"Yes, that's right. And from that first week, she developed an intense attachment to me. In retrospect, I should have certainly heeded it as a warning, but...well it's water under the bridge now."

"So what exactly happened?"

"Toricelli, Dr. Toricelli, I'm sure you can understand that issues of confidentiality prohibit me from giving a detailed account of her treatment. What I will say, however, and this is off the record, is that...she was not able to separate fantasy from reality in her therapy. For that reason I elected to discontinue her treatment."

"Well, even if I accept all of that at face value, it still doesn't explain all the secrecy about her being a former patient of yours. So what is it you've been trying to hide?"

"There is nothing I've been trying to hide, exactly. It's more...well...you see, this is a very, very troubled young woman . And I simply don't want her subjected to unnecessary and irrelevant intrusions into her private life, into her inner world, as it were. She is already traumatized enough by the death of Dr. Epstein."

"So you've been trying to protect her, is that what I'm supposed to be believing here?"

"You may believe whatever you like. I am only telling you that I have stepped in, in this time of crisis for this young woman, as a kind of protector. As a kind of, albeit unofficially, guardian for her."

"Uh-huh, and just what have those guardian duties of yours involved?"

"Well your tone tells me you're quite skeptical doctor," he said, "but I can assure you that I have only been motivated by a desire to serve this girl's best interests. And at no little cost to me, I might add."

"Fine, but you still haven't told me what you've been doing for her, and why."

"I'll tell you," he said, "I arranged for her move back to Moscow, I got all of her belongings shipped, and I even helped get her set up in an apartment here."

"Why?"

"Call it a lingering sense of responsibility, or perhaps guilt, it's difficult to separate the two. Maybe, I tell myself, maybe if I'd handled things differently in her treatment I could have helped her. And she wouldn't have gone to Dr. Epstein and, well of course, she would be in a much better spot today."

"And how exactly did she end up going to Epstein?"

He smiled and shook his head. "Dr. Toricelli, I told you she had or, more precisely, has a passionate attachment to me, didn't I? So is it so difficult to imagine it being transferred to the doctor with whom I share an office suite?"

"And what'd Epstein know about her former situation with you?"

"Everything. From time to time he and I would discuss her ongoing treatment, doctor. He was handling her case quite skillfully, I can assure you."

"So what's going to happen with her now, is she going to be getting treatment here in Moscow?"

"Of course she is. I've made all the arrangements, through some colleagues of mine at the Neuro-psychiatric Institute here. She'll be in very good hands and, just as importantly, she will be in her hometown, close to her family and friends. In time, I hope she will also be able to find work, respectable work that is."

"And how do you know about her work?" I said.

"Through Dr. Epstein. He told me about this so-called Daylight Club."

"And what'd he tell you about it?"

"Well, it is clearly a disreputable place, in all likelihood connected with organized crime."

"Uh-huh. And did you know I was almost killed outside of there the other night, after the bartender slipped me a Mickey and then someone tried to shoot me?"

"No, I didn't," he said, "but with the sort of element who must be around that place, it certainly doesn't surprise me."

"Anybody down there you know?"

"That I know? That I would know at this club? Well of course not."

"No hit men you know that could be affiliated with the place?" I said.

"'Hit men'? What are you talking about Dr. Toricelli?"

"Hit men. You know, guys you could hire to knock of Dr. Epstein...and me too, if I'm getting a little too nosy."

"Dr. Toricelli," he gasped "I...I...I mean honestly man, after everything I told you, have you completely lost touch with reality?"

"Maybe. You'll let me know in time. But tell me this, why is it that in Brighton Beach they're saying Ms. Frontenac moved out in a hurry and not so happily, aided by thugs, and at the behest of the Russian Mafia?"

"Well, Dr. Toricelli," said Roland, laughing "I...I really don't know how to explain such gossip, unless the men from the local moving company I hired frightened the neighbors in some way. But there was certainly nothing sudden or unhappy about her move. She and I had been planning it for at least ten days, and that you can verify with her Aunt Valentina."

"Okay. So what you're telling me is, you brought her back home, you paid for her move, you set her up in her own apartment, and got her a treatment referral; and all this out of the goodness of your heart, that's what you're telling me?"

"I could not argue with that account of things."

"And this conference here; what'd you do, whip that up at the last minute for a tax deduction on the trip?"

He laughed. "Not exactly Dr. Toricelli. The fact is, I'm in Moscow several times a year with conferences and other professional activities. I simply took advantage of this trip to help out...Sabrina."

"And what is the story with the names? Briand, Frontenac, what's that all about?"

"Sabrina Briand is her original name. Recently, she changed it to Wilhelmina Frontenac."

"And why?"

"Part of her pathology," said Roland, smiling sadly, "that is really all I can reveal to you."

"You know Dr. Roland, I'd actually like to believe you about all this. It'd sure start to tidy things up in this case. So what do you say you and I pay a visit to Ms. Frontenac or...Sabrina...and see if she'd be willing to talk about, and corroborate, everything you're saying."

"Yes, well, I'd really rather not. Frankly, I don't see how it is necessary or relevant to your investigation. And further, it risks disrupting the delicate emotional balance this young woman is struggling to maintain."

"That's all well and good, but we've got other priorities here. Like solving a murder case and making sure we're not going to convict an innocent man."

"Dr. Toricelli, with all due respect, you seem to be caught up in some sort of obsessional storm about the innocence of Nathan Volknick. For God's sake, man, he has already confessed to the crime and his story is consistent with all of the evidence the police have gathered."

"And I presume Volknick is still your patient?"

"That's right."

"And how did you feel when you heard about his confession?"

"I was deeply saddened," he said, "when his mother called and told me the news."

"But weren't you skeptical about the validity of his statement, given his mental state?"

"Having a psychotic illness, even actively so, does not preclude the veracity or accuracy of his confession Dr. Toricelli. For me, I'm sorry to say, his confessional statement had the ring of truth."

"And did you actually hear it from him?"

"No, he is not communicating with me, or anyone I know of at this time. But his mother faxed me a copy of the statement he wrote for the police, shortly after your interview with him, from what I understand."

"And, in your meeting with him Dr. Roland, did you ever discuss the Epstein murder with him or any possible part he could have played in it?"

"That topic was off limits in our meetings," he said. "I told Nathan and his family that from the start. I was in the role of managing his medications and advising regarding treatment referrals. I was not going to get involved in any forensic issues. That was up to the police, yourself included, to pursue."

"Uh-huh, well I say he's innocent," I said, "so, now tell me Dr. Roland; are you afraid to have me speak again with Sabrina Briand?"

"Yes I am, but not for any reason other than I think it may hurt her. I only appeal to you as a physician Dr. Toricelli, do no harm to this young woman, do no harm to this fragile, deeply disturbed patient."

"And the same goes for you with Volknick." I said, "So let's go together to see Sabrina Briand. That way you can be there if she starts getting real upset."

"It is a fool's errand Dr. Toricelli, that's what you're inviting me to partake in."

"Well...it's not exactly an invitation Dr. Roland. It's more like an opportunity for you to avoid charges of obstruction of justice."

"Obstruction of justice?"

"That's right. Like lying to the police, like you've been doing with me, about the identity of this woman."

"But...but this issue of Ms. Frontenac...or Ms. Briand, is not in any way material to your investigation. It's obviously irrelevant."

"It's not obvious to me," I said, "so I say, either cooperate now, or I'll call police headquarters and inform them of what you've been doing."

He shook his head and sighed. "You know Toricelli, I don't know what the world is coming to, I really don't. At any rate, if you'll excuse me, I will call my driver and tell him to pull the car out front."

He pulled a cell phone out of his pocket, punched in a number and proceeded to have a short conversation in Russian. As he was talking, I looked at him and thought to myself; there's a real good chance he's been lying to me, about everything. So where does that leave me if I hop in a cab with him right now, maybe face down dead in a ditch on the outskirts of Moscow? I didn't know, I really didn't know. But I just figured going with him, right now, to see Frontenac, was just a risk I was going to have to take.

After he hung up, he said, "All right, Dmitri will have the car out front momentarily. Let's go."

BY THE TIME we got to the entrance doors of the hotel there was a big, black BMW parked out front. We climbed in the back and Roland gave the driver the address and what sounded like directions. All I could make out was something about Komsomolsky Prospect. We rode out of the parking lot and along an avenue by the Moscow River.

"So," I said to him, "looks like you've got the language down pretty good, huh?"

"I'm fluent in five languages, Toricelli, though I think Russian is my favorite. It has a marvelous intensity to it. Marvelous, marvelous country, I might add."

"Yeah? What's so marvelous about it?"

"Look around you Toricelli. Everywhere you go there is passion, energy and change. The society is changing daily, and people are aware that they're living through a great historical moment."

"Some moment. Mainly what I've seen is broken down buildings, bad service and lots of poor people."

"Toricelli," he laughed "you're looking, but you're not seeing and, more importantly, you're not listening. You make the mistake that most Westerners do; you only see what you consider to be the surface, but not the great potential beneath it."

"The only potential I see is for chaos. But, anyway, how soon before we get to Sabrina's apartment?"

"Almost there, it's just up here on the right." Then he said something in Russian to Dmitri and we slowed down and pulled up in front of a big beige brick apartment house.

"Now I warn you, Toricelli," said Roland, "she will be very surprised...and upset...to see you here." He pulled out his cell phone. "I will call her and let her know we will be up in a few minutes."

"She'll get over it," I said, putting my hand on the phone, "so put it away and let's go."

Roland's jaw tightened. "If she becomes upset, it will be on your hands, on your...indelicate, over-zealous hands."

"So be it," I said, climbing out of the car, "Let's go."

We walked into the building entrance and through the little lobby, and took the elevator up to the sixth floor. Roland kept biting his lower lip and two or three times looked like he was going to say something, but he didn't. Then the elevator door opened and we walked down to apartment 6-M. Roland knocked on the door.

"*Kto tam?*" I heard Frontenac say, on the other side.

"Sabrina?" said Roland. "It's me, Bertrand. I'm...I'm here, believe it or not, with Dr. Toricelli. He...he wants to talk with us, together."

The door swung open and there stood Frontenac. She was all dressed up with high heels and a black dress and make-up and looked like she was heading someplace real fancy. She looked at me with a tight little smile.

"Dr. Toricelli," she said, "such a surprise to...to see you in Moscow."

"Is it really?" I said, "didn't Aunt Valentina tell you I was in town?"

She laughed. "Aunt Valentina? You have met my Aunt Valentina? But no, no, I have not spoken with her."

"Mind if we come in?" I said.

"Of course not doctor. Please, please come in."

She led me and Roland into her apartment, a huge place with high ceilings, beautiful furniture and a view over a park. We all sat down around a big coffee table in the living room.

"I don't have a thing in the house to eat," she said, "but perhaps you would like something to drink?"

"No thanks, Ms. Frontenac," I said, "or Sabrina, if I may..."

"Sabrina is fine doctor," she said and threw her hair back like she was nervous.

"Now I'll try to get right to the point," I said. "You sure left New York in a hurry and I'm real curious as to why you did that."

She took a quick look at Roland before she began to speak. "I consulted with Dr. Roland," she said, "we both thought it would be best for me."

"Right, exactly what he said. And why was it best for you?"

"Sabrina," said Roland.

"Hold on, Roland," I said, "let's hear it from her. Now why did he think that was best for you Sabrina?"

"Dr. Toricelli," she said, "you must understand how terrible it has been for me since Dr. Epstein died. He...he was everything to me. He took care of me, he protected me."

"Protected you? From what?"

"From me," she said in this little girl's voice, "no one else could do that, no one in New York, anyway."

"And in Moscow?"

"In Moscow doctor, I have many, many people whom I know. This is my home; here I may feel safe. I thought about it many days after Dr. Epstein died. What I should do, where I should go. I was confused, then I spoke with Dr. Roland. I called him because, I felt so terrible. He spoke with me a long time and helped me to see my situation, what was right for me. It was to return to my country, to my home."

"I take it starting up again as Dr. Roland's patient wasn't really an option," I said.

She looked over at Roland, and started to get real teary-eyed.

"It's all right, Sabrina," said Roland. It sounded like he was trying to sooth her.

"Dr. Roland's been trying to keep that a big secret," I said "that you were his patient once. He kept saying he didn't know you. Didn't know anything about you. Even with your picture right there in his book and all."

She didn't say anything.

"Now there's something I need to know, Sabrina," I said, "as private as it may be, and I want you to spell it out for me real clearly. Why did you stop seeing Dr. Roland , and start seeing Dr. Epstein?"

Now she started crying real hard. She put her face in her hands and wailed and even started rocking back and forth in her seat. I called her name a few times but it didn't do any good. She just kept whining and sobbing.

"Are you satisfied now, Toricelli?" said Roland.

"No, I'm not," I said. After a while, she settled down and took her hands from her face. Again, I asked her why she'd stopped seeing Roland. This time, instead of hiding her face in her hands, she started to speak.

"I...I don't want to talk about it, doctor," she said, "it's not your business. You can't make me talk about it. Can you?"

"Whether I can or can't isn't really the thing here, Ms. Front...Sabrina. Bottom line is, you've got to ask yourself what's more important, your privacy or the life of Nathan Volknick."

"Nathan Volknick?" she said, "why do you talk about him doctor. I don't understand."

"Toricelli," shouted Roland "that's enough."

I ignored him.

"Don't you know?" I said to her, "Nathan Volknick is under arrest for the murder of Dr. Epstein. He made a full confession three days ago."

"No," she cried "no, it's...it's not possible, it's a mistake, please doctor this boy would not hurt Dr. Epstein."

"That's what I say," I said. "No way this kid did it."

"I know for sure this is a terrible mistake," she said, "for sure he didn't do it. You cannot let the boy be hurt."

"How Sabrina," I said, "how do you know for sure Volknick didn't do it?"

"How?" she asked. Then she sat straight up in her chair and wiped the tears from her eyes. Her face got real calm and she got herself all pulled together again.

"Because, Dr. Toricelli," she said, "because I was not really on that yacht in Westport on that Friday afternoon. That was a lie. No, I was really in New York, and very specifically, in Dr. Epstein's office. You see it was I...who killed poor, poor Dr. Epstein."

"Sabrina," Roland piped up "what are you saying? This...this is nonsense."

"It is no nonsense," she said, looking straight at me. "I strangled him, that afternoon. After the boy, Volknick, went away."

"But I don't get it," I said, "why would you want to kill Dr.

Epstein?"

"It was an accident," she said, "it wasn't supposed to happen that way. We were playing, playing our game."

"Your game?" I said, "what game?"

"Sabrina," Roland was scolding her. "Please, please, this is all fantastical nonsense. You, you mustn't do this."

"No," she said, "no, I must say it now, before it is too late. I cannot see this boy go to prison, or maybe be executed. No, Dr. Toricelli, I must say it. I killed Dr. Epstein. He had wanted to play our game. He wanted me to tighten his tie around his neck and to whisper dirty words to him. Many, many times we had done this. But this time, I...I went too far. I don't know why. Maybe I was angry at him, because he was such a pig. But no, no, Dr. Toricelli, you must believe me, it was an accident. I didn't really mean to kill Dr. Epstein."

"Sabrina," said Roland, talking to her like she was some kind of bad kid. He stood up over her, as if he could get some control over her. "You must stop this right now," he said, "or you'll have Dr. Toricelli believing you if you go on like this."

"Leave me alone," she yelled. She stood up, about two heads taller than he, and pushed him over the coffee table and down to the floor. "You leave me alone or I'll kill you, do you hear me?"

I got up and helped Roland back to his feet and sat him down on the couch. "All right champ," I told him "you better let me handle things from here on out."

I was flabbergasted as hell by what she had said, but I thought at this point, it was better to get her arrested than to argue with her about who killed Dr. Epstein. I figured I'd get her down to the American Embassy, and let them take care of calling the cops and getting her back to New York. How exactly I was going to avoid getting identified and arrested myself I hadn't put together yet, but I expected I'd cook something up.

"Okay, look Sabrina," I said, "me and you and Dr. Roland are going to take a ride over to the American Embassy and let them handle your extradition..."

"Toricelli," Roland yelled, "you must be mad, this girl doesn't know what she's talking about."

"I know very well what I am saying," she said, "and I am ready to go as soon as possible."

"I wouldn't argue with her, Roland," I said, "it's not going to be very good for your health."

We waited for her to throw on a sweater and then we headed down the elevator and out to Roland's car. As we got near it I saw a couple of big guys sitting in the back seat.

"Wait a minute, Toricelli," said Roland, "I think we've got some sort of trouble here." Then, all of a sudden, somebody whacked me in the back of the head and I must have gone out cold before I hit the ground.

Part 8

THE NEXT thing I remember was waking up with a real sore head, sitting in the backseat of a limo barreling down some rough road out in the dark countryside. As best I could tell there was no one else in the car except me and the driver. I went to move forward to get a better look in the front seat, but I was roped tight to the backseat and my hands were cuffed in my lap.

"Hey," I called to the guy driving "hey, who are you?"

He turned his head to the side for a second.

"Hey," I said, "what's going on here?"

"No Angliski," he said, in this gravelly voice, "don't speak English."

"Where are you taking me? Where are we going?"

But he just shook his head and said again how he didn't speak English.

"Ah, shit!" I said, and tried to squirm out of the ropes pressing against me. But it was no use. I slumped back and looked out the window, and saw thousands of stars shining, like they'd been spilled into the sky, and the blurred silhouettes of trees rushing by. It went on like that for a long time, so all I could tell was we were way out from the city or any towns. Then the car slowed down and we took a right onto a dirt road that went through a big forest of birch trees. It was windy and narrow and full of potholes and a couple of times I thought that big beast of a limo was going to get stuck in the middle of the woods. But little by little we kept creeping along, and after awhile the road came out into a big field that spread out across a hillside. As we drove up to the top of the hill, a huge white mansion started to come into view. It was done up in a classical style and reminded me of one of those gaudy old plantation houses you see in the South. The grounds and the house were all bright with floodlights and when we drove up the gatehouse, maybe a hundred yards from the house, a big no-neck guy with an AK-47 came up to the car, looked us over real carefully, and then waved us on in.

We drove slowly past a big lawn with shrubs and groves of huge old trees, before we pulled up to the front door. Two guys in dark suits came out talking Russian to each other, and they untied me, and led me into the big entry foyer of the house. They pointed for me to sit down on a little settee against the wall, and next to a big Greek statue.

"What...what's going on here," I said to one of them, who was wearing a little cross of an earring on his right ear.

He put his finger up to his lips real quick. "No questions," he said, "and no conversation. You will wait to speak with Dr. Ognev."

"Who's Dr. Ognev?" I asked.

"Are you stupid?" he said, and looked like he was going to spit on me. "I told you, no questions and no conversation."

"Yeah, whatever," I said, "by the way, any chance I can get some water, while I'm waiting?"

"Shut up...and wait," is all he said, and I was getting a pretty good idea that hospitality wasn't going to be one of the strong points of this visit.

We waited around twenty or thirty minutes. The two guys sat in chairs across from me, chatting back and forth in Russian, and every once in a while taking a swig from a flask they passed back and forth. Then some French doors opened to one side of the foyer and this tall, lean guy with blonde hair combed straight back, and real cold-looking blue eyes, walked toward us. He looked straight at me with this sharp-toothed smile and reached out to shake my hand.

"Dr. Toricelli," he said, "good evening. Sorry to keep you waiting but, I hadn't expected you so soon."

I stood up from the settee and showed him my cuffed hands.

"I didn't know you were expecting me at all," I said, "but I know I'd feel a lot more welcome with these things off."

"Of course, of course," he said. He took the key from one of the thug guards and unlocked the cuffs. "There you are, Dr. Toricelli," he smiled and shook my hand. "I am Dr. Boris Ognev, it's a pleasure to meet you."

"Uh-huh," I said, "if you don't mind, I'll hold off on the pleasant introduction stuff until I find out what the hell I'm doing here."

"What you're doing here?" he said, sort of surprised. "You are here, Dr. Toricelli, in my house, as my guest, of course."

"Your guest? That's a funny way to be treating guests; assault, battery, kidnapping, handcuffs...should I go on?"

Dr. Ognev laughed. "No, no Dr. Toricelli, you need not. These circumstances you describe were rather...unfortunate and I sincerely apologize. My men overreacted, you see, to what they perceived to be a dangerous situation."

"Your men saw a dangerous situation? You're going to have to fill me in on that one. I don't get it."

"You see, Dr. Toricelli, I have...employees...whose specific responsibility it is to make sure that no harm comes to my cousin, Sabrina Briand."

"She's your cousin?"

"That's right. And...understandably they became quite alarmed when they saw her being whisked away, visibly upset, by two American strangers."

"Well if they'd taken a second to talk before whacking me on the head, they'd have found out she'd just confessed to the murder, or manslaughter at least, of her psychiatrist in New York."

At this, Ognev threw back his head and laughed a long time. The thugs standing around started to laugh too, but it wasn't real clear they'd even understood what I said. Then Ognev raised his hand, as if to tell everybody it was time to settle down.

"Dr. Toricelli," he said, "please, I hope you will forgive me, really I don't mean to mock you. But, if you knew my dear cousin, you would much better appreciate the absurdity of your statement."

"What exactly should I know about her?"

"This would take me a long time to explain, even if I thought it was proper to tell you. Suffice it to say that her character structure is profoundly unstable, and she is given to making fantastic utterances."

"That by itself doesn't dismiss her confession."

"Strictly speaking, you would be right. But to give any credibility to her statement would be, at best, naive. Besides, I read in the *New York Register* yesterday that another patient of her Dr. Epstein's has already signed a confession."

"That's bogus," I said.

"Strange that you would say that, doctor. I would assume you were one of the forensic specialists who helped to obtain this man's confession."

"I was. And it didn't sound any less weird than your cousin's. I figure two weird confessions adds up to one unsolved murder, for now at least."

"Your logic eludes me," he said. "I can only tell you that my cousin is as innocent as she is disturbed, and any attempt to extradite her to New York would be a futile and foolish project."

"Well I don't see it that way. And by the way, where's Dr. Roland?"

"You mean the little man who was with you?" said Ognev.

"Yeah, that's right. You know him?"

"No, not really. At any rate, I suppose he is back at his hotel. He made it clear to my men that he, unlike you, had no intention of taking Sabrina anywhere."

"Did he tell your guys to mug me?"

"Please Dr. Toricelli. No one tells my men to do anything, except me. In any case, Dr. Roland exercises no authority. From what Sabrina has told me, he is a former psychiatrist of hers, who has assisted her in moving from New York to Moscow."

"You know anything about their past relationship?"

"Nothing, nothing at all. And it is really not my business, nor is it yours."

"And what about her name change?" I asked. "Are you familiar with that?"

"If you mean Sabrina assuming other names, yes, I am familiar with it. It is a sort of hysterical habit of hers, which the family has known about for a long time."

"Including Aunt Valentina?"

"Valentina?" he said, looking puzzled for a second. "Ah yes, Valentina. She is the old aunt on her father's side. Well, I suppose she knows about my cousin's...difficulties. Though I don't think I've seen the old woman in years. But, Dr. Toricelli, this is all irrelevant chitchat. I only want to tell you, most emphatically, that my cousin is no murderer, and for you to arrest her would be a sad, silly act."

"I'll have to take that chance," I said, "and then figure out what her confession is all about. If nothing else, taking her into custody will get things confused enough to reopen the investigation. Then there's half a chance of finding out who really killed this doctor."

"Rather strange police methods, doctor," said Ognev, "of course I cannot say I am familiar with American investigative techniques. But I cannot allow you to use my cousin to solve or, I suppose, more precisely, to unsolve your case."

"It's not up to you to allow or not to allow. The woman confessed and she was cooperating with her arrest. That is, until you and your boys barged in. Now the way I see it, if you let us get on with things, I don't have to make a complaint about you obstructing a criminal investigation."

"That's very funny," said Ognev, laughing, "and to whom will you complain?"

"Don't make me have to think about that one too hard. Now where's your cousin?"

"You're quite serious about this, aren't you Dr. Toricelli?"

"Yeah, I am. So where is she?"

"At her apartment," he said, "just as you found her."

"I see. So, rather than wasting more time here, I'm going to ask that you get one of your guys to give me a lift back there. Now."

"Dr. Toricelli," said Ognev, shaking his head, "I had really hoped I might dissuade you from your foolishness. But I see now it won't be possible." He turned to one of his thugs. "Slava," he said, and then he went on in Russian with something that mentioned "Moscow" and "Sabrina." Then he turned back to me. "You are pigheaded and naive doctor," he said. "I will tell you now that by the time you arrive at her flat my lawyers will be there to greet you."

"Fine with me," I said, turning to walk out the door, "good evening."

Slava followed me back out to the limo and opened the back door for me to get in. Then he got in and cranked it up and we started back down the driveway to the gatehouse. Something felt real dangerous about Ognev and his whole setup, and I didn't trust anything he had to say , but I figured I had no choice except to get back to Sabrina's place and get her into the hands of the police. I hadn't bothered to press Ognev about Roland, but I figured he knew more than he was letting on. And I still had a strong suspicion that somehow Sabrina's confession, or whatever the hell it was, was eventually going to tie Roland into Epstein's murder. I just couldn't believe Roland's Good Samaritan bullshit about how he wanted to help get her back to Moscow.

When we got to the end of the driveway the gate was closed and no one was in the gatehouse. Slava honked the horn a couple of times and when no one showed up, he turned back to me and said, "Wait right here, please, I must find man to open gate."

He went off across the lawn and I sat back to catch a wink. It was after midnight and I was tired as hell. A few seconds after my eyes closed I smelled something kind of sweet in the car and then this warm, lazy, slightly electric rush came over me. There was some kind of white noise, like a fan or the sound you hear by the seashore, building up all around me and, little by little, I felt like I was shrinking into some tiny point deep inside my skull. I thought of reaching toward the door handle and getting out of the car, but it was like my will power dissolved as soon as I had the thought. Nothing seemed important anymore; and all I wanted to do was lose myself in the white noise that was building and building all around me. That's the last thing I remember before waking up in a huge brass bed in a big, bay-windowed room with sunlight flooding in from all over.

I FELT TOTALLY lost. I didn't know where I was or, for that matter, who I was. And after a few brief seconds of feeling paralyzed, I propped myself up in the bed and looked around. The room had high ceilings and polished, parquet floors covered with a couple of rich looking Oriental rugs. There was an antique desk in one corner and a big abstract painting by Kandinsky on the wall behind it. I got out of bed and put on my clothes, which had been neatly hung on a chair near the desk.

Then I ate from a tray of sandwiches that had been left on a table, and drank from a bottle of mineral water. When I finished, I walked over to the big window and looked out at a clear blue sky domed over a forest of birch swaying in a brisk wind. In the foreground was an impeccable green lawn. It was studded with shrubs and shade trees and, in the middle of it, there was a breeze-rippled pond with swans and ducks and lily pads. A red brick walkway circled around the pond and then spurred off toward a big porch in the back of the house, which I could see just to the right and below the window of my room. I turned around to look at the room again and caught a glimpse of myself in a long mirror hanging on a heavy oaken closet door. I stared at my reflection a long time and, it was the damnedest thing, I couldn't get a handle on who I was. It wasn't that I didn't recognize myself, because I did. I even whispered my name, "Joe Toricelli." It was more like I didn't feel like me anymore. I just felt like...nobody...like I was just one of those trees out in the birch forest. My name, my life, my identity, all of that felt like nothing. None of this felt bad and, as a matter of fact, I was feeling really laid back and lazy and started to laugh over nothing in particular.

I pulled a chair up by the bay window and sat and looked out over the sky and forest for a long time. "So be it," I told myself, looking at the trees. "I'm just like you, just one of you guys." On and on it seemed I kept having that same feeling of nothingness and, anonymity, I guess you'd call it. Hours passed while I sat in that chair and the shadow of the shrubs and shade trees grew longer and longer, 'til soon the light dimmed into dusk and then darkness, and then a million stars came out and shimmered and glowed in the deep black moonless sky.

I went back to lay on the bed and fell into long dreams that carried me out through the cosmos; past fiery rivers flowing into blazing red and blue stars, past rainbow colored planets and comets that gave off high-pitched, screaming melodies. I saw the faces of laughing men-in-the-moon and heard this deep basso voice-over narrator announcing "the end of time, as we know it." Through all the dreams I seemed to be laughing and felt this lazy, ticklish feeling. When I finally awoke, the light was graying into dawn and I felt like I just wanted to float out of bed and through the window and melt into the soft, dewy air outside. The only thing that kept me focused was my stomach, which was churning and hurting and calling out for food. After a while, I climbed out of bed and went to open the bedroom door. It gave way to a long marble-floored hall with polished woodwork and lush tropical plants arranged on either side.

I walked to the end of the hall and came out on the landing of a huge staircase. It wound down to an atrium with two fountains, lots of classical statues and a massive chandelier reflecting the light of the new morning sun. As I got to the bottom of the stairs, I saw a couple of French doors, off to one side of the atrium that opened up onto a patio. There were a table and chairs set up there, and I saw Ognev sitting back and reading the paper. It was only then that I realized I was still at Ognev's estate. I walked out to him, feeling, in a weird kind of way, almost drawn to him. He looked up from his paper as I approached.

"Ah, good morning, Dr. Toricelli," he said, "you are up very early. And how are you on this beautiful morning?"

"Good, good," I said, "Dr...Ognev, right?"

"Yes, yes, that's right," he said, laughing "you remember, after your rather long sleep. And are you rested now, Dr. Toricelli?"

"Believe so," I said, "and I feel pretty good."

"Good, good. Please sit down. And tell me, you must be very hungry, yes?"

"You bet," I said, sitting down "real hungry."

"Wonderful. Olga!" he called to a girl tending flowers nearby, "please, bring our guest a good breakfast." Then he turned back to me. "And tell me Dr...or may I call you Joseph?"

"Yeah, 'Joseph' is fine."

"And tell me, Joseph, what sort of plans do you have for your visit to Russia?"

"Plans? I, uh, I hadn't really thought too much about it."

"But, if I may ask Joseph, didn't you have some specific purpose to visit Russia? Perhaps for business? Or for pleasure?"

"Good question," I said, scratching the stubble on my chin, "why the hell did I come to Russia?" I thought about it for a few minutes before I could answer. "I guess the reason I came here," I said, "was to solve a kind of puzzle. It was to find Ms. Frontenac or, Sabrina Briand that is. She's your cousin, right?"

"That's right. My second cousin to be precise."

"Yeah, so it was to find your cousin, Sabrina Briand. She's hooked up with this Dr. Roland and somehow, I believe, in the murder of Horatio Epstein."

"I see. So you do have plans then, for your stay in Russia."

"No, no I don't. I don't know why, I don't even care to know why anymore...but none of it, none of it really concerns me anymore. Yeah, that's it. It just doesn't mean a damn thing anymore."

"Indeed," he said, "that is quite interesting."

"Yeah? Maybe for you."

Then Olga came back carrying in a couple of trays: one with different meats and salads and fish and all sorts of condiments. And the other with fruit and bread and cheeses and caviar and champagne.

"Look at that," I said, "now that's what I call interesting."

Ognev smiled. "Please Joseph," he said, "*Buon appetito*; enjoy, enjoy."

And that I did. I dug in and ate everything there was on both trays. Any other thoughts about the Epstein case, or for that matter anything else that I'd ever worried about, had more or less vanished from my mind. Ognev was quiet while I ate, and seemed to be watching over me. When I finished, he asked me, "Was it tasty?"

"Unbelievable," I said, "like no meal I've ever eaten."

"Wonderful, wonderful, Joseph. I want you to know, by the way, that you are free to stay here as long as you would like."

"Thanks, thanks a lot. I believe I'm going to take you up on that."

Just then Ognev looked behind me into the other doorway and seemed to nod real happily to somebody inside. In a moment I heard footsteps clicking onto the patio's stone floor and then I saw the rat-happy face of Bertrand Roland smiling and staring and hovering over me.

"Dr. Toricelli", he whined, "so good to see you again. and aren't you looking chipper."

"Thanks," I said, "you're looking...well, like the same weird wiry short guy I remember from New York."

His face seemed to fall into a scowl when I said that.

"Yes, indeed," he hissed at me, and pulled up a chair and sat down. Then he turned to Ognev. "Troublesome side-effect, Boris, this disinhibition, and more common than I'd like to see."

"Nonsense, Bertrand. Joseph's candor is rather charming. Besides, any comments you have, you should address directly to him."

Roland huffed and puffed and looked at me up and down. It didn't matter to me what they had to say about me, because I couldn't care less.

"So Dr. Toricelli," Roland started up again "tell me, what are your current views on the Epstein case?"

"The Epstein case? That's the second time I've been asked about that this morning. I don't know," I shrugged, "I guess you could say it's taken some twists and turns, hasn't it?"

"I'm not sure what you mean," he said, "can you be more specific?"

"Well...I don't know...is this really important to you...I mean to both you guys?"

"Only to the extent that it is important to you," said Roland.

"Well...it's not," I said, "it's not important at all."

"I see," said Roland. "Nevertheless, if you would Dr. Toricelli, what do you mean when you say the case has taken its 'twists and turns'?"

"Just that, I didn't expect to end up here. Didn't expect you to either, for that matter."

"And how do you feel about that?" he asked.

"Hey look, Dr. Roland," I said, "let's just glide over it, okay? Why don't you swig some champagne and kick back?"

I poured myself another glass and looked out over the green lawns stretching to the forest. I hoped Olga would come back soon. She had really big tits, and I was imagining how it would be to press my face into them.

"Enough," I heard Ognev say to Roland.

"Fascinating," said Roland, "a pure lesion of will...of purpose, just as you predicted."

"Enough," Ognev repeated "your chatter is tedious and... premature."

"My apologies," said Roland, "but really, I'm quite confident that Dr. Toricelli will be only the most friendly of chaps. Isn't that right, doctor?"

I looked over to him, his words drawing me away, momentarily, from my fantasies about Olga.

"Yeah, whatever," I said, "whatever you guys have to say, it's cool." I looked at them both for a couple of seconds. "Mutt and Jeff," I said, laughing. "Mutt and Jeff go to Moscow."

Then Roland scowled again, and I slipped back into dreams of Olga.

A few minutes passed, before Ognev looked behind me again. And this time his face lit up in a really big smile.

"Sabrina, my dear," he said, "please, please come join us."

Sabrina Briand sashayed past me and Roland and pulled a chair up close to Ognev and sat down. He took her hand to his lips and kissed it, and then clasped it and rested it in his lap.

"Hello, Dr. Toricelli," she smiled, and threw back her long, thick waves of auburn hair. "You are being treated very, very well I hope?"

"Ms. Frontenac," I said, "or Ms. Briand if you prefer. May I say I've never seen you look so beautiful. I love that white dress, and the perfume is heavenly."

"Thank you, Dr. Toricelli. You are too kind."

"Please, call me Joseph," I said.

"As you wish. Of course. I hope you know, you are welcome here as long as you want to stay."

"Thanks. Thank you."

"And I think you could use a vacation now that Dr. Epstein's case is clearly closed."

"Right, sure." I didn't really know specifically what she meant by that but, on the other hand, it didn't really matter to me anymore. I remember Roland and Ognev looking at each other, like they had some kind of secret.

"Yes," said Roland, "I think it's come as quite a relief to us that the Volknick boy has been released, after new forensic evidence indicated that indeed Dr. Epstein's death was due to self-strangulation."

"No kidding?" I said, almost as a reflex. "When'd you hear that?"

"Just today," he added, "I was speaking to Mrs. Volknick."

"And are you surprised to learn that Dr. Toricelli?" asked Sabrina "after you received confessions of murder from two of his patients?"

"Sometimes an innocent person has a guilty conscience," I said, "and if their mind is weak, like Volknick, they can get crushed by its power."

I took a sip of champagne and felt its fizz gently on the back of my throat. For me the Epstein case was feeling like a parlor game. I didn't mind playing, so long as I didn't have to work too hard.

"And what about me Dr. Toricelli?" she said, "do I have a guilty conscience?"

"You?" I laughed "Nah. I figure you were just trying to buy a ticket out of...MuttandJeffland."

"Where?"

I looked at Ognev and Roland. "These two jokers," I said, "you wanted to get away from them."

She giggled and snuggled up close to Ognev. "You are half right," she said, "sometimes I do think Dr. Roland is a very dangerous man. Someone you must not stay too close to."

"Whatever," I said, while I was eyeing Olga's breasts. "It's all water under the bridge now."

"You don't seem very interested in the case anymore," said Roland.

"Hey look," I said, "you got to know when to cut loose. I'm on vacation, remember?"

"Yes, of course, Dr. Toricelli," smiled Roland, "I just find your capacity to detach...well," he looked over at Ognev. "Remarkable, that's all. Absolutely remarkable."

"Joseph's detachment is selective, Dr. Roland, I assure you," said Ognev, who must have been watching me getting an eyeful of Olga. "However, I think that a man of his status deserves something better than this fat little cow."

He stood up and gestured for me to do the same. "Come with me Joseph," he said, "I want to introduce you to some very interesting women I have...working for me."

I got up and he put his arm on my shoulder and we walked across the big green lawn toward the edge of the birch forest. The morning sun was brightening up all the flowers and shrubs, and I had a delicious light feeling inside me, like I was caught up inside a picture by Monet. We walked quite a ways down a path in the birch forest, and came into a clearing where there was a four story building that must have been half a block long. It was done up with real rich looking red brickwork, and looked like it should have been sitting on some fancy big-city avenue, instead of here in the middle of the woods.

"So what's this?" I asked "you running some high-class whorehouse in the middle of the woods?"

Ognev laughed. "Not quite, Joseph. But you will find the women here quite accommodating. Provided you have the right connection of course."

"Meaning you," I said.

"Exactly."

We walked through the front entrance and down a hallway directly to the back of the building. It opened up onto a quadrangle with lawns and walkways and three other buildings, similar to the first one, arranged around it.

"This looks like a college, Boris," I said, "so it's a college for whores you're keeping, is that it?"

"Quite a one-track mind you have, my friend," he laughed. "I never thought of it that way but, perhaps, in a way, there is some analogy."

We crossed the quadrangle, walked into the building opposite the first one, and went up to the fourth floor and knocked on one of the doors. This gorgeous looking brunette with short curly hair, black eyes and long legs answered the door.

"Good morning, Andrea," said Ognev.

"Good morning, Boris," she whispered. She gave him this real sexy, come-hither smile.

"Andrea," said Ognev, "I want to introduce you to a new member of our community. This is Joseph. Joseph Toricelli."

"I'm very pleased to meet you," she said, in what seemed like a Spanish accent, "did you just arrive?"

"Yeah," I said, licking my lips "a couple of days ago from New York." This girl was giving me a charge of horniness like I'd never felt in my life.

"Andrea," said Ognev ,"I want you to take Joseph under your wing, so to speak. You will give him a warm welcome, yes?"

"Of course, Boris," she said, smiling at me and looking me over.

"And," said Ognev, "of course you will introduce him to other members of the community."

"It will be a pleasure," she said.

WITH THAT, OGNEV left us alone and Andrea and I went into her apartment. It was a huge, sun-flooded room, arranged with a little kitchen, a big living area and a sleeping alcove. I was on fire for her and she was real cooperative and pleasant about knowing what I needed.

"Joseph," she said, taking me by the hand and leading me toward the bed "you may take off your clothes and put them on this chair." Then she unzipped her jeans and tugged them off, pulled off her blouse, and hopped into her bed deliciously naked. "I wait for you Joseph," she said, "with great...anticipation."

I nearly tripped over myself pulling off my shoes and clothes, and more or less flew into the sack from across the room. We got into it real quick and spent the rest of the morning and all afternoon playing out, I believe, every known sexual position tried in the heterosexual world. She was unbelievable in the way she knew how to take care of me, and I couldn't imagine being with a more exquisite woman. Every once in a while we'd take a little bath and eat fresh fruit and drink champagne and watch the light change on the trees and grass and flowerbeds outside. But mainly it was one high-energy, wild-ass ride down the bumpy whitewaters of sexual desire, and the only reason we finally let up was because there was a knock on the door in the late afternoon.

I stayed under the sheets while Andrea put on a robe and answered the door. In a minute she came back and sat down on the side of the bed. "I missed you," I smiled. She leaned over and kissed me on my forehead.

"So who was that at the door?" I said.

"Michael," she said, "he wanted to know if I was going to the dinner."

"Dinnertime, already, huh?" I said, "but what dinner does he want to take you to?"

"Twice a week we have dinner in the main house, all of us, before we go to Boris's lecture."

"Yeah? And who exactly is 'all of us'?"

"The members of the community. There are about thirty of us."

"No kidding. And what do you guys do with Boris anyway?"

She got a real serious look on her face before she answered me. "It is not really what we do with Boris, Joseph," she said, "it is all about what Boris does for us."

"That's cool. So what's old Boris do for you all, then?"

"Everything."

"Everything, huh? That's, uh, that's quite a lot. But, how do you mean, 'everything'?"

"He takes care of us. He is...our father, our mother, our...everything. He teaches us all good things—about life and beauty and philosophy— about all the good pleasures of the senses."

"I see. I think I do, anyway. And I guess I've been getting myself a taste of this...philosophy, huh?"

She smiled. "Pleasure, Joseph, it is the highest gift and should be taken in its full measure. Always."

"Always, huh?" I turned that one over in my mind, or what was left of it, for a while, and it seemed to make more and more sense.

"You know," I said, "I could see myself really getting into this...philosophy."

With that, I pulled her down to me and felt her soft, full lips against mine, and her warm smooth skin press against me all over. We had sex, one more time, before getting up and going to dinner at Boris's place.

BY THE TIME we got there, the long table in the dining room was about full. Boris was seated at the head, with Roland at his side. I don't remember seeing Sabrina there. Andrea and I sat together toward the middle of the table. Waiters came around to pour champagne for everyone and then Ognev stood up to speak.

"Friends," he announced "I would like to begin our discussion this evening by asking you all to extend a warm welcome to a very special guest in our community, Joseph Toricelli, from New York. Let us raise our glasses and wish him a good visit."

Everybody toasted me and said, "Welcome" and Andrea kissed me gently on my cheek.

"Thanks, thank you," I said, "I'm real happy to be here."

Then we all dug in to this lavish seven-course meal, while some soft sort of New Age music spilled out of speakers overhead. A light buzz of dinner conversation developed, with people speaking in this real mellow tone to each other, mainly about the things they'd been doing all day. As I remember it, there was an amazing amount of talk about sex, and people thanking each other for what a good time they'd had. The rest of the conversation seemed to be about the food they'd eaten and what a beautiful day it had been. Ognev and Roland mainly spoke to each other, and every once in a while I'd hear Roland say "Remarkable, remarkable."

After dinner we all moved into the living room, and Ognev went up to a podium while everyone else sat in chairs that had been set up in several rows. I remember sitting next to Andrea and holding her hand and smelling the sweet perfume she'd put on before we went out. Ognev cleared his throat to speak.

"Friends, good friends," he began "as always, it warms my heart and energizes my spirit to see you all gathered here this evening. From each of you emanates an aura of transcendent happiness, wisdom and peace. I ask now that we bow our heads for a moment and reflect on all that is beautiful and pleasurable."

Everybody, including Ognev, bowed their heads.

In a few seconds he looked up and started to speak again. "Now my friends," he said," tonight I want us to address, as we do periodically, our most sacred task and responsibility, that of deliverance. For the time has come, once again, for one of you to be chosen to venture out of our realm. In so doing, you will seek out and deliver to us a new member, and in return you will ascend to the highest realm of ecstasy, far away in space and time from our present paradise. I look out to you now and wonder; who feels best prepared, and willing, at this time to embark on the quest for deliverance?"

For a minute or so there was silence in the room. Then a young guy in the back row stood up and started to speak.

"Boris," he said, "I am ready, I feel it as we are gathered here. I am ready to leave my friends and ascend to the highest realm."

"And Charles," said Ognev, "can you tell us more about how you know this?"

"I believe I have learned all that I need to know about the pleasures and experiences of this realm," he said, "I am ready for new knowledge, and ready to bring a new soul to our community."

"Good. Very well then," said Ognev, "we shall now congratulate Charles, and tonight we shall celebrate his decision and forthcoming departure to a realm of higher pleasures. Let us now all stand and raise our faces upward toward the next realm. Let us all wish Charles a good journey."

Everyone, including me, stood up and gazed up toward the ceiling. It was in the shape of a dome and had a retractable roof that was opened up to a black, starry sky. I got this feeling that somehow seemed to come in from outside of me, this feeling of hope that someday I could go where Charles was going.

We spent the next several hours drinking and dancing to all kinds of piped in music, and just mixing it up among one another. The community was about evenly split between men and women and nobody seemed to be specifically hooked up to anybody else. All the women were gorgeous, and I started to really hanker after one of them, Elizabeth, this tall redhead with a Boston accent. Andrea didn't mind at all, she was already in the embrace of old Charles, and covering him with kisses and wishing him one helluva bon voyage. Elizabeth and I danced 'till well past midnight, and then went back to her apartment on the quadrangle where we bedded down for the night.

THE NEXT THREE days pretty much blurred into each other, and each was centered around the pursuit of sex and food and dance and champagne; with a few naps thrown in, in between. When you wanted a little outdoor activity, you could stroll the woods and meadows and lawns of Ognev's estate, or go swimming in a big pool he had set up a little ways from the house. Now and then I'd even find time to shoot the bull with some of the house staff , those that spoke a little English anyway; mainly about American movies and sports and cars and stuff like that.

Then, late in the afternoon of my third day there, I was lazing in the twilight between just waking, and sweet dreams of sex with my latest girl. I can't even remember her name now, let's call her Charlene. I was lying alone in her bed in one of the apartments on the quadrangle, and I seemed to be slowly opening and closing my eyelids and dreaming, or seeing, Charlene sitting over me. But Charlene then seemed to turn into Sabrina Briand, and then back to Charlene, and then to Sabrina again, and so on. After a while, I clearly opened my eyes and in fact, right there over me, was the smiling, radiant face of Sabrina Briand.

"Ms. Frontenac," I said, "or...Sabrina...nice to see you. I, uh, I thought you were Charlene."

"She is out by the pool," she said. "But Dr. Toricelli," her voice got low in a kind of whisper, "how are you?"

"Fine. Just fine."

"But how are you feeling?"

"Fine," I repeated "I mean, to tell you the truth, I never felt better in my life."

"Really?"

"Yeah, really."

She looked kind of confused.

"I mean," I said, "why do you ask?"

"I...I don't know. Maybe it's a mistake but, Aunt Valentina, she thinks you are very, very sick."

"Aunt Valentina?" I said, "she...what could she know about me?"

"I...I don't know exactly," she said. She was looking more confused and sort of pouty. I was getting real horny and reached out to touch her breasts.

"Dr. Toricelli," she pulled back "what are you doing?"

"Nothing. What's the problem?"

"I told you," she said, now sounding more angry than confused. "Aunt Valentina thinks you are sick. But it is a secret. You and I must tell no one."

"Say, what is it with your Aunt Valentina, anyway?" I laughed. "She's that wacky old woman who wouldn't let me in her house, right?"

She seemed to ignore what I was saying. "She came to visit me this morning," she said, "Boris arranged for her to come to the house. I had already told her by phone you were Boris's guest."

"Yeah, so...good for me, right?"

She pulled a little box out of her purse and gave it to me.

"She brought this for you," she said, "it is a secret that you and I must tell no one. That is what she said."

"A secret gift huh? Now that's real sweet of your old aunt, isn't it?"

"I must go now," she said, "you must not tell anyone...you must not tell Boris, or anyone about this. Do you promise?"

"Do I promise?...promise?" I repeated. It was like I had to get a handle on the meaning of that word. "Yeah, 'promise,'" I said again, "yeah, got it...sure why not? I promise not to tell anyone."

"Good," she smiled "goodbye Dr. Toricelli."

She hopped off the bed and left.

I sat up in bed and unwrapped the little box. "A present," I said to myself ,"isn't that nice. I didn't know Aunt Valentina was such a sweet old bird." I opened up the box and found a note, a hypodermic needle, and an injection bottle. The note said:

Dr. Toricelli,

My best wishes to you. Please take an injection of this as soon as possible. You will find a pleasure you can't imagine. But tell no one.

I looked at the bottle, all the label showed was a chemical formula: C19 H21 NO4 and "+++ other analogs." I stared at it awhile. It seemed like I'd seen it, that formula , before, but I couldn't place it. "Big molecule," I said to myself. I looked at the hypodermic, then back at the bottle. All right, Doc, I said to myself, laughing kind of goofy, "let's give it a shot." I drew up the stuff about halfway into the syringe and aimed the needle at my left deltoid. "Is this weird, or what?" I said, before I buried the needle into my muscle and pushed down the plunger.

There was no pain at all, at least for a few minutes or so. And then, bing-bang-boom; all of a sudden I felt not only the prick of the needle but, all around me, came this real heavy, sick, sad feeling. "Son of a bitch," I said to myself ,"son of a fucking bitch." I got to feeling real nasty and I looked around the room and wanted to bust up everything in it. "You rotten bastard!" I shouted at nobody in particular. I felt like throwing up, and I was real dizzy, but somehow I wanted to get out of bed, and just stand up, and walk. I got up and stood by the bed, real unsteady, yeah, like I was seasick. And at the same time my skin felt all wooly and like I had to pull it off.

I staggered, little by little, over to the mirror. I just had to take a look at myself. And there was this image, butt naked in the glass. At first I couldn't quite figure out who it was I was looking at. I mean, it was me, but, it was me with a whole different story. Or maybe it was the same story, but the different parts of it had shifted in what they meant, and what was important. The guy in the mirror, I gradually came to understand, was Joe Toricelli, who'd come to Moscow to solve Horatio Epstein's murder. Who'd come to Moscow courtesy of Tim Landsdowne because...because I was about to get framed for the killings Horace Crassidy had done. I shook my head back and forth a few times. Then I went over to the sink and splashed some water on my face. "Son of a bitch," I was saying to myself "what the hell is going on? La-la Land, that's what," I told myself, "I've been hanging out in some kind of drugged up state." I took a look around the apartment. Beautiful place, I thought, and a beautiful woman lives here.

Over on the kitchen table I noticed a bowl of fruit, some cheese and a stopped-up bottle about a quarter full of champagne. Must be in what they give us to eat, I thought, that's where the drug is. But what? It had to be one helluva drug...or a bunch of drugs. I went back to the bed and looked again at the bottle Valentina had sent. There was that formula: C19 H21 NO4 and "+++ other analogs." What the hell is it? I wracked my brain to name that formula. Then, all of a sudden, it hit me. Naloxone. Yeah, that's what it is, I thought, fucking Naloxone! The party pooper drug. The total opiate antagonist. The drug that'll get you straight if you've got heroin or morphine on board.

"Holy shit!" I muttered. Ognev had bought me a ticket to...to some kind of zombie-Eden, courtesy of morphine and whatever the hell else he was giving me. Yeah, it was definitely more than just opiates. That's why the antidote had to include this "+++ other analogs" stuff.

Then I started to feel a kind of familiar rush again. A real warm, juicy, lazy, goofy, kind of rush. And I heard this sound of white noise. All just like the first time I must have been hit with this stuff. Yeah, I thought, it must have been in that sweet smelling stuff that blew into the car when I passed out there at the gatehouse, on my first night here. And man, it felt good then, and it felt good now. It was unbelievable how good it felt. But no, no, I thought. I can't. There ain't no returning to la-la land, no fucking way. I put on my trousers and pulled off the belt and tightened it hard around my left arm. Then I grabbed the works and drew up a full syringe of Valentina's stuff again. Then I drove the tip of the needle up into the main line and gave a slow, steady push to that nasty crash recipe Valentina had cooked up for me. Yeah, there it was again. Pain, surliness, nausea, and this weird empty sadness where I felt like crying. Yeah, that's it, I said. That real shitty feeling that hurts so good.

I picked up Valentina's bottle to check out how much of the stuff I had left. I estimated maybe another half a dozen shots or so. Who knows how long this stuff, presumably Ognev's stuff, is going to stay on board, I thought. I only hoped to hell it wouldn't outlast whatever I had left in

Valentina's bottle. A wave of dizziness suddenly came over me and my hands started to shake real bad, and I dropped the bottle on the floor. "No!" I heard myself shout. I grabbed it back up and looked it over for any cracks. Thank God, it was okay. It was the only thing that stood between me getting out of here or being one of Ognev's zombie... "members," as he'd put it.

Then there was a knock on the door.

"Doctor?" I heard a familiar voice whine. "Dr. Toricelli," called the voice I could only know as Roland's. "May I come in?"

"You fucking slimeball," I muttered under my breath, while I stuffed Valentina's bottle and works underneath the pillows. "Sure," I called out, sitting on the side of the bed and trying to sound like a nice, pleasant, numbskull. "Sure, c'mon in."

Roland strode in with a big smile on his face. He'd been visiting me every day and asking me a bunch of questions. Now it dawned on me that he must have been keeping tabs on my response to this morphine-plus stuff. Steady, I thought to myself, be steady.

"Well, Dr. Toricelli," he said, standing over me. "How goes it today, old man?"

"Fine," I said, I thought my voice sounded a little shaky. "I mean, beautiful."

"Good, good. And I trust you're getting along well with your latest roommate, yes?" He gave me this grotesque wink.

"Roommate? Oh yeah...her. Oh, yeah she's, she's a real peach of a girl."

"Yes, I quite agree. And spectacularly endowed, I might add, judging from the figure she cuts at poolside. I just saw her there now."

"Oh, right," I said. "Have to get over there myself, real soon."

"Of course, of course you will, old man, and I won't detain you long. Indeed this will be my last visit for quite awhile, as I'm off to New York this afternoon."

"No kidding? That's, that's too bad. I'll miss you."

Suddenly, his right eyebrow arched. "Is that so?" he said, each word coming out slowly. "What do you mean it's 'too bad, you'll miss me'?"

"Uh, gee," I said slowly, "I dunno, just one of those expressions, I guess."

"And specifically, what does it mean to you, Dr. Toricelli?"

I paused a minute to think. Wrong phrase, I thought to myself, there's nothing "too bad," and nothing to "miss" in la-la land. I smiled at Roland. "You know, I really don't know what the hell it means," I said, laughing, "I really don't."

Then Roland slowly smiled, and lowered his brow. "Yes," he said,

"I don't suppose you would."

"But I really do hope you enjoy your trip back to New York," I said, "like the song says, it's a helluva town; isn't it?"

"Yes, it is. And do you...find yourself missing it? Perhaps longing to return?"

"Oh, no, not at all. This is fine, just as fine as it gets, right here."

"Um-hum, I quite agree, Dr. Toricelli. I quite agree. Well then," he said, extending his hand "hope to see you again, soon, on my next visit."

"Sure thing," I said, standing up to shake his hand, "always, always a pleasure."

I walked him to the door and tried to keep some kind of mellow, nitwit smile fixed on my face. He opened the door and then suddenly turned and seemed to look straight into me.

"One more thing, doctor," he said, "I trust you have been eating properly?" He looked past me to the table in the kitchen area.

"Oh yes I have, thank you. Three squares a day and plenty of good snacks, sure."

He looked at me again, squinting slightly. "Good, good," he said, shifting his eyes around like he was trying to think through something. "Well then," he said, "without further delay, doctor, I bid you goodbye, until our next visit."

"You got it, Dr. Roland. Bon voyage."

Then he turned and walked out the door.

"Son of a bitch," I muttered, and grabbed the works and bottle back out from under the pillows and gave myself another shot. I'd felt myself getting pulled, little by little, back into the drug fog, even while I'd been saying goodbye to Roland. Nonetheless, he must have suspected there was something wrong. I'd made a mistake saying "too bad, I'll miss you," and I wasn't sure he was just going to let it go.

I paced around the room awhile, trying to get through that nauseous feeling that came over me after I took a hit of the Naloxone. I tried to piece together what was going on and what I was going to do. For sure Ognev and Roland were teamed up in cooking up this feelgood shit. And they were dosing up everybody in the compound here, and then keeping tabs on what they did, what they felt, etc. But why? Were they running some kind of experiment? And who the hell were these people? Where'd they get them? Where'd they come from?

And what about Sabrina? Okay, so she'd once been a patient of Roland's. But what is she doing with Roland, and Ognev, now? She's supposed to be Ognev's cousin, but it seemed to me she acted more like his girlfriend. So, if she is hooked up with Ognev in some way, then why the hell did she give me this antidote, courtesy of her Aunt Valentina? And finally, where does Epstein fit in here? Was he in on all this? Or had he just found out about it, and learned too much for his own damn good. Who the hell knew? I just knew my best bet was going to be to get the hell out of here and get the police—Moscow, New York, whatever—to start asking all these questions. Problem was, I wasn't exactly going to be able to call a car service to get me off the grounds, and Ognev was going to get real sore if he found out I wanted to leave.

Just as I was turning all this stuff over in my head, I looked out the window and down below saw Ognev and Roland walking across the quadrangle, toward the front door of the building I was in. Aw shit, I thought, now they're both coming back to look me over. I didn't fool him, I thought, I'm not going to fool anybody.

I was on the top floor of the building, and I figured they'd be at my door in about two minutes, so I had to move fast. I picked up the Naloxone and hypodermic, and figured I'd better hide it real well because...who knows?...they might even start nosing around the room. I looked around real quick where to put it. Under the mattress? Behind the fridge? In the bookcase, somehow? Then I looked up at the ceiling, where there was a board that lay over a little trapdoor entrance. I pulled up a chair and stood up on it, and then lifted up the board and slid it aside. When I poked my head in the trapdoor, I saw it was pretty dim up there, but it looked like it opened up into a little crawlspace of an attic. That's it, I told myself, that's it, nobody's home, for now anyway. I jumped back down, put the chair back against the wall, put Valentina's stuff back in the little box and stuffed it in my pants. Then I jumped up and grabbed the edge of the trapdoor hole, and hoisted myself up into the crawlspace. I slid the board back over the entrance and lay up there real quietly.

IN A HALF A minute or so there was a knock on the door. Then, after a few seconds, I heard Ognev's voice.

"Hello? Joseph? Hello?" he said.

Then, after another couple of knocks, I heard the door open and the footsteps of Ognev and Roland.

"So," said Ognev, "you say he was not at the pool?"

"No," said Roland, "I told you, I checked."

"Probably in another apartment," Ognev said "or elsewhere on the grounds."

"Strange," said Roland, "I...I don't like it. I tell you he looked different. He may even be trying to escape, right now."

"And how?" Ognev laughed "how will he penetrate a high-voltage steel mesh perimeter which is four meters high, two meters deep and under twenty-four hour surveillance?"

"I...I don't suppose it is possible," said Roland.

"And where is his motivation?" Ognev asked. "Even, even if he had not eaten or drank all day, and by the way, I saw with my own eyes how he ate a big lunch today; the half-life of KG-2 is 15 to 18 hours. So he would still have effective blood levels."

"All right," said Roland, "I...I grant you your logic. I don't know how it's possible...but I tell you...he was different. And why did he say 'too bad, I will miss you'? It is absolutely inconsistent with how his world should look...it..."

"Please, please Bertrand. You should consider it a kind of verbal tic. It means nothing, do you hear me, nothing."

"No," said Roland, "I...I feel there is something wrong. Maybe...the drug is not establishing its effect...properly. You know...we should have tested him...from his first morning on the drug with the Torento-Toricelli story."

"Absolutely not," said Ognev, "it would have been wildly premature, and would have profoundly disrupted the full development of the drug effect, especially if he'd become violent."

"I suppose..."

"I'm afraid, Bertrand, that you are having a crisis of nerves about phase three."

"No," Roland gasped "absolutely not, Boris, you have my word."

"Really? Then why did you, shall we be delicate and say 'excuse' yourself, from the autopsy and organ processing?"

"That's not true...you know I had a call from New York. I had to..."

"There was nothing you *had* to do," said Ognev, "I'm sure it could have waited. But neither your stomach...nor, perhaps, your heart...would allow you to witness young Charles as a specimen and, if all goes well, as our first source of a new line of commodities."

Roland was quiet.

"You have nothing to say?" said Ognev.

Still no response from Roland.

"Your silence tells us everything, doesn't it?" said Ognev. "You were a fool to grow attached to the young man. You will be a fool to grow attached to any of them, do you hear me? Are they somehow special to you, because they once paid you money to participate in your seminars?"

"That is nonsense," said Roland, and then cleared his throat, "Though perhaps there was something about Charles, his lips, his eyes, his soft skin."

"But you must understand, Bertrand, they are our material, our raw living material, in the research and manufacturing process. Nothing more."

"I understand," Roland whispered.

"I hope you do," said Ognev, sounding dark, "because if you do not, you will allow sentimentality and guilt to infect you, and the entire enterprise. Do you see how dangerous that is?"

"I...I do," said Roland, "but Boris, I assure you, no such thing will happen."

"But you see, Bertrand," said Ognev, with his voice lowering as if he had to contain his anger, "it already has. That is why we are standing here now, looking for Toricelli. Your guilt about Charles is shaking your judgment. So, you come to believe that Toricelli is no longer drugged, and has found you out."

"I...I don't know," Roland whispered ,"I will feel better after you have examined him."

"And that I will," said Ognev, "in due time. But at the moment you are assuming responsibility for our highest priority...do you foresee any problems in New York?"

"Absolutely not. The truck is already at the airport and a very handsome bribe has been negotiated with Customs. I will be convening a meeting at Daylight tomorrow evening regarding the first stage of distribution. In all likelihood we will start with the project houses in Red Hook."

Ognev laughed. "So the Negroes will be our first test market, yes?"

"Prudence dictates it," said Roland, "as I said, any bad reactions will maintain a low profile there. Let's save the suburbs for when we're sure the product is fully tested."

They walked toward the door with this last exchange and in a second I heard the door close and could hear their muffled voices fade and disappear down the hallway. I stayed up there a few more minutes, giving myself another shot of Naloxone-plus and trying to plan out my next move. One way or another, I figured, these maniacs would kill me. Maybe it would be like they did to young Charles there, or maybe like the way they must have with Epstein.

As best I could tell, their scheme was about testing this KG-2, that's what Ognev called it, on people they'd kidnapped from Roland's seminars, and then getting it ready for distribution in America, with Club Daylight as a base of operations. Why exactly they killed Charles, Ognev had said he was a specimen, but also a source of commodities, I wasn't sure about.

But, sure as hell, I had to get my ass out of there ASAP. Roland may have been nervous, just like Ognev said, but he'd definitely picked up that I wasn't gaga on KG-2 anymore. And what was this stuff about the "Torento-Toricelli Story?" That'd sure sent a shot through me. But what else could it be, but that the news was out about the fingerprints, and that I was now officially on the lam. Well, I figured, I could trust these bozos wouldn't rat on me. No, I'm sure they've got a lot more ambitious plans for me.

I slid back the trapdoor lid and jumped back down to the apartment. I was revved up with Naloxone and adrenaline and ready to, somehow, make a getaway. I just hoped I wouldn't run into Ognev in the meantime, and give him any reason to be suspicious.

I pulled the chair back under the trapdoor and put the lid back just like it had been. Then I decided to take the cheese and fruit snacks on the table and dump them down the toilet, just so no one would think I wasn't keeping up my KG-2 ration. I was just about ready to get rid of the champagne as well, to pour it down the sink, when an idea flashed through my brain. Why not save it up in a jar I could carry? Just in case I might get the opportunity to give old Ognev a little taste of his own bubbly.

I emptied out a bottle of vitamin pills I'd found in the bathroom, filled it with the champagne, and screwed the lid on tight. After another hit of Naloxone, I got fully dressed and put on a sport jacket. I put the vitamin bottle in one inside pocket of the jacket and the Naloxone works in the other. Then I left the apartment and walked into the chilly air of what was now mid-evening, first down the path through the birch forest and then across the big lawn toward Ognev's mansion.

AS I CAME TOWARD the shrubs and gazebo, just near the front of the house, two big guys came out from the portico and started walking towards me. Be cool, I told myself, real cool. When they got close, I was able to recognize one of them. He was a big goofy-looking guy named Gennady. I'd remembered he could speak a little English, because I'd gotten into some bull sessions with him yesterday about his favorite American actors. He'd said Bruce Willis or Sylvester Stallone or somebody like that.

"Hey, Gennady," I called out, "seen any movies lately?"

He guffawed a couple of times. "No, no, Mr. Joseph not today."

"Bruce Willis, right? He's the best," I said.

"Yes, yes of course Mr. Joseph. But now I must bring you to Dr. Ognev. He said me that if I see you to please bring you to him for conversation."

"Sounds great," I said, while I felt my insides go cold, "where is the big guy, anyway?"

"This way Mr. Joseph, this way."

I walked with my escorts to the patio on the other side of the house, where we found Ognev alone, reading a book and sipping some tea. When we approached him he looked up from his book, smiled, and seemed to study me with those cold blue eyes.

"Joseph," he said, "good evening. Please, please sit down."

"Thanks Boris," I said, sitting down. "Beautiful evening, isn't it?"

"Yes, I quite agree," he said, and signaled to Gennady and his buddy to leave us alone.

"And would you like some tea, Joseph?" he asked.

"Oh, uh, no thanks. Just had some champagne and uh, just want to enjoy the buzz for awhile."

"Yes, I see," he said, looking me up and down, "by the way, I understand Dr. Roland came to say goodbye to you today."

"Oh yeah, Dr. Short-stuff," I said. "Yeah, I wished him a big bon voyage and all that."

"And how do you feel about him going back to New York?"

"Feel?" I said, "gee, I don't know. It's fun to travel, I reckon, and they say New York's a helluva town."

"Any other reaction to it Joseph?" he kept his eyes riveted on me while I sat back and did my best to look real laid back.

"Reaction? Uh, gee, no, Boris. I mean I'm not quite following you here. Are we playing a game right now, or something?"

Ognev laughed. "A game? No, no not at all Joseph."

"Okay, whatever. Hey, look Boris," I tried to get his eyes off me, "aren't the stars looking fantastic tonight?"

He looked up a moment. "Yes, yes they are Joseph, quite magnificent." Then his gaze returned to me. "And Joseph," he went on, "how have you been feeling today? Your...mood, in general, that is."

"My mood? Uh, tell you what Boris, I don't give it any thought, you know? I mean like...everything's just real fine, copascetic. Know what I mean?"

"Yes, Joseph," said Ognev, his eyes now looked a little bit less cold. "Yes I do know what you mean."

We talked a little more, about the good late summer weather, my latest roommate, and how much I was enjoying my "visit", that sort of thing. I had a gut feeling I was coming across just fine with him, though I kept worrying about a rebound rush of KG-2, and whether I'd be able to keep it together enough until I could mainline some more Naloxone. In fact, seeing as there was no obvious opportunity to spike his tea with my champagne stash, I wanted to cut this visit short and start casing around for a way to escape this joint. So after awhile I stood up, breathed in some night air, and told him I had a real hankering to go find Andrea...or Elizabeth...or Charlene...or whoever I could get my hands on.

"Of course, Joseph," he said, "it is your privilege. But, just one more thing before you go."

"Sure, what's that?"

"I heard on the American news channel today that your cousin,

Jacob Roma, I believe his name is, was killed yesterday."

As he said this, his cold blue stare drilled into my eyes and everything inside me wanted to shout out "No! Fuck no, it can't be!" But I did my best not to miss a beat and try to keep a lid on things.

"Is that so?" I said, trying to sound casually surprised, "and what exactly went down with dear old Jake?"

"The television said he was shot dead by thieves, after he had come to the assistance of his fellow policemen in a bank robbery."

"Curious situation," I said with a shrug, "chasing robbers isn't in his normal line of work."

"Yes," said Ognev ,"the report mentioned that. It was just by chance that he was walking by the bank when it happened."

"No kidding. Well, that's fate I suppose."

"I think not," said Ognev. "No, I think it is directly because of you, Joseph, that he died, and that his death has achieved such prominence."

"Yeah?" I said, smiling, "how do you figure that?"

"Because it was he who brought you into the police department, Joseph. You, Joseph Torento, the famous killer of the famous boy who drove the taxi."

"Hah," I laughed, "I like the way you put that, Boris: 'the famous killer of the famous boy who drove the taxi.' But I guess I don't really get the connection you're trying to make."

"It is very simple, Joseph," he said. "Even the TV newsman made a comment about it. When this scandal became public knowledge, that you, Dr. Toricelli are also the murderer Joseph Torento, your cousin felt terrible embarrassment...and responsibility...for giving you a police job. There are also, of course, rumors that he was protecting you. And so, to prove that somehow he is really a good policeman, he tried to become a hero in this bank robbery. Imagine, he confronted two criminals carrying assault rifles. And he had only a pistol. Well, I think you can understand the picture, yes Joseph?"

"Sure, I follow you Boris. But them's the breaks, right? So anyway, you seen any of my girls around? You know...like Andrea, especially?"

He didn't say anything, but kept his eyes fixed on me, real hard, like he was looking for something, like he was looking for some kind of sign of something resembling a normal human reaction to what he'd said to me. But I wasn't going to give it to him. No way. And, in fact, I kept telling myself, whether I believed it or not, that he was just trying to fuck with my head, to see if I was doped up just right, and nothing more. No, I thought, old Jake was really alive and kicking, regardless of how mixed up he must have felt about me and Joe Torento being one and the same.

"So Boris," I said, "the cat got your tongue or what? You ain't seen any of the girls around here tonight?"

"Try the solarium Joseph," he smiled ,"you may have some luck there."

"Thanks Boris, thanks a lot," I said, turning to leave, "maybe I'll see you around later tonight, all right?"

"By all means, Joseph, please go and enjoy yourself."

I walked back around the front of the house, stepped inside the shadows of some bushes, and gave myself a quick and dirty IM shot of Naloxone. I'd already gone through half the bottle and figured if I didn't get out of here tonight, I'd run out of Naloxone before the KG-2 washed out and then I'd be sure to end up as a permanent member of Ognev's Zombie Academy.

I ran out of the bushes and walked up toward the portico. There was a big black ZHIL parked underneath it. I went up to the driver's side and nosed around to see if the keys were in the ignition lock. No luck. But what difference would it make, I thought, they'd blow my head off before they'd let me get past the gatehouse anyway. Still, I felt like taking that car was my only chance out of there.

Just then, I saw Gennady again. He came lumbering down the front steps of the house and called out to me.

"Hello, Mr. Joseph," he said, "it's a beautiful night, yes?"

"Lovely," I said, "real crisp." I took a deep breath and leaned back against the driver's door of the ZHIL. He came up to me and reached behind me and grabbed a flask off the dashboard of the car.

"It's good car," he said, and then took a swig from the flask, "very strong, very heavy, very good motor."

"Right," I said, "looks like one real serious machine."

"Yes," he laughed, "very serious machine." He held out the flask to me. "You want?" he offered.

"Sure, why not," I said. I took in a mouthful of what must have been straight vodka. "You know," I said, smacking my lips, "this'd be one hell of a car to drive around in America. Everybody'd wonder what the hell it was."

"Yes?" he said.

"Sure," I said, and passed the flask back to him. "Why...you'd get all kinds of attention. Women would think you were one cool dude...you'd probably get the car full of them."

"No, Mr. Joseph," he said ,"you are joking."

"No, not at all, Gennady. I'm telling you, you have the right car, especially something kind of edgy or...exotic...like this beast, and man, there's no telling how many women'd come after you."

"It's unbelievable," he said, like he believed every word of it, and was already thinking of how he could pack himself into one for express, overnight delivery to the States.

"Believe it, pal," I said. "And just picture yourself now; you're sailing this baby around the streets of, say, Hollywood or Las Vegas. You're sporting some sunglasses, a little ponytail, an earring or two. You got yourself some long side-burns and you're wearing a bright green polyester shirt. It's...oh man, I'm telling you Gennady, you and this car, I mean the pussy's going to come purring around you like...like you're Sylvester Stallone or something, you know what I mean?"

But he didn't say anything. The big turkey just stood there, struck dumb, so to speak, by whatever steamed-up fantasies were swirling around in that thick, sledgehammer skull of his. Then his buddy called out to him from the front door, something in Russian ,and all I could make out was the word "telephone." Whatever it was, it kicked him back into reality mode.

"*Da, da,*" he said, "*momyent.*" Then he handed me the flask. "Wait me here, Mr. Joseph," he said, "I come back in one moment." He turned and went up the stairs. Meanwhile, I looked at the flask and felt for the jar of champagne in my jacket and got the distinct sensation that somebody up there liked me. Real quick, I dumped about half the flask of vodka out on the grass. Then I reached in my pocket and got the vitamin bottle, and unscrewed the top. I couldn't believe how shaky my hands were, which had to be from some combination of nerves and withdrawal from KG-2. I poured most of the spiked champagne into the vodka flask, but when I got toward the end I got real clumsy and dropped the vitamin bottle, and it cracked into a few pieces on the cement. Bad move I thought to myself, bad, klutzy move. I looked around for a second, and then kicked the shards of glass underneath the car.

Okay, big boy, I said to myself, I'm ready for you now, come on back. Mr. Joseph's got something that's going to addle that dick brain of yours real good.

In a few minutes he returned, and the first thing he did was wipe his lips with his hand and reach out and take the flask from me. He guzzled a few mouthfuls and then handed it back.

"It was call from Moscow," he said, "soon I must go to receive package."

"Oh yeah?" I said, and faked taking a swig from the flask, "you know I ought to hook you up with these hot girls I know from LA, they're three models, who're doing a shoot in Moscow. I think they'd really go for a guy like you."

I handed him back the flask and he took another swallow and sniffed a couple of times.

"Yes?" he said.

"Oh, definitely. They're over at the..." I tried to remember the name of a posh hotel somebody'd told me about on the airplane, "the, uh, Metropole...you know where that is?"

"Yes, of course, very good hotel." His smile started to get a little crooked, and it looked to me like the old KG-2 may be kicking in.

"'Course, you'd need an introduction, which I'd be glad to provide...if you want to take me along with you."

"Take you? To Moscow, tonight?"

"Yeah, why not? You'll have the time of your life."

He got this kind of pained, serious look on his face, like he was up against some kind of problem he'd never imagined could come up.

"But it's not possible!" he gasped. "No, no Mr. Joseph, it's impossible. Dr. Ognev said us, many, many times, absolutely no students must leave without him. He worries about safety of students...always."

"Of course he does. He's, uh, he's a real sweetheart that way. But you see, Gennady, you taking me, this is okay, it really is. I'm going to show you a great time. And you're going to smuggle me out in the trunk here, so nobody knows...and worries about me. And we'll be back later...feeling real safe and sound and happy, see?"

His eyelids were already starting to droop a little and his smile was getting more crooked. This was going to work, it had to, I could feel it.

"So what do you say, Gennady, huh? Let's get me in the trunk right now and let's get rolling to Moscow...to see these beautiful American girls."

He stood there dumb for a few seconds, kind of staring off into space. Then he opened his mouth real slow and waited...it looked like he was waiting for some thought to pass. Then he cleared his throat and said, "Okay."

WE WALKED TO the back of the car, he opened the trunk lid, and I hopped in and pulled it closed over me. Then he went and cranked up the car and soon it started rolling down the driveway. In another few seconds we slowed to a stop by the gatehouse. I heard some muffled conversation back and forth, and then we were moving again, first down the last part of the gravel driveway, and then along the bumpy dirt road through the forest. It's going to work, I thought to myself in that dark, stuffy trunk, it's really going to work.

After we came out on the highway, we drove for quite a while, and then the car gradually came to a stop. I didn't hear a sound; no doors slamming, no traffic noise, no nothing. After this went on for a bit I figured it was time to get out. I flipped open the trunk lock from the inside, jumped out on the road and walked over to the driver's side of the car. There was old Gennady, his head resting against the window, and sleeping like a baby. Just like I must have been on that first night in the car. So, I figured, this stuff must be pretty much guaranteed to knock you on your ass, before you build up a tolerance to the sedative effects.

I opened the door, pushed him over to the passenger's side and got behind the wheel. Through the windshield, I could see a dome of sky glowing over the city lights of what had to be Moscow, maybe thirty miles away. I drove in pretty fast, getting to the city's outskirts in about half an hour, and then actually managed to follow some signs and make my way into the center of town.

I pulled over and parked the ZHIL, with Gennady still passed out, along a little side street off Tverskaya. As it turned out, it wasn't far from the Metropole Hotel. "Good luck, Gennady," I whispered to him, as I got out of the car, "look me up if you ever visit the States."

Then I hailed down a gypsy cab and told him the address of Valentina's place. We got there in a jiffy, which was a real good thing because I'd already taken the very last hit of Naloxone, quite a while ago now, and I could feel a nice warm surge of KG-2 creeping up on me pretty strong.

BY THE TIME I was rapping on Valentina's door, it had to be two o'clock in the morning. I kept banging away without hearing a hint of noise inside, and hoped to hell it was just a matter of time before I roused her from her sleep. As I stood there, it crossed my mind that she must have gotten wind of the Toricelli-Torento stuff. If she did, I figured she'd let me know soon enough. Otherwise, I sure as hell didn't plan to bring it up. Finally, I heard footsteps creaking the floorboards and heard her raspy voice whisper "*Kto tam.*"

"It's Joe Toricelli, Valentina," I said. "I made it."

I heard the locks turn and unbolt one by one, and then I saw the door swing open. There was Valentina, white-haired and frail looking in her nightgown, and squinting hard to get a good look at me.

"Thank God you escaped," she said, "please come in."

I followed her down a narrow hallway and into a small living room, where we went to sit down.

"How do you feel?" she asked.

"I'm okay," I said, "except my hands are a little shaky."

"It is normal," she said, "and you still have some antidote?"

"No. Took the last of it, maybe an hour ago."

"I see. I have just a little more. I will give you last dose."

She left the room for a minute and came back with a dosed up syringe and hypodermic. I took off my jacket and shirt and she gave me a shot in the left deltoid.

"When do you think you had KG-2 last?" she asked.

"I think probably around two or so in the afternoon."

"Then you should be okay after several hours," she said, "maybe by eight this morning. Effective half-life is eighteen hours, maybe a little less. This is very strong dose of antidote, it should protect you."

"That's good."

"Tomorrow I shall go to my laboratory at Physiological Institute and arrange for more synthesis," she said, "but now tell me, how did you make this escape?"

"Drugged one of the drivers with this stuff, and got him to smuggle me out in a car. After awhile he passed out and I drove the car into Moscow."

"Very good. I expected you would be clever. And where is car now?"

"Parked near the Metropole. I took a cab to you from there. No way anybody could have followed me here."

"You are probably right...for now, at least."

"But look," I said, "I don't get it. Last time I was here you didn't want to talk to me, and you lied to me about Sabrina. Now you decided to save my life. So what's going on?"

"In case of Ognev, it is very dangerous for me to tell anything to any police, including you. Ognev will kill anyone who talks to police. So, when you first come here, obviously I think it is best to say nothing."

"So what changed your mind, then?"

"After you leave that day, I start to feel very bad. For two days I think to myself, for how long I will be afraid of Ognev? And what is it really he can do to me? I am already old and sick. My heart is very bad. So, for how long should he hurt and kill people? As, of course, he had Dr. Epstein killed."

"You know that for sure? He had Dr. Epstein killed?"

"Of course, I know this for sure, Dr. Toricelli. Dr. Epstein was very good doctor and he treat my Sabrina very well. Unfortunately, little by little, he find out too many things about Ognev...and Roland. And so, it was necessary that they kill him."

"But what? What did Dr. Epstein find out?"

"Exact details I am not sure. But it looks like he found some documents that indicated Ognev and Roland had plan to smuggle KG-2, this is drug they gave you."

"Yes, I know."

"To smuggle very big quantities of KG-2 to United States, for selling to many people."

"And how do you know Epstein may have been on to this?"

"From time to time I would speak to him by telephone, with Sabrina's permission, about her different relations, including with Ognev and Roland. He knew how bad they were to her. Maybe one week before he died, he told me he wanted to go to police with information about

Roland and Ognev. I told him to wait. For one reason Ognev was too dangerous and, for another, I did not believe Ognev could have large supply of KG-2

"Why not?"

"It is too difficult to harvest, and extract."

"Really? How do you know?"

"I know, Dr. Toricelli," she said, with a little smile "because this is my discovery."

"What? Now wait, let's back up here. This KG-2 stuff, this is your discovery?"

"Yes it is."

"How, I mean, where...where'd you find this stuff?"

"It is from Krasnaya Gribe, red mushroom," she said "I found this species on my second trip to Lake Baikal. So, I call it KG-Number Two. This was twenty years ago."

"So it's some kind of mushroom extract?"

"That is right. At time of my discovery Ognev was medical student in my laboratory."

"Ognev? He was your student?"

"That's right. And even now people in my laboratory remember he was most brilliant, and most sick scientist to work at First Physiological Institute. Anyway, he and I make many good experiments with mice with this drug. We show that they are not afraid and do not feel pain with drug. Even when cat appears, and attacks them, they are absolutely peaceful."

"Scary," I said "and I know just how those mice felt."

"Not exactly, because Ognev made special mixture for testing on monkeys. He mix with morphine, and greatly increase effect of pleasure...and craving. This is mixture he want to sell in America, I think some mix of KG-2 and morphine."

"So that's what I've got on board?"

"Yes. This I know when my Sabrina described to me on phone, that you were guest of Ognev's and were very happy there. It was only explanation."

"Right, right. But I don't get how Sabrina fits into all of this. Calling herself Frontenac, saying she killed Epstein, acting like she's Ognev's girlfriend and...and then rescuing me with your 'present'."

"Sabrina is very confused girl, doctor...and very troubled—this I think you know."

"Yeah, but I still don't understand..."

"I will tell you," she interrupted me "because I raised her as my own daughter from time she was five years old. After her parents, my nephew and his wife—wild, drunk children they were—died in car accident in Leningrad."

"Gee, that's awful sad."

"Yes, but it give me great pleasure to raise this girl, she is only family I have. And she was very clever and good-natured child. But terrible problems begin when she was teenager."

"What do you mean?"

"Many changes of mood, very angry, many lies. And more and more she forget where she has been and what she is doing on this or that day."

"So did she get checked out or get any help?"

"Oh Dr. Toricelli, she received very complete examination," she said, shaking her head and curling her lips up in anger, "by very brilliant young neuropsychiatrist, Dr. Boris Ognev."

"Ognev? Why'd you take her to him?"

"At time, Dr. Toricelli, I loved Ognev as my own son. He did very good work in my laboratory and was also excellent clinician. I did not see or, perhaps, did not want to see dark side of his character. All I saw was charming, intelligent young man."

"Uh-huh. So what exactly did he do to Sabrina who, from what Ognev says, is his cousin?"

"Cousin?" said Valentina "that is stupid lie he tells people, to explain why he helps her. Anyway, he examine her and do many psychological and neurologic tests. Finally, he diagnose her with, how you say, multiple personality. This, by reason of her father mmm...again, how you say...molesting her many times."

"Really? Did that make sense to you?"

"Unfortunately yes. My nephew, Dmitri, he was very strange, strange boy."

"So what kind of treatment did she get?"

"What kind of treatment, Dr. Toricelli? She received the worst possible you may imagine. From Dr. Ognev."

"What?" What did he do?"

"He take her...he take beautiful fifteen-year-old girl, whom he tells she must come to see him for hypnotherapy five days a week and...and he make her his...his private prostitute."

"Horrible," I said, "unbelievable."

"It is truth, Dr. Toricelli. And this for three years. It only stop when Ognev become too busy with different Mafia business to see her."

"Mafia business?"

"Yes. This was always main interest of Ognev. Money. And to use people. Unfortunately, I see this only too late. So, he became involved in many activities, and he throw away my Sabrina like some little doll."

"So what'd she do?"

"She try to kill herself, with many pills. I brought her to hospital, thank God they save her. And then she tell me everything about Ognev, and how much she is in love with him."

"Shit. And anything you could do to Ognev?"

"Impossible. He was already too powerful, too rich, with too many friends. But, because he decided Sabrina was embarrassment to him, he arranged to send her away, first to Italy where he arrange for her to receive false Italian passport and documents, and then to America. He have her go to Brooklyn, to live in apartment home of some criminal friend of his."

"And how long ago was this?"

"Maybe seven years ago," she said. "In beginning she was okay there. She work as model and make some money and have friends. But all the time she write me that she feel very bad inside, very ugly. Then one day she hear about famous doctor in New York who write books about people who are 'Beautiful Outside, Ugly Inside,' and she go to see him."

"Bertrand Roland, of course."

"Yes. And, at first, she very happy with him. He seem to understand her so well, he let her take special course with him in Caribbean, and so on."

"But then it must have gotten like Ognev again," I said, "all over again."

"Yes, but this time she is stronger. It is true he use her for sex, for several months. But then she choose to stop to come to him, because she feel too dirty. And for this reason, he became very crazy. He try to beat her, and he say he will kill himself, and so on. Nonetheless, she would not continue to see him."

"Good for her. But tell me something. Is that how Ognev and Roland met, through Sabrina?"

"Yes, Dr. Toricelli, this is how they met. Roland call up Ognev at beginning of Sabrina's treatment. In order to get clinical history. I think soon they see they have same very bad, very evil character."

"I'm sure. They picked up each other's slimeball vibes real quick. But...then how did she end up with Epstein, and didn't she feel just a little weird coming back to the same office suite?"

"I will tell you. Some time after she leave Roland, she have good success as model and make some money and get her own apartment in center of Manhattan. She change her name to Wilhelmina Frontenac, she tell me because she want to destroy her past life and many bad memories."

"Uh-huh, and what about 'Briand'," I said "that doesn't sound Russian."

"No. Her mother was French woman, and my nephew decide he want his daughter to have his wife's family name."

"I see."

"So, for maybe four years she do very well. She have money, she have boyfriends, she is very happy. But then it become very difficult for her to continue to get work as model. Many new girls come to agency, and she does not receive good jobs. Soon she is poor and very frightened."

"So what'd she do?"

"Unfortunately, she call Ognev again. All the time she continue to love him, despite that she is only little doll for him. Anyway, he say he is coming to New York soon, to open nightclub..."

"Club Daylight I presume."

"Yes. And when he open club, he give her job as dancer, and arrange again for her to have apartment in Brooklyn."

"So she's on a real merry-go-round with Ognev."

"Yes, round and round. And at first she feel okay. She is making money again. But in time, she come to feel very, very bad. Her mood is always changing, and many hours of day she does not remember what it is that has happened. She knows she needs doctor but doesn't know whom she can trust."

"Which we can't exactly blame her for," I said.

"No, of course not. And she become more and more confused girl, and she even thinks she must call Dr. Roland again."

"Now that's really crazy."

"Yes, it is crazy but, in any event, she goes one day to walk by his office. She does not see him but, as she walks by front door, she sees other doctor, Dr. Epstein, come out. She does not speak with him, but later that day she calls him for appointment. Something about him, she feels, his eyes, the way he smiles, make her think she can trust him."

"All right," I said, "so she starts seeing Epstein. And pretty soon he hears all about her past, and all about Ognev...and Roland. So things have got to start to get pretty tense between Roland and Epstein, right?"

"This is possibility, but remember Dr. Roland is very clever and...how you say...very sneaky man. When Dr. Epstein present him with Sabrina's story, Roland tell him she very crazy girl, and make up many fantasies of sex with him. He remind him this is common case with such diagnosis."

"And does Epstein buy it?"

"At first, of course, he believe his colleague. And he try not to make this central part of treatment. Instead he give her medication to help her with mood, and he spend many hours discussing her early life. He also speak with me then, to get early history."

"Did you tell him about Ognev...as well as what she'd told you about Roland?"

"Yes, yes of course. And he listen, but with much skepticism. Once he even try to call Ognev, but Ognev would not speak with him. Anyway, over time, as he get to know her more and more, Dr. Epstein did come to believe what my Sabrina say about Roland."

"So then what'd he do? Did he confront Roland?"

"No. No. Instead, I remember he tell me this, maybe two months ago, he say he will one day find very important evidence in Roland's office."

"What? What kind of evidence?"

"It seems, from what Sabrina told him, Dr. Roland took many Polaroid photos of her, without clothes, in his office."

"No kidding."

"And Dr. Epstein said one day he will find these photos in Roland's office, and this will prove everything."

"And so, did he? Did he find the photos?"

Valentina sighed and shook her head. "As far as I know, he did not. But then, quite by accident, he find something much more dangerous: the documents of Roland and Ognev, that indicated some plan to sell KG-2."

"And did Roland know he'd found them?"

"This I cannot say for sure, Dr. Toricelli. But what else can you think if Dr. Epstein is dead a few days after he finds these papers?"

"There's nothing else to think," I said. "Roland found out, Epstein got knocked off, and Volknick got framed for it. But wait, you just now said it was only a few days before his death that Epstein found the papers. Before you told me a week. Now let's think about this real precisely, exactly when did Epstein tell you he found these papers?"

"Hmm, if I remember...ah yes, on Monday...yes, Monday... because next Monday I hear from my Sabrina he is dead."

"Okay, and what exactly did he say?"

"As I said, he find some papers several days ago, he said, showing plans with Ognev to sell KG-2. This is when I advise him to be careful please, and don't go to police."

"Because you were afraid Ognev would kill him."

"Yes, yes. I also call him back some days later, again to tell him be careful."

"Some days later?"

"Yes...I think on Friday. But he could not talk because of guest."

"Guest? On Friday? When?"

"Oh, I am not sure. I call him very late, of course, because of time difference. I was still at Institute."

"Well, roughly, what time?"

"Oh, maybe one, maybe some minutes before one."

"Yeah? What, uh, what's the time difference between Moscow and New York anyway?"

"Eight hours."

"So it's...son of a bitch...excuse me...so it's maybe five or earlier in the afternoon. And he had a guest? Who?"

"Oh, I don't know, it is important?"

"It may well be, Valentina, that's the estimated time of his death, Friday afternoon."

"But I thought he die on Saturday, No?"

"That's when they found him. But the best estimate says he died the evening, or afternoon before. Maybe right around, or just after you were talking with him, see? So think now, what did he say to this guest, did he say a person's name?"

She knitted her eyebrows and ran her hand through her stringy white hair.

"No, Dr. Toricelli...no, I don't remember name."

"Well tell me, think now, what do you remember?"

"I call him, he say hello, I begin to advise him, again, about danger of Ognev. Then...ah!...then, then he say 'Excuse me...what a surprise...'"

"'What a surprise? What, who...who's the surprise? There must have been a name!"

"No, no none doctor, this I promise you, no name. But...ah!...he say 'What a surprise...I didn't expect...' no 'What are you doing in'...mmm, how you say...'the neighborhood' yes, that's what he say."

"Wait, now let me get this straight, he said. 'What a surprise, what are you doing in the neighborhood'?"

"Yes, yes. That is what he say. Then he tell me 'I must go, we will be in touch.'"

"And that was it?"

"Yes, I never talk to him again."

"Is that right? Well, I'll be," I said.

By the time we went through all of this the wheels in my head really started whirling. If she was anywhere near right about these time frames, and I believed she was because we went over it again and again, it meant that Horatio Epstein got a visit by somebody after Volknick ended his appointment and maybe just before Roland's call from Monotoc. It was obviously somebody he knew, and somebody he didn't expect to see "in the neighborhood." Now that ruled out any quick re-entry by Volknick. So whoever it was, it could damn well have been his killer, couldn't it? I had a gut feeling it had to be. But who? Roland had his alibi, he was in Monotoc. And it had already checked out that he called Epstein...close to five, as a matter of fact. Was that somehow planned to connect with this "guest?" Or was that guest really Roland, and had he arranged to have someone else in Monotoc making a call on his credit card, at that time? But who? Maybe his wife, I thought, maybe she's in on all of this. So what's her alibi? We'd have to check it out.

But then something else occurred to me, something I really didn't want to think about, much less discuss with Valentina. "Her Sabrina," I recollected, had seen Epstein at noon that Friday, three and a half hours earlier than her usual appointment, because she'd wanted to get an early start on that weekend in Westport. And she'd had three people back up her story that she was on some Wall Street geek's yacht from Friday at two until Sunday evening. Could they have been lying, as she had said in her little "fantasy" confession? But no, I said, that's too crazy. Why am I suspecting her of killing Epstein? I mean, the girl had just brought me the "present" that saved my life, and her aunt's just told me how much she trusted Epstein. But still, why is she with Ognev now? Because she's nuts about him, literally, that's why. So could he have induced her to knock off, or help knock off, Epstein?

But wait a minute, I told myself. Take it easy. You're going too fast, faster than you got time to sort things out. Now slow down, slow down. Meanwhile, as I was thinking all this, Valentina had gone to the kitchen and come back with a tray of hot tea and black bread and preserves. I poured myself some tea and sat back for a minute and listened to the purr of her tomcat, who was lazing and napping on the windowsill nearby. I reached over and stroked him between the ears, and his eyes widened for a second, and then narrowed back into his own sultry little dreamland. Okay, I thought to myself, now let's take it slow, and step-by-step, with Aunt Valentina.

"All right Valentina," I said "so I guess we've established you were one of the last people to talk to Dr. Epstein."

"From what you say to me, it is quite possible. But can this information really help you?"

"Maybe, Valentina, maybe. I mean, I don't know. But let's change the subject for a minute, and go back to your Sabrina. There's still a lot I don't understand there. For one thing, what's she doing with Ognev now? I mean, she's sleeping with the enemy, so to speak, isn't she?"

"You may put it that way," she said, smiling, "but Dr. Toricelli, I have sensation now that perhaps you suspect Sabrina gave help to hurt Dr. Epstein."

"No, Valentina. I mean, well, not exactly. But she's a real wild card in all of this, you know? So, for starters, what is going on with her and Ognev?"

"Ahhh, she sighed, "you see, of course, my Sabrina has trouble to have one mind, one heart. For example, she knows that Ognev and I have absolutely bad relations, yes? We are enemies. But she have trouble to decide to whom she must be loyal. Do you understand?"

"I'm following you so far."

"So, now she is happy to stay with Ognev, with whom she remains in love. But, it is my opinion, she knows nothing of KG-2 plan or who exactly kill Epstein."

"No?"

"No, Dr. Toricelli, Ognev would not trust her with such knowledge. I say to you again, she is only little doll for him, little doll to whom he feels little bit of kindness. This is why he take care of her, this is why, because he know she love me, he allow me to visit her on his land from time to time."

"Like yesterday," I said, "when, lucky for me, you brought her my present."

"Yes, of course," she said, smiling.

"But she had no idea what it was, right?"

"No, no doctor. There is no good reason to give her those details. I only tell her it is secret present for you and she absolutely must not tell nobody. Not Ognev. Not nobody."

"I sure as hell hope she's able to keep that secret."

"I hope so too."

"And what about her sudden move to Moscow?" I said. "I take it Ognev's goons just came in and packed her up and shipped her out?"

"Yes, but only after Dr. Roland try to hide her for few days in another apartment in Manhattan. He became very nervous that police will find out that he have unethical relations with Sabrina and come to suspect him in murder of Dr. Epstein."

"I remember how nervous he was."

"At first Roland try to hide these relations from police. And he have Sabrina make secret plan with girl in Canada."

"Jayne Le Grande?"

"Yes, this is her name. He tell Sabrina to tell this girl that when police call about some photo in book, that Le Grande girl should say she is Sabrina. Sabrina tell her she need this favor because she is having trouble with American immigration and they must not know she was out of United States at time of photo."

"And Le Grande almost pulled it off, until she spilled the beans to me about where she and Sabrina really were in that picture."

"Yes, I think so," said Valentina "but as far as I know, she still keep many thousands of dollars Roland arrange to pay her for this favor."

"Wow. Good pay for being such a lousy stooge. So after the Le Grande scam goes haywire, Sabrina gets packed off to Moscow ASAP, courtesy of Roland and Ognev."

"Yes."

"But then I show up on her doorstep, with Roland no less, and before I know it she's telling me she killed Epstein. Now what's that all about?"

"I will tell you," she said. "When you told her schizophrenic boy...whom she knows..."

"Volknick."

"Yes, when you told her this schizophrenic boy is going to prison, because he kill Dr. Epstein, she become very, very angry."

"Why?"

"Because she already had sensation that Roland kill Epstein, to hide his scandal with her. And when you tell her about this...Volknick, she think suddenly that Roland use him to take blame for murder."

"All right. But why does she make this confession?"

"At that moment, she became so angry at Roland that he use this boy, that she want police—you—to take her back to New York, and then she plan to tell police everything about her and Roland."

"But," I said, "unfortunately Ognev's goons were waiting outside her building, and then mug me and take me to his estate."

"Yes, yes. And very soon after this, she arrive at Ognev's house too, and Roland and Ognev tell her they receive news from America that Dr. Epstein really commit suicide, and Volknick boy is free."

"But that's gotta be bullshit. That is...a lie. There's no evidence to support a suicide."

"Yes, yes, I am sure," she said, "but my Sabrina accept this story, maybe because most important thing for her now is she is happy to be with Ognev."

"Right. And she's probably not going to hear any news story here to contradict these lies."

"No, of course not. This case mean nothing in Russia."

"Yeah," I laughed, "I'm sure it doesn't. No Epstein case...no O'Connor case...no nothing."

"What is O'Connor case?"

"What's the O'Connor case?" I said, and then Ognev's story about Jake being killed hit me again. "Well...that's another real doozie of a case Valentina. But uh, before I can tell you, I want to make a call to New York."

"Of course," she said, and handed the phone to me. She showed me how to dial out, but when I tried all I got was some fast busy signal.

"I'm not getting through," I said.

"You may try again later. Sometimes, to call to America is difficult."

"Right. And I don't suppose you get CNN on your TV, do you?"

"Television is broken, doctor. But you say this...O'Connor case, I have not heard about it. You say it is 'doozie' case. What it means this 'doozie'?"

"Oh, it means it's really out there," I said, "it's...extraordinary, very extraordinary."

"And why?"

"Well, we don't have a lot of time to go into it Valentina, so I'm going to give you the short version. Basically, I'm accused of a murder, a very famous murder, in America. Which I promise you I did not commit. I will be arrested and jailed as soon as I get back to the States."

"You will go to prison?" she said, " when you return to America? But it's impossible, no?"

"No. It's not one bit impossible."

"But...but, you are very good policeman, yes? And American system...it will want to believe you are innocent, yes?"

"Well if I were a policeman, maybe that'd help. But I'm not, Valentina. I'm just a doctor, more or less, who my cousin hired to help out on the Epstein case."

"But, if you say you are innocent..."

"I am innocent. But, because of all sorts of weird circumstances, the government has a real whopper of a case against me."

She looked me over for a minute, and wrinkled up her already wrinkled up forehead. "But you know, Dr. Toricelli," she said, "you have very pleasant face. Nobody will believe what government say, that you are murderer."

"That's awful nice of you to say, but I don't think looks are going to get me too far in this case. I've just got to face up, so to speak, to the fact that when I return to New York, I'm going straight to the calaboose—jail that is."

"So, you must not return to America. You must stay here in Russia, and nobody will find you."

"Stay here? In Russia? And how...how am I going to pull that one off?"

"It will be very easy," she said, "I know little village, very beautiful, on Black Sea, near Sochi. Beautiful mountains, beautiful blue water. You will stay there with my friends."

"But what do I do there? I don't speak Russian, I don't have much money. What kind of work could I do?"

"My friends will help you. Also, there are very beautiful girls in this village. You will be very happy. In time you will see, everything will be good for you."

"You know, Valentina," I smiled, "you're actually starting to sell me on this place."

"Yes, of course, and very healthy climate too. Soon you will forget all these terrible, silly troubles."

"That'd sure be something, wouldn't it?" I said, "kind of like heaven. But what about the KG-2? What if Ognev and Roland really do start moving this stuff? And, I didn't even tell you this, they've got a whole bunch of people they're giving this stuff to. And I know for sure they killed one of them to examine his organs."

"I am not surprised."

"So they've got to be stopped. We...or you, have got to get the police out there, right?"

"Russian police will not get very far with Ognev. He have very powerful friends. No one will seriously investigate."

"Then we get him with the Epstein murder," I said, "we get the United States involved, to demand an investigation."

"Yes, maybe, if you have opportunity to present some evidence. But you just told me you will go directly to prison if you return to America."

"Then it's what I'll do, and I'll still get the case solved. I'm obligated to, for a lot of reasons. For one, I made a promise to the Volknick kid, that I'd look after him, that I wouldn't hurt him, or harm him in any way."

She looked at me and smiled. "You are idealist, Dr. Toricelli. And maybe you think you can be hero. But you must know in the world there are many bad things and bad people. Will you risk your life in prison to try to stop one or two? It will change nothing."

"You're telling me I should hide out then? In that little village of yours? And just let all this bad stuff go down?"

"I am telling you, Dr. Toricelli, that life is very short. And if, as you say, you will go to prison in America, how will you prove Roland and Ognev are criminals? You will be criminal yourself and unable to do nothing. Who will listen to you?

"I...I don't know", I said, looking down at the floor. "Maybe you've got a point there."

Then we sat in silence for a while and sipped tea and I looked out the window and up at the stars floating overhead. Somehow, I wished the sun would rise, but I didn't think it was much past three. Good deeds, I thought, lots of good deeds. And none of them coming to any good end. Like helping Vera find the cash for the thrown out stash of coke, that worked out real well, didn't it, with her and her kid ending up getting killed. And helping Wilcox get off all those meds, that were clouding up his brain, so he could finally face down his demons and settle his score with all those memories from 'Nam. Yeah, he sure settled things all right, brain dead and bottle-fed on the neuro ward at Pershing. And, of course, let's not forget what happened to my old man. Taking a bullet in the head trying to stop a lousy little dope deal in some burnt out tenement in the South Bronx. Now there's something worth dying for, don't you think? Buying the farm, just to make life a little more complicated for some punk drug pusher in the neighborhood. So to hell with good deeds, I thought, to hell with good intentions that leave you pissing in the wind. I should have learned my lesson once, after Wilcox, but now it seemed I had to learn it all over again.

Well it'd be all right this time, I thought. I'd pick up some Russian, little by little, and come up with a new name, of course; and see what kind of deals I could get in on down in this little village by the sea. A new Crossroads, I thought, that's what it would be. But this time, I told myself, it'd work out right, and I wouldn't ever leave.

But then I thought of Wilcox, in that hospital bed in D.C., and the promise I'd made to him, brain dead or not. And then I thought about Volknick, holed up in a prison cell at Rikers, somehow convinced that he'd killed Epstein, and turning it over and over again in that addled brain of his. And finally, I thought of all those poor zombie bastards at Ognev's, who thought they were living in paradise, and were really no better than a cattle herd lined up for the slaughterhouse. No, no—I told myself—I don't give a damn if I do go to prison, or how it all turns out. I'm going to do everything I can to nail Roland and Ognev, even if it kills me, that's right. And I'll leave the unforeseen consequences of good deeds to whatever hand holds the power over such things and shapes whatever destiny we're chosen to play out. So that's it, I told myself, and that's how it's got to be. I got to do what I got to do. Then Valentina's voice shook me out of my reverie.

"So Dr. Toricelli," she said, "I am afraid that soon Ognev will come to my house. He will suspect that somehow I help you to escape. We must make plan for you to go to Black Sea."

"Valentina," I said, "your offer doesn't sound half-bad, it really doesn't. But I thought about it and I'm not going to do it."

"And why doctor?"

"I've got to go back to New York, and see what I can do to solve the Epstein case."

"But you will go to prison," she said, "you told me this."

"I know. But me going back is the only way Epstein's murder is going to get put to bed, and the only way I can see that Roland and Ognev are going to get nailed."

"And can you be executed for this murder, that government say you did?"

"Oh, yeah. In Florida, you bet. But that doesn't matter. I'm not letting this Volknick kid rot in prison. And I'm not letting Roland and Ognev get away with what they're doing."

She looked at me and shrugged. "If this is really the case doctor," she said, "you must hurry. I told you I have feeling Ognev could be here very soon."

"I hear you. And I'm out of here."

We stood up and I gave her a hug and kissed her. Then she wished me good luck, and we said goodbye.

I grabbed a cab back to my room at the Rus, grabbed my bag with my passport and visa, paid up for the last several nights, and headed out to Sheremetyevo to catch the next flight to New York. I tried calling Jake before I left the hotel, but only the machine answered at his house. The hell with it, I thought, they're probably all out in the yard. And the hell with Ognev and all his bullshit about Jake. It was bullshit, that's all, just made up to rattle me. And nothing more.

Part 9

I SLEPT REAL sound for most of the trip back and found that going through Customs was a real breeze. As I walked through the terminal at Kennedy, I passed a newsstand, and saw the morning's headlines in the *Tribune*: "Police Psychiatrist At Large in Murder of Francis O'Connor—Nationwide Manhunt for Joseph Toricelli Continues." I made my way over to a payphone near the exit, and slipped in a quarter to call Jake. Let the game begin, I told myself, and let the chips fall where they may.

The phone rang six or sèven times, and I wondered if Jake was in the office yet. But he must be, I figured, it's already eleven o'clock. Poor son of a bitch, I thought, he never bargained for this mess when he first hired me to help him out. Then the phone picked up.

"Roma," I heard Jake say.

"Jake?"

"Yeah, who's..." Ah shit...Joey, what the fuck...where the fuck are you?"

"I'm here, Jake...in New York, I mean. I want you to come pick me up."

"Pick you up? You crazy fuck. You're a goddamn fugitive...I got to arrest your ass, don't you know that?"

"Yeah, yeah, I know that. But we got to talk first. You ain't solved the Epstein case yet, and there's all kinds of shit going down there...stuff you're not going to fucking believe."

"Joey, are you out of your fucking mind? You are a fucking fugitive from the biggest goddamn murder rap of the century, and you're talking to me about Epstein?"

"Don't exaggerate," I said, "it's not that big."

"Not that big, not that big? You asshole. I'll tell you how goddamn big it is. My ass is on the fucking line here, okay? I'm the numbskull who fucking hired you, remember? Do you know what kind of deep shit I'm in?"

"Nothing compared to the shit I'm in. But look, Jake, I didn't kill anybody and you damn well know it."

"So where the fuck have you been then? What the fuck did you disappear for?"

"Jake, I'm going to explain everything to you, I promise. But look, I didn't kill anybody. Now you got to tell me you believe that, you hear me?"

"Did you know this O'Connor kid?" he asked.

"No. I didn't know the fucking kid. I'm telling you, it's all a big mix-up, see? Now, tell me you don't believe I killed this kid."

There was a silence on his end.

"Jake?" I said.

"Fuck it."

"Just tell me you believe me. That's all I want to know."

He was quiet a few more seconds, and then he said, "All right, Joey. I believe you."

"Honest? Honest to God?"

"Honest to God, Joey, I believe you," he said. "Now where the hell are you?"

"I'm at the airport. I just got in from Russia."

"Russia? What the fuck?"

"That's right, Russia," I said. "Now look, I told you, I'm going to explain everything. I want you to meet me, right away, at that wildlife park on Jamaica Bay, as soon as you can make it. And for Pete's sake, come alone, huh? And don't tell anyone about me, not yet. We got to talk things over."

"I got to arrest you, Joey."

"I know that. You already told me. Now I'm taking a cab to the wildlife park now, okay? I'll be sitting on a bench near the front gate, near the ranger's station all right?"

"Yeah sure, nature boy," he said ,"I know where you'll be. Jamaica fucking Bay. I'll be there within the hour."

"And alone Jake, you hear me? And you tell no one."

"Yeah, yeah, you got it. I'll be there. Within the hour."

WE HUNG UP AND I caught a taxi to the park. Poor Jake, I thought, I did feel bad for the spot I'd put him in. But he'd get over it. And by the time I helped him crack the Epstein case wide-open, he'd be up for a promotion, he'd see. Then again, I thought, what the hell am I worried about him for? I'm about to go into the hoosegow and I got a pretty strong feeling no judge is going to be springing me out on bail any time soon.

I paid the cab fare and walked over and sat on the bench in the park. I took in the hot noonday sun and watched a stand of cattails sway in a light breeze. After a little while, I heard Jake's voice call from behind me.

"Joey?" he said.

I turned around and saw him standing there, with a little bit of a goofy smile on his face.

"Jake," I said, "good to see you man. Come on over and sit down."

He came and sat down next to me and put his arm on my shoulder.

"Good to see you Joey," he said, "boy, I was worried as hell about you."

"I'm all right...all things considered."

"So look...sport," Jake said, "what the hell are we doing here now? We gonna catch up on some bird-watching or what?"

"No, that's not on the agenda. But, before you do your duty and, uh, you know...haul me in, I got to tell you everything first; the whole story about this O'Connor mess, and then the lowdown on what's behind the Epstein murder."

"I'm all ears, Joey," he said, shaking his head, "so lay it on me."

So I told Jake everything: all about Vera and the lost coke stash and me going to Danny Corona to cover her for it, and all about how Crassidy tied me up, and how he'd really killed O'Connor, and then how he'd managed to take advantage of all the confusion to cover his ass and stick the rap on me.

"Unbelievable," said Jake, "fucking unbelievable. But hey, you should have come forward right away, why the hell did you keep hiding?"

"C'mon Jake," I said, "I never fucking thought they'd find Joey Torento. He'd disappeared. How the hell did I know you were going to give the police department a set of my prints, without me even knowing about it?"

He just shook his head and kept repeating "Unbelievable, un-fucking-believable. And what the hell was with this 'Torento' shit anyway? What were you doing going around with an alias for? But no, wait a second," he said, raising his hands "don't tell me why. I don't want to know nothing about it. I don't want to know nothing about no aliases and nothing about why you've got buddies in the Miami mob."

"Look Jake, whatever bad stuff I did, well, I'm not doing it anymore. And I can guarantee you that, at this point, I don't have anybody I could call a 'buddy' in the Miami mob."

"You're probably right about that."

"But the fact is," I said, "this Torento tag, and whatever I did while I was him, it was just a way of trying to erase the past, after the stuff that happened back in Doboy. Stuff I'll tell you all about one day. But that was the whole idea I was operating with, that I could erase the past."

"You're a crazy son of a bitch, Joey. You know that? You're one hundred percent nuts."

"Maybe," I said, "maybe I was. But not any more."

"Well, I'm going to personally take care of this, you'll see. I'll be on the phone with the cops in Florida, and we'll crack this fucking scumbag Crassidy. His bullshit ain't going to fly much longer, you'll see."

"I hope so, Jake, I really do. But look, if you think this Crassidy shit is weird, wait till I tell you what I found in Russia. It's going to blow everything you thought you knew about the Epstein case right out of the water."

"Go ahead. But nothing's going to surprise me after this Crassidy and Torento bullshit."

"Well, Jake," I said, "you wait and see about that, big guy."

So I told him all about how Frontenac's really Sabrina Briand and how she used to be a patient of Roland's and how he'd put together the Le Grande scheme to try to cover it up. And I told him all about Ognev and Roland and their kidnapped zombies, and how they'd drugged me with the KG-2, and how Epstein had stumbled on the plans to sell the stuff, while he was secretly rifling through Roland's files. And finally, I described what Valentina had told me about this "guest" that surprised Epstein in his last call to him, and the timing of all that, and my hunch that this guest was the one who'd knocked off Epstein. By the time I finished, Jake had this blank look on his face and just kept looking at me with his mouth open.

"So," I said, "what do you say?"

"What do I say?" he said, "what do I say?" Then he paused a minute. "I say...we'd better re-open this goddamn case. That's what I say."

"That's right, and right away. 'Cause I'm sure that Roland's heard I escaped by now, and he figures I'm going to get to you as quick as I can."

"You got it," said Jake, "I'm going to call headquarters from the car. We'll get a couple of guys to bring him down for questioning right now, and we'll send over detectives to check out the Daylight Club."

"Perfect. And you've got to call Valentina and get a statement from her as soon as possible. And try to get her police protection too."

"We'll do the best we can," said Jake, "now let's go."

WHEN WE GOT to headquarters, Jake took me in through the basement, real quick and low-key, and brought me upstairs to get booked. I got my fingerprints and mug shots in a jiffy and was sitting in my jail cell downstairs in half an hour.

"Don't worry, Joey," said Jake, as they locked me in "this Crassidy joker's going to be confessing before you can say 'extradition,' you hear me?"

"I hear you Jake," I said, "but for now, let's make sure we nail Roland."

"Sure thing, buddy-boy. You just sit tight."

About an hour or so went by, and I had time to look over the *Herald* one of the guards handed me. There was nothing new on Crassidy, just the same old garbage from him and his attorney, about how they wanted to help the O'Connor family in every way they could. But then something else caught my eye that surprised me and made me feel real sad. The item was headlined "Landsdowne Condition Still Critical After Stroke." The story said that Landsdowne had suffered a "massive stroke" shortly after resigning from the presidential advisory staff on Thursday, August 23rd. He was in a coma, and receiving steroids for cerebral edema. Son of a bitch, I thought, he couldn't face the pressure of a public confession, and public disgrace, after all. For a second I thought: that's what you get for following my advice, you poor bastard. But then I thought, no...no, this isn't the time to be thinking that way. Landsdowne had made the right choice and, besides, maybe there's even some chance for recovery. I sure hoped so.

A little while after I put down the paper, Jake came back to my cell.

"How's it going?" I said to him. "Did we reach Valentina yet?"

"Not yet."

"And what's happening with Roland, is he hiding behind his attorney?"

"Not exactly," said Jake, shaking his head and looking real serious. "Joey, the guy's real pissed off, he's threatening to sue the police department, and he says, I quote, 'I demand to face my accuser this instant.'"

"He's got more balls than I gave him credit for. So take me to the son of a bitch and let's rock and roll."

JAKE AND TWO uniformed cops handcuffed me and shackled me and brought me up to the conference room on the tenth floor, the same place where I'd gotten that crazy confession out of Volknick just the week before. When I passed the secretaries on the way in, they both looked down, like they were real embarrassed to make eye contact with me. I was happy at least that I didn't see Moore around, but I did think that if they'd taken her advice in the first place, and hired somebody else for the job, I wouldn't be in the fix I was in now.

They sat me down at one end of a long table, facing Roland at the other end. He was alone, without an attorney, and I thought to myself, the little snake's decided to bluff, in the last hand, and with all the chips down.

Jake sat down between me and Roland and began by reading over a summary of what I'd told him: about Briand and Roland, Frontenac and Epstein, the Le Grande cover-up, Valentina (and her mention of Epstein's surprise "guest"), Ognev, KG-2, the kidnapped subjects, and Epstein finding out about the secret drug distribution plans. Then he asked me if I had any comments.

"The summary's perfect," I said, "now just make sure you turn Club Daylight upside-down before they get rid of their stash of KG-2."

Roland turned his mouth down slightly, like he was real disappointed. "You know, Lt. Roma," he said, "with all due respect to the New York City Police, as well as your family,"...he looked at me and raised his eyebrows "...these...charges, if you will, are absolutely preposterous. Their content is obviously fantastical and their source is...well, to put it delicately...quite unreliable. This man has been running away from first-degree murder charges for three weeks; he has presumed to operate as a forensic expert, absolutely untroubled by his lack of training; and he has been stalking me for the last two weeks, first at my office in Manhattan and then, incredibly, on my recent trip to Moscow. He is obsessed with somehow demonstrating that I am a charlatan, a murderer, a sexual pervert, a drug dealer and an all around agent of mayhem and evil. I submit to you, Lt. Roma, again with all due respect, that your cousin, Dr. Joseph Toricelli, is a deeply disturbed, deeply troubled young man, and should be receiving a comprehensive medical and psychiatric evaluation. Indeed, if a diagnosis of paranoid schizophrenia can be established, it may go far in mitigating the punitive consequences of his murderous deeds."

"I tell you what, Roland," I said, "you sure can talk your ass off. But what are you going to say when your little stooge, Jayne LeGrande, who, just by coincidence, made the same mix-up as you did in the book photo, gives us a detailed deposition, huh? Telling us all about that payoff, for lying to the police about that picture of Sabrina Briand."

Roland just laughed and looked over at Jake. "Again, Lt. Roma, I appeal to your common sense. My 'mix-up,' as Dr. Toricelli puts it, was due to my mis-reading the photo that I have on file. I was in a hurry at the time, and I didn't realize I was looking at a reverse print of the photo in the book. As for Ms. LeGrande, I cannot speak for her or her alleged error. Though it may well be that initially, your men were not clear in their questioning of her. But of course, I urge you to call the LeGrande woman, I am quite sure you will find no corroboration of these...outlandish assertions."

"And I suppose you have no knowledge of Ms. Frontenac suddenly moving out of her apartment in Brighton Beach either," I said, "and showing up in Moscow as Sabrina Briand, at the exact time that you happened to be there, visiting her former quack shrink, Dr. Ognev."

"Lt. Roma," said Roland, "I thought I would be able to speak directly to your cousin, in regard to his accusations. But I now see that doing so will only give him and his rantings a dignity they do not deserve. So I will repeat to you what I stated earlier: If, indeed, this Ms. Frontenac has moved from her apartment in Brooklyn, it is news to me. And if indeed Sabrina Briand is in Moscow, this is also news to me. I certainly have no knowledge of, nor do I have any reason to believe, that Ms. Frontenac and Ms. Briand are one and the same person. Nor do I have any knowledge of Ms. Briand ever being a patient of Dr. Ognev's, or being sexually molested by him. And if you must search my files on Ms. Briand to satisfy yourself of all this, then do it."

"I don't know how the hell you think you can keep lying about it all, Roland," I said, "Valentina Lubimova's not afraid anymore to talk. And as soon as your partner Ognev gets busted, he's going to turn on you. You wait and see."

"Lt. Roma," said Roland, "I must tell you again, I don't know to whom your cousin is referring, with this name of 'Valentina Lubimova.' As for Dr. Ognev; as I've said, I've had the pleasure of knowing him as a colleague and friend for several years now. Dr. Ognev is one of the most distinguished neuroscientists in the world, and I did indeed have the privilege of staying at his dacha on my recent trip to Moscow. I will say, again now, that Dr. Toricelli followed me to Dr. Ognev's house. He was repeatedly turned away at the gate, before finally being removed by Dr. Ognev's driver, to the nearest Moscow Metro station. At any rate, these paranoid delusions of Toricelli's, that Dr. Ognev and I are conducting human experiments with dangerous psychoactive drugs, and that we conspired to kill Dr. Epstein when he discovered this; well, on the face of it, this is absurd and there is absolutely no evidence to support it. Least of all this mysterious visitor theory of yours, implying that I could possibly have been in Epstein's office that afternoon of his murder."

"And where exactly were you at five o'clock on that Friday afternoon?" I asked.

"As I have told you from the beginning," he said, with his teeth clenched, "I was in Monotoc, on the phone with Dr. Epstein. It was a routine call, to receive any information I needed for weekend coverage of his practice."

"I'm going to ask you again, Dr. Roland," said Jake, "did you have knowledge of anyone being in the room with him at the time of the call?"

"And again, Lt. Roma, I tell you I do not recollect anyone being with Dr. Epstein when I called him. Of course I assume the Volknick boy must have been nearby, based on his confession."

"Yeah, let's get the 'Volknick boy' back here," I said, "maybe we'll get to the bottom of how you brainwashed him into thinking he killed Epstein."

"Lt. Roma," Roland whined, "I really must appeal to you as a police officer and a professional. Must I continue to be subjected to these paranoid accusations?"

"All right," said Jake, "that's enough for now. We're all going to sit tight for a while until we get a chance to check this out."

"'Sit tight' Lt. Roma," said Roland, "and exactly what does that mean?"

"It means you're going to wait a while so we can check some of this out."

"Am I to understand you are detaining me here? On what grounds?"

"I just explained it to you, doc," said Jake.

"But this, this is an outrage!" Roland yelled. "I have appointments, meetings. You are totally disrupting my schedule, on the basis of this man's...this criminal's disturbed, unfounded accusations."

"I'm just doing my job, sir," said Jake. "Now if you'll excuse me, I'm going to take care of things as quick as I can."

THEN JAKE AND I got up, and I followed him, cuffed and chained and with my guards in tow, into his office downstairs. Then we sat down on either side of his desk and he told the guards to wait outside.

"You know, Joey," he said, "if I didn't know you like I do, my own kid cousin that I grew up with, I'd swear this fucking Roland is right on about you being a nut job. You know what I mean?"

"Right. You'll see how nuts I am. I'm going to call Valentina's place right now. Meantime, you better call up LeGrande, she's too nervous to lie about anything anymore, and you better make sure your detectives down at Daylight are taking a good look around."

"What? So you're running the show now, from jail?"

"Jake, I don't have time to screw around, all right? They're probably going to haul my ass down to Florida tomorrow, see?"

"You'll be all right, Joey," he said. "No way that bozo's story is going to hold up down there."

"Easy for you to say. Now how do you dial to Russia on this phone?"

"Punch '0'. You got to go through the switchboard."

The operator dialed Valentina's number, and the phone rang over and over, but there wasn't any answer. I looked at my watch, it was almost three, which meant it was close to eleven at night in Moscow. Maybe she stayed late at the lab, I thought.

"No answer?" said Jake.

"No. I'll get information, and try where she works."

I got the number to the First Physiological Institute and called them up. After a few rings there somebody answered, but they couldn't speak any English. I kept saying "Dr. Valentina Lubimova" over and over again, and that I only spoke English. Finally, someone came to the phone I could talk to.

"Hello?" I said. "This is Dr. Joe Toricelli, calling from America. I need to speak with Dr. Valentina Lubimova. Is she there?"

"Who?" said the woman on the other end.

"Valentina Lubimova, Dr. Valentina Lubimova. Is she there?"

"No...there is no one here with this name," she said.

"No one there with that name?" I repeated. "But, she works there. She has her own laboratory. Dr. Valentina Lubimova. She's an old woman, maybe seventy, eighty, I don't know. But she's a scientist there."

"I tell you, absolutely, there is no one here by this name."

"And this is the First Physiological Institute?" I asked. "In Moscow?"

"Yes."

"And you have no scientist or professor there named Valentina Lubimova?"

"No," she said, "I told you this already."

"But...there's got to be some kind of mistake. This woman...she told me she worked there, that she had her own laboratory."

"I don't know. And I cannot help you."

"Any other institutes in Moscow" I said, "with a similar name? Maybe I've got this confused, I..."

"I don't know," she said, "only there is one First Physiological Institute, and I am working here two years as scientist. And I tell you absolutely there is no one here by this name. I never hear this name before. Never in my life."

"Okay," I said, "fine. Thanks a lot. Goodbye."

I hung up.

"So what's that all about?" said Jake.

"I don't know. I really don't fucking know. But there isn't anyone who works at the First Physiological Institute in Moscow named Valentina Lubimova."

"Huh. So, it's some kind of mix-up, maybe."

"I don't know what the hell it is," I said. "Maybe some kind of mix-up or maybe somebody just made her disappear. Who knows? But look, let's get Jayne LeGrande on the phone, before anything else goes haywire."

"Whatever you say, buddy boy."

I dialed up Jayne LeGrande's number in Montreal while Jake

listened in on his other phone.

"Let me talk to her," I said, "I know exactly what to ask her."

"Fine," said Jake, "I'll take notes."

Then Le Grande answered the phone. "Hello?" she said.

"Hello, Ms. Le Grande?"

"Yes."

"This is Joe Toricelli, New York City Police Department. You remember we spoke last week?"

"Yes. I remember."

"Good. Now the reason I'm calling is, that I need to go over that photograph with you again. You know, the one in Dr. Roland's book, where you originally got the positions mixed up, between you and Sabrina Briand?"

"Yes," she said," I know. But I thought we cleared all that up, officer. I told you...I was confused about the questions from the first time the police called up and asked me about that picture."

"Right," I said, "you were confused. But I want you to listen real carefully now, Ms. LeGrande, because I've got my partner here on the other phone, and we're going to be real clear about what we ask you, and we're going to make sure we write down everything you say."

"What do you mean?" she said, "what is this? I've already told you I made a mistake about the picture. A very human mistake, that's all."

"Uh-huh. Well I'll accept that you made a mistake, and now I'm going to advise you that you don't make any more."

"What is that supposed to mean?"

"It means, Ms. LeGrande, that I know you made a mistake, and took a bribe to lie about that picture, to lie to the police, about your position in that picture."

"What?" she said. "What are you talking about?"

"I'm talking about money you received. Thousands of dollars for you to conspire with Sabrina Briand, and lie to the police about who was who in that picture. You thought you were going to protect her from an immigration investigation, and make some real easy money for it. Right?"

"I really have no idea what you're talking about, officer, but it sounds crazy. It sounds like something Sabrina would say."

"It does, huh?" I said. "And tell me, when was the last time you actually heard Sabrina say something to you?"

"I...I told you officer. It must have been a year ago or more. She's not exactly a close friend of mine."

"Now I know you spoke with her more recently than that. And it'll be a cinch for me to get the phone records to show that. So why don't you just tell us the truth about what the two of you talked about?"

"I have nothing to tell you," she said, "because I don't know what you're talking about."

"Ms. LeGrande, if it's a matter of you being threatened to keep quiet about all this, we will give you whatever police protection is necessary."

"Threatened? Police protection? This is really getting wild," she said, "now what are you trying to accuse me of? I..."

"Ms. LeGrande," said Jake, interrupting, "this is Lt. Roma on the other line here. Now look, nobody's interested in getting you in any trouble here, see? This has got nothing to do with you. We just want to know if you made some kind of deal, with this Sabrina Briand, or Dr. Roland, to lie to the police about your place in that picture. Now did you?"

"No!" she cried, "No, no, no. This, this is all crazy. And, as a matter of fact, you people are harassing me."

"Now take it easy," said Jake, "nobody's harassing you here. We're just trying to follow up on some information we received."

"Well I don't know who gave you this information," she said, "but it's crazy, and it sounds like it's from Sabrina Briand, who's a real head case anyway."

"Well let me ask you a few questions about this Sabrina Briand," said Jake.

So Jake proceeded to ask Jayne LeGrande about anything and everything she knew about Sabrina Briand; where she came from, what her relationship was with Dr. Roland, if she ever mentioned her Aunt Valentina, where she lived in New York, what she did for a living, what she looked like, if she'd ever gone by the name Wilhelmina Frontenac, and so on. LeGrande pretty much repeated to Jake everything she'd already told me the week before, with the addition that she thought Sabrina Briand was from France—she'd never heard her mention Russia—and that she didn't recollect Briand ever saying anything about an Aunt Valentina. By the time their conversation was winding down, it was pretty clear we weren't going to find any smoking gun, and the only thing we really had was the obvious occupational and physical similarities between Wilhelmina Frontenac and Sabrina Briand.

"So what do you think?" I said to Jake after we hung up the phone, "somebody's got a gun to her head, right?"

"Maybe," he said, "or we're just barking up the wrong tree."

"No, it's the right tree, that I guarantee you. But Roland and Ognev are doing a real good job of covering their tracks, so far anyway."

"So far, Joey, so far. But we're checking out this Daylight joint real good. From top to bottom, so to speak, and I don't mean just the girls. We ought to be getting a report real soon."

"Yeah fine," I said, "but I'll bet whatever of this KG-2 shit they might have stashed there is long gone by now. And everybody's going to be real button-lipped about Ms. Frontenac."

"We'll see, we'll see. We'll get in their faces pretty good, and do whatever we got to do."

"Meanwhile, we got to get Volknick back up here," I said. "I mean, Roland must have done some kind of number on his head, to get him to confess to Epstein's murder. We got to talk to him now, while we're still holding on to Roland."

"We'll try," said Jake, "but I tell you, that kid's been like...what the hell's the word?"

"What do you mean?"

"You know, where they just stand there, like they're some friggin' statue..."

"Catatonic?" I said.

"Yeah, that's it. The fucking kid's catatonic. He ain't said a word to nobody in a week now."

"Is that right?"

"And he's refusing to take his medication."

"Damn! All of Roland's goddamn handiwork, huh? He's literally got the kid dummied up."

"That's about right," said Jake. "But anyway, I hope to hell we find some kind of evidence at this Daylight Club. Something we can use to nail Roland good."

"Right. And hey, let's look at his phone records again. Maybe there's even a call on there, something we missed, like to Daylight or something. Now that'd give us something to sink our teeth into."

"Good idea," said Jake. He opened up one of his desk drawers and got Roland's phone records out of the files.

The records went back about three months, and we went over them real carefully, looking for any calls to Daylight, or to Frontenac's number in Brooklyn, or to LeGrande in Montreal, or to any places in Russia. Nothing turned up except three calls to the front desk of the Kievskaya Hotel in Moscow. Not even anything to Ognev.

"No luck," said Jake. "Tomorrow, we'll get records going further back, and check out any other phones he has."

"Tomorrow, tomorrow," I said, "tomorrow we're not going to find jack shit. Because Roland's not that stupid, see? He's not going to leave us any fucking trail of clues."

"Well, who knows, maybe you can get Volknick to talk, Joey. And maybe we'll find out Roland actually hypnotized the poor kid, to kill Epstein."

"No. No I don't buy that. Hypnotizing Volknick to believe he killed

Epstein; yeah, that I can accept. But not to kill him. No way."

"So maybe Roland drugged him then," said Jake, "like with this shit they gave you, and then directed him to kill Epstein."

"No, it doesn't work that way," I said. "You're not aggressive on this stuff. No, I'm telling you, somebody else was in Epstein's office, after Volknick left. Somebody Epstein knew. That's who killed him. And I say, somehow, it was Roland."

"Well, I wish I knew how we're going to show that" said Jake. "The little wimp's got himself an airtight alibi."

"I wouldn't be so sure about that."

"What do you mean? Two hundred people saw him at Monotoc that Friday afternoon. We got phone records showing he called Epstein at five. And he wasn't back in Manhattan 'till eight at that dinner party at his club. We know he took a limo back from Monotoc to the city; leaving Monotoc at about six and arriving in Manhattan just before eight. We got a limo driver and his receipt to vouch for that."

"Yeah," I said, "but...but maybe that driver lied, and that limo business is part of Ognev's operation. And somebody else made that call to Epstein from Monotoc, using Roland's credit card, so it'd just looked like he made it. And meanwhile Roland could have already been back in New York taking care of Epstein, see? And that fits in with Epstein being surprised to see somebody he knows 'in the neighborhood.' He figured Roland was up in Monotoc and he didn't expect him back so early."

"But it don't hold up, Joey," said Jake. "This conference of Roland's, it didn't end until two-thirty, we know that for sure. Now Roland didn't just run from the podium the second it was over. He hung around, he schmoozed at least until two-forty-five or three. We know that."

"All right. So let's say he leaves Monotoc at three; he goes at a good clip, he can be in Manhattan at five."

"But the limo..." said Jake.

"Assume the limo stuff is phony, as well as the phone call. Now we got a nice little window for Roland to get his slimy ass back to his office, just in time to kill Epstein. You see? It's perfect."

"Son of a bitch. Son of a bitch Joey, you may really have something there, you really might."

"Did we ever check specifically to see if anybody actually saw Roland at Monotoc between, say, three and five that afternoon?"

"I don't know," said Jake, "but I'm going to say, probably not."

"And did we ever check specifically, to see exactly what phone that alleged call of Roland's originated from?"

"Not exactly," he said. "I mean, it says in the records that the phone number's from New Pawling, that's where Monotoc is. But why are you asking that?"

"What if," I said, "what if this hypothetical phantom, this stand-in for Roland, made a mistake? Like, let's say, made this call from a hotel room he was registered in, or from some dive in New Pawling. Some place that'd give us a clue as to who it could be, or some place that Roland would have a hard time explaining how he could be there. See what I mean?"

"Yeah," said Jake, stroking his chin. "Yeah, I do. So then let's do it Joey, let's nail down where this phone in New Pawling is."

We both got on the line and I called up the phone number. We let it ring maybe fifteen or twenty times, before somebody finally answered.

"Hello?" said this guy on the other end. He sounded slightly peeved. "Who are you looking for?"

"Who am I looking for?" I asked.

"Yes," he said, "was somebody supposed to be waiting for your call here?"

"Is this a payphone?" I asked.

"Yes," he said, sounding real condescending, "in the lobby of the Monotoc Hotel."

"Is that right?" I said. "Where exactly in the lobby?"

"Is this a joke?" he said. "You know I'm very busy."

"You work there?" I asked.

"Yes," he hissed, "at the front desk."

"No kidding," I said. "Look—uh this is Joe...Roma, New York City Police. What's your name?"

"Alan. Alan Blaning."

"Look, Alan," I said, "bear with me here now, because we're involved in an investigation."

"An investigation? About what?"

"Well...it actually has to do with your payphone there. You're pretty close to it from where you work there, at the desk?"

"About fifteen feet, sir. It's just off to the side of the check-in area."

"Uh-huh, I see. Now tell me something, Alan. Were you by any chance working there around five in the afternoon on Friday, August third? That'd be about three weeks ago, or so."

"The third? Let's see...the third" he said, thinking for a few seconds. "Oh yeah, sure, I remember. I came on at four, after that conference...with Dr. Roland."

"You were there, at Roland's conference?"

"Oh yeah, it was fabulous. It was this whole talk on beauty and spirituality and...well, but anyway, yeah I was at the desk here afterward.

At four."

"Okay," I said, "and did you by any chance see Dr. Roland, or maybe talk to him after the conference?"

"No," he said, sounding disappointed "I had to get ready for work."

"Did you happen to see him afterward? I mean, standing around in the hotel, in the lobby, for instance?" I looked at Jake and shook my head, hoping that Alan would say 'no.'"

"No, no I didn't. But why? Is this investigation about Dr. Roland or something?"

"No, not exactly, Alan," I said, "but now think. Just think for us now. Just to make sure. Any recollection at all of seeing Dr. Roland? Say, while you were behind your desk?"

"No...but...hey, wait a second. No, I do remember seeing Dr. Roland. Yes, of course, it's coming back to me now. I was behind the desk and he was standing right here, where I am now, talking on the phone."

I could feel my heart sink. "He was?" I said. "After you went on duty, behind the desk?"

"Yes, yes," he laughed, "I remember. Little Dr. Roland, right on this very phone."

"And you're sure it was after you started working? It was definitely after four on that Friday the third?"

"Oh yeah. I'd probably been on about an hour or so. But the thing that was so funny, so strange...was how angry he was."

"Angry?" I said. "How do you mean?"

"Oh God, he was just pacing around the lobby. Yeah, I remember...he asked me where there was a payphone. I said 'right behind you, Dr. Roland' and he said 'Don't you have something with more privacy?'"

"'Privacy'?"

"Yeah. And I pointed out the phone booths to him down the hall. But he said they were occupied."

"So what'd he do?" I asked.

"Well, he used this phone. But he was so angry, he even started yelling at the person he'd called up."

"Really? What'd he say?"

"Oh, boy, I don't remember," he said, laughing again. "It was just so...totally ironic, you know? Dr. Wisdom and Enlightenment, in a big snit on the telephone."

"Right, real ironic. But, you must have heard something of what he said, right? I mean, you were watching him. He was just a little ways from you. So do you remember anything?"

"Oh...let's see...oh, I don't know officer," he said, giggling, "just that he was so damn mad at something...he wasn't going to take it anymore...like in that movie...*Network.*"

"*Network?*"

"*Network.* Yes, you know, with the crazy newsman? Who says he's not going to take it anymore?"

"Sure," I said, "I know the movie. But is that it? Anything else you remember? Names? Things he said? Anything?"

"No, sir. That's really it, I can't think of anything else. But, is it important or something?"

"It very well might be."

"Well, then I can call you if I think of anything else, would that be okay?"

"Sure," I said, "you do that, Alan."

I gave him our number and said goodbye. After we hung up the phones, Jake said to me, "So he was real pissed off about something, huh, Joey?"

"Yeah, who the hell knows," I said, "probably arguing with Epstein about keeping a lid on things."

"I'll question him about it," said Jake.

"Yeah, go ahead, for all the good that's going to do. But, bottom line is my theory's down the toilet. Roland was right where he said he was. That's all there is to it."

"Yeah, but something's got to turn up, you'll see. And Roland knows the heat's on, so the guy could easily be rattled and make a mistake."

"But when?" I said. "He's in pretty good form so far."

"Well, let's see what turns up at this Daylight Club, Joey. And maybe you'll be able to talk to Volknick. Who knows? Maybe the kid will give us some kind of clue about Roland."

"Maybe," I said. "But the payoff's going to be with other people who knew Epstein. We've got to double-check everybody's alibis. His wife, for instance. Who the hell knows, maybe she's in on this."

"Mrs. Epstein?" said Jake. "Where'd you pull that one out of?"

"I don't know, but let's double-check her story anyway. And his weirdo kid too. He'd told me how much he hated Roland. Maybe it was all a smokescreen."

"All right. We'll double-check."

"Hey," I said, "and what about Roland's wife, huh? Now that's somebody we never even interviewed, right?"

"Right."

"But look, I distinctly remember him going ballistic with her one afternoon at the office."

"What do you mean?" said Jake.

"Oh, he was really ripping into her about how stupid she was and stuff. Really heaping on the abuse. So how's this? Maybe she came into Epstein's office when Valentina called, and then stayed there when Roland called. She strangles Epstein while Roland's on the line and maybe, who knows, she makes some kind of mistake after she kills him, she talks to Roland about it, and he starts going bullshit on the phone, see?"

"I don't know," said Jake. "Did you ever hear anything about her being in on this KG-2 scam?

"No. But it all fits. Even how she was so sad, like maybe too sad, when she was talking to me about poor old Dr. Epstein. I'm telling you, we got to check her out."

"All right," said Jake, "we will, we will."

Then the phone rang. It was the detectives Jake had sent down to Club Daylight. They told Jake they'd talked with the manager there, and all the available staff, and everyone had been real cooperative and let them search all around the place. But they turned up absolutely nothing. All they had to report was how worried the Daylight people were about the sudden and mysterious disappearance of Ms. Frontenac. And, of course, everybody assumed that Ms. Frontenac was from France, not Russia and nobody'd ever heard the name Sabrina Briand.

"It figures," I told Jake. "So far Ognev and Roland have got everything covered. One hundred percent."

"So far. But I'm going to see what Roland has to say about why he was so pissed off on the phone in Monotoc."

"Go for it," I said, "and let's make sure we check out his wife real good."

"Definitely, Joey. We'll get a real detailed statement from her."

Just as he finished saying that, Moore walked into the office, and stood over us by the desk. "Hello Dr. Toricelli," she said, with her eyebrows slightly knitted, in this look of pity. "The building is already abuzz with the news of your arrest."

"I'll bet," I said, feeling like this was the last person I wanted to face right now. "And how have you been?"

She glanced at Jake, smiling slightly, and then turned back to me.

"Actually, quite concerned," she said, "for your safety, as well as for the impact this...scandal, is having on your cousin, and our department."

"Appreciate the concern," I mumbled.

"You were wise to turn yourself in," she said. "I only wish you hadn't chosen to hide in the first place, especially in our department."

"Probably not the best P.R.," I said, "but then again, that may be the price you've got to pay, for me making sure you crack the Epstein case."

"Yes, I'm sure," she said real fast, and then turned to Jake. "You know I just passed Dr. Roland in the hallway upstairs. He is absolutely livid, and I was incredulous, as well as embarrassed, to hear all he had to say. Am I to understand that we are re-opening our investigation of Dr. Epstein's murder? And focusing on Dr. Roland as a suspect?"

"That's right, Madeline...or Dr. Moore," said Jake. "You don't know anything yet, but Joey's dug up all kinds of stuff on Roland. He was with him in Russia as a matter of fact."

"Yes," said Moore, looking at me, "Dr. Roland just told me how you were following him."

Then she turned back to Jake. "But Lt. Roma," she said with her voice rising in anger, "given the embarrassment your cousin has already brought to the department, and to our investigative team in particular; don't you think we should be proceeding with extreme caution, in considering any allegations, or ideas, or...fantasies your cousin may be expressing?"

"Fantasies?" I said. "You don't know a fucking thing about what I've seen, you dumb, arrogant bitch."

"Joey!" said Jake. "Settle down, will you?"

Moore got red as hell and her lips tightened up and got real small. "Lt. Roma," she said, "I have only the sincerest sympathy for the situation your cousin is currently in, regardless of what the facts turn out to be in the O'Connor slaying. But I really must appeal to you, on behalf of the professional integrity of all of us. Are we really going to continue to entertain your cousin's allegations? No matter how unfounded? No matter how irresponsible? No matter how damaging to the people whom he subjects to his preoccupations?"

"We're going to follow things up," said Jake, "and check out everything real systematically. Once you learn all the details, you'll see. We're doing the right thing."

"Perhaps," said Moore, "but I would like to remind you now, we have already obtained a murder confession, and solved this case!"

"Okay, look Dr. Moore," said Jake, standing up, "we're not going to get anywhere arguing here, all right? So I'm going to go ask Dr. Roland some more questions, then I'm going to fill you in on the whole story."

"As you wish," sighed Moore.

"Meanwhile, Joey," said Jake, "you might as well head back downstairs for now. We're going to keep trying Valentina, and I'll come see you later on today."

"Sure," I said, "I'll talk to you later."

JAKE CALLED the guards back in and they brought me back down to my jail cell. I tried to nap there for a while, but my mind was racing with thoughts about Roland and Ognev and any angle we could get that could help us finally nail them. I hoped to hell something would turn up with Roland's wife. She damn well could have done it, I figured, and we'd better get to her now, before Roland or Ognev get wind of our suspicion. And Ognev. Ognev, that son of a bitch. I hoped that Jake could get somebody to get the Moscow cops to bust in on the guy's property and raid the place. And I sure hoped to hell he hadn't hurt Valentina, wherever she was, and whatever the story was about where she worked.

A couple of hours passed while all this stuff cycled through my head, and then I heard the sound of Jake's voice down the hall. He and the guard came down and opened my cell door, and then Jake came and sat down next to me on the cot. The guard locked the cell door and left us alone.

"So Joey," he said, "how are you holding up?"

"About the same as a couple of hours ago," I said. "So what gives? Did we find anything?"

"Zilch, so far. First of all, I asked Roland about his call to Epstein. He said, yeah, he was angry, but it was no big deal. Supposedly him and Epstein were always disagreeing about how to treat this or that patient, that's all."

"Sounds like bullshit," I said.

"Maybe, but try to prove it. And then there's Roland's wife."

"Yeah, what'd you find there?"

"Nothing that's going to help us. She was on some kind of retreat in New Jersey from Thursday to Sunday, continuous. No way she was near Epstein's office."

"No?"

"No."

"And what about Ognev?" I said. "Can we get the Russian police, maybe the KGB or the FBI on his ass?"

"I got some calls in, Joey, but that's real complicated shit. Especially with this guy being such a big shot over there and all."

"Yeah, right. And what about Valentina, any news there?"

"Nothing. Still no answer."

"Shit," I said, "maybe she's out at her country house. I just hope Ognev's guys haven't nailed her."

"I don't know Joey. But that's real strange that nobody'd ever heard of her where she's supposed to work. You sure this old lady's on the level?"

"Yes, one hundred percent. She saved my life, remember? No, I just don't know what the confusion is about where she works. But anyway, where the hell do we go from here?"

"That's a good question. For starters, we're going to have to let Roland go."

"Let Roland go?" I said. "You gotta be crazy. That son of a bitch is a fucking murderer and a kidnapper and you're going to let him go?"

"We're going to keep a real close eye on him," said Jake, "so he ain't going to go too far. But I got orders from upstairs to let him go, for now anyway. Seems his lawyer called up the commissioner, and really laid into him, about our 'arbitrary and capricious' interrogation of the son of a bitch. And how we don't have any evidence to support our allegations."

"But didn't you tell your bosses everything I told you about him?"

"I told them most of it, Joey. But, believe it or not, your, uh, credibility with the department's been taking a real nosedive lately. Know what I mean?"

"Yeah, I know what you mean," I said, "but..."

"And so has mine," he said, interrupting me, "and I think you can see why. So we aren't exactly dealing from a position of strength here, see? So far, we've got no evidence against Roland. And if you want to know the truth, I'm lucky if I get to continue this investigation at all."

"Oh, c'mon Jake, don't let anybody bulldoze you now."

"Nobody's going to bulldoze me. But, whatever I do in this case from now on, it's going to be with both hands tied behind my back. Now we're going to double-check the alibis of Epstein's wife and his kid. And we're going to check with the airlines and INS for anything they got on a Wilhelmina Frontenac or Sabrina Briand. If nothing turns up with any of that, I got to see what we're going to do next."

"Ah, shit," I said. "You know what? I hate to say it, but now I'm seeing a fucking dead end, to this whole damn thing. You know that? These guys...these fucking guys are two steps ahead of us all the time. No matter what we do, or what we think we're going to do, we don't find squat."

"I don't know," said Jake, "we'll see."

"We'll see, we'll see. And meanwhile I'm on the jailbird bus to Florida tomorrow. What a fucking world of shit, you know what I mean?"

"Could be better, Joey. Could be better."

I laughed. "Now that's some fucking understatement, huh? And you know what Jake, it's true, if you keep pursuing this investigation the department's going to think you're as fucking screwy as I am, you know that?"

"Probably. But who knows? I got Moore listening to me, so maybe she'll be on our side."

"That's encouraging," I said. "Did fucking her have anything to do with that?"

"It ain't exactly like that. She's...she's all right, she really is."

"Aw now c'mon, Jake. Don't add to the bad news here, now. You're not falling for her, are you?"

He didn't say anything.

"Oh shit," I said, "I don't believe this. And when Nina finds out, she's going to divorce your ass, you know that, you dumb fuck?!"

"Joey," he said, all of a sudden raising his voice, "you don't know how it's been for me since that fingerprint shit came up and you disappeared. Do you know the fucking position you put me in?"

"Look, Jake, I'm sorry. I know it was rough for you."

"No you don't fucking know. But I tell you what, Moore...uh, Madeline...she was there for me, all right? Me and her, we had to deal with it together, and keep it real quiet. You know, for a while there Joey, your identity, and for that matter even the possibility of your identity, was kept real hush-hush. Besides me and Moore, only two guys in personnel, the top brass and FBI knew that you were Joseph Torento."

"Is that right? And why's that?"

"Well I'll tell you why Joey. In fact, I'll tell you the whole friggin' story, from the beginning. Now, you remember how you were supposed to go give your prints again, on that day Volknick confessed, right?"

"Sure. I remember it, real clearly."

"Well the reason was, that the old fingerprint card I'd given to personnel got rejected by the computer. It was unreadable, see?"

"Yeah, okay."

"Now, that by itself don't exactly get anybody excited, except that this little nerd down in personnel, DeFrancesco's his name, he's already got your application flagged, okay, because he's already got this bright fucking idea that you're really Joseph Torento."

"How did he come to suspect that?"

"'Cause he's fucking crazy, that's why. He'd been following this O'Connor bullshit real closely, okay, and, at the same time, he's got your application sitting on his desk all week, with your friggin' passport picture staring at him all day long."

"So what are you going to tell me, that he started thinking my passport photo resembled the police composite of Joe Torento?"

"You got it," said Jake.

"But those were some lousy likenesses they came up with, weren't they?"

"I seen worse. And they got better after the FBI got that video shot of you in Corona's driveway. But all the composites did look kind of similar to the passport picture. Remember, you had a beard and long hair when that picture was taken, many moons ago."

"Shit, you're right," I said, "I'd forgotten about that."

"So anyway, DeFrancesco doesn't say anything about what he's thinking at first. Even he thinks he's nuts for thinking that you, my own doctor cousin, could be this scumbag murderer Joseph Torento. But still, he can't get it out of his mind; the way the faces look in the pictures, the way the physical description put together by the police pretty much matches up with your height and weight and age as I'd wrote it down in your application; and plus, the fact that your last address was down in Florida. So anyway, he figures he'll wait and see if your prints clear the NCI computer, before he says anything to anybody. But then, well you know what happened with that."

"Oh yeah."

"And it don't take too big an imagination to figure out how DeFrancesco, and his supervisors now, reacted when you didn't show up that afternoon, or the next day, or the next fucking day, to redo your prints, right?"

"It could start to look a little suspicious," I said.

"And it could look even more suspicious when they get the fingerprint unit to look over that old card, and they say: yeah, there's a real good possibility there could be a match here with what the cops got on Torento down in Florida."

"So what did they do then?"

"Well Joey, by this time it's what, two days since I've seen you, okay? And I'm trying to locate where the hell this place was that you were renting, 'cause you never gave me the address. Luckily Nina dug it out of some old newspapers, where you'd circled a few apartment ads, and we managed to track you down to this dump on West Fifth Street."

"Hey, what are you talking about?" I said, "that was a nice little studio."

"Yeah right, if you're some fucking weirdo trying to hide out from the world. And speaking of weirdoes, you should have seen this guy who lives next door. He was going absolutely bullshit, saying how he had some freakin' vision ten days ago of you ending up in jail."

"That weirdo would be Jackie."

"Yeah, whatever," said Jake, "crazy fucking fairy, with a crazy fucking dog with a bell around its neck. But anyway, the landlady lets us into your place, and, let me tell you, she was one pissed off old broad. And, of course, we don't find you there. So then we start lifting prints from all over the place in that room of yours. And by the next day—bingo—we had the fucking match."

"So how bad were you feeling about then?" I asked.

"Real fucking bad Joey, real fucking bad, believe me. But I told them, and Moore backed me up on it, I told them: let's keep it quiet, just for a little while if we can. We got a better chance of finding you, or you coming to us, without this being all over the papers."

"You thought I might not run, huh?" I said, "quite so far, or so fast."

"That's right. But after a couple of days the big guys said: the hell with it. And you got famous real quick. Me and Moore were against it, but we didn't exactly have a say in the matter."

"So you and Moore came together to try to protect me," I said. "Now that's real sweet, the way this crisis brought the two of you even closer, huh?"

"Don't bust my balls, all right Joey? Believe it or not, she's sympathetic about you. She don't think you killed O'Connor, for one. And, like I said, she's listening to me about all this stuff you've found out."

"All right, all right," I said, "might as well take help wherever we can find it."

Jake and I talked a little more, about defense attorneys in Florida, contact he'd had with the cops investigating Crassidy, and a private investigator in Miami who might be able to help me. All in all, he tried to give me a pep talk about how I'd deal with what was ahead. Then he looked at his watch and said it was time to go. He was due back home with the family in an hour.

"And by the way, Joey," he said, "Nina and the kids don't believe for a second you had anything to do with killing O'Connor, or anybody else. They believe in you, all the way Joey, just like I do."

"Thanks, Jake. I appreciate it."

"And look," he said handing me his cell phone, "keep this with you while they're holding you here. Nobody's going to say anything. This way we're in touch with each other, all the time, right?"

"Sure", I said, "thanks, thanks a lot. You give my regards to the family and, I'll see you tomorrow."

"You got it, Joey. Later."

THAT EVENING, the guard told me I was slated to take the bus to Florida at three tomorrow. I crashed out pretty early and slept long and deep all through the night. I had all kinds of dreams; Landsdowne asking me why I couldn't tell him everything about me, he said he'd have understood; Valentina telling me she was dead, and how it was real peaceful; Ognev and Roland digging a grave for me, with blood dripping from their hands. Then I dreamed of Jake and Moore in a wedding ceremony, and them congratulating me for proving that Crassidy killed O'Connor. But it wasn't clear how I did it. When I woke up in the morning, I felt pretty rested, and real tranquil in some weird kind of way. It was, somehow, like I'd passed through the darkest hours and made it, and it wasn't going to get any worse than this.

The guard came by and passed a cup of coffee through the bars, and asked me if I wanted to see the morning paper.

"Yeah sure," I said, "but I didn't know I was going to be getting room service when I checked into this joint."

"You're getting the four star treatment doc," he laughed, "seeing as you got family connections."

"Beautiful. I love being a VIP"

He handed me the paper and went back to his post. I sat down and unfolded it and saw my mug shot right there, on the front page of the *Tribune*, under this headline: "Police Psychiatrist Toricelli Arrested in New York—Fugitive in O'Connor Slaying Turns Himself In." That I did, I said to no one in particular, that I did. The accompanying article didn't say anything about me being in Russia, just that I'd contacted Jake yesterday afternoon and "requested to be apprehended at the Jamaica Bay Wildlife Refuge." I thought: that doesn't make me sound too bad, now does it?

Then the story went on to review how the police and the FBI had kept my story hush-hush, for two days, just like Jake had told me, until they decided they had to go public with it last Sunday evening, now five days ago. But then something kind of shook in me, like something didn't exactly fit right. It was the time frame they were talking about; last Sunday, five days ago, it didn't seem that long, not long ago enough for some reason.

Then I tried to remember what Ognev and Roland had said, when I was listening to them from up in that attic. It was something about how Roland had wanted to hit me with the "Torento-Toricelli story" from—what the hell did he say?—the "first morning," from the "first morning" on the drug right? I racked my brain, trying to put together time frames. My first day on the drug: that'd be the first morning right? And of course it would be Moscow time, which was eight hours ahead of New York. Now I'd assumed that Ognev and Roland had read about me in the papers, but now I was thinking: Did they? Could they have? Because the first morning on the KG-2 had to be what; at least, as best I could think about it, was at least 5 days ago New York time. Weird, I thought, did they have some kind of inside connection with the FBI maybe? But no, that's crazy. And anyway, I couldn't feel that confident about the precision of my memory, especially after being on that KG-2.

I put down the paper and sipped my coffee. They brewed it as bad down here as upstairs but, what the hell I thought, it's the least of my problems. I looked at my watch, it was already eleven in the morning.

Four more hours and I'd be on the bus to Florida. I hadn't seen Jake yet, and I figured I'd call him up on the cell phone and see when he was coming down.

He answered on the first ring.

"Hello, Jake?" I said.

"Yeah, Joey, how are you? Look I'm just about to head down to see you, got caught up in a meeting this morning."

"Gee and here I thought you forgot about me."

"No way. No, as a matter of fact...hey, hold on a second...hey Madeline...Mad..." he called out to Moore. "It's Joey on the line. Let's take a walk down and see him, all right?" Then he came back to me. "Joey, look I...me and Dr. Moore, we're coming down in a minute."

"The both of you, huh?"

"Yeah. Look, I want you to talk to her, about what you saw in Russia. She's real interested in hearing what you've got to say."

"All right," I said, "if you think it'll help."

I hung up and waited for a few minutes for them to come down. Not exactly the way I'd wanted my exit interview as a "police psychiatrist" to go, I thought.

Then something shook inside me again. It was about the time frame, again, between the fingerprints, and the cops going public with the Torento/Toricelli identity. I counted over the past several days again. Today was Friday, I thought, and the news of my identity broke last Sunday evening, two days after the fingerprint match on the preceding Friday. Then I thought of when I'd left for Russia: the day before that fingerprint Friday, on Thursday; and then my "first morning" on the KG-2, in that bedroom, what would have corresponded...to the wee hours of last Saturday, a.m., New York time. Now if Roland had wanted to hit me with the "Torento story" as early as that, then that was at least a day before my identity was public knowledge. So how could he have known? As I thought about all of this, my brain was just whirling around, somewhere between confusion and revelation, and I was getting literally dizzy. That's when something else hit me, I mean really slammed into me hard: Madeline, I thought, yeah "Maddy...or Mad...". Yeah "Mad," that's it. Isn't that what Jake had just said before?: "Hey Madeline...Mad"? So how about, being mad...mad as hell. Now that was something like what Roland was yelling, on that phone in Monotoc wasn't it? So was he really mad as hell? Or was he just calling out, nervously maybe, to his good friend, and colleague—and co-conspirator—Madeline Moore? But, no, I thought, it's too far out. I must still be weirded out on this KG-2, and I'm getting into all kinds of crazy paranoid shit. But, on the other hand, I thought, it's possible, isn't it? Epstein knew Moore, and she could have popped into his office that

Friday afternoon, and surprised him. So he says: "What a surprise, I didn't know you were in the neighborhood." And her little visit was then supposed to coincide with Roland's call, making sure Epstein was properly occupied while she comes up behind him and closes down his windpipe. But then something didn't go exactly as planned and Roland got nervous. Yeah, he got real rattled and started calling her name: "Mad, Mad damnit, what the hell is going on!" Something like that. But then I thought c'mon, we're talking about Moore here, Madeline Moore. I mean, she's got problems, but, murder? That's wacky, isn't it?

But how wacky? It sure as hell could explain how Ognev and Roland knew about my fingerprint match, and my "Torento-Toricelli" story, a day before the New York papers. And why she ragged on me for even suspecting Roland, and why she was in such a hurry to nail Volknick. And it sure would explain how she's taken a liking to Jake; just to fuck with his judgment. I mean that's one odd couple, isn't it? No, that's it, I thought, she did it, she and Roland. But how could I prove it, and do it quick, before they haul my ass out of here? I looked at the cell phone I'd been turning over in my hands, and got an idea. That's it, I thought, I got it. We're going to administer Dr. Moore a little psychological test and see what kind of score she comes up with. We'll get the results real quick.

Just then I heard the door in the corridor open, and Jake and Moore greeting the guard. Then I heard their footsteps coming toward my cell. Okay, Dr. Moore, I thought, here it comes, ready or not.

"Joey," said Jake, coming up to the cell door, "how you doing man, you sleep okay?"

"Hi Joseph," said Moore, giving me a big, stiff smile, "you're looking rested."

The guard unlocked the door, and they entered the cell and sat on the cot across from me. The door was left ajar while the guard went back to his post.

"I just wanted to tell you, Joseph," said Moore, "that I apologize for my reaction yesterday. After what Jake has told me, well...I'm very interested to hear about everything you saw in Russia."

"Well, I'll tell you what," I said, "that's already ancient history. Because I've got great news, and I was waiting 'till you all were down here to tell you."

"What's that?" said Jake. "What's going on?"

"Consider Roland nailed," I said.

"What?" said Jake. "What do you mean? What'd you find out?"

"I just got off this very cell phone with him," I said, "a little while ago. And he said he's going to confess everything, including who killed Epstein. It's incredible, isn't it?"

"Are you serious?" said Jake. "But how? How the hell did you do it?"

"Yes," said Moore, "how? I...I just can't believe it."

"It's too good to be true, right?" I said. "But believe it. Here's what happened. Late last night I called Epstein's son. You remember how he's keeping all his father's files? Well, I got this hunch, that maybe Epstein had somehow filed away some stuff on KG-2, or his conversation with Roland about Frontenac—Briand in another folder, see? Just for safekeeping, in case Roland tried to steal the Frontenac records."

"Good thinking," said Jake, "something I should have come up with, right?"

"Yeah, sure. Well, anyway, the Epstein kid liked this idea, and spent all night going through all his old man's files. And guess what? This morning, just about an hour ago, he hits the jackpot. He's got everything we need, filed under another patient's name."

"What do you mean?" said Moore. "He found a document?"

"Oh, he found a document all right," I said. "Let me tell you what he found. He found a bunch of notes going back six, eight, nine months ago and more, summarizing conversations he'd had with Roland about his favorite patient, Sabrina Briand; notes that show that Roland knew that she was now being treated by Epstein under the name Wilhelmina Frontenac."

"Son of a bitch," said Jake, "so we got him. He lied through his teeth about all that. So he's nailed on obstruction of justice at least."

"Oh no, Jake," I said, "that's small potatoes, it gets much better than that. We got notes by Epstein going back to two weeks before the murder, saying how he found files in Roland's office about the experiment with KG-2 and the whole distribution scheme with Ognev."

"Unbelievable," said Jake, "this is fucking gold."

"But wait just a moment," said Moore. "How do we know about the authenticity of these documents? They...they could have been fabricated."

"Fabricated?" I said. "These are dated notes, see? And clearly in Epstein's handwriting. And believe me, when I called Roland a little while ago, he didn't even mention anything about "authenticity," see? He knows when he's nailed."

"So what'd he say?" said Jake. "Did he tell you who killed Epstein?"

"No way. He's not that stupid. He wants to use what he knows to negotiate some kind of immunity, see? He wants to make a deal. He told me he'd meet with you today, in his office at two, with his attorney."

"I'll be damned," said Jake. "What a fucking find. Joey, you're a genius."

"Let's not get hysterical," I said, "but I do think some congratulations are in order."

"Yes..." said Moore, "but I'm stunned...absolutely stunned. A man of Dr. Roland's reputation, involved in murder?"

"It's unbelievable," said Jake, "just when you think you've seen it all, right?"

Then, suddenly, Moore looked at her watch. "Well, I'm going to need to go," she said. "I have rounds at Charity at noon."

"Wait a minute," said Jake. "I thought we were going to lunch. And besides, we got to both prepare to deal with Roland."

"Yes, yes. I know," she said, standing up, "but I have to attend these rounds. I meant to tell you earlier. It just slipped my mind. I have to go. I'll see you back at the office, in about an hour."

"But..." said Jake.

"Really," she said, "I have to go. Goodbye. And good luck Joseph."

"Thanks," I said. "See you."

As soon as she left I grabbed Jake by the arm. "Everything I just said is bullshit," I said.

"What?"

"That's right. I never spoke with Roland. I never spoke with Epstein's kid."

"So what...what is this", said Jake, "some kind of joke?"

"It's no joke," I said. "Now go follow Moore. My bet is she's going right to Roland's. There ought to be some kind of scene there real soon."

"What?" said Jake. "What the hell are you talking about?"

"I don't have time to explain everything Jake. But, it looks like she and Roland cooked up a plot to kill Epstein. Now she thinks Roland's going to double-cross her and she's going to go confront him."

"Joey, are you nuts? Do you realize what the fuck you're saying?"

"I do Jake, believe me," I said. "But it's just got to be, see? You told me my fingerprints were a big secret, right? Until five days ago."

"Yeah."

"Well, I'm telling you Roland and Ognev knew about those prints at least six days ago. Now how do you explain that?"

He didn't say anything.

"There had to be a leak, Jake, an informant who let them know. Now who's that? You? The FBI? The police commissioner? Or somehow, somebody down in personnel? No, I don't think so, Jake. It's your little Mad Maddy: that's the name Roland was calling out in Monotoc. 'Mad' not 'mad as hell' see, just 'Mad'!"

"But how? said Jake. "Where's the friggin' evidence?"

"You're going to find it. But you gotta move fast. You see how suddenly she left? Now look, you got to head uptown before she does.

You gotta go into Roland's building through the lobby entrance, and then go wait behind the service entrance door to Roland's office. I'm betting you're going to hear her come into Roland's office, and start giving him all kinds of hell for double-crossing her. Be ready to bust in, and try to bring a tape recorder."

Jake just looked at me with his mouth open. "Joey," he said, "you're way the fuck out there on this one. I mean you're still reeling from that mushroom shit, you know that?"

"Just follow her, all right? Do it for me. It's my last fucking request before I get locked up in Florida, okay? Look at it that way."

He took a deep breath and shook his head. "All right, Joey," he said, "I'll do it, just for you, okay? One more turn on this friggin' fucked-up merry-go-round, okay? Just for you."

"Atta boy, Jake," I said, "and just stay on your feet, when you find out how she's been taking you for a ride."

Part 10

I GOT PACKED into a van to Florida before Jake ever got back, so I didn't hear what happened 'till I called him that night, from a truck stop just north of Richmond, Virginia. I sure hoped to hell I hadn't steered him down some nasty stretch of dead end road.

"Jake," I said, as soon as he said hello, "so what the hell went down today?"

"What went down?" he said, sounding sort of sad. "One hell of a lot, that's what."

"So tell me, tell me," I said, "I got to get back in the van in a few minutes."

"It was like this," he said. "I got to Roland's building, and just like you told me, I went in through the lobby and went over by the service entrance."

"Yeah, and..."

"Well, I'm waiting there a few minutes, feeling like a damn fool, with my hands in my pockets and dodging the guys bringing the garbage out and I don't hear nothing from Roland's office. Then, all of a sudden, I hear what sounds like Roland's voice on the other side, and he's saying 'Madeline?' Then maybe a minute goes by, and I can only hear some kind of mumbling. Then, comes Moore's voice, screaming at the top of her lungs; 'You fool, you twerp, you idiot, they scared you into making a deal with them, don't try to deny it!'; And Roland's saying 'No, no, it's all a lie, a bluff. They're trying to trap us.' But Moore hollers out 'Don't lie to me you worm, don't insult my intelligence...you never took the time to go through his files. And now you will identify me as the murderer, and save your own wrinkled, candy ass!'"

"She said that, really?" I said. "Gee, that's beautiful."

"So then I hear Roland start to whine, he keeps saying: 'No Madeline, no...Mad...they are bluffing. You...don't understand...' Then things are quiet for a second, before he picks up again, hollering and yelping, like some little dog: 'No!' he says. 'Stop it...you're crazy...stop it...you're going to...' Then he starts screaming: 'Help, help, help!' At that point I pull out my gun, shoot the lock open, go through the door and see Moore on top of Roland on his desk, with her hands squeezing down real tight around his little neck."

"Son of a bitch!" I said. "Imagine that...you saved the little bastard's life. I hope he thanked you."

"Believe me, Joey, he was too shaken up to say anything. But Moore, man, she looks at me, like some wild fucking animal and starts screaming out, 'What the fuck are you doing here you...dickhead!'"

"She called you a dickhead, huh?" I said. "Well if the shoe fits, wear it."

"Ah, fuck you," said Jake. "Anyway, then she comes lunging at me and tries to take my gun from me. We struggle for a while, before I got to coldcock her crazy ass to the floor."

"Ouch," I said. "You sure you didn't go a little overboard there?"

"No way," he said. "But meanwhile Roland's curled up behind his desk, shaking and crying and whining his ass off. When I go to get him he tells me, 'I'll tell everything, Lieutenant, I swear...everything. But you must believe me. I never laid a hand on Horatio Epstein...it was she...she was the one who strangled him.'"

"So you heard it from her as well as him," I said, "beautiful. But tell me how exactly did they pull it off?"

"What happened was, Moore had made this appointment with her skin doctor, for four o'clock that Friday. Guess where his office is?"

"In the very same building," I said.

"You got it; with one door off the street and the other off the lobby. She comes in the street entrance, has her appointment, and then leaves through the lobby side. But instead of exiting the building, she hangs a quick left to Roland's service entrance..."

"Which he'd left unlocked for her," I said.

"Exactly. So she goes into Roland's office, and waits until five, after Volknick's gone, and when Roland's supposed to call Epstein."

"But," I said, "there's one little glitch. Valentina calls at about three minutes to five, and Moore, thinking that's Roland's cue for her to enter, walks into Epstein's office."

"You're right on top of it," said Jake. "So then Epstein is surprised to see Moore and, because what he's got to discuss with Valentina is a big secret, he tells her he doesn't have time to talk now and hangs up."

"Did Moore suspect he was talking to Valentina?"

"Nah," said Jake. "From what Roland told me, Epstein told her it was just a drug rep on the line."

"I see," I said. "By the way, is everything you're telling me from Roland?"

"Oh yeah, Roland's talking a blue streak. On the other hand, Moore ain't telling us nothing, she said she's got to talk to her lawyer first."

"Right."

"So anyway," said Jake, "the next minute after Epstein hangs up with Valentina the phone rings again. This time, Moore says 'Go ahead and take it, I'll wait.'

So Epstein picks it up and starts talking now to our boy Roland. Meanwhile, as per the plan, Moore's supposed to open up a box of chocolates she's brought for Epstein spiked with this KG-2 stuff, okay? It's the pure stuff, and not detectable by the department's toxicology, see? She's supposed to offer Epstein a few tasty morsels while he's yacking on the phone with Roland."

"Why chocolate?" I said.

"Supposedly Epstein was some kind of chocolate fanatic, see? So he's supposed to start eating a few pieces of this stuff and then, little by little, get real weak and goofy. Moore is supposed to be watching for the stuff to take effect, and then take a little stroll behind him, and real nice and easy, unroll this necktie from her purse, and tie a lethal little granny knot around his neck."

"So what happened?" I said.

"Well, it looks like our busy little Dr. Moore didn't have time to go down to the Daylight Club and pick up the spiked chocolates; but she knows she's got to kill Epstein at five or else the plan's down the toilet. So she figures she'll just take him out without the KG-2; if not nice and easy, then real rough and ready."

"But Roland doesn't know she's going to operate without anesthesia right?" I said.

"That's right. He's expecting Epstein to start slurring and slowing down and, fading out, okay. But instead, he starts hearing gasping and yelping and some kind of struggle going on.

Then the phone receiver drops out of Epstein's hand, and it seems to Roland like somebody's covered up the phone while there's screaming in the background. He gets nervous, he gets scared, he doesn't know what the hell is going on. Maybe there's other people in the room. The little shit goes into full panic mode, and he starts yelling into the phone, 'Mad...Mad...What the hell!...damn it Mad?'"

"Within earshot," I said, "of our friendly clerk in Monotoc."

"Exactly. So then, in another couple of seconds Moore's finished off Epstein and picking up the phone to tell Dr. Jerk-off what happened. He's all bullshit at her for not bringing the chocolate, and being so 'brutal' with his old buddy Epstein. And he's mad that the whole thing scared the shit out of him like that. But then, after Moore convinced him the job is done and everything's okay, he calms down and they hang up with each other. Then she goes back to Roland's office, out through the service entrance and exits through the lobby entrance of the building. That way nobody sees anybody else going out of Epstein's and Roland's suite entrance."

"Son of a bitch," I said, "and when Roland comes into the suite on Saturday, he makes sure he locks up the service entrance before he 'discovers' his unfortunate colleague, in a state of advanced post-strangulation."

"That's right," said Jake, "and he makes sure of something else, that he cleans out any incriminating pages from Frontenac's file, including the note that originally tipped him off that Epstein was on to the KG-2."

"How do you mean?" I said.

"Well, like this Valentina told you, Joey, Epstein had been nosing around in Roland's office a couple of weeks before all this happened. That's when he discovered these papers of Roland's, right?"

"Right."

"Well, unbeknownst to Epstein, Roland noticed that things were a little out of whack in his file drawer and got a hunch Epstein had been snooping where he wasn't supposed to snoop. So he sneaks into Epstein's office, goes right to the Frontenac file, and sees that Epstein had written down what he'd seen in Roland's file about the KG-2 scam."

"Ah-hah," I said ,"so that's how Roland finds out Epstein knows too much, and then he's got to cook up something real fast with Moore and Ognev."

"Oh yeah. And what they figure is, Moore's the perfect candidate for the killer. Nobody'll even remotely suspect her, though she's had a big stake in this KG-2 scam for a long time."

"And," I said, "to make it even sweeter, they know Volknick shouldn't be too hard to frame; him being the last guy out and all."

"Yep. That's why they choose a time right after Volknick's appointment. And for extra insurance Moore hypnotizes the poor sap in her first police interview with him, when she's got him all alone. She plants the idea in him that he killed Epstein."

"Evil fucking witch. No wonder Volknick got the creeps and didn't want to talk with her in their interviews. But how the hell did they get him to go berserk that afternoon, after his appointment with Epstein?"

"Oh that was Ognev's handymen," said Jake, "working out a little bit of mischief. Ognev had a couple of goons from Daylight dress up like plumbers and go to Volknick's apartment to fix some kind of bogus leak."

"When?" I said.

"A few days before the murder," said Jake, "so they got into Volknick's bathroom, and replaced his psychiatric pills with some other kind of stuff. Sinemet, I think Roland told me."

"Son of a bitch," I said, "if you're schizophrenic, that stuff can make you nuts. Especially if it's in place of the psych medication."

"That's what I understand," said Jake. "And Volknick was popping that shit for four days before the murder."

"The poor bastard. But still, how did he go berserk that very afternoon, of Epstein's death?"

"Believe it or not," said Jake, "that was just dumb luck on their part. I mean, they knew he'd blow, but they didn't think the timing would be that perfect."

"I'll be damned."

"Yeah, they got him set up real good, just so you could jerk that nice confession out of him."

"Yeah, real nice," I said. "But now we've got Roland as our star witness, laying out the whole slimy scheme."

"And he's aching to get started, and try to save what's left of his ass."

But just then I felt a hand on my shoulder and the deep voice of my guard saying, "We gotta go now, doc."

"Sure, sure," I said to him, "but just hold on a second. Look, Jake, I'm being called back to the bus, so to speak. Twenty more hours down the road to the Sunshine State. But look, I'll be in touch with you okay?"

"Sure buddy," said Jake, "goodbye, and good luck."

Epilogue

UP TO NOW, these last couple of weeks I've spent in the Coriolis County Jail have been pretty dark, and there hasn't been much to brighten up my mood, except the good news that's coming out of the Epstein case.

Jake told me the FBI and the KGB have arrested Ognev, and liberated all the zombies in the compound. Turns out they were from all over the States and Europe and had, at one time or another, attended Roland's seminars. Roland had gathered information on them, showing they were all single, living alone, and not too social. A few weeks after each of them had gone through the seminar, Ognev had his goons kidnap them, drug them with KG-2 and smuggle them to Russia. There they were used as human guinea pigs , addled with KG-2, and on occasion killed and autopsied to study the brain effects of different dosages of the KG-2 cocktail. There was also some plan to extract KG-2 brain metabolites from them, and to try to synthesize some even more potent, and addictive, super psychedelic opiate.

As far as that half-baked hedonistic bullshit they were spewing, it'd been cooked up and fed to them by Roland, just to see how he could influence their blown out minds. I hope to hell they'll get deprogrammed all right.

As for the Epstein murder case itself, old Roland's talking up a storm and it doesn't look like Moore's going anywhere except to prison, though I heard she's pleading innocent and now trying to say Roland made Sabrina Briand do it. But, besides the fact that Sabrina's staying in a Moscow sanitarium, with no clear prospects for discharge or extradition, I'm sure that yachting alibi of hers is going to hold up and she'll be safe from Moore trying to frame her.

On the other hand, Sabrina's Aunt Valentina ended up in a real bad way. The day I left Moscow, she had a fatal "accident" and fell down a long escalator in the Moscow Metro. The "official" cause of death was a heart attack, but the timing, obviously, was real suspicious. As far as nobody knowing her at the Physiological Institute, that was real simple. She just hadn't worked there in over ten years, but apparently wanted me to believe she still did. Who knows? I guess she wanted to believe it too.

But as far as I know, old Valentina was on the level about everything else she said, including the Jayne LeGrande deal. Jayne LeGrande had definitely lied to the police initially about that picture, with Sabrina's promise that she was going to get paid twenty-grand to protect Sabrina from immigration. And then she had to deny that she'd lied; the first time with me, because she didn't want to get in trouble; and then later, with Jake and me on the phone, because Ognev's guys had threatened her with dismemberment if she spilled the beans. The last thing I heard on her now, is that she's filed a malpractice suit against Roland, claiming negligence, misrepresentation and willful misconduct. Well, I get a feeling she's going to be standing in a real long line with those complaints.

But one guy who's not complaining, as far as I know, is Nathan Volknick. He's just real happy to be out of jail, and he's jumping for joy to find out he really didn't kill Dr. Epstein. And I'm glad to hear that his family's real grateful to me, for saving their boy from a life of incarceration. As a matter of fact, they're making arrangements to foot the bill for my legal defense, as well as to pay off Danny Corona the forty grand he hadn't forgotten I'd borrowed from him, way back when. But, like I said, up to now, other than the good news about the Epstein case, things have been pretty damn dark here in jail. The case against me couldn't've looked worse. And old Horace Crassidy, unpleasant as it must have been for him to see me alive and kicking, hasn't flinched one little bit in his rendition of my murderous rampage.

But just now, on account of what I read just a little while ago, I've got a hunch everything's going to change. You see, I've hired this private eye, who's been shadowing Crassidy's girlfriend in all her comings and goings. And it seems she keeps going into this bank in Miami, maybe three or four times now, and on each occasion she comes out with a brown paper parcel. Then she drives down Route 1 to Key Largo, and pays a visit to a certain guy living in a shack on the South Side. A guy who's lately reported to have become a real big spender in town. But the funny thing is, he's recently unemployed. It looks like he quit his job about a month ago, as the night manager of the Crossroads Key Marina. Now that's a real coincidence, isn't it?

Well, I've got a feeling we're going to be setting up a meeting with this guy real soon, and we're going to find a way to persuade him to give up blackmailing for a classier and more heroic role, to become the courageous witness who wouldn't be intimidated any longer by Horace Crassidy's threats; and is now ready to come forward and identify him as the real murderer of Francis O'Connor.

Yeah, it's going to work, it really is. And I've been feeling so good about it, that I had to call up Anya and tell her the news, just a few minutes ago. Oh yeah, by the way, I've been talking to her just about every day now.

Somehow, when I first got back down here, and was feeling pretty down and lonely, she's the one person I wanted to reach out to. And every time I call her, I feel all warm inside. She's always real happy to hear my voice. I told her just now I'll bet I'll be sprung out of here within a week; and then I know just what I want to do. She asked, "what's that?" And I said to her that I wanted to come up to New York, and sit at a cozy booth in her restaurant, and drink hot tea and look into her beautiful green eyes. She said she really likes that idea. She even says she knows a place in the neighborhood where I could stay pretty cheap, before I, or maybe even we, figure out exactly what I do next.

Well, I guess that's looking a little too far ahead; but who knows? It could well be in the cards, or let's say the stars, that we could really fall in love. And she could run her restaurant and I could...well, I got this idea, see, that I could take a stab at some kind of forensic work. I mean, I haven't done half bad so far, and from what Anya tells me, she thinks I've got some kind of talent for it. Just the other day, over the phone, she told me: "You see, Joseph, you made one good case, now you may do another."

"Maybe," I said, "maybe you've got something there."

And then I thought to myself, one good deed, just one good deed. It's one good step toward forgiving and forgetting all the others. And so, hold onto this one good deed. And take care to see that it's followed by another.

~*~